PENGUIN BOOKS

RECAPITULATION

Wallace Stegner (1909–1993) was the author of, among other novels, *Remembering Laughter*, 1937; *The Big Rock Candy Mountain*, 1943; *Joe Hill,* 1950; *All the Little Live Things*, 1967 (Commonwealth Club Gold Medal); *A Shooting Star*, 1961; *Angle of Repose*, 1971 (Pulitzer Prize); *The Spectator Bird*, 1976 (National Book Award, 1977); *Recapitulation*, 1979; and *Crossing to Safety*, 1987. His nonfiction includes *Beyond the Hundredth Meridian*, 1954; *Wolf Willow*, 1963; *The Sound of Mountain Water* (essays), 1969; *The Uneasy Chair: A Biography of Bernard DeVoto*, 1974; and *Where the Bluebird Sings to the Lemonade Springs: Living and Writing in the West*, 1992. Three of his short stories have won O. Henry prizes, and in 1980 he received the Robert Kirsch Award from the *Los Angeles Times* for his lifetime achievements. His *Collected Stories* was published in 1990.

RECAPITULATION

I

1

The highway entering Salt Lake City from the west curves around the southern end of Great Salt Lake past Black Rock and the ratty beaches, swings north away from the smoke of the smelter towns, veers toward the dry lake bed where a long time ago the domes of the Saltair Pavilion used to rise like an Arabic exhalation, and straightens out eastward again. Ahead, across the white flats, the city is a mirage, or a mural: metropolitan towers, then houses and channeled streets, and then the mountain wall.

Driving into that, smelling the foul, exciting salt-flat odor, Bruce Mason began to feel like the newsreel diver whom the reversed projector sucks feet first out of his splash. Probably fatigue from the hard day and a half across the desert explained both the mirage-like look of the city and his own sense of being run backward toward the beginning of the reel. Perhaps his errand had something to do with it; it was not the first time he had returned to Salt Lake to bury someone. But those previous returns, dim and silvery in his memory, almost subliminal, were from the east, through the mountains. This route suggested something else. This was the road out which, at sixteen or seventeen, he used to drive much too fast in stripped-down Ford bugs with screaming companions in the rumble seat. They must have driven back, too, but he remembered only the going out. To see the city head on, like this, was strange to him.

He had not prepared himself for this return to the city of his youth, had made no plans beyond the obligation of seeing his aunt properly buried. And he had no psychological excuse or nostalgia, had not been left skinless and purified by a serious illness, had had no cause for reviving memories of his forgotten adolescence. Yet anticipation leaped up bright and unexpected in his mind, and his eyes were sharp for landmarks and reminders as he passed the airport and the expanding edge-of-town industries and the old fairgrounds, and slowed for the first streets of the city.

Forty-five years had made differences, but they did not seem critical. The city had spread a good deal, and he was surprised, after the desert, by the green luxuriance of its trees. But the streets were still a half mile wide, and water still ran in at least some of the gutters. It really was a pleasant town; it looked young and vigorous and clean. Passing the Brigham Young monument, he nodded gravely to the figure with the outstretched hand, and like a native coming home he turned at the light in the middle of the block and pulled into the parking garage that had replaced the old Deseret Gymnasium. That change jolted him a little. The old rattrap gym had held a lot of the boy he used to be.

The doorman collared his bag, a youth climbed in to take the car underground. Still running pleasantly backward into the reel, he went into the not-much-changed lobby and registered, and was carried up the not-much-changed elevator to the kind of room he remembered, such a room as they used to take when they held fraternity and class dances in this hotel, back in Prohibition times. During at least one of those years he had been on a diet for ulcers, and couldn't drink, but he used to retire religiously with the boys, gargle raw Green River red-eye, and spit it out again in the washbowl, only for the pleasure of lawbreaking and of carrying a distinguished breath back to the ballroom and the girls.

With his bag on the rack, his hand still holding the handle, he stood still for a second, remembering his giddy and departed youth.

Later, fresh from the shower, he picked up the telephone book and hunted up the Merrill Funeral Parlor. But when he had found it he was troubled, struck by the address: 363 East South Temple. On the Avenues side, somewhere around D Street, near the cathedral. He tried to visualize that once-familiar street, but it was all gone except for a generalized image of tall stone and brick houses with high porches, and lawns overtaken by plantain weeds. One, the one Holly had lived in, had a three-story stone tower.

That tower! With all the Jazz Age bohemians crawling in and out. Havelock Ellis, Freud, Mencken, *The Memoirs of Fanny Hill, Love's Coming of Age, The Well of Loneliness,* Harry Kemp, Frank Harris. My Lord.

He was flooded with delighted recollection. They were all there before him—reed-necked aesthetes, provincial cognoscenti, sad sexy yokels, lovers burning with a hard, gem-like flame, a homosexual or two trying to look blasted and corroded by secret sin. Painters of bile-green landscapes, cubist photographers, poets and iconoclasts, resident Dadaists, scorners of the bourgeoisie, makers of cherished prose, dream-tellers, correspondence-school psychoanalysts, they swarmed through Holly's apartment and eddied around her queenly shape with noises like breaking china. He remembered her in her gold gown, a Proserpine or a Circe. For an instant she was slim and tall in his mind and he saw her laughing in the midst of the excitement she created, and how her hair was smooth black and her eyes very dark blue and how she wore massive gold hoops in her ears.

He wrote the number down in his notebook and tucked it into the pocket of the seersucker jacket laid out on the bed. But when he had dressed and gone down and was walking in the blazing heat up South Temple past the Church offices, Beehive House, Lion House, the Eagle Gate, the Elks Club and the Alta Club, the old and new apartments, he began to look at numbers with a feeling that approached suspense, and he searched not so much for the Merrill Funeral Parlor as for the house with the stone tower. Finally, just past the cathedral, he saw it lifting across the roof of a mansion gone to seed, and in another thirty paces he could see the sign and the new brass numbers on the riser of the top porch step. It was the very house.

Quickly he looked around for something that would restore

and brace his memory. The street did not look much changed. Some of the old maples and hickories he remembered were gone, and the terrace rolled down with an unfamiliar smooth nap of grass. The porch no longer carried its sagging swing, and porch and steps had been renovated and painted. The door was as he remembered it, with rays of colored glass in its fanlight, and the doorknob's massive handful was an almost startling familiarity. But inside, all was changed. Partitions had been gutted out. The stairs now mounted, or levitated, a spiral of white spokes and mahogany rail, from an expanse of plum-colored carpet. Instead of the cupping old parquetry his feet found softness, hushedness. The smells were of paint and flowers.

He was eying the stairs when a young man came out of the office on the left and bent his head leftward and said softly and pleasantly, "Yes, sir. Can I help?"

Mason brought himself back to what he had driven eight hundred miles to do. He said, "I'm Bruce Mason. My aunt, Mrs. Webb, died day before yesterday at the Julia Hicks Home. They telephoned me that she'd be here."

"Oh, yes, Mr. Ambassador," the young man said, and put out an eager hand which Mason found narrow, cold, and surprisingly strong. It was like shaking hands with a perching bird. "We've been expecting you. It's an honor to meet you. My name is McBride."

"How do you do," Mason said, and added, "Let's forget the 'ambassador,' shall we? That was a while back."

"As you wish." McBride regarded him, smiling, with his head tilted. "Did you fly in?"

"Drove."

"By yourself? From San Francisio?" He seemed surprised to learn that an ex-ambassador could drive a car.

"I slept a few hours in Elko."

"It wasn't so bad, then."

"Oh, no. Not bad at all."

This young McBride, Mason was thinking, might be left over from one of Holly's parties. He looked better equipped to write fragile verses than to deal with corpses.

"She's in the back parlor," he said. "Would you like to see her? She looks very nice."

That would be McBride's function. He would be the one who made them look nice.

"Later," Mason said. "I expect there are some details we should settle."

"Of course. If you'll just step in here. You have a family cemetery plot, I believe. This should take only a few minutes." He motioned deferentially at the door.

A few minutes sufficed. They rose, facing one another across the desk coolly glimmering in muted light. "Now would you like to see her?"

Clearly he took pride. He probably stood back estimating his effects like a window dresser. Mister McBride, the mortuary Max Factor. "All right," Mason said. "Though it's not as if I had any tears to shed. I barely knew her, and I haven't been back since I left, and she's been senile for ten years."

McBride guided him around the unfamiliar stairs to where the plum carpet flowed smoothly into what had once, perhaps, been a dining room. "She does look nice. Very sweet and peaceful."

Which Mason couldn't believe she did when she was alive. He went forward to the table with the basket of house chrysanthemums at its foot. To remind himself that this was his father's sister, the only relative on that side that he ever knew, made him feel nothing. It was only a freak that she had come to Salt Lake at all, hoping to attach herself to his father, and arrived for the funeral. Mason had acquired her as an obligation when he least needed obligations. Though he had helped take care of her for half her life and more than half of his own, he could stir up no feeling for her wax figure. He supposed that if he had been attached to her he might think her peaceful, as McBride instructed him to. But all he could think was that she looked well embalmed.

Old Aunt Margaret, a stranger who had imposed herself on him as an obligation and an expense that at first he didn't want and couldn't afford, thrust her sharp nose, sharp cheekbones, and withered lips up through the rouge and lipstick and was only old Aunt Margaret, mercifully dead at eighty-six. He couldn't even see in her face any resemblance to his father, and he felt none of the conventional disgust with young McBride, who tampered

with the dead. Considering what he had had to work with,
McBride had done pretty well.

Back in the hall again, he stood looking up at the spiral stairs,
apparently as unsupported as the Beanstalk, and remembered a
time when Holly and two roommates—not Nola, she came later
and was here only a few weeks—came down the shabby old
steps arguing about the proportions of the perfect female figure,
and he met them on the second landing and like a chorus line
they raised their skirts and thrust out their right legs before him,
demanding to know which was the most shapely. An undergraduate Paris and three demanding goddesses. He had picked
Holly. Why not? Though if Nola had been there then, it might
have been another story. That would have been obsession, not
judgment.

"We've just redone the whole place," McBride said. "It was the
home of a Park City silver king originally, but it was all run
down."

Mason continued to look up the stairs. McBride's information
was no more important than the decorative changes, but up
there was something that *was* important, or used to be. It pulled
at him like an upward draft.

"I used to know this house years ago," he said. "Some people I
knew had an apartment on the third floor."

"Oh? Front or back?"

"Front. The one with the round tower window."

"Oh yes. We haven't done much to that yet—just painted it."

"I wonder," Mason said, and made a little deprecatory gesture
and felt irritably ashamed, like a middle-aged man recalling last
night's party, and his own unseemly capers and his pawing of
the host's wife. It was fatuous to want to go up there, but he did.

"Go on up if you like," McBride said. "The only thing, there's
a woman laid out in that room."

"Well, then . . ."

"It doesn't matter, if you don't mind. She's presentable."

For a moment Mason hung on the word. McBride's professional vanity was one of the odder kinds. And he was annoyed
that a corpse should intrude upon a sentimental but perfectly le-
gitimate impulse. Then he put his hand on the mahogany rail.

"Maybe I will."

The second-floor hall, at whose doors he had knocked and entered, was as much changed as the ground floor, but up the second flight of stairs he mounted into a growing familiarity. And he climbed against the pressure of a crowd of ghosts. The carpet ended at the stairhead. He put his feet down softly and held his breath with the wild notion that he heard voices from the door of Holly's old apartment. Up these stairs, a hundred, two hundred times—through how long? a year?—he had come with books or bottles or manuscripts in his hands and (it seemed to him now) an incomparable capacity for enthusiasm in his heart. From the high burlap-hung window of the apartment they had let their liquid ridicule fall on the streets of the bourgeois city. He half expected, as he moved into the doorway, to see their faces look up inquiringly from chair and couch and floor.

But in the room there was only the dead woman, and she was not looking at him.

She lay on a wheeled table, with beside her one stiff chair and a taboret bearing a bowl of withered lilacs, all of it arranged as if for a macabre still life. Looking toward the window across the woman's body, he saw how the light of afternoon blurred in her carefully waved hair.

For a few seconds he simply stood in the doorway, stopped partly by the body and partly by the sensation of obscure threat: he was walking in a strange neighborhood and needed his own gang around him.

In Holly's time the tower bay had held an old upright piano, its backside exposed to the room like the hanging seat of a child's sleepers. Afternoons, evenings, Sunday and holiday mornings, the place had sounded to "Twelfth Street Rag," "St. Louis Blues," "Mood Indigo." On at least one Christmas morning they had sung carols around the piano, syncopating them wickedly. That was the morning when he had brought Holly the facsimile copy of *The Marriage of Heaven and Hell*, a mutinous book full of mottoes for their personalities and their times.

But what he remembered now, hanging in the doorway, was how in some lull in the bedlam that always went on there they had found themselves smiling foolishly at one another by the piano, and she had put up her hands to his face and kissed him sweet and soft, a kiss like a happy child's.

He felt the stairs in his legs, the years in his mind, as he went in softly past the woman who lay so quietly on her back, and when he had almost passed her he turned and searched her face, as if he might surprise in it some expression meaningful to this wry and confusing return.

She was a plain woman, perhaps fifty. McBride had not yet made her look nice. She wore a simple black dress, but she had a Navajo squash-blossom necklace around her throat. It struck Mason as a remarkable piece of realism—perhaps something she had especially liked and had stubbornly gone on wearing past the age when costume jewelry became her. It gave her a touching, naïvely rakish air.

Yet she shed a chill around her, and her silence spread to fill the room. Hardly a sound came through the stone walls. In the old days there had always been the piano banging, the phonograph going, two or six or sixteen voices making cosmic conversation. And he could not remember ever seeing the apartment in daylight. The windows were always shrouded in their artificially frayed burlap, and the light was from lamps, most of them low on the floor and some of them at least with red bulbs in them. And always the smell of sandalwood.

Like a Chinese whorehouse. Pitying and entranced, he sat down on the window seat overlooking the reach of South Temple. Directly across was a Five Minute Car Wash with a big apron of concrete and a spic dazzle of white paint and red tiles. In the times he remembered, that lot had held a peewee golf course where men in shirt sleeves, women in summer dresses, young couples loud with laughter, had putted little white balls along precise green alleys of artificial grass and over gentle predictable bridges and causeways into numbered holes.

"Look at them," Holly had said to him once as they sat in the tower bay looking down at the after-dinner golfers moving under the floodlights. "*Toujours gai*, my God! Someday I'm going to build a miniature golf course with fairways six inches wide and rough six inches deep. I'll fill the water holes with crocodiles and sow the sand traps with sidewinders. How would it be to hide a black widow spider in every hole, so that picking up your ball would earn you some excitement? What if you sawed the supports of all the little bridges nearly in two?"

Live it dangerously. It was strange to recall how essential that had once seemed. Go boom, take chances. He ran his hand along the sill, thinking that this was the pose, sitting right here and looking out, that Holly had assumed when Tom Stead painted her in her gold velvet gown.

Probably that portrait wasn't anything special. It couldn't have been. The chances were that Tom Stead was painting signs somewhere now, if he hadn't drunk himself to death. But then, in this room, in the presence of its subject whose life overflowed upon them all, that slim golden shape with the velvet highlights was Lilith, Helen, Guinevere, *das Ewig-Weibliche*. And it was hardly a day before other girls, less fortunately endowed or graced, began dropping comments on how *warm* that Holly-Stead romance was getting, and hinting that there was tucked away somewhere, in the best Goya fashion, a companion portrait, a nude.

Well, well, what a bunch of bohemian puritans. Mason did not believe in any nude, or in its importance if there was one, though at the time the possibility had bothered him, and he had been malely offended, surprised that she would *lower* herself.

What he had meant was that his vanity was hurt if Holly accorded Stead any privileges she did not accord to him. And he didn't really believe that she accorded any to Stead. What truly shone out of that golden portrait, as out of Holly herself, was not glamour but innocence. Under the sheath she was positively virginal, a girl from Parowan who had made the big step to city excitements but remained a girl from Parowan. If you cracked the enamel of her sophistication you found a delighted little girl playing Life.

Once more he felt on his lips the touch of that soft, childlike kiss by the piano on a Christmas morning, and stood up so abruptly that he startled himself with the sight of the dead woman, whom he had forgotten. It *was* innocence. Holly could put away the predatory paws of college boys, twist laughing from the casual kiss, pass among the hot young Freudians as untouched as a nun, shed like water the propositions that came at her seven to the week. There she sat in her gold gown by her window opening on the foam: a maiden in a tower.

Like someone tapping at a door, wanting to interrupt a private conversation, Nola was there in his head asking to be asked in. He found it curious that he didn't want to ask her in, not just now, though she was surely a more significant part of this lost place and past time than Holly. It was Holly he wanted to talk to just now; she seemed fresher with possibilities, not so tainted with old sullen emotions. The two had briefly shared these rooms, but it was Holly whom the rooms remembered.

He crossed to the door of what had once been her bedroom, wanting to look in on her intimately. In this room, now completely bare, aseptically painted, he had sat many times when she was ill or when on Sunday mornings she made it a charming point of her sophistication to entertain in bed. While she lay propped with pillows he had read to her, talked to her, kissed her, had his hands fended away. The empty space was still charged with the vividness she had given to everything. There was one night very late, two or three o'clock, when he had sat on one side of the bed and a mournful and lovesick jazz trumpeter had sat on the other, neither of them willing to leave the other alone there, and all that night he had read aloud into the smell of sandalwood the life story of a mad woman from Butte, Montana. *I, Mary MacLean*, that one was called.

What an occasion she had made of it, laid up with a cold, hemmed in by rival young men, covered to the chin in an absurd, high-necked, old-fashioned nightgown, taking aspirins with sips of ginger beer, laughing at them alternately or together with that face as vivid on the pillow as a flower laid against the linen. It was innocence. In that crackpot bohemian pre-Crash wonderful time, it was innocence.

How he and the trumpeter had broken their deadlock, what had ever happened to the Tom Stead flurry, what became of Holly's string of other admirers—all gone. She sent them away, or they quarreled at her over their bruised egos, or they became upset at finding her always in a crowd. Plenty of self-appointed hummingbird catchers, but no captures.

And yet, maybe.

Summer and winter, day and night, were telescoped in his memory. How old would he have been? Nineteen? Something like that. He was still in college, and even though he had stayed out most of one year to work, he had still graduated when he was twenty. And twenty, for him at least, had been very different from nineteen. Say it was 1929. Say he was nineteen, Holly two or three years older. There was neither beginning nor ending nor definite location in time to what he vividly remembered. What they had been doing, whether they had been out to some university dance or to some nightclub, hardly any details came back. But they were alone in a way they seldom had been.

They must have been talking, something must have led up to it. It could have been during the time of gossip about Stead, for Holly was upset. It could have been only some occasion when she found her job as secretary of the American Mining Congress, or the attentions of her boss, or simply being absolutely independent and self-supporting, more of a strain than usual. But there she was, floodlighted in his mind, pressing against him with her face against his chest, clinging and crying, saying, "Bruce, get me out of this! I can't take any more of it. This is all no good, it leads nowhere, it's grubby and I hate it. I've got to get away, Bruce. Please!"

Both the tears and the way she clung excited him. But the game had been played through all their acquaintance under different rules. And if she was an innocent, what was he? He went on in the old way, alarmed but still kidding, burlesquing gestures of consolation, patting the crow-wing hair, saying, "Well now, hey, don't let it get you down. Brucie fix it, whatever it is." Inanities, idiocies. She wore an evening dress cut very low in the back, and he played his fingers up and down her spine. He slid his hand in against her skin, slid it further, expecting the competent twist and shrug and fending, and the laugh that would mean the emotional fit was over. But his hand went on around, clear around, and with a shock like an internal explosion he found it cupping the frantic softness of her breast.

Even remembering, all his sensations were shocking to him. He remembered how smoothly the curve of her side swelled upward, how astonishingly consecutive her body was. Also, and almost with revulsion, how rigid and demanding the nipple of her breast. Innocence—he had never touched a girl there, bare—never imagined, or imagined wrong. Stupefied by the sudden admission to her flesh, made uneasy by the way she crowded and clung, a scared schoolboy where she needed a man, he stood wrapping her awkwardly with his hand paralyzed against her discovered body, and kissed her and tasted her tears, and thought with alarm and conviction of Stead and the rumored nude, and was anguished with eagerness to escape.

He remembered not a scrap, not a detail, of how he got away. She offered herself, and that was all. The peewee golfer putting his little white ball up the little green alley of his youth came suddenly on the sidewinder in the sand trap, the crocodile in the artificial lake.

He closed the door on the memory. It had begun to occur to him that he was an extraordinary young man, and not everything that was extraordinary about himself pleased him. Innocence? Maybe, though there were more contemptuous names for it. Amusing certainly. If he were not caught in this queer emotional net he would have to laugh. You simply couldn't tell a story like that without drawing smiles. But he was not telling a story. He was standing in Holly's denuded bedroom trying to understand his emotions of nearly fifty years earlier. No matter what he had pretended, at that age he was hungrier for security than for taking chances. A fraud, he would gargle the whiskey he would obediently not drink. A great yapper with the crowd, he would tear up the turf coming to a stop when the cat quit running, he would break his neck not to catch what he was after.

He told himself that he had been a very young nineteen. He told himself that the bohemian excitement boiling around Holly was an absurd and perhaps touching and certainly temporary phase of growing up. He told himself that he had not been ready.

Like a bubble of gas escaping from something submerged and decaying in deep water, there rose to the surface of his mind one of Blake's proverbs of hell that he and Holly had admired together that long-gone Christmas morning. It burst, and it said, "Prudence is a rich ugly old maid courted by Incapacity."

The last time Mason had seen Holly, she was boarding a train for Seattle, on her way to Shanghai and a job they all publicly envied and would probably not have risked themselves. Whatever happened to her, her life could not have been dull. She had probably spent it flying around the world like a piece of space hardware. As Mason himself had done, however inadvertently.

Holly had burst out of Salt Lake's provincial security by choice.
He had been thrown out like a bum through swinging doors.
The result might have been the same, but the motivation was
not; and remembering the night when she stopped playing
make-believe and presented him with an option that would have
totally changed his life, he half regretted his youthful unread-
iness as if it had been a flaw of character and nerve. He
disliked that cautious image of himself.

His watch told him it was nearly five. Starting for the door, he
passed the dead woman's table and looked again into her waxen,
dead-white face. The skin was delicately wrinkled like the skin
of a winter-kept apple, but soft-looking, as if it would be not unpleasant to touch. The barbaric silver necklace somehow defined
her. What it said about frivolity, girlishness, love of ornament
and life, made him like her. But it lay very soberly on the black
crêpe breast.

He thought how she had been tampered with by McBride, and
how further touches of disguise would redden cheeks and lips
and complete her transformation from something real and terrible and dead to something that could be relinquished and forgotten. He turned away, frowning with a regret that was almost
personal, a kind of rueful sorrow. He did not want her to have
died.

As he reached the door he threw an apologetic look back at
the room as quiet and empty as a chapel, and at the corpse that
lay so quietly at its center. There was a dread in the room that
he would not stay for. He meant to tiptoe out, but he heard almost with panic the four quick raps his heels made on the bare
floor before they found the consoling softness of the stairs.

2

Smiling, with a manila envelope and a slip of paper in his hand, McBride intercepted him at the bottom. "Find anything you recognize?"

"Too much. Even the body."

McBride's eyebrows flew up. "What? Really? You mean . . . ?"

"No, no. Figuratively. Ghosts."

"Oh. Yes. Yes, of course, I suppose it *would* be rather disturbing, wouldn't it? I'm sorry if I . . ." He handed Mason the manila envelope. "These are some things Mr. Philips brought down from the Home. Your aunt's watch, wedding ring, and so on. And there's this box. I don't know if you'll want to take it now, or get it later." He stooped inside the office door and brought out a cardboard box tied with cord.

"Box?" Mason said. "What's in it, do you know?"

"No. It's marked with your name, so Mr. Philips didn't feel he should dispose of it with her other things."

Mason hefted the box. It was not very heavy. "That's strange she'd package up something for me. Her mind's been gone for years."

"It was something she was keeping for you, I think. I gather it's been in her room there a long time. I can keep it here if you'd rather take it tomorrow."

"No, I can take it along now. It's only two or three blocks."

"All right. And there's this," McBride said, and handed Mason a slip of paper. "Someone telephoned, wants you to call her."

At first Mason would not accept the piece of paper. He had the unpleasant sense that he had been shadowed, his disguise penetrated, his cover cracked. "Telephoned me? Nobody knows I'm here. Unless my secretary. Was it from California?"

"No, local. She'd read in the paper about Mrs. Webb's death, and guessed you might be coming. She called the Home first, and they directed her here."

Mason let his fingers close on the paper. There was nothing on it but a number. "She didn't leave her name?"

"No. If you want to use the telephone, there's one right in here."

Briefly Mason considered and rejected the fantasy that by some incredible coincidence the call might have been from Holly —that he had wandered down this rabbit hole into the past and that now anything was possible, even likely. Absurd, of course. He said, "Was there an obituary notice that named me as a survivor?"

"I don't know," McBride said. "Probably. It would be a natural thing, considering who you are. Go ahead and call, if you'd like."

But Mason stuck the paper into the breast pocket of his jacket. "Thanks, I'll call from the hotel. Will you do me a favor?"

"Of course."

"If anyone else calls for me, or this woman calls again, you don't know where I'm staying. Take their numbers, and their names, too, if you can."

"I understand."

"What time should I be here tomorrow?"

"There's only the graveside service. No reason to come until we're about ready to start for the cemetery. Say eleven-thirty?"

"Good. I'll try to have some flowers sent up."

"That will be nice." McBride bent his head sideward in deferential agreement, like a Goan houseboy, and Mason picked up the box by the cord and went out into the unabated heat.

The afternoon sun glared in his eyes. The sun glancing off the pavement lifted into the air a dark, wet-looking mirage. Cars going townward into the rising heat waves began to blur, grew as tall and square and black as the old Dodges of his youth, stretched and lifted off the street darker and higher until, tall as towers, they merged with the buildings downtown.

All his impressions suffered from distortion and ambiguity. Looking at buildings, he couldn't say whether he remembered them or whether his memory was filling the street with things it wanted familiar. Though he had been vaguely prepared for changes, he had not foreseen how strangeness and familiarity might fuse. He knew the street but was made uneasy by it. Was that because the person who saw and the person who remembered were not the same, though they used the same eyes?

He knew this Bruce Mason who walked down South Temple Street carrying a cardboard box of his aunt's unwanted leavings. He had lived with him a long time, knew what he could do and how he would respond to different situations. But Bruce Mason walked double. Inside him, moving with the same muscles and feeling with the same nerves and sweating through the same pores, went a thin brown youth, volatile, impulsive, never at rest, not so much a person as a possibility, or a bundle of possibilities: subject to enthusiasm and elation and exuberance and occasional great black moods, stubborn, capable of scheming but often astonished by consequences, a boy vulnerable to wonder, awe, worship, devotion, hatred, guilt, vanity, shame, ambition, dreams, treachery; a boy avid for acceptance and distinction, secretive and a blabbermouth, life-crazy and hence girl-crazy, a show-off who could be withered by a contemptuous word or look, a creature overflowing with brash self-confidence one minute and oppressed by its own worthlessness the next; a vessel of primary sensations undiluted by experience, wisdom, or fatigue.

Put aside, postponed, schooled, overtaken by events, he was never defined, much less fulfilled—hardly even remembered until Mason came around Black Rock that afternoon and saw the old lake bottom littered with the stumps of the pilings on which the Saltair Pavilion used to ride above waist-deep water, and turned eastward to see the mirage city rising against its mountains, and heard the ghostly unmuffered roar of Jack Bailey's bug.

When he took off his jacket, and a drift of air bushed his

sweating forearms with a chill like liquid nitrogen, it was the
boy's skin that cringed with remembrance of what evaporation
can do in super-dry air. And when he looked at the people he
met, half expecting to encounter someone in whose altered features he could decipher a face once known, it was the boy on
whom he relied for recognition. He himself would not know an
old acquaintance, no old acquaintance would know him. Actually, he would not have liked meeting anyone the boy might
know. He didn't want either the boy or himself to be recognized.
He wanted them to see without being seen, as if they looked
through one-way glass.

They met only strangers. In the hot street the sound of tires
was sticky. The sidewalk was hot through his soles. Inhabited by
his Doppelgänger, exhilarated by the sense of being invisible, he
passed the old Church offices with their flower beds, and the garage ramp that had usurped the space of the old gym, and was
sucked through a whirl of reflections into the Utah Hotel's cool
lobby.

For the last block he and the boy had been marching to the
beat of a scrap of poetry, a little 4/4 tune risen from the same
cistern that had produced Blake's proverb of hell:

> You need not be a chamber to be haunted.
> You need not be a house.

In his room, where a chilly wind blew out of the air condi-
tioner, he threw box and jacket on the bed and called Room
Service for ice and tonic water. They came promptly—this had
always been a first-class hotel, quintessentially Mormon both in
its friendly efficiency and in the air of moneyed confidence it
wore. More and more pleased to be here, he got the bottle of gin
from his bag—before leaving he had remembered that Utah sold
no liquor by the drink—and made himself a gin and tonic.

His was a corner room. The west windows, which looked
across Main Street toward Temple Square, he left shrouded, for
he could feel how the undiminished heat would burst in at him
if he drew the drapes even inches apart. But the south windows
were shaded, and he pulled the drapes wide. Sipping his drink,
he looked down on the intersection of Main and South Temple, a
corner once as familiar as his own face.

Progress had been at work on it. Old buildings had been replaced by newer, taller ones, and something drastic had happened to Main Street. Its sidewalks had been widened well out into the former traffic lanes, and the street narrowed to half its former width. The sidewalks thus expanded had been encumbered with planters, fountains, flower urns, and stelae, all made of a substance that looked like granite but probably wasn't. The effect was rather like the Soviet exhibit at a World's Fair, something created by Heroic Workers. Merely human activities would be diminished on such a street. God pity the adolescent who in his exuberance, talking to his girl, turned around and walked backward. God pity the woman who window-shopped as she walked. Ass over teacup into a fountain or a bed of golardias.

On the other hand, it did get flowers and young trees into the downtown concrete. It did demonstrate that community pride, half Mormon and half Chamber of Commerce, that had always made Salt Lake a clean and pleasant town. What if the imitation-granite things were too heavy and too many? What if someone now and then did fall into the fountains or the flowers?

As far as he could see down Main, the wide encumbered sidewalks continued. Though he leaned, he couldn't quite see to the entrance of the old pool hall. Was that smelly cave still there? Probably not. It would be incompatible with beautification and downtown renewal. But he felt its possibility down there, just out of sight, and he was aware of a prompt, defensive caution, like the caution he would have felt if he were walking along a mined road. He kept to one side. He circled.

Brigham Young's frock-coated figure, standing where the Gentile jingle left him, with his back to the temple and his hand to the bank, cast its shadow almost to the bank's doors. A car turning the corner burrowed under the shadow like a cat under a rug. When it had passed, the outline of Brother Brigham settled back upon the pavement as intact as revelation.

Then something strange. The intersection drifted and became a double exposure, as if a transparent overlay had been slid across it. Over the modern corner with its striped pedestrian crossings and its wide cluttered sidewalks hovered the image of an older, simpler meeting of streets. From his window he saw three foreshortened figures pass below him and turn to cross South Temple. The camera cut to street level and he saw them plain: three sunburned boys of sixteen or seventeen or eighteen, one of them very tall, with red hair, one dark and curly-headed, one thin and blond, all of them in white shirts whose sleeves were rolled nearly to the shoulder, and in white Navy-surplus bell-bottomed ducks with laces at the back of the waist.

Slim-hipped identicals, walking with a spring that could at any moment break into a run, they grin back over their shoulders at the camera. Three abreast, they pass out of the frame, out of sight, out of time—glimpsed and gone, irrecoverable, their presence written on the hot summer air of a period as irrecoverable as they: Joe Mulder, Jack Bailey, Bruce Mason, fixed for a few seconds by a Pathé News cameraman filming a Salt Lake City street scene in the summer of what? 1925? 1926, the summer after their freshman year in college.

The day was there intact. They had just come from the tennis club, where Mulder and Mason had won a doubles match that put them into the third round of the state tournament. From the club they had accompanied Bailey to the Mission Home, which he would enter tomorrow to be briefed and purified for his coming mission to Tonga. They were now on their way down to Second South to have a hot beef sandwich at the workingmen's restaurant known as Joe Vincent's. On Mason's palate, either as remembrance or as anticipation, lingered the flavor of that slab of white bread and slab of overdone beef smothered in brown Formula 57 gravy.

The vanished trio left him brooding with the cold edge of the glass against his upper lip. Irrecoverable, but fantastically more real than anything in the modern street, much more real than the planters and fountains of downtown renewal. He had seen them plain, living, solid, as unchangeable as history. They *were* history. That Pathé newsreel must be preserved somewhere. He could go to the archives and borrow it and project it and turn his momentary hallucination into actual images. Just before the boys appear on camera, President Calvin Coolidge has been crowned with a warbonnet by some tame Sioux in the Black Hills. Just after they pass out of sight beyond the bank corner, a forlorn family will start picking through the wreckage of their home in a tornado-struck Oklahoma town.

Je suis une chose qui dure. So said Henri Bergson, whom he had probably not thought of since reading him as background for a college paper on Proust half a century ago. *Je suis une chose qui dure.* I am a thing that lasts.

But not, it was clear, unchanged. New shapes took over from old ones. Memory had to be—didn't it?—a series of overlays. I remember, therefore I was. I was, therefore I am. I both contain and commemorate myself. I am both grave and gravestone.

Mason had left Salt Lake sick with hatred of Jack Bailey. But grievance and injured vanity did heal, and other recollections seemed to have lasted almost as well as the grudge. He wouldn't mind seeing Bailey again, if only out of curiosity. And if Bailey, then certainly others, the ones who once made his world for him, Joe Mulder especially, who all but created Bruce Mason.

Would he call Joe? Of course, why not? Though if he was still alive, as he might not be, their meeting could be an awkward effort by two strangers to reconstruct one another from memory. He had a vision of himself ringing a doorbell and being confronted by some old baldhead or some grandma with a hearing aid. "Remember me? I'm Bruce Mason, we used to know each other back in the nineteenth century."

The prospect both daunted and intrigued him. He had often enough imagined coming back and restoring all the relationships, filling himself in on all that had happened in his absence. But now that he was here, it did not seem an easy thing to do. He made himself another drink before he checked the telephone book.

Then he had it open, his finger went down the M's, and suddenly there it was, the name, even the same address, Joe's parents' house, which for two or three years had been more home to him than his own. Delighted, he hunted for a pad on which to write down the number, found none, and ended by fishing out of his jacket pocket the slip that McBride had handed him. He scribbled the number on the back of it, shut the telephone book, told himself that he might as well make this other call, too, whoever it was. Then he turned the slip over, looked, turned it back. The number was the same on both sides.

Adrenalin went through him. He made a short, incredulous sound of laughter. Right in the same house, as if waiting! While the absentee tried to make up his mind whether to restore old friendship, the stay-at-home acted as if it had never been broken. But it was a woman who called. His wife, presumably. It struck Mason as not completely protocol that the instant, infallible restoration of contact should not have come in Joe's own voice.

Just the same, nothing in a long time had given him this much pleasure. It made him, in fact, slightly giddy. He took a little impulsive walk across the room. The stiffness of the long drive lurked in his muscles. His skin had glazed over in the air-conditioned chill. As he sat down on the bed he had an unsteady moment, a darkening of the sight. Then it cleared. But it had lasted long enough to check his dialing finger. Wait, wait. A gap that wide couldn't be closed in a minute. There would be plenty of time after dinner. Call him then.

3

In the old days the Roof Garden had been open, with awnings and pots and planters and the smell of freshly watered flowers. Now it was the Sky Room, enclosed for elegant dining. The sun had found clouds to hide in, and the windows were unveiled. Below his window table were the geometric paths of the temple grounds and the brown turtleback of the Tabernacle, and right opposite him, pasted against the clouded west, was the temple itself, spiny as a horned toad. Though he found that he couldn't admire it architecturally, it struck him as comforting and safe—he felt protective about it. It was one of the shapes of permanence he remembered.

The place was crowded with early diners, and the service, though assiduous, was slow. Mason did not mind. He ate his salad and looked out of the window while the sky began its phases from gray to red, red to purple, purple to saffron. At a certain moment floodlights sprang to life at the bases of the temple's clustered spires and improved them, deepening the round windows and brightening the Angel Moroni on his steeple point. The light was gentle outside, even gentler inside, accentuated by a blade of candle flame on each table.

Then he noticed that the flames had begun, all together, to

waver, and about the same moment he felt the faint touch on his face and hands. The windows along the east and south had been opened, and were catching the canyon breeze flowing down from the mountains to fill in under the air still rising from the warm lake.

One touch, and his skin remembered. Magic. He sat drenched in another of those showers of sensation that had been passing over him ever since he arrived.

He was on the lawn behind Joe Mulder's house, flat on his back, arms wide in cool grass, his eyes full of stars. If he rolled his head to the right he saw the dark crowns of trees rising out of the gully. If he rolled it to the left he saw, over the roof of the bungalow, the rim of the Wasatch smoking with imminent moonrise. Others were sprawled around him. Who? Joe, for sure; probably Jack Bailey; probably Welby Kreps. The Phi Delt quartet. They had probably been practicing for the Spring Sing, gathered in Joe's back yard harmonizing Tin Pan Alley moon songs: "When the Moon Comes over the Mountain," "Moonlight and Roses," and the one Bailey called the sheepherder's song, "The Same Old Moon, the Same Old June, But Not the Same Old Ewe."

The smells were of mown grass and damp earth and the rich rotting of compost over the gully's edge. The mood was idle, easy, contented, open to every sort of nocturnal yearning. Their recent harmonies hung in the air that moved cool and secret down the gully and spread along the grass, but no one suggested another song or another run through an old one. They were quiet, flopped loosely, waiting for nothing in particular. His ear, close to the ground, heard dim stirrings as if night crawlers were oozing out of their holes—as if, with a flashlight, you could startle their reddish gleam among the grass blades.

The edge of the moon dazzled over the rim. Someone sat up, a silhouette edged in silver. The leaves of the maple between house and garage glinted silver and dark, moving as if the light beyond were forcing them aside. In the gully, hidden among the stir of cottonwood leaves, a mockingbird awoke and sang.

Incredulously Mason backed away from that vision. What a Rube Goldberg wiring job a man was! How enduring were the circuits stamped into a boy when he was dizzy with hormones

and as vulnerable to experience as dry blotting paper to water!
Push the right button and you floodlighted him like the temple.
Push another and you got a whole *son et lumière*.

And what programmed the memory for such instant recall was
not necessarily profound or even important. He supposed people
were often programmed by important things; he had been himself—teachers, great books, painful deaths, family conflicts, the
midnight miseries that had marked even such a deceptively safe
adolescence as his own. But what sprang out of revisited Salt
Lake City to confound him with forgotten emotions seemed to
be mostly trivia, the sort of thing to which he had paid no attention at the time and had never recalled since.

What is an event? What constitutes an experience? Are we
what we do, or do we do what we are? The circumstances that
had poisoned Mason's boyhood, the events that in a malign con-
junction had gathered to drive him from this town, seemed to
have lasted less well than a kiss behind the piano on a Christmas
morning, or the feeling of fellowship, almost beatitude, that
came from the shadowy presence of friends not even firmly
identified on a dark lawn, where the air breathed romantic yearning and trembled with the sound of cottonwood leaves, and had
only just ceased vibrating with June-moon harmonies rehearsed
for a forgotten Spring Sing.

Dangerous to squeeze the tube of nostalgia. Never get the
toothpaste back in. He could end up embarrassing himself. Because the fact was, the darker things he had to remember about
this town were at least as numerous as the sentimental and satisfying things, and merely by remarking that he didn't seem to
remember them, he brought them back. If he would let them,
they could swarm at his mind like autumn flies at an attic window.

His dinner came, with profuse apologies from the young waitress, and he took his hands off the table to let her fuss at setting
him up nicely. He ate with his eyes turned out the window and
his mind turned backward.

All his earliest years in Salt Lake had been an effort, much of
the time as unconscious as growth itself and yet always there as
if willed, to outgrow what he was and become what he was not.
A stray, he yearned to belong. An outsider and an isolate, he

aspired to friends and family and the community solidarity he saw all around him in that Mormon city. A runt, he dreamed of athletic triumphs. Insignificant, he coveted the kind of notice he saw given to football heroes, sheiks, slickers, and campus politicians with glib tongues—all of whom, he felt in his heart, which was arrogant even when most envious, were inferior to him in brains and potential.

Convinced that everything private to him and his family was the reverse of respectable, he agonized considerably about goodness and guilt and God. Once he found a place in the Boy Scouts he went up through the ranks like a rocket from Tenderfoot to Eagle, cheating a couple of times to get merit badges he wasn't qualified for, and suffering bleak contritions when he thought over his sins in bed. All sorts of sins, comic now but not then. He was the original of the kid who slept with boxing gloves on.

Most means of gaining attention were unavailable to him, but none was beneath him; and though all through high school he had no real friend, he did not go unnoticed. At thirteen, when he started the tenth grade, he was barely five feet tall and weighed barely ninety pounds. But he learned very soon to speak in the voice of Polyphemus or the Bull of Bashan. Kidded or persecuted by bigger boys, he offered to tear them to bits and scatter their bloody parts for the sea gulls. Very early he understood the exact shade of hyperbole that would startle but could not be taken seriously. Beneath notice, he compelled it.

Because he was too small to take the required ROTC—the only kid in school not in uniform—he became a violent anti-militarist, full of contempt for the regimentation, the itchy woolen breeches, the rolled puttees, and the choking blouses of the chickenshit soldiers. Then in his senior year, when he suddenly started growing, he took up the military life so enthusiastically that at the year-end parade and inspection he was leading a platoon, wearing a Sam Browne belt, shoulder pips, leather puttees, and a sword. He even spent part of the following summer at a Citizens' Military Training Camp, of which the less said, the better.

In gym classes he was a joke, added to teams as an afterthought or a handicap. Embedded in the sedimentary strata of

his mature descendant were cherty nodules of humiliation, as
when a hulk of a retarded athlete surveyed him with astonishment in the shower one day, remarking, "My God, shrimp, you
haven't got knockers big enough to knock up a chicken!"

Bushwah, you big dumb ape. Come fooling around and I'll
show you how to knock. I'll knock your teeth so far back you'll
grin out the back of your neck. I'll kick you so hard you can
carry your ass in a knapsack.

He pushed his comic ferocity ahead of him like a shield
behind which siege forces advance toward a defended wall. Born
mascot, midget, he muscled secret bricks. He ran around the
block a lot, mostly at night when he wouldn't be seen. He
dreamed. The dreams were not remarkable, and they neither
stopped nor changed after he started to grow, but continued on,
even into college. Athletic prowess, casual heroisms, and the adoration of perfumed women comprehended them all. He got his
clues from movies and popular songs. For a good while he was
in love with the great pansy eyes of Corinne Griffith, and in his
fantasies he closely resembled Wallace Reid.

The mere recollection of the shrimp he once was made Mason
shake his head incredulously. He saw the waitress start from her
place, apparently thinking he had found something inedible
among his dinner, and he had to smile and nod her back with intimations of pleasurable surfeit. Looking back out into the fading sky, he thought with some exasperation that the twenties
have been badly misrepresented by moviemakers and social his-
torians too young to know what they are talking about, and
badly misunderstood by contemporary kids who have roared
more by the age of thirteen than the slickers and flappers of the
Roaring Twenties roared in their whole mythical lifetime. The
twenties as Mason remembered them were the age of innocence.

Or was it that, famished for acceptance, he himself had
rebelled backward, away from his father's lawlessness? He didn't
think so. Everyone he had grown up with had been pretty mild.
Holly, the most sophisticated creature he had ever seen, was, as
he had decided this afternoon, a small-town innocent creating in
stodgy Salt Lake a pale lavender version of Greenwich Village.

Good Mormon girls would not only not take a drink, they
might refuse to go out with someone who smoked: they didn't

dare come home with the smell of cigarettes in their clothes. The
line between nice girl and chippie was as firmly drawn as a national boundary, and if challenged, would have been defended
by all the red-blooded youths who spent much of their time and
treasure trying to lure nice girls across the border. What they
were all headed for, perhaps after a brief fling by the males, was
"My Blue Heaven," sung in a male alto by Gene Austin. A smiling face, a fireplace, a cozy room, a little nest that's nestled
where the roses bloom. Just Molly and me, and baby makes
three. Much more sweet than hot. Mason remembered billboards
(put up by whom?) with pictures of chubby infants and the
caption "Utah's Best Crop."

For better or worse, the place he derived from. Precisely what
made him smile fascinated him. He seemed to have passed
through some barrier into an earlier and simpler time, and at the
same time to have exposed himself to feelings that he had
thought completely outgrown. Was this a worse place to grow
up in than some more worldly city? Didn't Salt Lake, once, save
him, or let him save himself? Would delight have been any more
delightful, or friendship any warmer, or young love any more de-
lirious, or unhappiness any bleaker, or the terror and awe of adolescence any more potent, in another town and another society?

He had not come back, consciously, to look up the past. Yet if
you wanted to hunt the yeti, you went where he lived. If you
came to find young Bruce Mason, and more and more that
seemed to be what he was doing, you looked where he had been
seen.

And found him, if you went clear back to the beginning, rat-
eyed and watchful in some corner, or gnawing his own trapped
limbs in his agony to escape. In the Sky Room murmuring with
voices and the discreet sounds of service, while dusk came in the
west windows and the canyon breeze freshened the conditioned
air, Mason sat abstractedly eating, remembering a day during his
first months in this town.

4

When his Latin teacher said she had always wanted a scale
model of a Roman *castra* so that pupils reading Caesar's *Gallic
Wars* could see exactly how the legions built their defenses, of
course Bruce volunteered. He was always volunteering. The year
was 1922, he was thirteen years old. Around East High School he
drew two kinds of attention, one kind from teachers and another
from boys, especially the big boys and most especially the stupid
ones. He would have given a good deal to be big and stupid so
that he, too, could sneer at his little peaked face focused on the
teachers ready to cry answers, and his little skinny arm flapping
at every call to special duty.

"A *castra*? I'll make one!" he said. "I know a slough where
there's good clay. I'll get some tonight after school."

"Now that, Bruce," said Miss Van Vliet, "is the spirit I like to
see."

They lived then on Seventh East, across from Liberty Park.
The slough was clear down on Seventeenth South below Fifth
East, where streets began to fade out into big truck gardens with
shanties and staked-out goats. A good sixteen blocks, more than
two miles, added to his walk home. A month before, he had

made another volunteering expedition out there to get hydras and paramecia and amoebas for his zoology teacher, but this trip, in late November, was not quite the sunny autumn holiday the other had been. By the time he was laying his books on dry ground at the edge of the slough, the afternoon was already late and blue. The wind went dryly through tules and yellow grass, and the sky over the mountains was the color of iron.

It was too cold to take off his shoes and wade. He had to hop from hummock to hummock until he found a place wet enough to dig in. The clay lay under the sod like icy blue grease; it numbed him to the wrists as he filled his lunch pail. He saw a mouse dart through the reeds, and the sad cry of a marsh hawk coasting over made him feel little and alone, and wish that he had brought someone along. He had to remind himself that though it was less fun to do things alone, there was more distinction in it that way. Anyway, who would have come?

The slimy clay stuck like paint to his hands, and it was impossible to get to open water where he could wash. He wiped them as well as he could on the grass, but he had a hard time, working with wrists and elbows and the very tips of his fingers, trying to get his books tucked down inside his belt without smearing them and his clothes with mud.

His way home led across fields and down wide streets with many vacant lots, some of them planted to gardens now gone by. As he walked, the day grew bluer and colder, the wind cut his face, his hand carrying the heavy lunch pail stiffened into an iron hook. Every time he shifted the pail from hand to hand he had to stick out his stomach hard to keep the books from sliding down inside his corduroy knickers. If they had slipped clear down he wouldn't have dared, with those hands, to get them out.

The heroic and indispensable feeling he had started with, the spirit that Miss Van Vliet liked to see, had leaked away. He was not a hero. He was thin and pale, weak, stick-armed, a baby. And no matter how he hawked and shuffled, no matter how many times he cleared his nose through his mouth, a clammy and elastic gob began to droop lower and lower on his upper lip.

His muddy claws couldn't have handled a handkerchief if he had owned one. They couldn't have got it out of his pocket. Working his face against the sting and stiffness of the wind,

holding his stomach pouted out against books and belt, miserably snuffling and spitting, he went crabwise down a road, across
a corner shortcut, past a yard where a dog leaped out roaring. At
last he came to the big cabbage field, still unharvested, that
spread over considerable ground below the Surplus Canal along
Thirteenth South; and passed it with his face sideward to the
wind so that the cabbages made changing ranks and then diago-
nals and then new ranks down the gray field; and finally, his
shoulder blades aching and his arms dead and his hands numb
and bloodless under the mud, he made it through the sagging
picket fence and up onto his gingerbread-framed front porch.

There was a car in the drive. There often was. He was too far
gone to pay it any attention. The books were held by one slip-
ping corner, the clot sagged frantically under his nose. It was
like a nightmare in which he had to get to some special place before whatever was behind him made its grab. This time he made
it to the door, fell against the jamb, and braced the books there.
Some rule would be violated, something would happen bad, if he
set the pail of mud down before he was clear inside. He hung on
to it, braced against the jamb, and pressed his frozen thumb on
the bell.

Down each side of the door, relics of some time when this had
been a fairly pretentious house, went a panel of leaded panes of
glass of many colors. Through a violet one just level with his
eyes was a neat bullet hole. Nobody knew how it had come
there. It hinted of old crimes, feuds, jealous lovers, better days.
Sometimes, inside the hall, he had felt through it a thin cold secret draft like the stream of air a dentist squirts into a cavity to
dry it out before he fills it. Now he put his tongue to the bullet
hole, but there was no draft, only cold glass. He remembered
that the doorbell hadn't worked since last week, and raised his
dirty fist and pounded. Instantly such pain went through his frozen knuckles that he moaned in fury and kicked the door.

The books slid down inside his pant leg. The clot dropped a
dangerous eighth of an inch on his lip. Then his father opened
the door.

He was very annoyed. "Have you lost the use of your hands?"
he said.

Desolately snuffling, tilted into agonies by the contrary strains of the heavy pail in his hand and the heavy books in his pants, Bruce whined, "I was all *muddy!*"

His father looked him over in silence. His look was like a hand in the scruff of Bruce's neck. Then he said, "What's the matter with your handkerchief?"

He was extraordinarily fussy about things like that. A runny nose or somebody who smacked at the table or the sight of somebody's dirty fingernails could drive him half wild. And Bruce *had* gone off to school again without a handkerchief. He said once more, "I'm all *mud!*"

Somehow he sidled past into the hall, wonderfully warm with the dry breath from the register. But he didn't dare set down the pail or relax, so long as he was being looked at that way. "Jesus Christ," his father said finally. "Thirteen years old and running around with a lamb's leg under your nose, making mud pies."

That stung. Bruce whirled around and howled, "I was not! I'm supposed to make a *castra.*"

"Oh you are," his father said. But he was stopped for the moment. Bruce knew he hadn't the slightest idea what a *castra* was, and wasn't going to ask and expose his ignorance. He knew things that his father had never heard of: that was a sweet fierce pleasure.

In the parlor somebody had started to play Bruce's new Victrola record, a piece called "Nobody Lied," with a big slap-tongue baritone sax solo embedded in it. The clot drooped, and he dragged at it wetly, his nose stuffed shut with the warmth of the hall. His father's lips turned inside out. He gave Bruce a push on the shoulder. "Go get yourself cleaned up, and stay out of the front room. There's company."

He didn't need to say so. Company meant there were people in there buying drinks. That was what they were, a speakeasy. Practically all his life they had been something like that, something shameful and illegal and not to be spoken of.

He had no inclination to go into the parlor, but he said to himself that he wished the damned company would quit wearing out his record. He started for the kitchen, spraddling because of the books in his pants, and his father said after him, "For God's sake, have you messed your pants, too?"

That really made him bawl. He started yelling, "No! My books slipped down, and I couldn't . . ." But his father cut him off with one furious motion of his hand. The kitchen door opened and his mother, with an instant cry, stooped to help him. He had finally made it home. Behind him, as the parlor door opened and closed, he heard his father saying something humorous to the company.

"Great day!" his mother said. "You've got yourself tied hand and foot. What on earth!"

She wiped his nose. She pried the pail out of his frozen fingers. She slid his belt buckle open and reached down and got the books. Then she stood him at the sink and ran warm water on his hands until they stung and tingled and grew clean and red, while he snarled and complained. Last she rubbed lotion into the bleeding cracks in his knuckles and put him at the kitchen table and made him a cup of cocoa.

All he would tell her when she asked what he had been doing and why his lunch pail was full of mud was that his Latin teacher wanted him to make a *castra*. What was a *castra?* she wanted to know, and he flew out at her bitterly. It was a thing for school, a thing the legions built, what did she suppose? Finally she found out that it was something he was going to build with clay on some sort of board base, and gave him an old breadboard to build it on. Before supper he spent an intent hour, sitting stocking-footed soaking up the warmth pouring from the kitchen register, drawing a *castra* to scale on the clean bleached wood.

Life in that house was full of tensions. For one thing, they were afraid of the law, and were constantly poised to move, though a move meant losing customers who might never find them again. For another, Bruce's mother was the wrong woman to be the wife of a man who ran a speakeasy. She had been brought up in a stiff Lutheran family, and without being at all religious, she had a yearning belief in honesty, law, fairness, respectability, and the need for self-respect. When Bruce looked around him and envied the home life of students he vaguely knew, he was envious mainly for himself, but also in part for his mother. She would have loved being part of some friendly town or neighborhood, she would have been immensely thankful to have friends. When company came, she stayed in the kitchen. If the party in the parlor got loud, she sat wincing as if she had cramps, and threw looks at Bruce, with grimaces and jerky movements of her shoulders. She was a humble, decent woman married to a boomer. All it ever took to remind Bruce of how abused he was, was to catch sight of her face when she didn't know anyone was looking.

His father was a perfectionist, he had standards, he aspired to run a classy and genteel joint. Even in the old tin-wainscoted, Congoleum-floored houses they rented, he went around with a towel on his arm, always flicking and dusting, cranking the Victrola, making conversation, setting up a free one for good spenders. When, as sometimes happened, he needed help, he expected his wife and son to hop.

Bruce escaped him all day at school. His brother Chet escaped completely, for as a halfback on the high school football team he was living at the team's training camp on the coach's farm in Murray. Lacking so thorough an escape, Bruce relied on homework. He saw to it that he had loads of it. At home he was not a volunteer, and his mother abetted him, for though they never spoke openly about it, they were in mutinous league against their life.

That night new customers came in after six. His father took a plate into the dining room, which could be shut off by sliding doors from the parlor but from which he could hear the customers if they wanted anything. Bruce and his mother sat in the kitchen. Once, coming in for hot water to make a toddy, his father stopped in the doorway to talk for a moment. He parted his hair in the middle and slicked it down like some old-time German bartender with a sense of vocation. As he stood flicking his towel, his eyes drifted over to the table where the breadboard lay with its walls and ditch half molded and its wad of blue clay in the middle. His glance came back across Bruce's like saw teeth across a nail. Through the register, sounding plain but far away, there was a dark, remote throbbing, the last beats of the slap-tongue sax, and the voice started chanting, with what seemed inappropriate vivacity,

> Nobody lied when they said I cried over you.
> Nobody lied when they said that I 'most died over you
> Got so blue I don't know what to dooooo.
> All my life before me looks so dreary and so black
> I think I'll choose the river and I'll never come back . . .

"Don't you want some pie?" Bruce's mother said.

"I'll get it later," his father said, and took the teakettle and left.

After supper Bruce went straight back to the *castra*. He wanted to take it to school with him in the morning and dazzle Miss Van Vliet with the speed of his accomplishment, and force reluctant admiration from the big and stupid, and set the girls to twittering. One girl in that class thought he had a roguish face—someone had told him. The knowledge was like a secret twenty-dollar gold piece in a deep pocket that no one knew of.

Carefully he went on smoothing the clay into walls, gates, rows of little tents. He would make such a *castra* as Caesar and all his legions had never thrown up in all the plains and mountains of Gaul—roguish Bruce Mason, that bright little boy, with the spirit the teachers liked to see.

Behind him his mother tipped the coal scuttle into the range. From the sound, he knew there was nothing in it but dust and papers, but he did not rise to get her a new bucket of coal. He bent his head and worked on in great absorption while she went past him and the door let a cold draft across his feet and closed again, while the returning scuttle knocked against the door and then went down solidly on the asbestos stove mat. Later there was a noise of dishes in the pan, the smell of soap and steam. Nothing disturbed him. Eventually she stood behind him and he heard the squeak of a towel on china.

"Oh!" she said, pleased. "It's a little fort!"

"It's a *castra*," he said in scorn. "A Roman camp."

About seven-thirty his father came in again. "Have your pie now," Bruce's mother said. "I've kept it warm. Who's in there?"

He took the slab of pie in his clean, round-nailed hand. "Just Lew McReady and his lady friend, now."

"His lady friend. One week he's here with his wife, and the next with his lady friend. Which one, that nurse?"

"Yeah."

"I wonder if she knows he's got children seventeen years old?"

"Oh, Lew's all right. He just likes a change."

He was trying to kid her, but she would not be kidded. Glancing up under his brows, Bruce saw her unbelieving look. "What a life we lead," she said. "What friends we have."

"If you can't tell the difference between a friend and a customer you don't know which side your bread's buttered on."

"Maybe that's the trouble. All we have is customers."

"If we're starting on that again," he said, "I'm going back in the dining room and read the *Post*."

With a push of the shoulder he was gone from the doorway. Bruce's mother smiled at him bleakly. He made no response—went on smoothing with the back of a paring knife the triangular bits of clay that served as tents. Their wrangling was not his concern. He did not live in that house. He lived at school, where teachers lighted up when he came around and girls thought he had a roguish face. In this country inhabited by hostile barbarians he erected his defenses and mounted guard.

"It's beginning to look real good," his mother said after five minutes of clock-ticking, stove-ticking, tap-dripping silence. "You do a nice neat job of things."

Praise made him businesslike. "I wish I had a little eagle."

"A what?"

"An eagle. Legion standards had eagles on them. In camp they planted the standard in front of the commander's tent."

"I guess . . . I don't quite know what a standard is," she said.

He didn't bother to answer.

For a while she read a magazine at the other table. Bruce had not heard any noise, either from his father or from the company in the parlor, for some time. The radiator puffed its warm breath against his legs, the dust puppies fluttered in its grill, the tin pipes sighed and popped.

"I've got a pin shaped like a bird," his mother said. "Would that help you? Maybe you could fasten it onto this—standard—some way."

She bothered him, trying to horn in on this thing she didn't even understand. On the other hand, maybe he *could* use the pin. He leaned back. "Let's see it."

"We'll have to wait till they go, in there. It's in my sewing basket."

"I think they're gone."

"I haven't heard the door."

"They're gone. I'd hear them through the register."

He was already up, skating on stocking feet across the slick linoleum. "Well, I'll have to find it for you," she said. "You'd never know where."

Down the darkish hall, lighted only by a high dim bulb that brought a shine out of the newel post and tangled in the shadows of the coatrack, he stroked with skating strides, made a detour to pass his hand across the cold stream of air at the bullet hole, and slid up to the half-open parlor door.

He was there just a split second before the tap of his mother's heels startled them. Lew McReady was bent far over his girl on the sofa, whispering in her ear or kissing her, Bruce couldn't see which. But he could see, in the spread of light that the table lamp shed, the white satin of the lady friend's blouse, and Lew McReady's fingers working like a cat's claws in it.

Then they heard. McReady snapped around and spread his arm in a big elaborate gesture along the sofa back, and yawned as if he had just been aroused from a nap. The girl made a sound like a laugh. Behind Bruce his mother said in a tight voice (had she seen?), "I'm sorry, Bruce needs something for a thing he's making at school. Excuse me . . . just a second . . . he's making something . . ."

McReady crossed his legs and made a sour mouth. Bruce knew his son at high school, one of the big stupid ones, a football player who was supposed to star if he ever got eligible. But he couldn't keep looking at McReady. He had to look at the nurse, who smiled at him. She seemed extraordinarily pretty. He couldn't understand how she could be so pretty and let old McReady paw her. She had a laughing sort of face, and she was lost and damned.

She said, "What is it you're making?"

"A *castra*—a Roman camp."

"For Latin?"

"Yes."

His mother was rummaging in the sewing basket. He wished she would bring the whole basket so that they could get out of there, and yet he was glad for every extra second she took. McReady, still spread-eagled elegantly over the couch, lighted a cigarette. He had a red face with large pores, and the hair on top of his head was thin, about twelve hairs carefully spread to cover as much skull as possible. When he took the cigarette from his lips and looked at the tip and saw the pink of lipstick there, he put the back of his hand to his mouth and looked across it and saw Bruce watching him. So he separated himself from the others and interested himself in a long wheezing coughing spell. His eyes glared out of his purpling face with a kind of dull patience, waiting for things to die down. The nurse smiled at Bruce, and loathing her he smiled back. She said, "I took Latin once. *'Gallia est omnis divisa in partes tres.'*"

"My Go-guho-guhod!" McReady said through his coughing, and his bulging eyes stared at her glassily. "An unexpec-uhec-uhected talent!"

Bruce's mother was surprised, too. He saw both her surprise and her pleasure that something from the world of his school meant something to somebody, even though she herself couldn't share it and even though the one who could was this lady friend of McReady's.

Maybe she was as mixed about the girl as Bruce was, and he was truly mixed. He could still see that hand in her breast, and the softness under the satin was like the voluptuous softnesses that coiled around him in bed some nights until he lay panting and glaring into the dark, feeling his ninety-pound body as explosive as if his flesh were nitroglycerin packed on his bones. The girl looked at him with clear eyes, she had several wholesome freckles, she laughed with a dimple. Above all, she quoted Caesar (and what if it was only the first line, it was *correct*— most dopes said *omnia* instead of *omnis*) He could hardly have been more shaken if he had run into Miss Van Vliet having a snort of Sunnybrook Farm in his parlor. Actually that would have shaken him less, for Miss Van Vliet would never crawl naked and voluptuous through his dreams, and this one would. Oh, this one would!

He said sullenly and stupidly, *"Quarum unum incolunt Belgae."*

"Elsa," Lew McReady said, "we are dealing with a pair of real scholars."

His mocking face was exactly the face of any number of the big and stupid at school. Bruce hated him. He hated his whiskey breath and his red face and the memory of his hand in this lost girl's breast. He hated the way he called Bruce's mother by her first name, as if she were some friend of his. He hated everything about McReady, and McReady knew it.

"Ma," he said passionately, "I got to . . ."

"Yes," she said, coming, but hesitating out of politeness for a few more words. "You'd think the world depended on it," she said to the nurse. "He's making this *castra* and he needed a bird for the standard. That's what we came in to get. School is awful important to him," she said with an abrupt, unexpected laugh. "If I didn't chase him out to play he'd study all the time."

The dining-room door slid back and Bruce's father came in. His eyes were heavy on Bruce's mother and then on Bruce, but only for a moment. He said heartily, "Well, well, old home week. Everything O.K.?"

"Just getting ready to beat it," McReady said.

Bruce's father flicked his towel across his hand. "One for the road?"

"Nah, we got to go." McReady wadded out his cigarette, looking down with smoke puffing from his mouth and nose and drifting up into his eyes. The elk's tooth on his watch chain jiggled with his almost noiseless wheezing.

The nurse rose. "I'll bet he's bright in school," she said. (And what did her smiling mean? Did she find his face roguish?)

His mother said, "We hadn't been here but two or three weeks before they moved him ahead another whole grade. That's two he's been moved up. He's only thirteen. He won't be quite sixteen when he graduates from high school."

Bruce could have killed her, talking about him in front of those two, with her proud proprietary air. Their eyes were on him like sash weights—his mother's full of pride, the nurse's crinkling with her smile, his father's suspicious, McReady's just dull and streaked. Then McReady picked up a book from the end table by the sofa and knocked it on his knuckles. "This something you read in school?"

The book was Bruce's all right. They must have been looking at it earlier, and seen his name in it. It was by Edgar Rice Burroughs, and it was called *At the Earth's Core*. It was about a man who invented an underground digger in which he broke through the crust of the earth into the hollow inside, where there was another world all upside down, concave instead of convex, and full of tyrannosauri and pterodactyls and long-tailed people covered with fine black fur. So McReady cracked it open and of course it opened to the page that Bruce had most consulted, a picture of the tailed furry girl who fell in love with the hero. She didn't have anything on.

He showed it around. He and Bruce's father laughed and the nurse smiled and clicked her tongue, and Bruce's mother smiled, but not as if she felt like smiling. "You better stick to Latin, kiddo," McReady said, and dropped the book back on the end table.

All of Bruce's insides were pulled into a knot under his wishbone. He shivered like a dog. If asked, he could have given a very logical explanation of why McReady chose to humiliate a runty thirteen-year-old. The thirteen-year-old was too much smarter than his own dumb son, he had walked in on their necking party, he might talk. On that point he might have saved his worry. About things that happened in his house, Bruce never said anything, not a word, not to anyone, even his mother.

But though he could have explained McReady's action, he didn't survive it. It paralyzed him, it reduced him to a speck in front of them all, especially that girl. He left them laughing— *some* of them were laughing—and vanished. When he heard them leaving, he was back before the *castra* in the kitchen.

Almost as soon as the front door closed, he heard his parents, their voices coming plain through the register.

"What went on in here?" his father said. "Something drove him away. He was good for all night."

"He was good for all night if we'd provided a bed," said his mother in a strange, squeaky, trembling voice. It burst out of her in a furious loud whisper. "What a thing for him to see in his own parlor! Oh, Bo, I could . . . if we don't . . ."

"What are you talking about? Talk sense. What went on? What do you mean?"

"I mean Lew and that girl. We came in to get something from my sewing basket, we didn't hear them, so we thought they'd gone. They were so . . . They didn't even hear us coming. His hands were all over her. Bruce couldn't help seeing, because *I* saw, and I was behind him."

The register sighed with its empty rush of air. Bruce's father said, "Well, God Almighty, I've told you a hundred times to keep him out of here. How do you suppose people like to have kids peeking around the corners when they're out partying? Kids that know your own kids, for God's sake! Do you think he'll ever be back? Not on your life. Kiss him goodbye, and he was good for twenty or twenty-five dollars every week. Oh, God *damn*, if either of you had the sense of a . . ."

Bruce's hands were shaking so that he could hardly stick the decapitated match stem down into the clay before the commander's tent. When he pressed the pin into the end of the wood he split it, and threw it furiously aside. His mother was saying out of the register's warm rush, "Will you tell me why—just tell me why—a boy should have to stay out of part of his own house, and hang out in the kitchen like the hired girl, for fear of what he'll see if he doesn't? Is that the way a home should be? How can he grow up right, how can he have any self-respect, how can he even know right from wrong, when all he sees at home is people like Lew McReady?"

The sigh and steady rush of air. Bruce's father said, "This is a place of business, too, remember? This is how we make a living. We stop this, we don't eat."

"Sometimes I'd rather not eat," she said. "So help me God, I'd rather starve." She stopped, as if she had said more than she intended. Then she said, "I wonder how we'll feel if he turns out bad. What if we make him into a thief, or worse?"

"Into something like me?" Bruce's father said in a voice so soft and ugly that Bruce held his breath.

"I'm as guilty as you are," she said. The register boomed so that with all his straining Bruce heard only a mumble. Then words again " . . . to pretend it was only bad times, sooner or later you'd get into something else. Do you have any idea how blessed it was, even though we were poor as mice, up there in Saskatchewan? Before you went back into the whiskey business? Bo, I . . . There's a limit."

"Yes," he said heavily. "I guess there is."

Bruce sat with his eyes squeezed half shut. His ears repudiated the quarreling voices. He was frozen in a frantic, desolate rejection of everything that threatened him. He hated this new outbreak of an old quarrel, with its threat of breakup. What they had, bad as it was, was better than the caving-in of everything. Did they ever think what might happen to *him*? He would be pulled out of school, he and his mother would have to move. Everything that he escaped to, as well as everything he escaped, would go if his mother pushed her quarrel too far.

The *castra* with its *vallum* and ditch and rows of tents swam distorted and watery. He ground his teeth in shame and rage. The register was silent. He could imagine them in there, glaring at each other, speechless.

A noise at the door made him turn. His mother came quietly in. Her face was white and still. She smiled and spoke, and her voice was low and matter-of-fact. "Does it work?"

It took him a moment to understand that she was talking about the pin. "No," he said then. "It's too big. It splits the match." Accusingly he glowered at her where she wavered in the big lens of tears.

"Why, Bruce," she said. "You're crying! Oh, poor kid!"

She started for him, but he kicked his feet into his unlaced shoes and stumbled to the outside door. Down the steps he lurched and recovered and ran, and stopped in the shadow where the old pear tree tangled its branches with the overgrown lilac hedge. His mother's silhouette was in the lighted rectangle of the door. "Bruce?" her high voice said. After that one call she stood still, listening. Then she bent her head and turned back in, and the rectangle of light narrowed and was gone.

Under the pear tree's darkness it was still and cold. When he went out through the hedge he saw his breath white against the arc light. He stood with his fists clenched and his teeth clenched and his mind clenched against the sobs that rattled and shook him. He could hear the sounds of traffic from Ninth South, but in the park opposite, and up and down the street, there was no sound. It was as if they lived not merely at the edge of the park but outside the boundaries of all human warmth, all love and companionship and neighborliness, all light and noise and activity, all law.

He had never been able to bring a companion home from school with him, or even a neighbor boy casually encountered on the block. Once, when a good-natured older boy rode him home on his handlebars, he gave the boy a wrong address and stood at a strange gate until he went away. The very sight of his house, divided within itself but enclosing its secrets behind thick hedges, drawn blinds, closed doors, shook him with self-pity. He set off up the sidewalk, which along the Surplus Canal became a dirt path, and as he walked he cursed aloud in the filthiest words he knew.

He cursed his father and Lew McReady and the wicked girl who had started all this; she was as repulsive to him as if he had caught her copulating with animals. He shed tears for his mother and himself, forced to live in a way they hated. After a while, exhausted by tears and cursing, he stood shivering under trees that rattled stiffly in a little night wind, and imagined revenges, triumphs, ways of becoming rich and famous. He magnified himself in years, strength, confidence, and nerve. He whipped his father with his tongue until he cried and begged forgiveness for all his impatience and contempt. There was a brief tableau in which he stood humbly by while Bruce broke all the bottles of home-made Sunnybrook Farm, until the cellar was flooded with whiskey and they stood knee-deep in broken glass.

Stumbling along the path again with his mind full of carnage, he saw Lew McReady in a dozen postures of defeat, collapse, and cowardly apology. He saw the girl, too. She came up to him soft and beguiling, and for a moment his picture of her was totally obscured by the image of his own scornful eyes and contemptuous, repudiating mouth. But within seconds of that magnificent rejection he was thinking how it would be to touch her, and he was beside her in some very private place with a grate fire and soft music when he came to himself and fell to cursing again. Thinking how close he had come to letting her into those dreams of coiling limbs and silky skin, he shook with self-loathing. Passing a tree, he smashed his fist against it and howled with outrage at the pain.

There was a moon like a chip of ice; the air smelled of smoke and frost. He was the loneliest creature alive. With his hands tucked into his armpits, his eyes glaring into the dark, his throat constricted by occasional diminishing sobs, he went on. Now he was at the edge of the big cabbage field he had passed that afternoon. Out of the shadows the heads lifted in even rows, touched by the moon with greenish light.

Reminded of the *castra* with its rows of tents, he yearned for that job he had begun. He wanted to be back above the warm register, removed, intent, and inviolate. He saw the kitchen as sanctuary: though he had fled from it, he had already had enough of the cold and dark. And anyway, what he had fled from was the parlor. In the kitchen was not only warmth but the true thing that made it sanctuary—his mother, sitting with her magazine, glancing across from her isolation to his, making tentative humble suggestions that might for a few seconds gain her entrance to his world.

Understanding and shame dawned together, coming on like the rheostat-controlled light in a theater. He had had all the contempt he wanted, that day, but now he heaped more on himself. With his chin on a fence post he stared across the glimmering cabbage field and gnawed his chapped knuckles, thinking. There was this one person in the whole world who loved him, only this one he could fully trust. If he thought himself lonely, friendless, and abused, what should he think of her? Ever since they had left Canada she had been without friends, without even acquaintances beyond the company that came to the parlor. He had school, he was almost as used to praise as to contempt. Outside his hateful house he was able to gather approval with both hands, and bring it back to her and have it doubled. Who praised *her*? Who helped *her*? What did *she* have? He remembered the scuttle of coal he had deliberately not roused himself to get for her.

His father said, "If we don't do this, how do we eat? Did you ever hear of money?"

She said, "It might be better to starve. So help me, sometimes I'd rather."

Bruce said, "I won't let us starve. I'll get a job. I'll quit school if I have to. We won't take anything from him. I'll look after you."

The roguish one, the ninety-pound volunteer.

In the moonlight the cabbages went row on row like the crosses in the poem. Their ranks swam and melted and reformed greenishly, shadowily, a great store of food left carelessly unharvested, while at his house they ran a speakeasy because it was the only thing his father knew how to do. His mother submitted because she must, or because of Bruce.

In his nostrils, shrunken in the cold, lay the sourish smell of the field. He dove under the fence and in a moment was wrestling with an enormous cabbage, trying to unscrew its deep root from the ground. Before he defeated it he was crying again with exhaustion and anger, but there it lay at last, a great cold vegetable rose. Stripping off its outer leaves, he rolled it under the fence, crept through after it, gathered it in his arms, and went staggering toward home.

He heard the phonograph the moment he opened the door. His mother was sitting alone in the kitchen. Her life was right where he had left it. As he stuck his head and half his body inside, she stood up. Her eyes went from his face to the front of his sweater, where dirt from the cabbage had rubbed off on him, and from that to where his hand was still out of sight holding the cabbage behind the door.

"Where did you go?" she said. "Are you all right?"

Already his confidence in what he had done was leaking away. The last block of the way home, the cabbage had weighed like solid lead. It seemed to him that all that day he had been carrying weights too heavy for his strength up to that house he hated and took refuge in. Now by its root he dragged the upended cabbage around the door, and watching her face for her response, said, "I brought you something."

She was standing straight beside her chair. Her head did not move as she glanced at what he offered her; only her eyes flicked down and back up. She said nothing—not "Oh, how nice!" or even "Where did you get it?" Nothing.

Panic began to rise in him, for here in the kitchen he could not pretend that the cabbage was anything but ridiculous, a contribution to the household that would have made his father snort in incredulous contempt. Moreover, and this was worse, it had been stolen. His mother knew at once that it was a theft he brought home. He remembered her angry whisper coming with the rush of warm air through the register: "I wonder how we'll feel if he turns out bad. What if we make him into a thief, or worse?"

"Ma . . ." he said.

It was more than he could do to support her still look. Still clutching the cabbage root, he let his eyes slide away until they settled on the *castra*. There lay reassurance. The daubed wall was tight and neat, the tents stood in mathematically precise

rows. Like a dog on a track his mind ducked after his eyes, and
he found himself repeating other words like *castra* that had a
different meaning in singular and plural: words like *gratia-gra-
tiae*, and *auxilium-auxilia*, and *impedimentum-impedimenta*, and
copia-copiae; and even going over some of the words that cus-
tomarily took *in* with the accusative: names of towns, small islands, *domus, rus*. Such words, though really exceptions, were
supported by all the precision and dependability of law.

Out of the register came the squawk of the needle being taken
carelessly off the record, a big burst of laughter, a woman's
squeal, shouts whose words he refused to hear, and then the
music again, good old "Nobody Lied," his own contribution to
the parlor fun.

He brought his eyes unwillingly back to his mother, opening
his mouth to say, "I . . ."

She was looking at him with odd intentness. Her hands hung
awkwardly before her as if she had forgotten them there. Her
mouth twitched—smile, or grimace such as she made when the
parlor grew rowdy?

Perhaps the true climax of that rueful day, perhaps the culmi-
nation of that depressed period of their life as a family, was that
tableau in which Bruce after a fashion presented and his mother
in some sort accepted the grotesque vegetable he had stolen to
compensate her for the uncertainties and deprivations of her life.
He brought her this gift, this proof of his love and loyalty, and
they stared at each other with emotions mixed and uneasy.
What should they have said there in that kitchen? What another
family might greet with great belly laughs they could not handle
so easily. They had no margin for laughter.

The slap-tongue sax was pounding through the pipes. He
wanted to say to her, "I'm awful, I have filthy thoughts, I steal, I
cheat on merit badges sometimes, I'd even cheat in school if I
couldn't get on the dean's list any other way. I'm a crybaby and
people laugh at me and I'm sorry, I . . ."

He said none of it. She said, with her eyes glittering full, "Ah,
poor Bruce!"

She put out her arms and he dropped the cabbage and crept
into them. Hugging each other in the sanctuary kitchen, they
were both about half comforted.

5

Mason came up from a long way down to find that his assiduous waitress was standing by his table, a healthy-looking blonde girl who smiled so brilliantly that he felt like shading his eyes. "Anything else? Dessert? Coffee?"

"Just coffee, please. And the check, if you will."

She went away. Opposite his window the golden angel tiptoed his floodlighted spire. In the pale sky beyond, the colors of sunset were almost gone. Venus hung over the bony silhouette of Antelope Island.

An hour ago he had wondered why coming back here revived only the trivial and sentimental. Now he sat like someone whose car had just crashed, and who was not quite sure he could climb out. That night in November 1922, recovered from and forgotten, needed only to be remembered and it was as virulent as it had ever been. His childhood had been a disease that had produced no antibodies. Forget for a minute to be humorous or ironic about it, and it could flare up like a chronic sinus.

Which was unjust—his father was not always like that. It was just as possible to remember times when he had filled his son with admiration and pride. Was he an incurable grudge-holder?

Was he going to pursue the poor devil with his hatred as if he had never survived adolescence? Was he never going to be reconciled to his mother's unhappy submissive life? If he had known that this would be the net result of his returning, he would not have returned.

Since 1922 he had been packed and stored with later experiences, emotions, acquaintances, affections, languages, bodies of learning, cautions and wisdoms. He was thirty years older than his mother had been on that evening of the *castra* and the cabbage. Yet that single miserable evening, with its hatred of him, its loyalty to her, and its self-pity for himself all intact, hung in his head as unalterable as a room that disappears when a switch is touched, and appears again the moment the switch is turned back on. He hadn't turned on the light in that room for years, but there it still was, implacable.

The waitress brought the coffee and poured it from its metal pot with gestures that were graceful and self-conscious. Mason picked up the check from its tray, added a twenty per cent tip, signed it, and turned it over again. At once respectful and pert, the girl stood there. "Enjoy your dinner?"

"Very much."

"I saw you looking at our sunset."

Did she think she ought to trade some cheery chat for the good tip? Had she been trained to give diners the friendly-Mormon-girl treatment? Did she think maybe he might turn out to be Stanley Kubrick?

"Spectacular," he said.

"Salt Lake's supposed to have the best sunsets in the world."

The old local brag. "I know," he said. "I used to live here."

The girl made a comic face. "Nice try, Alice," she said. "When?"

"When?"

"When did you live here?"

"I left in 1932."

"Oh, wow. I bet it's changed."

"Some ways. Not the sunsets."

He watched her through the steam of the raised coffee cup, thinking that some things changed hardly at all. This was a type he had known by the dozen, just such a girl as he might have met at the kitchen entrance after her evening's work, and taken out to the Green Dragon or the Old Mill to dance till the band folded. Just the sort of peppy date who would have necked happily in the car, parked in front of her house, and on the porch before going in, but would have briskly made him keep his hands to himself. Just the sort of date from whose enthusiastic but restricted kisses he had so often gone home (would anyone now believe it?) satisfied and pleased with himself.

"But you weren't born in Salt Lake," he suggested.

"What makes you think that?"

"Evidence."

This was her kind of game. With her hip against the table edge she shot a look in search of the hostess, did not see her, cocked her eyebrows, and smiled down on Mason her brilliant smile. "Where does the evidence say I'm from?"

"Somewhere north. Malad? Brigham City? Cache Valley?"

Comic dismay, real puzzlement. "What are you, a medium or something? How'd you know?"

"From the way you say 'carn bread.'"

Now an uncertain glance through her lashes. "Oh."

"What's the matter? Don't you like being from—where is it? Cache Valley?"

"I'm sorry if I talk like a hick."

"Oh now, come on," Mason said, contrite. "Who said you talk like a hick? You talk like somebody from up around the Idaho border. You made me feel I'd come home."

"Yes," the girl said, rather sullenly, he thought. She was still smiling, but the smile had flattened against her marvelous gleamy toothpaste-ad teeth. As if indifferently, she looked across the Sky Room's wavering candles. "Jist give me a year," she said. "If I could git out of here and down to the Coast I'd sure wear the Cache Valley out of me. You wouldn't know then where I'm from."

"Maybe you're better off here," Mason said. "Don't knock Cache Valley, or Salt Lake either. You might not like California half as well."

"Mmm."

"California food doesn't taste the way this dinner did. They do something to it. It isn't served as pleasantly. The sunsets are watery."

She blinked and smiled and found something to deal with somewhere else in her section. How standard, touching, in the end uninteresting. Dissatisfied provincials, exportable dreams, upward-and-outward mobility. Mason knew all about it.

Venus, in the few minutes his eye had been off it, had slid down behind Antelope Island. He drained his coffee cup, ready to leave. From the second table down, against the windows, a party of four came past, holding him for a minute in his chair. Their table stood disheveled under its soiled dishes and crumpled napkins. A busboy, his face fiery with acne, wheeled up a cart and began to clear away.

Click. Involuntary narrowing of the eyes.

He moves dazed through magic. If you should draw him, you would have to put x's where his eyes should be, like a funny-paper character who has been hit on the head. He is fourteen, and enchanted. His motions are somnambulistic and his mind numb, but his senses are wide open. The breeze that sweeps through the wall-less pavilion brings in midway sounds: nasal chanting of barkers, thunder of the roller coaster with its obbligato of squeals, shuffling of many feet, cries and mutterings, the rumble and twitter of voices. And midway odors: taffy, popcorn, cotton candy, rancid grease from hot-dog and hamburger stands, the encompassing smell of the salt flats. The shore breeze blows them into the pavilion and through the tables and across the dance floor and through the unused tables on the other side, picking up in passing all the dining-room odors of roast beef, barbecue sauce, spare ribs, coffee, vinegar, floor wax, a sudden sourceless onion smell of female perspiration, an equally sudden and sourceless whiff of perfume. Tangled and braided, smells and sounds blow through the room and through Bruce and are swept out over the lake.

The lake side, where he is standing, is dark and quiet. Only a mangy velvet rope holds the tables in; beyond are timbers and the sense of water. When the music stops, he can hear the slosh of brine against the pilings down under, and from far off, as if

they came floating on the water, the clear voices of bathers over
on the north side, where Chet works. The darkness isolates and
protects him. From here in the shadow, when there are no tables
to be cleared, he can look and listen.

His eyes are dazzled by the tent of hazy luminance through
which he sees. The revived saxophones sob through his soul.
The people at the tables are more dressed up and romantic than
ordinary people. Some are eating, some have already begun to
dance. He watches a pair of girls go by, dancing with one another for lack of male partners. Does one of them look at him
with an interest not quite covered by her gum-chewing
indifference? He wishes he had a white coat that fitted him. The
one he has to wear has sleeves six inches too long, so that he has
to turn back the cuffs, and the shoulders are broad enough for
someone twice his size.

The members of the band on their platform all wear ice-cream
pants and blue jackets and straw skimmers. They are playing
"Ain't We Got Fun," and the people at the tables begin to join
in, singing and clapping like people at a picnic.

There's nothing surer,
The rich get rich and the poor get poorer (laid off, children),
In the meantime
In between times
Ain't we got fun.

Near Bruce a boy and girl are doing the Charleston. He is a
slicker in a four-button pinch-waisted suit with bell-bottomed
pants. The girl's red dress is so short that he can see her stockings rolled below the knee. Her mouth is red and laughing, her
shingled head is like a boy's. Her feet move in swift twisting motions, following the twistings of her partner's bell bottoms. They
hang on to each other's arms and put their noses together,
watching their feet and laughing.

Bruce can do the Charleston. A high school acquaintance
whose mother is a dance instructor taught him one afternoon at
Warm Springs. But he is not sure he would do it here. Whole
dance halls have been shaken down when a lot of people start
doing it. It works like an earthquake. It gets everything going to

a rhythm, and pretty soon the hall vibrates apart. He watches these two, and is both envious and contemptuous of the bell bottoms and the sideburns, and thinks with disapproval that the girl shouldn't show her knees in public this way, and wonders what it would be like to put his arm around her red silk waist, and with his face only inches from her laughing face, Charleston her around the floor.

He moves to ease the swelling in his pants. What's the lightest thing in the world, Mr. Gallagher? Your pud, Mr. Sheen, it rises with thought. All by himself, he snickers.

Then he spots a family—father, mother, somewhat fat daughter—leaving a table. With one hand in his pocket, hiding his condition behind the cart, he starts toward them. Ed Mueller, the manager, is watching him, he sees, and he hurries, wanting to impress. Almost at once he feels it is safe to take his hand out of his pocket and be businesslike with both hands on the cart handle. In his mind, as he starts stacking the dishes, is a tableau in which Mueller, at payoff time, publicly praises him. *Watch this Mason kid. He may be little but by God he's on the job. He could teach all of you something.*

His glance brushes the glance of the fattish girl. She turns away so indifferently that he knows she is only lighting a Murad. Back of that nonchalance there is a gleam of curiosity, interest, invitation.

In the grease on one of the plates he finds a nickel embedded, and hastily digs it out and darts after the departing family. "Mister? Sir? You left this."

Young Lincoln, he waits for their praise. He hopes Mueller is still watching. But the man toward whom he holds the nickel does not accept it. His face is full of heavy astonishment. The fat girl is staring, the mother smooths her dress over her high corseted rump. Slowly comprehension dawns. Bruce's face grows slowly hot. "Oh," he says vaguely, and turns away, too confused for thanks or anything else. Three tables away, Ed Mueller, who *has* been watching, is breaking up in laughter.

Sullenly Bruce finishes loading the cart and starts off toward the kitchen around the dark edge of the dance floor. He has an impulse to throw the nickel as far as he can throw it out into the water, but instead he wipes it off on a napkin and pushes it down into his watch pocket, where his ten-dollar paycheck from the news company where he works during the week is folded tightly around the silver dollar his mother makes him carry in case he should run into what he scornfully calls a Dire Emergency.

His mother doesn't like his working here. She says it is too much for a boy of fourteen, and not strong at that, to work ten hours a day, six days a week, at the news company, and then ride out fifteen miles on the train and work all Saturday and Sunday night. By the time he gets back to town and catches the Owl streetcar home it is way past midnight. It isn't like Chet, who sleeps at Saltair, under the Pavilion. And Chet is older. Bruce will ruin his health. He will stunt his growth, which, though she refrains from saying so, seems to be stunted already.

He did not win her over by argument. He simply threw such a tantrum, followed by sulking, that she gave in. This is his second weekend. Though he has been working since eight this morning, and has had for supper only the extra sandwich his mother put in his lunch sack, he is not tired. He is only furious with that stupid man and that fat girl and that Ed Mueller with his horse laugh.

He will show Ed Mueller. Suppose the pavilion caught fire, and while everyone else ran around in panic, trampling each other, suppose here came the one they call Shrimp (unknown to them, he is an Eagle Scout), burrowing along the floor where the air is better, dragging people to safety, grabbing confused Ed Mueller and getting *him* out, plunging back in after others. He comes upon a body with the flames all but swallowing it, and as the fire sweeps up and away and the smoke clears for a moment he recognizes the flapper in the red dress and the shingle bob. Her slicker escort has run like a coward, leaving her to her fate. Fallen, she is wonderfully helpless; her white legs are exposed above the knees. He takes up her soft body (who would have thought he was so strong?) and carries her to safety. Under cover of the smoke he cops a feel.

At the swinging doors to the kitchen he backs around, pulls the cart through, and unloads it onto the table behind which four pearl divers in their undershirts, their tattoos shining with sweat, stand armpit-deep in greasy suds. They are not men to be fooled with—impatient, savage, dangerous. Though the most dangerous of all, according to Chet, are fry cooks. Fry cooks will take after you with a cleaver if you so much as look at them cross-eyed.

Keeping his eyes open and his mouth shut, he finishes unloading and backs out through the swinging doors. The music comes loud in his face. His sullenness is already forgotten. Out past dancers and diners, above the bright midway, the scrolls and scrawls of the roller coaster lift out of the light into obscurity. A red car is crawling up the first long pitch. He hears the screams and then the thunder as it tips and falls.

What a keen place! As the moon moves through the sky he moves through that dreamland. As swimmers float unsinkable on the brine of Great Salt Lake he floats on blended saxophones. The girl in red and her slicker friend are up again, still doing the Charleston. From time to time one of the band members stands up and sings through a megaphone.

He assures: "It ain't gonna rain no more, no more." He exhorts: "Horsie, keep your tail up, keep the sun out of my eyes." He warns: "You got to see your mama every night or you won't see your mama at all."

Eventually it is eleven, the last table has been cleared, they hang around the kitchen waiting to be paid. When Mueller comes in, finally, Bruce accepts his dollar and a half and his train ticket back to town. The long day has come down on him like an avalanche of feathers. Rubber-legged, blind with yawning, he gropes out of the kitchen and staggers across the midway toward the gates beyond which the train waits on the causeway. Behind him the band is playing "Moonlight and Roses," and the dance floor lights go dim. The nearly empty midway stares, too brightly lighted. Its concessions are closed, all except the check stand, where the attendant is killing time by throwing an ice pick underhanded at the wall.

A crowd has gathered at the gates. They are tired, yawning, subdued. Somebody grumbles that if they'd jist open the gates a man could at least go out to the train and lay down. There is a slow, ponderous leaning as people stack up behind. Everybody is pressed close together, closer to the gates. Packed bodies hold Bruce up on every side. He is down below, and can see little—

could see little even if his eyes were not so heavy. They drag
shut against all his efforts to hold them open. Asleep on his feet,
embedded in the crowd, he drifts.

A shift, a stagger, somebody steps on his foot, he feels himself
losing his balance, and comes awake to find that he has grabbed
hold of a girl's arm. As if his own fantasies were writing the
script, it is the girl in red. Muttering an apology, he lets go and
straightens himself. She gives him only a glance, yawns loudly,
laughs, raises her hands to take hold of her boy friend's shoulders, and twists him around facing away from her so that she
can lay her cheek against his back, pretending to sleep.

Bruce's fingers tingle with the memory of her skin. Sunk down
below everyone, he can't see out, but he can see, close to him,
the girl's red dress and bare raised arms. Lifted that way, they
pull her breast up and out so that it juts alive and bold against
the red silk. In Bruce Mason the lightest thing in the world stirs
and lifts. No longer sleepy, he folds his arms—it is dusky, he is
jammed among people, there is no need of getting a camouflag-
ing hand into his pocket even if there were room to do it. He is
as aware of the bulge of her breast as if it were a sparking live
wire. With his arms folded, and if he lifts his hands a little high,
the fingers of his left hand are within inches of that softness. He
is thinking that if the crowd should shift again as it did a minute
ago, and if he were again bumped off balance, his fingertips
might just brush against her as if by accident.

It does not take long. The crowd does shift. It leans. Instead of
bracing against it, he lets it move him. His fingers touch her.

Snap! Her arm clamps down on his hand, pinning it to her
side. Her furious face is a foot from his, she has pointed teeth,
she is shouting. But he is deaf, his mind has gone white with terror. Frantically he yanks, but she has him. Then she reaches for
him with her other hand, and he breaks loose. The boy friend is
struggling to turn and get at him. He dives low and burrows,
lunging ahead. Hands grab at him, voices rise, but he twists,
breaks away, gets beyond the surge of the turmoil he has
created. He feels with his body that the gates have just been
opened, and he shoves between a man and woman, sees an opening, hits it, and is through onto the causeway and up onto the
steps of the open excursion car. Through the car, off the other

side, up along the train in near darkness, he outdistances everyone, slides into the end seat of the front car, facing backward
and watching the train fill up.

Every glimpse of red stops his heart. He is prepared to jump
off on either side if he sees them. He will jump into the lake,
swim under the causeway and hide among the pilings, drown
there in the dark if he must, but he will not be taken. His heart
pounds so hard it hurts him, he has trouble getting his breath.
He is frantic with the fear that they will somehow get close before he sees them, and will pop up on both sides of the car, trapping him. He will be collared and dragged off, a cringing,
babbling, weeping, skin-and-bones crybaby with guilt and de-
pravity written all over him.

He cannot see them anywhere. People are boarding his car,
but none of them pays any attention to him. But in his sliding
back and forth across the seat with his neck craning like a baby
bird's in a nest, he attracts attention, and then he freezes, sitting
with his breath still as short as if he were being strangled, and
his guts full of fear.

But the train jerks and starts, and nobody has come. They
leave the causeway and gather speed, rocketing across the flats
toward the far glow of the city. The tainted wind tears at him;
he gulps his lungs full of it. Gradually his heart quiets and the
constriction of his throat eases. Driven to know where they are,
and whether they are still hunting him, he starts cautiously back
along the steps, hanging to the poles that support the roof. But
the steps are preempted by necking couples who do not enjoy
being disturbed, and it is hard to see by the one dim light at
each end. What if they are lying in wait for him? If they should
jump up suddenly in front of him, what will he do? Jump off the
train? The flats rush by below him, the pole he clings to throbs
with speed. Intensely aware of the ground rushing past, he visu-
alizes and pities his own death.

It is too dangerous. He retreats to his front seat, where at least
he should be safe until they reach the city. His mind, running
ahead, tells him that from here he can beat anyone off and
through the station. But streetcars are brightly lighted. What if
he should board one and they should get on behind him? He
doesn't want to see that girl ever again. The memory of her furi-

ous face and pointed teeth, the way her arm snapped down and trapped him against her side, will do him for a long time. How could she have known that his fingers were not an accident? Where did a girl like that get so strong?

He will have to walk home, twelve long Salt Lake blocks, nearly two miles.

The car is dusky, and people are quiet, but he does not dare let his eyes close. When they slow for the station, he is off like a slingshot rock. For the first two blocks he runs, tired as he is. Then he plods.

The streets, growing brighter as he approaches Main, are almost deserted. Occasionally a car goes by, and now here comes the first streetcar from the station, brightly lighted, nearly full. He stands behind a tree while it passes.

At West Temple, rather than go into the brightness of Main Street, he turns south, but at Third South he must turn again across the bottom of the business district, across Main and then State. At each of those intersections he waits until there is nothing in sight for a block each way, and then forces his dead legs into a trot. Beyond State Street it grows darker, shabby houses replace business buildings, there is a nighttime odor of damp lawns and poplar trees. Between the widely spaced arc lights the trees hang heavy and dark. The sidewalks are humped and uneven. His eyes burning with rage and humiliation, he plods one interminable block after another, stumbling and cursing and pitying himself. His head is often turned back over his shoulder, for he is as afraid of the dark as he has previously been afraid of the light. How could such a contemptible thing as he defend itself against thieves and murderers? His body will be found with its throat cut, thrown under some hedge.

Starting at every rustle of a disturbed bird, his heart stopping and then starting again with great bounds, his eyes bulging from his head, he finally takes to the middle of the street, away from the fearful dark along the sidewalk.

As he enters his own block, the clock in the City and County Building tower booms out one heavy stroke. His feet have hardly touched the porch steps before his mother is at the door in her bathrobe. She takes him by the arm; she says in a voice unusually angry for her, "Bruce, this is just too much! You'll *kill* yourself! I'm not going to let you work out there any more. You've got to promise me!"

He mumbles something about missing the Owl. He lets her lead him into the kitchen, he accepts a glass of milk and a cookie, he staggers off to his room with her arm around his shoulders, he submits when she drags off his clothes. In his underwear, he falls into the bed like something falling from a roof.

He has made her no promise. But he understands that he won't go back the next night, nor the next weekend, nor ever again. He will get his mother to telephone that he is sick. When she has turned off the light and gone softly away, he lies grinding his teeth, his eyes squeezed shut on angry tears. Already his arms, legs, shoulders, head, his very hair, are falling away, disappearing, weightless in sleep.

6

Once again Mason came up from a long way down. He watched the acned boy clear the table and wheel away. He shook his head with a wincing kind of sympathy. Pretty unlikely material. But who could say? Some survived. Half apologetically, he tried to catch his waitress's eye as he went out, but she was busy with other things.

His watch said eight-forty. He should now go and call Joe Mulder and reestablish contact with his amputated youth. But the initiative in that particular reunion had so far been with the youth, not with him. It kept blurting into his awareness: unschooled yokel, country cousin, full of itself. He was not prepared to shut it up and take over. Procrastination, as he freely admitted, kept him from the telephone, led him out through the lobby into the street, and seduced him across Main Street and under the wall of the temple block until he stood opposite the Temple Square Hotel.

It was smaller than he remembered it, but it still looked as if it were used by good Mormons coming into town for Spring and Fall Conference. That was the clientele the church had built it for. When it was brand-new, Nola Gordon had lived there for one week. Bruce Mason had been perhaps an indirect cause of her moving in. He was certainly the cause of her moving out.

They were already what his mother called "in deep." Nola was wearing his fraternity pin. He was wearing the West Point class ring that had been given her by a previous steady, a fellow from her home town. There might have been an omen in that ring, if Bruce had been in a mood to read it.

That was the year after he stayed out of school to work full time so that Joe's father could take the family to Europe. What year? 1929? 1930? He was beginning to discover that the memory had no calendar. Inside there, all was simultaneous. A sense of time had to be forcibly imposed on it.

But it was still in charge of him, random and disjointed though its reminders were. It simply outboxed him, it danced around and hit him at will. Time's patsy, he came straight from being peppered by a lot of adolescent humiliations and found himself facing this hotel whose only association was Nola. What had made him walk this block and stop here? A need for some sort of reassurance? It was an interesting notion. Until this moment he had managed pretty effectively to exclude her from his rerun of old pictures. He had hardly said her name in his mind.

Unappeased grievance, or habit? For a long time he had worked hard to dis-create her. He had willed her never to have existed. So now, without conscious intention, he walked straight to where he could be reminded of no one else. So far as he could remember, he had never been in the Temple Square Hotel in his life except during the week she lived there.

Holly had scared him off because she took the offensive. She grabbed. He was too young and green, his bones hadn't hardened. By the time he had come to Nola, only weeks later, he was farther along. And Nola was a different girl, altogether other.

Books and ideas put her to sleep, art bored her. Only music meant anything, and in that, by a freak of nature, she had a real gift, which, by the accidents of her nurture, remained undeveloped. How did a girl from a cow town on the edge of the slick rock country, a girl with obvious Indian blood in her from some time when a polygamous grandfather, on the advice of the priesthood and with the aim of getting glory in heaven, help around the house, and pleasure in bed, took a Ute wife—how did such a girl from a starving and primitive little town get born with perfect pitch and the ability to play almost any instrument, after a try or two, by ear? Where did she learn so well to sing parts in her husky contralto? Was is the compulsion of a gift that drove her to sing, or Mormon tradition and habit, the practice of a pentecostal hymn-singing frontier reinforced by choiring Welsh converts? Merely youth? Did all the young sing? Were they all like Dryden's countryman who whistled as he walked, for lack of thought? Whatever it was, everybody Bruce Mason loved in his home town sang, and so did he, and so, more than anyone, did Nola.

Singing, she was a warm and happy energy. Joy came out of her mouth. Knowing nothing about music, knowing only ballads and popular songs, she loved the congruency of long sonorous chords. "You're so *true!*" she cried to Bruce the first time they found themselves singing in a crowd. He hoped she meant the remark more than musically. But it was in singing that they first came close. They entangled themselves in songs, they converted emotion into harmony. Whenever they were together they hummed like prairie telegraph wires, and their repertory covered every sentimental occasion but specialized in the ecstasies of new love. Right now, without trying, he heard the song they used to sing most significantly, leaning their heads together, closely harmonizing, baritone and dark warm alto. *Their* song.

It made Mason feel like a sentimentally scored movie. If he were telling this to anyone, he would have to laugh to keep from looking foolish. But he was not telling it to anyone, and he didn't much care, at the moment, if he looked foolish to himself. He often had. What fascinated him was that that moonstruck boy and he were the same person. What a thing a human life was!

Where Holly was all vivacity, Nola was all repose. There was a deep quiet about her, the air of complete self-containment that Mason had often noted in animals, seldom in humans. She did not chatter—it struck him now that she had told him remarkably little about herself, her family, her background, her growing up. When things bored her, she curled up and slept. Her hair was dark, heavy, and unbobbed: *luscious* hair, Holly said enviously. Very early in their acquaintance—and the acquaintance of a boy and girl that age, in those times, was as alert and responsive as boxing or table tennis—she took it down and proved to him that she could sit on it.

Her eyes were as dark as her hair and voice. They were less speaking eyes than Holly's, they did not flash or sparkle, but an unquenchable life glowed in them, deep down or behind, looking out from a center that was untroubled and untroublable, serene, acceptant, complacent, maybe even devouring. Mason never saw them bleached out, streaked, or tired. Her face was Indian-looking, a little heavy in the bones; olive-skinned, expressionless in repose, dark-browed, with a small triangular scar above the right eye that managed to be an accent, not a blemish. She had a magnificent scowl, and she walked with a straight back and neck like a barefoot woman carrying a head burden, the proudest, most unselfconsciously female walk he ever saw. On a horse she was marvelous: she had grown up on a ranch, and her brother was a rodeo rider. For all her quietness, her soft-voiced withdrawal, the placidity of her dark eyes, she compelled notice—his notice, at least. Simply by being there as if waiting, she took his attention away from brittle, witty, febrile Holly. She smoldered without apparently being aware that she was afire.

In psychology classes they used to argue, with all the exhilaration of emancipated thinkers, that mind is only the high integration of the physical, and that unless the spirit can be proved to have its location in some organ, it has to be a fiction. Nevertheless, the head, Mason was thinking now, the head, which probably developed as the seat of the first sense organ, feelers or eyes or whatever, and went on developing from there, is a very different part of the physical apparatus from the body. The body eats, evacuates, winces, and reproduces. The head senses, comprehends, responds, and plans. That was not quite the way St. Paul put it, but never mind. There were head people and body people. Holly, for all her calculated glamour, lived above the neck. Nola, with no intentional glamour at all, lived below it.

Holly understood that, and understood where Mason himself belonged. One spring night, a while after they had their queer, unresolved parting, they were sitting together on the porch swing while Nola was up in the tower changing her clothes. Bruce thought, in a dim way, that he owed Holly some sort of explanation, if only an after-the-fact explanation that was essentially a lie. So he told her what was by then becoming a fact, that he was in love with Nola.

It was dark. He could barely see her at the other end of the swing, but he felt her turn toward him. "You're joking," she said in her light, high voice. A vanilla voice; Nola's was caramel, or chocolate.

"No. I am."

"In the good old-fashioned way?"

"In the good old-fashioned way."

"Meaning you're going to marry her?"

She jolted him. She often jolted him, being two or three years older, and used to thinking not in collegiate terms but in the terms of real life. Marriage had never entered Bruce's head. He was afloat, or adrift, on the present like a fly on meringue. But having said what he had said, he had no alternative but to go on. "Sometime," he said. "Not right this week."

He heard her long earrings jingle as she shook her head. It seemed to him that by contrast with Nola's unadorned femaleness, Holly was false and empty, just as her light voice was made for jokes and quips and society verse where Nola's husky whisper had a thrill in it like the rattle of a snake.

"But eventually," Holly said. "And get buried in Salt Lake."

"Not necessarily."

"Necessarily," she said. "Oh, Bruce, she doesn't have a *brain!*"

"She's got anything I want or need," he said. They didn't say much more. He was angry. So, he supposed, was she. Very shortly after that, Nola moved out of the tower. It was just too awkward.

She didn't come to the Temple Square because it was a church hotel. Her family were as much cowboy as churchgoer, and she herself was no more religious than a lizard on a rock. She had a summer job in a downtown department store. The hotel was new, clean, and convenient. Perhaps there was also at work in her a residual country girl timidity. In the city she had lived in her sorority house or with roommates, never alone. Living alone would be pleasanter for her and Bruce, but she may also have felt it more dangerous. This was Utah, 1929 or 1930. Perhaps she picked the church's hotel to ensure the supervision she had just discarded.

Mason had no more idea now than he had then why she had chosen as she did when their growing involvement led them away from the awkwardness of being around Holly. Looking across at the bright entrance behind which a precise memory lay waiting to be examined, he first examined himself to see if there was any mold of old emotion on any of this, and decided that there was not. It was as clean as a bleached bone, without power to do more than make him smile.

It was late, well after midnight. He saw the two of them enter the lobby, he saw that walk of hers that made him, even in passionless retrospect, want to pat her on the haunch the way one might pat a muscled quarterhorse. He saw himself only vaguely, assiduous but in tow. He saw the elevator man stand up from his stool inside his lighted cage, rocking on one heavy built-up shoe.

Nola gave him her warm, sleepy smile. Bruce too smiled at him. He would have smiled at anyone on earth, and not simply because by that time he had been trained to smile for business reasons by J. J. Mulder. They were young, happy, and in love. They were what all the world is supposed to love, and they loved all the world. Probably they had in mind the same program: He would take her to her room, they would neck a while, they would part lingeringly, unwilling but not questioning the forms, and then he would go home. Tomorrow after work he would call her. They would go to a movie, take a walk, window-shop up and down Main Street, maybe drive up on Wasatch Boulevard and park above the valley lights. Summer stretched ahead of them, a succession of such days and nights.

Nola stepped into the elevator. But as Bruce started to follow, the steel door slid briskly across in front of him. The elevator man looked at him through the crack. "Not upstairs," he said.

Bruce completely failed to take him in. "I don't live here," he said foolishly. "I'm only taking her to her room."

"Not in this hotel."

Still not sure he wasn't joking, or that he had not misun-

derstood, Bruce tempted his good nature with a disarming smile.
"Why? What might I do?"

The elevator man's eyes were as round as the eyes of a fish,
and seemed to be surrounded by rings of cartilage. They goggled
and stared, unamused. "Rules," he said. "After eleven."

Past his head, Bruce could see Nola. Instead of storming out,
as he half expected her to, she only looked astonished. "Come on,
this is a bum joke," he said to the elevator man. "What kind of
hotel is it where you can't go up to a room?"

"She can go up."

"Suppose we want to talk a minute?"

The goggle eyes rolled, indicating the empty lobby, lighted like
a stage set.

"What if we'd rather be alone while we talk?"

Shrug.

"Good Christ!" Bruce said, unbelieving.

"No need to blas*pheme*," the elevator man said meanly. *Clang*,
the door slid shut. The brass needle above it started to creep up
around the half circle of its dial.

Furious, Bruce darted around the corner and sprang up the
carpeted stairs three at a time. Inside the wall he could hear the
laboring sigh of the cable, the click as the slow cage passed the
second floor. He was at the third floor ahead of it, but stopped
short of the hall, his hand against the wall at the top step. There
was an irritable series of clicks as the operator jacked the cage to
the floor level, then the rattle of the folding iron grate, then the
clash of the door. Bruce heard no talk. Did she bawl him out?
Was she going to make him take her back down to the lobby,
where he presumably was?

She appeared, walking past the stairhead. Her head turned
very slightly, her eyes touched his with their very corners, at her
left side her hand made a small, natural flicking motion. She
went on without pausing.

In two bounds Bruce was down to the landing and around the
corner out of sight. Just in time. Above him he heard the
shuffling of what he supposed was the operator's heavy shoe
and the rasping of what he knew, holding his own breath, was
breathing. He listened like a tourist in the tabernacle waiting for

the pin to drop. His ears were sticking two feet above his head, his heart was pounding so hard he was afraid the operator would hear it. It was like a movie chase out the windows and across the rooftops and through the alleys. He was pumped full of adrenalin and absolutely delighted. The operator of course couldn't be sure he had come upstairs; he only suspected he had. And if Bruce couldn't outfox that gimpy-legged cross between a bishop's first counselor and a house detective, he was slower and less smart than he thought he was.

Shuffling. Breathing. Then nothing. Was he sneaking down the stairs? No, he couldn't be that quiet. Bruce waited. After quite a time he heard the elevator door slide shut, then the inner grille. But the shaft, encased in the wall right beside his ear, gave up no sigh of the descending cage. Within fifteen seconds he heard the door softly open again. The operator was standing up there waiting to see if his pretense of departing had decoyed Bruce into the open.

He badly underestimated his opposition. Bruce went down to 2, where he could watch the dial. For a while it sat dead on 3, then it started down. He leaped back up to 3 and watched the dial there.

The operator was a most suspicious snoop. The needle stopped at 2, but instead of going on down to the lobby, it started up again. Ready to explode with excitement and triumph, willing to play hide-and-seek all night if the fathead wanted, Bruce slipped halfway down and around the corner. Again the sound of doors, again a wait. Finally the sighing of the cable within the walls. Bruce went up to 3 and watched the needle descend clear to L and stay there. All right, then. He must have satisfied himself that the rule-breaker was not in the building.

But he was, he was there like the Thief of Baghdad in the harem. The numbered doors flowed past him till he came to the right one. There he laid his cheek against the wood and scratched softly with his nails.

She opened, pulled him in, closed and locked again. She had let her hair down, and she was laughing without noise, whispering, "How did you duck him? He was sure you'd come up. When I passed you, he was right on my heels almost."

"He's got to be better than he is if he's going to catch me."

He was breathless, boastful, aggrandized. The chase had worked on him; the whispering secrecy of her room, made illicit by the elevator man's suspicions, worked on him more. His hands were full of her clean, thick, slippery hair, their bodies were locked together, there were long close kisses in the close hallway. They made a stumbling sideward progress, without unlocking lips or arms, until they reached the sofa and fell into it. There, temporarily jarred loose, they looked into each other's eyes with their noses two inches apart.

"Ah!" she said, and with her eyes wide open brought her lips close and put them with deliberate fierceness against his. "Ah, you!"

Bruce said nothing, burrowing into her throat to kiss a knob of collarbone. She had a sweet warm odor. Her hair smelled of pine soap, a simple village folk smell that somehow defined her.

"Sometime, sure," he had told Holly on the porch of the tower house two months before. "Not right this week." But here they were locked together, hungry, devouring one another. The escapade with the elevator man had quickened her as well as him. She was not phlegmatic, remote, or amused. She was aroused, and so was he.

But he had not yet naturalized the idea that a girl he was in love with, a nice girl, might be so emotionally excited that she would go, as the phrase went, "all the way." They necked passionately for a while, and then after an unmeasured time—half hour, hour—she pushed him away and sat up and stretched. Her eyes looked unfocused, the pupils enlarged to fill the whole iris. "Well," she said, and laughed softly, and at once grew serious again and said, "How are you going to get out of here? You'll have to walk right past the elevator."

"I'll have to stay here all night and go out with the crowd in the morning."

He said it jokingly, programmed as he was for the game of assault and resistance, siege and defense, scaling ladders and boiling oil, that was their accepted pattern. He said it hoping that against all precedent she might agree, and half terrified that she would, and sure all the time that she would not.

Erect on the sofa, her hair a tangled dark mass over her shoulders, she looked at him out of the corners of her eyes. He could see the glint of white eyeballs, and in the dark pupils a dot of red reflected from the down-on-the-floor lamp. They stared at each other, precarious between opportunity and inhibition.

Then he saw that she was not going to give in. "No," she said. "No. Not now."

"When, then?" Safe, he could be importunate.

Her eyes moved on his face, memorizing him. She leaned and kissed him slowly. He took a handful of her hair and pulled it across her mouth and kissed her through it, an exciting, sexy kiss that at once relinquished and asserted.

"Soon!"

"Ah, you!" she said again. "I can't seem to get enough of you tonight." Then she removed herself from him, without moving at all. "How are you going to get past him?"

"That's my problem. When are you going to move out of this old ladies' home?"

"I've paid a week in advance."

"Don't stay any longer. Let's start looking for some other place tomorrow."

"All right. But you've got to go now. You've got to go go GO! My name will be mud if they catch you here."

"What can they do?"

"I don't want to find out. Write my father, maybe." She took him by the ears and wagged his head back and forth, pecking him with kisses that hit and missed. "You!" she said a third time. "Get out of here! You're driving me wild."

He yielded. He had always been going to yield. He knew the rules. But as they went through five more minutes of panting good-nights, as he finally broke away and sneaked down the stairs and with ridiculous ease caught the elevator man dozing on his stool, and slipped out the side entrance unseen, he was full of the awed realization that the rules were about to change. One of these days, the next time the opportunity presented itself, he would press her again, and the answer would be yes. It was yes tonight. There was no way to think around a fact like that. All he could do, driving home, was visualize that coming event in a dozen ways, each softer and more secret than the last.

So there she was, retrieved by his computer along with all the rest of it. The old way of thinking of the memory as an attic was absurd. In attics things gathered dust. There was no dust on any of this. It was as fresh as if he had reached back only an hour. He could feel the humorous violence with which she took hold of him, he could smell pine soap.

Without ever crossing the street to look into the hotel, he turned back along the wall of the temple block to where Brigham Young stood at the bright beginning of Main Street. The night was mild, with a steady flow of air from the mountains. The street reaching southward was Anystreet, Anywhere, and yet he knew it in its special and local identity. Simply by the way it lay on the earth he knew it. It lay on his mind that same way.

He turned down it among the thin evening crowds.

7

As he walked, scraps of a poem were bothering the back of his mind. Something about being sick for home for the red roofs and the olives, something about It is a strange thing to be an American. McLeish? Whoever it was, Mason agreed. He had felt it all during his years abroad, when he represented in foreign countries a country to which he himself belonged only tentatively and temporarily and partially, but by which he had been shaped, evoked, limited, given opportunity, perhaps warped or damaged. Many a time he, too, had been sick for home, not for red roofs and olives, but for this city planted between the desert and the mountains. Yet as he walked in the shirt-sleeve night among the paragranite urns, planters, fountains, and stelae that crowded the tiled sidewalks of transformed Main Street, there was little that evoked memory or nostalgia. Home was another word for strange.

His initial inclination to think well of it, to accept Progress, withered as he walked. Urban slick. He might have thought it attractive in Montreal or San Francisco, cities about which he held no illusions. But it wasn't Salt Lake. A flock of bronze sea gulls rising from a sunken garden in front of the Prudential Building, new to him, revived his approval briefly. Then more paragranite, and fountains whose jets wagged like sheeps' tails. What he remembered was shabbier, homelier, friendlier than this. A salmon turning inland after years in salt water should taste with certainty and gladness the waters of its birth.

Something was missing, and it took him nearly a block to realize what. Streetcars. Now it was buses rank with diesel exhaust, silent on rubber. Then it was yellow streetcars with square wheels, clanking, pounding, groaning on curves, audible for blocks (and welcome, too, for their shelter in the rain, warmth in the cold). Their retracted front trolleys stuck out like unicorns' horns, their rear ones popped blue sparks at the switches, and now and then jumped the cable and rained blobs of fire until the conductor hopped down and pulled the trolley away from the wire and set its wheel in place again. It was a favorite sport for boys to jerk the trolley and scatter, hooting derision as the conductor stormed out.

If there were a streetcar in sight now he would take it; any number, it wouldn't matter. 5, up First South to the university, or 6, down State Street to Murray, or the one, whatever number it was, that went north around Ensign Peak to Beck's Hot Springs. On this alien new-city sidewalk he was homesick for the smell of ozone, the slickness of a caned seat, the *dang* of the motorman's bell, the *pink* of the stop signal, the pneumatic sigh of opening and closing doors, the familiar car cards above the windows: Arrow Collars, BVD's, Lux, Listerine (even your best friends won't tell you), Paris Garters, Knox Hats, Stacomb, Lydia E. Pinkham's Vegetable Compound. And Herpicide, with its pictures of three stages of human defoliation: one of a man with thinning hair (Herpicide can save it); one of a man with only a fringe (Herpicide can still save it), and one of a man gone stony bald (too late for Herpicide.)

It would be pleasant to ride clear to the end of some line, while the car emptied by ones and twos until at the last stop the motorman would rise from behind his curtain and open his door and step out and stretch, and leisurely engage the front trolley for the reversed trip back, while the conductor came down the aisle yanking on the brass handles of seats, two at a time, facing them the other way.

Ends and beginnings, familiar and repetitive routines. When

he first came to Salt Lake he had never even seen a streetcar—
had barely made the acquaintance of the water closet. The pure
American frontier savage, with everything to learn about how
people live in groups, he had ridden every line in town, just to
see where it went. For a while he had believed that the conduc-
tors carried little revolvers in the holsters next to the change
boxes on their belts, and he was shamed by his own ignorance
when he found they were only the punches with which they
punched out transfers.

Simply by its public transportation, Salt Lake had opened the
door to membership just when he most needed something to belong to. It served native and stranger, young and old, Gentile
and Mormon, alike. It prompted the beginning of a wary
confidence. He knew where he was and how to get somewhere
else, and he had a book of blue student tickets that would take
him there.

But this face-lifted street bled away a confidence that he had
taken for granted. He felt the absence of old friends. He failed to
recognize what he saw.

The light was different, too. He remembered Main Street as
white, lighted by electric signs outlined by scores of individual
bulbs, some of them comfortably burned out. Now the whole of
downtown, like downtown of every city in the world, was lurid
with red and green and blue. He would never have noticed this
anywhere else—he expected neon. But here where he remembered an earlier stage he found neon garish.

Had he expected that the city would stand still in fact as it
had in his mind, a Pompeii silenced and preserved as it was before neon, diesel buses, streamlined cars, balloon tires, parking
meters? Before television, before even radio in anything but its
crystal-to-superheterodyne forms? Before World War II, Korea,
Vietnam, the counterculture? Before the Fall? Before sin and
death? Did he think he could walk down Main Street as into a
black-and-white, silent, wheels-running-backward 1920's newsreel?

Apparently he did. He wanted the womb kept warm.

Nevertheless, there were some things, passing First South, that
he carefully did not look for.

At Fourth South, where rehabilitation ended and the old shabbiness resumed, he was not tempted to go on into the shabbiness in search of familiarity. Instead, he crossed the street to the post office and started back up the other side. Most of what he walked past on his way back to the hotel was not there. It was as if the things he passed were inventions or dreams. But if inventions, persuasive; if dreams, indelible.

He stopped before a place called the Cat's Meow (and there was an echo in that—for a while in the twenties everything was the cat's meow, or the bee's knees, or the snake's hips). It dealt in gifts and art objects, but throughout his years in Salt Lake it, or a building very close to it, was a clothing store, Mullett Kelley's. Beyond the plastic and chrome and leather of the displays, beyond the reflections of lights and pedestrians and his own peering face, he saw the dim aisles and counters of 1923, the year of his summer job with the news company and his brief flirtation with the fleshpots of Saltair. There he stood with his hoarded pay in the pocket of his knee pants, selecting his first long-pants suit (electric blue) and his first grown-up shoes (Selz Sixes, so called from their six-dollar price tag)—Scotch-grain brogues with wing tips. And black silk socks.

Not even the dazed adulthood of the long pants that the mirrors reflected back at him could give him the pleasure those black silk socks did. For months he would not look down at his feet in their shiny Selz Sixes and see his sleek ankles without a thrill of gratification. He was that way about gloves, too. He couldn't help playing with them, pulling one on and snugging it around his fingers and clenching the fist to see the stitched back tighten into a wonderful smoothness, turning the upper part down to reveal his wrist merging into leather elegance. To any outsider, a scrawny kid, a plucked chicken. To himself, a creature of infinite interest, a marvel, transformed by clothes.

All by himself he came to Mullett Kelley's. Strange that his mother had let him. Perhaps because he had earned the money himself, perhaps because she understood his need for independence. Even the electric-blue suit she never criticized, though after one wearing he himself knew he had made a terrible mistake, and his father, at sight of it, threw a fit.

There were other ghosts back in the night-lighted aisles of vanished Mullett Kelley's. His later dudism would not be tentative, uninstructed, and solitary, as was that first attempt, but social and imitative. He would dress the way his friends dressed. He could see them in there, crowding toward the windows in Oxford bags with twenty-two-inch cuffs, in Cantbustem white corduroys and crew-necked sweaters, in ROTC breeches and prospector's boots, in pegged whipcord and British leather, in straw skimmers with rainbow bands, in narrow-brimmed hats of rabbit-fur felt dyed red or green or orange—a brief fad borrowed from some movie, perhaps *Brown of Harvard*. And in white flannels and white buck shoes, in golf knickers and Argyle socks, in three-buttoned, short-lapelled suits made by Hickey Freeman or Hart, Schaffner and Marx out of (apparently) grain sacks. What one wore, all wore. Witness those Navy-surplus ducks he had seen disappearing down Main Street before dinner.

He stood and stared in past the little scene of the window display to where Bruce Mason at eighteen or nineteen, the Bruce Mason of the Holly phase or just before, surveyed himself in triple mirrors, a creation almost too perfect for profane eyes: white linen plus sixes, black stockings, black-and-white shoes, black sleeveless cable-knit sweater, black knit tie, white shirt with long arty "studio" collar points. The grasshopper at summer's end. Medium-big man about campus, editor and tennis player, poeticule, fop.

With a refocusing of his eyes he made it a year or two earlier, say spring of his sophomore year in college. He was seventeen. Joe Mulder was with him, a couple of years older and cubits bigger. They had peeled off their red athletic sweaters with the white U's on them and were being shown the new line of suits by Jack Bailey, just returned in disgrace from his aborted mission to Tongatabu.

Bailey had always been a scandal. In high school he spent his time playing football and tennis and his nights in what he and his peers called cunt-hunting. Their reports on how the hunting had gone drew crowds in corridors and locker rooms. Twice he had wrecked his father's car, the second time killing the girl who was joyriding with him. In his one year at the university he had raised so much hell that his father had conspired with the bishop of their ward to get him called on a mission.

Tonga was not a good choice. Bailey was not exactly repentant about getting recalled. He admitted that he had been teaching the girls on the beach at Nukualofa more than the story of the Golden Plates, and that they had taught him more than the ukulele. With small encouragement he would detail what he had taught and what he had learned.

It was Bailey's theory that women like it. He believed that there was not a woman alive he couldn't do it to, given time and circumstances. That was very interesting to virgins like Bruce Mason and Joe Mulder. Having experimented with how far a nice girl would let you go, they demanded to know how Bailey would go about persuading a girl who was saving it. He replied that he would ding their clitoris. Ding their clitoris and they fell like ducks in a shooting gallery. Oh, sure, they said, hooting. How you going to ding their clitoris? Just go ahead and ding, is that what they're going to tell you? You have my permission?

Who said anything about permission? said honest Jack Bailey.

As a haberdasher's clerk he was a natural. He would appraise your leg and tell you whether you should wear plus fours or plus sixes. He would instruct you in the right style of Arrow collar to wear with your tux. He would show you how to keep your shirt from ballooning out over your belt by attaching a rubber band between a lower shirt button and the top button of your pants. He bought his clothes at a discount and looked snappy in them. He wore his belt buckle snuggled against the point of his left hip. He was a husky, curly-headed, laughing satyr with a good tenor voice, an encyclopedic knowledge of clothes, cars, female anatomy, and the postures of fornication, and no interest in anything else. Joe, with his large tolerance, found him enormously amusing. Bruce found him fascinating because of the possibilities he suggested.

Bailey had the supreme confidence that he could talk his way out of anything. He liked to tell of the night he was parked with a girl out by the mouth of Mill Creek Canyon, and had to leak so bad he was dying of it. So he got out, saying he'd better take a look at the right rear tire, it had been feeling soft, and while he looked he took out old Elmer and let fly, and while letting fly he talked a blue streak to his girl in the front seat, ten feet away, so that she wouldn't hear the waterfall against the wheel.

Chortling, he raised his eyes and sang:

> Just a piss in the park,
> 'Twas to her just a lark,
> But to me 'twas relief supreme . . .

The story he was telling now topped them all. Probably he was right, probably he *could* talk his way out of anything.

"We're on her porch," he was saying. "I've been working her over and she's hot as a firecracker. But there's no porch swing or anything, so I've got her backed up against the wall beside the door. You ever try it standing up? With a tall enough woman it's O.K. Not like a wheelbarrow—oh, mama!—but O.K. So we're giving it to each other good. Every time I sock Elmer to her he lifts her off her feet. Every time she comes down she buckles my knees. Sometimes I don't get in but three or four pumps before I come, but last night I got in ten or fifteen. And then just when I'm coming, and it's all pinwheels and skyrockets, her old lady opens the door."

Cries of disbelief. Laughter. "Bailey, you liar, you could sell that to the Mulder Nursery for ten dollars a ton."

"Swear to God," Bailey said, with his hand raised.

"So what did you do, you bullshitter?"

"What *could* I do? Jesus, I'm in her, I'm going off like Big Bertha. And there's her old lady three feet away with her nose against the screen door. I couldn't even quiver. If she turns on the light I'm gone. There we'd have been, stuck together like a couple dogs. So all I can do is hold old Agnes up on my pecker, and brace my hands against the wall like I'm penning her in, trying to kiss her or something, and I say to her old lady, 'Mrs. Larson, I've been trying to get a good-night kiss from your daughter and she won't give me one. Have you got any influence with her?'"

"You didn't!"

"I sure as hell did. 'I know I'm keeping her up late,' I says, 'but she's been holding us up here for fifteen minutes.'"

Bailey rolled his eyes toward heaven; his cocky, square-jawed face wore a look like prayer. "Jesus, it was me holding *her* up, and Elmer was losing his holt. There's no way I can turn away, or get her skirts down, or button up, or anything. I just have to lean there against her and spill this line to her old lady about what a stingy daughter she has, won't even give a guy a good-night kiss. 'Maybe if you told her to,' I says, 'she'd give me one little smack and I could go home and we could all go to bed.' All the time old Agnes is fainting down the wall, and I'm scared shitless her old lady will turn on the light, or come clear out."

"Penis erectus non compos mentis," said Joe, who had a lawyer brother.

"And then what happened?" said Bruce Mason, snake-charmed by this tale.

"So I lean on old Agnes and I sing a little song in her ear," Bailey said. "'How about a little kiss, Cecilia? A little kiss you'll never miss, Cecilia?' Just like Whispering Smith."

"Bailey, you're the goddamnedest . . ."

"If my boyish charm don't work, I'm ruined," Bailey said. "I'm still into Agnes about a foot. . . ."

"Ah, ah," Joe said. "Vanity, vanity."

"And then her old lady says, 'I don't find any of this very funny, Mister Bailey. Agnes, I want you in here in two minutes, you hear?' And shuts the door. Oo woo. Oh boy."

"So then you screwed her again, I suppose."

"No," Bailey said. "As soon as she shut the door, I discreetly withdrew."

They shouted with laughter, and Bailey, with one eye on the office door in the back where the boss might be listening, began straightening up a rack of ties. (*Laughter*, Mason thought, staring through the window at that embryo of himself inside. Could there have been a time when he thought Bailey *funny?* And answered himself: yes.)

But Bailey's grin faded, he twitched his little mustache and knocked irritably, twice, on the counter. "Shit, though. I went away from there still wearing the condom, and when I got home I threw it in the can and flushed it down and went to bed. But it didn't go down, and this morning my old lady goes into the bathroom and sees this evidence floating there, and there's hell to pay. I don't know if I dare go home. If she tells my old man, I won't."

Back in the dim aisles they huddled and commiserated, reflected in triple mirrors, images of outgrown images, and outside the window of the Cat's Meow Mason stood wanting to laugh and found that he couldn't, quite. He found Bailey unpleasant and troubling, actively hateful, as if time had earned him no perspective at all. Personal grievance? Injured vanity? Or was he troubled by Bailey because, hateful as he once was, he demonstrated the attractiveness of amorality and self-indulgence and irresponsibility? Id. Principle of Evil. Lord of the flies. Why should Bruce Mason have caught, like another childhood disease, the sexual morality that was properly Bailey's inheritance, not his?

In the window he watched a gray-haired man, his seersucker jacket hung over his shoulder on a bent forefinger, frown and turn away.

He walked on up the street, but at Second South, thinking ahead to the next block, he felt the old pool hall coming, and that could have been as troubling as Bailey. Swerving with the green light, he recrossed Main and went up the other side, past where the Paramount Theater used to be. In its glass cage Olive Bramwell used to sit dispensing tickets, smiles, and in slack periods, chatter. A nice girl, a really nice girl, never Bruce Mason's steady but a girl he genuinely liked. She warmed his memory by appearing in it.

He and Olive understood some of the same things, without ever discussing them. He had, even then, the feeling that she kept her counsel as he kept his, and that she lived her life in compartments as he did: home, school, work, dates. Picking her up at her apartment (a girl could not conceal her home the way Bruce did) he had seen how shabby a place her family lived in, how proud they were of her, a college girl, how respectful of him, a college man. Her father was a fireman. Once or twice he had got Bruce and his friends the use of the firemen's and policemen's gym to practice basketball in. Or was it the police chief who had done that for them—the police chief who was a friend of Bruce's father's?

Like Bruce, Olive worked her way through school, first at the ticket window, later at the organ, which she learned to play in order to upgrade her job. Though she was pretty enough to turn heads, hers was screwed on right. A gay and game companion, she knew what she liked to do, what she wouldn't do, how far she would go, what she *had* to do. Neither a gold digger nor a fast one nor a teaser nor a dull and timorous dame, just a good-looking girl who had looked over her inheritance and her necessities and gone to work.

Once, walking down this same block with her after a movie, Bruce had looked at her animated face and her good figure in the pony coat she had just bought herself, and had said impulsively, "Olive, you know something? You're O.K. You make me feel good. I like just walking down the street with you."

In the middle of the sidewalk she had stopped, staring. Bruce was not one from whom girls expected compliments. Some of the bluster of his runt years clung to him. He affected the humor of belittlement and insult, he specialized in the outrageous. Hello, Double-Ugly. Hey, Repulsive, give us a kiss.

Dumbfounded in the stream of the after-movie crowd, she had stared at him with her mouth open. "Is this you?"

It embarrassed him to see that he had touched her. She had her own defenses, which he respected, and which were more breachable by stealth than by assault. He was afraid she might do something as awkwardly unprotected as he had just done—get tears in her eyes, or peck him with a kiss right there in the middle of the sidewalk.

"Don't tempt fate," he told her. "In a softheaded moment I said you're O.K. Give me any of your lip and I'll revert to type."

He swept an arm around her, felt her first resist and then give, and there they went varsity-dragging down the pavement while he leered lustfully into her face. Laughing, she broke free. People around them were laughing, too. That kind of attention-getting Bruce Mason never evaded. Whatever the occasion, he could be counted on to end up showing off.

Nevertheless, a moment that it pleased him to remember. Mark that page in the album.

The Paramount seemed to have been cut in half and renamed the Utah 3. Olive was not in the cage. A girl with buck teeth gave him an indifferent glance as he went by. Some other business, he didn't even notice what, had replaced the Keeley's Ice Cream parlor next door. In its windows he saw the gray-haired man with his jacket over his shoulder change direction to avoid

running into one of the paragranite fountains. Saved from collision with the intractable present, he renewed his inspection of
his own unsmiling reflection until it hit the window edge and
vanished.

Now he was at First South, where coming down he had not so
much as turned his head, preoccupying himself with thoughts of
streetcars and old-fashioned electric signs like someone who
stared intently into a store window to avoid greeting an acquaintance passing behind him. Not through fear. All that was
years and years ago, it had been worn smooth by time, and covered over with later deposits like a geological nonconformity.
More than that, he had had it in his mind that it was one of the
things he would revisit and confront, if only to test what time
had done to his response. But there was a reluctance in him, related to his procrastination about calling Joe Mulder. An influential part of his consciousness would have been perfectly content
to leave that whole horizon buried.

The WALK sign was on, and he almost obeyed it. But he didn't.
He stopped at the curb and looked left across Main Street and
down to the second building from the corner.

Gone. No sign in the shape of a pool table outlined in lights,
no steps leading down below the street level. A new tall building
had replaced the old four-story stone front; the patterned sidewalks of downtown rehabilitation had paved over that lowest
point in his life, the place where he had last seen his father alive,
and where he had cut every tie that bound him to his origins.

Now he turned and looked east up First South, searching for
the shabby front, the dim apologetic sign, of the fleabag hotel
where he had killed himself. It, too, was gone. All the buildings
on the block must have been razed. Slick high rises confronted
one another across their decorator sidewalks. It was as different
from the old street as the man standing on the corner was
different from the tense student who decades ago, summoned
from his law school graduation in Minneapolis, entered the now
vanished door and saw the washed area on the grimy wainscot,
the tack-holed floor of the corridor from which the carpet had
been removed, the door at the end with the hole at breast level
through which had gone the first bullet, the one that killed the
woman.

It was there as detailed and uncompromising as a photograph: you could have put a magnifying glass to it and read the flyspecks, the numbers and names scrawled on the wall beside the telephone. And then an overlay slid across it and he was seeing another bullet hole, perhaps prophetic: the one in the colored glass beside the front door of the first house they had lived in in this town, the hole against which, at thirteen, he used to put his experimenting tongue to feel the thin stream of icy outside air. That air blew at him out of the past right now. His teeth ached clear to the jawbone, and he was filled with a weary sense of predestination, helplessness, the inevitability of things.

In just a few months, he said to somebody, some *ficelle* or confidante, I buried my brother, my mother, my young love, and my innocence. In a few months more I buried my father and my youth. Put that way, it sounded like a bleat, a plea for pity to match some burning and unassuaged self-pity, and he despised himself for the way it had phrased itself in his head. Yet he was offended to see the pool hall obliterated, and his father with it. He wished his father could have been perpetuated through the places he had frequented. He wished change could have happened without wiping him out—that he could still exist on First South and Main as he existed in the memory, in the neurones which, alone among all the cells of the body, are never renewed. Mason wanted him preserved, he began to realize, so that he could return to him and settle something.

And if with him, then with others, too. With Bailey, if he was alive. With Joe, whom he had cut off with the others though from Joe he had never known anything but kindness. With Nola, of whom he had asked more than she could give. With all of them, dead or alive, he had binding treaties to make. With his mother, no. She was the one person whose memory he didn't need to placate, whose forgiveness he had without asking. For all his thoughtlessness and egotism, he had loved her with a whole heart, and she had known it. She lay quiet; they understood one another. The others were more demanding.

But he was not even yet ready for them. As after a long plane journey, he had some sort of historical jet lag to get over. His clock needed resetting. And also, he told himself, he must not, must never, exaggerate the pain and anger of his youth, because however he may have felt at the time, his youth was something that he now looked back on with fascination, disbelief, and a wincing sort of pleasure.

As a matter of fact, for five or six years this city had been so rich and full for him that every morning trembled with possibility like a wall on which sun and wind throw the flicker of leaf shadows. The days and nights could not contain him. He walked his routes to the university, or rode the streetcars to his job in Sugar House, or drove out on a date, or sat up late over books and went to bed with his brain exploding like an ammunition dump, or put his name on the sign-up sheets of tennis tournaments or his lips on the warm lips of girls, with the feeling that any hour could bring him some unimaginable, gorgeous fulfillment. He had no ambition, he did not plan toward any future, he felt no high resolves, he comprehended no goals. He simply lived the full present, and every morning opened his eyes on a new installment of it, and he trusted the new installments never to fail.

The light changed. He left the corner where the associations were all dark and heavy, and walked the obstacle course among urns and fountains back to the hotel, and straight past it to the garage entrance. Within five minutes he was driving up South Temple. In another three or four he was coasting along Tenth East, where the trees overhung so leafily that they obscured the arc light at mid-block, and his eyes were searching the dark east side of the street for the entrance to the old tennis club.

It was not there. A broad low building occupied the space where it had once been. The parking area was gone, superseded by a slope of lawn, in the middle of which was a sign. Looking through and beyond those structures of the present, he saw those of the past, the place where he had gone through a metamorphosis so complete that it had felt (and felt now) like a reincarnation. He could see the old entry, the high fence solid with Virginia creeper, and beyond that the five clay courts belted with their nets, the bungalow-like clubhouse to the left of the gate, the spectator area reaching from the clubhouse to number 5 court, shaded all the way by the grape arbor from which, in late summer, fat clusters of Concords hung down. The courts blazed in the brillance of summers gone but never lost. Under the arbor, in the weathered, creaky, unraveling wicker chairs, sprawled the figures in white flannels and ducks who were first his idols and then his friends.

If we were cloned, Mason was thinking, if we were cloned instead of being reared by amateur parents, would we still have the illusion that our personal experiences are unique? Who could say? In any case, his separate individualized remembering was an indulgence that he insisted on just now. All right, he said to the disapproving elder in his head, *je plains le temps de ma jeunesse.*

But his memory was a sloppy housekeeper, and had trouble concentrating on one thing at a time. It seemed that he was not only sitting in his dark car under the dark trees of Tenth East Street in Salt Lake City, looking across at the summers from 1925 to 1930, but he was also sitting over a drink at a glass-topped table on the terrace of the St. Georges Hotel in Beirut, a place that had since been so shot up by civil war that it didn't exist except in heads like his that had known it before. Motor-boats towing water skiers were cutting circles around the bay. Every now and then one swooped like a swallow through the sea cave in Pigeon Rock. The sound was abruptly cut off, the air was hollow with its absence, the boat and its spidery tow were swallowed up. Then the bow bolted into the open, the sound blared out, the skier swerved in a wide arc toward the beach and away again, the wake spread and chattered against shore and terrace. In the soft November Mediterranean sun he was talking to someone, someone female and sympathetic, who pursed the mouth that he might later kiss, and half dropped the lids that he might later kiss shut, and said with pity and disbelief, "But you had to *hitchhike* out of your childhood! You could so easily have been lost."

"Yes," he said, "if I hadn't been lucky."

"Lucky you had a father like that? Lucky to be sickly and small and an outsider? You couldn't have been more out of it if you'd been black."

"Oh yes I could have."

"But anyway you surmounted it. You made that scared inward little boy into something. You outgrew him."

"Maybe. Maybe not."

"You had to make your own chances."

"Oh no. They were given to me."

"Who ever gave you any chances?"

"My mother. Friends. Professors. Even my father."

"You said your parents never even finished grade school. How would they know what a bright boy needed?"

"I wasn't thinking of the bright boy. If he's really bright, he'll find out what he needs. I was thinking of the runt. I was thinking about confidence. I was thinking about plain physical competence. That meant more to me than being bright. Anything Bruce Mason ever did he owes to the Salt Lake Tennis Club. Shall I tell you about the summer of 1925?"

She is one of those imaginary women so generous and supportive that she calms the winds. She slows the pulse rate like transcendental meditation. "Please do," she says.

8

Unlikely as it seemed, they were a close family. The internal strains that tore them apart also forced them together. Because they lived outside law and community, they had no one but themselves to share themselves with. They belonged to no neighborhood, church, profession, occupation, or club. In Saskatchewan they had been part of a small town that they knew and were known in. Here, what happened outside their family did not touch them, and what happened inside it had to be contained there. Secrecy and caution affected even their name. At home his father was Harry Mason, but in Los Angeles, to which he now made frequent trips by car, he was Harry Barnes. The neighbors, such of them as they let themselves become acquainted with, were given vaguely to understand that Harry Mason was in mining. That would explain his frequent absences and his obvious lack of a steady job.

Sometimes Bruce wondered, long after they were dead and he had left Salt Lake behind, if the unhappiness that he and his mother felt had worked both ways, if his father was as little contented with them as they were with him. Even in illicit enterprises there would probably be professional pride and parental vanity. A pickpocket might be pleased if his children, in their play, paid him the compliment of imitation. Even Harry Mason, proud of his ability to make long drives, stay awake thirty-six hours at a stretch, keep out of trouble, smell danger in advance and avoid it, might have been glad of company on his trips if either his wife or his sons had ever indicated a desire to go with him. Perhaps he resented their resentment of him. Perhaps he thought of himself as a good provider inadequately appreciated.

Perhaps. Bruce never knew exactly how Chet or his mother felt, because the circumstances of their life suppressed communication. But he supposed the old man might have been a good deal happier with an easygoing, uninhibited, morally slovenly wife, and sons who got in fist fights and saw the world not as a club they wanted to join but as an enemy camp suitable for raiding. On the other hand, maybe not. In his way, Harry Mason was as conventional as they were. He simply didn't see himself as they saw him.

They were no longer a speakeasy. Now his father made those forced trips to Los Angeles, and between trips delivered heavy suitcases to certain habitual houses, pool halls, shine parlors, and hotels. The family knew of but did not know the customers. They no longer came to the house, so that they lost even that connection with the city they lived in. Sometimes Bruce felt that his mother would almost have welcomed a return to the time when the parlor had been full, even though the people in it were people she deplored and avoided.

As a family, they shared nothing with anybody in Salt Lake except its streets and streetcars, its hot thunder-broken summers, its smoky winters, sometimes its movie houses, sometimes its ball park. On Sundays, instead of visiting anyone or having friends in, they often took a drive, all by themselves, up a canyon or out to Holladay, ending up with a quart of solitary ice cream.

Outside the house, each of them except Bruce's mother had another life—he and Chet at school, his father downtown in those places where men of dubious occupation gathered to conduct businesses that operated without a business address. They were bootleggers, pimps, leasers of illegal slot machines, merchants of curios and pornographic postcards, promoters of doodlebugs guaranteed to locate gold and silver underground. Now and then his wife could make friends with the woman next door,

if Harry Mason thought her safe, and if she had no children to
be around the house and see too much. But her acquaintances
were few and soon lost, with a move. Much of the time she was
alone.

For a long time she had been sleeping and eating badly. In
June, right after Chet and Bruce graduated together from high
school, she broke down; and Bruce's father, with an understanding that surprised him, sent her up to Brighton, in the
mountains, for a rest. Bruce camped down on Big Cottonwood
Creek and came up every day to take her for walks—up to a lake
called Solitude, over the divide to Alta, up around the slope of
Mount Majestic, along the old tramway that led to Park City, or
simply along the dirt roads through the firs and aspen.

That idyll lasted less than ten days, and ended when federal
prohibition agents raided the house in town, where Chet and
Harry Mason were batching, and hauled them both off to jail.

Harry Mason fixed it. He was usually able to fix things, for a
lot of people liked him, including the chief of police and several
deputy sheriffs, none of whom had any particular affection for
federal prohis. Some of those doors to which he carried suitcases
after dark were perhaps the doors of judges, district attorneys,
people who could quietly squelch a prosecution. The grand jury
was supposed to be preparing an indictment. It never did.

But if Harry Mason could patch things up with the law, he
wasn't able to, this time, with Chet. Chet had been pitching in
the semipro Copper League. He was scheduled (Harry Mason's
doing) for a late, informal tryout with the Salt Lake Bees of the
Pacific Coast League. With luck, which he never had, he could
have ended up pitching in the big leagues, as his principal rival
in high school did.

But the prohis had hauled him off to jail. Even though he had
been booked as Chester Barnes, and immediately released, his
address had been in the paper, recognizable to those who most
mattered to him. He was humiliated before his friends and his
girl. Before forty-eight hours were up he had lied about his age,
which was only seventeen, married his girl Laura, and left town,
headed anywhere outward. In a week he was brought back, dou-
bly and triply humiliated, and his marriage annulled. Within another week he was gone again, it could almost be said for good.

He was the real casualty of that summer. And yet it seemed to his survivor and brother, brooding backward to those times, that he was never so helplessly a member of that little clenched family as when he left it in anger and pride.

Instant adulthood. He probably felt it was forced on him. Bruce did, too. In the last year he had suddenly begun to grow, and he came into the summer six feet tall and weighing about a hundred and twenty-five pounds—a greyhound, a willow switch. He wouldn't be sixteen until December. So what did he do? He, too, lied about his age, saying he was eighteen, which must have been a pretty transparent lie, and before the end of June was in a Citizens' Military Training Camp at Fort Douglas, on the bench above town. It was the only way he could think of to get away from the house. And he had recently had a taste of military glory, marching down Main Street in the Memorial Day parade in his leather puttees and his Sam Browne belt.

No Sam Browne belts in camp. He was a buck private in the Signal Corps. If he had deliberately tried to keep himself in the role of runt and weakling he could not have found a better way.

He was all sapwood, without strength, and years younger than anyone else in that citizen army. The first day on the pistol range, he found that he simply couldn't lift the boxes of ammunition that the others picked up and staggered off with. Couldn't budge them, they might as well have been bolted to the ground. Then at the weekly parade and inspection he got dizzy in the heat and threw up, splashing those next to him in line. The sergeant took one disgusted look and told him to fall out and go somewhere and stay the hell out of the way. He spent the rest of the morning under a tree at the edge of the parade ground watching his fellows sweat out there in their woolen uniforms. He knew exactly what they thought of him, and he agreed.

The whole miserable camp went that way. In the second week they had a sham battle. He was stringing field telephone lines, and he got fouled up and didn't get them to the command post in time, so that the apricot orchard held by the Blues was overrun and captured. Everybody knew who was responsible. And a while after that, on the pistol range again, Bruce had just reloaded and was standing at raise pistol after shooting 68 out of a possible 70 at twenty-five yards, and the colonel was standing

by him giving him his astonished commendation, when Bruce's
index finger, which should have been up along the barrel of the
.45 automatic, accidentally wandered inside the trigger guard.
The gun went off right beside his ear and almost in the colonel's
face. When Bruce could see again, and the colonel had recovered
from his leap backward, Bruce saw that he had shot a scallop
out of the brim of the colonel's campaign hat. The colonel gave
him such a scared, furious bawling out—exactly like Bruce's father, he sounded—that Bruce lay awake most of the night trying
to choose between desertion and suicide.

All he got out of camp was some sharpshooter medals, rifle
and pistol. But he couldn't believe that those were any sign he
was growing up. Saskatchewan and his father had given him
those, not the citizens' army. He had been a good shot by the
time he was ten.

Camp didn't even get him entirely away from home, for the
National Guard officers and mess sergeants and cooks had no intention of getting stuck on that baking shelf on weekends. The
men had passes forced on them, and there was no place to go except home.

The very sight of Bruce's beanpole figure in its badly fitting
khaki wool made his father tighten his lips and breathe hard
through his nose. And when one Saturday he suggested that they
all go to the ball game, and told Bruce to change into some
civilized clothes, and Bruce told him that they were under orders
to wear the uniform even on pass, he clutched his head in both
hands. Who the hell was going to know whether a fifteen-year-
old snotnose wore his silly monkey suit or not? Bruce replied
that though his father might shoot him he could not make him
disobey orders. His father asked whose orders counted around
here, the stupid army's or his. Bruce fell mulishly silent. His father said passionately that by God he was not going to be a
laughingstock, sitting in the grandstand next to any comic-opera
soldier, and he took Bruce's mother off to the game.

She didn't try to smooth it over. She knew Bruce would rather
stay home and read than go to the ball game with his father anyway. Laughingstock! said Bruce darkly to himself, prowling
around the house. Who'd be a laughingstock sitting next to *who?*

Finally he sat down in the cool dusky parlor and read about the discovery of New South Wales in Captain James Cook's *Account of a Voyage Round the World in 1769–1771.*

It wasn't the likeliest book to find in a rented house. Probably it had been brought back by a Mormon missionary—all the world travelers in Salt Lake City were missionaries—who had had his horizons enlarged by carrying the church's message into the islands of the sea. Somebody more broadly educable than Jack Bailey. It fascinated Bruce because it spoke of escape, adventure, far places, the unknown, the search for *Terra Australis.* Its most prosaic lines reverberated with possibility: *In the afternoon we came upon the dung of an animal which fed upon grass. . . .*

By the time camp was over, Bruce was out of the Signal Corps and carrying the front end of the bass drum in the band. Then he was released into the hot, endless, companionless vacuum of summer. He could find no jobs except the occasional mowing of a lawn. He knew no one in their neighborhood, and there was no one in any other neighborhood that he felt close enough to to look up.

The days were glaring hot, the house cool under big old trees. He lived in books and in his mind, which was numbed by the consciousness-changing drugs of adolescent physiology. He was so stunned with hormones that he hardly answered to his name. He read the days through, in all positions: sitting, lying, on his back, on his belly, upside down, hanging over the arm of the couch with his book on the floor, lying on his back with his feet on the sofa and the book held up in the air. Every sort of book passed through his hands without affecting his trance. In a sort of catalepsy he read through their unknown landlord's glass-fronted library—Conrad, James Branch Cabell, Galsworthy, Arnold Bennett, Shaw, Knut Hamsun, Aldous Huxley. He turned hundreds of pages in the Harvard Classics with no more comprehension than if he had been sniffing glue.

To the remarks, questions, and orders that disturbed the air around him he responded, if at all, with murmurs that would postpone or evade action, until after three or four such inattentive non-responses his father would fly off the handle and drive him out of his trance and force him, confused and sullen, to do what he had been asked.

Sometimes he spent an hour at a time simply sitting, lost in some daydream, and now and then when he came out of it he had the unpleasant shock of finding his father watching him. His face at such times was judging and exasperated and full of scorn. But Bruce couldn't have changed his behavior if he had wanted to. He simply took to avoiding his father whenever he could.

Then one afternoon deep in endless summer, he stood up from the chair where he had been flopped, glassy-eyed and lost to everything, and announced aloud some indecision arrived at a thousand light-years away. "Well, I don't know," he said, and went out into the kitchen to get a glass of milk from the icebox.

With the glass in his hand he started for the back yard, but when he felt the glare and heat of the afternoon come inward at him, he let the screen door bang shut without going through it. As he sat down at the kitchen table he heard his father's angry, intense voice. ". . . crazy! Out of his head!"

"He's at an awful hard age," his mother said. "He's beginning to grow up."

"Then why *doesn't* he grow up? Why does he sit by the hour with a stupid look on his face? Tell him something, he doesn't hear you. Tell him three times, he still doesn't hear you. Tell him at the top of your voice, he still doesn't hear you. You have to pull the chair out from under him before he notices. Stands up talking to himself. 'Well, I don't know.' What was that about?"

"He's alone too much," his mother said. "He needs friends, and things to do."

"Then why doesn't he find some? He isn't going to find any standing on his head in front of that bookcase."

"Maybe he can't," his mother said. "Maybe he doesn't know how. Maybe he's ashamed of what we do, have you thought of that? Maybe he thinks the other kids laugh at him. I know he used to. I wish . . ."

Bruce hung there waiting to hear what she wished, for it was sure to be something about him, and he was a subject in which he took the greatest interest. But they had fallen silent, perhaps sensing that he hadn't gone outside after all, and might still be within earshot. Easing the screen open, he slid out through it, let it close softly, and sat down quickly on the porch rail in a narrow band of shade.

His mother came into the kitchen. She gave him a worried, encouraging smile through the screen. "You're in the house so much," she said. "Couldn't you find someone to play with? Baseball? Maybe just play catch?"

"I don't know anybody."

"Oh, you know dozens of boys at school!"

"None of them live around here."

"Maybe if you went down to the Municipal. It seems to me that when we lived down by there, Chet could always find some game going on."

"It's too hot."

"Maybe you could go swimming."

"Where? There's only Warm Springs, and last time I was out there I got a bealed ear."

"Yes," she said, troubled. "I'm afraid that place isn't as clean as it should be. Well, isn't there someone you could telephone? Somebody who has a bike, and could come over? It would be all right. You could play cards or something. I could get Pa to go out and get some ice cream."

"It's all right. I'm O.K."

The last thing he wanted was to hunt somebody up and invite him over. Anybody worth asking would be doing something else, anyway. And anybody was likely to see or feel something, catch some family tension, or hear his old man bawl him out about something.

He set the glass in the sink and went outside and read on the lawn, under a tree. When his mother at supper asked him what book he had had his nose in all afternoon, he gave her a mumbled answer. He did not like to talk about books in front of his father, who despised them, or at least despised their capacity to pull him away from reality. But also, he lived his life in compartments, and his mother no more belonged in the compartment of school and books than his father did. The only compartment in which she had a place was the home one, the one in which his physical needs of food and clothing and sleep were taken care of.

Nevertheless, it was she who found the tennis club. And how

did she find it? By going along with his father when he made a delivery to the little Italian called Murphy who managed the place. If the old man hadn't been the club bootlegger she would never have discovered it, and neither would Bruce.

He could imagine, remembering, how it would have seemed to her when she came into that blazing white space insulated inside its high walls of vine. She would have sat in the deep shade of the arbor while the old man and Murphy conducted their business inside. She would have felt the intense seclusion, the privilege, of that modest little temple to sport. She would have heard the strange musical ping of rackets on balls, and heard the running feet, the gritty sound as someone slid into a shot on the clay, the burst of laughter and release at the end of a rally. She would have seen the bare-legged girls in white dresses, tanned and healthy, and heard their chatter and laughter, and thought how pleasant their company would be for her solemn solitary son, reading himself blind back at the house. She would have watched youths in white ducks fight each other for points out on the bright courts, marvels to her of coordination and skill, and wished she could somehow make it open and accept him.

She had a way of being quietly and single-mindedly efficient when she wanted something for Bruce. She must have gone to work on his father the minute he and Murphy came out of the unused bowling alley and stood by her under the arbor.

A night or two afterward, she started quizzing Bruce at supper. Had he ever played tennis? Did he know how?

He could see that she had in mind some scheme or other, something she wanted him to do for his own good, and he answered evasively. Yes, sure, he had played a few times.

Did he like it?

Like it? Sure, it was all right.

He hadn't played tennis this summer, even with a lot of time on his hands. Was that because he didn't like it, or didn't have anybody to play with, or didn't have a racket, or what?

He didn't know. Some of everything, he supposed. Anyway, the only public courts were away down in Liberty Park, and always full besides.

Wasn't there a tennis club in town? Had he ever heard of one?

Yes, but that was where the *good* players played.

Did he know anybody who played there?

He didn't know. Maybe some of the high school tennis team did.

Would he like to play with them if he had the chance?

They wouldn't play with him, they were way too good.

But he could learn.

Oh, sure, he supposed so.

Would he like to *belong* to the tennis club?

What for? He didn't have a racket or anything.

But if he had a racket?

Maybe. But those guys were all a tight little crowd. You couldn't just crash in.

He didn't like the way she couldn't keep from smiling. And his father was listening, looking almost agreeable. It was some kind of conspiracy. His mother got up and went into the kitchen and came back with her hands behind her.

"Because you *do* have a racket!" she cried, and produced it. It was secondhand, with stained adhesive tape spiraled around the handle. Bruce took it, pretending pleasure, and tapped it on the heel of his left hand. Dreadnaught Driver, it said on the throat.

"And you *do* belong to the tennis club!" His mother said. A pink flush had appeared on her cheekbones and she could not control her smiling. "Pa's bought you a membership for the rest of the summer. I got the racket from Murphy, it's just been restrung. And here's two new balls. I got you some tennis shoes and some white pants, too, that's what they all wear."

What could he say? Thanks. Gee whiz, Ma, thanks. Thanks, Pa. This is swell.

"Murphy said he'd introduce you to people. He's a customer of your dad's so you'd have to be a little . . . careful."

"Yeah, sure."

But that killed it, if it had ever been alive. His father sat watching him, and though Bruce had in his hands, and heard in his mother's happy voice, evidence of his good will, what he felt was his father's opinion of his son's response. His lack of enthusiasm disgusted him. The boy was unappreciative and mule-headed. He had thrown away his money. Maybe he thought Bruce was thankless, maybe he understood that Bruce wanted nothing to do with Murphy or any other customer. He veiled his eyes and finished his supper in silence.

Just the same, he had to go down the very next morning. It would have been like hitting his mother in the face if he hadn't. He had to get dressed up in his new white embarassing ducks and sneakers. She practically forced him out the door, she watched him go down the block. He was scared to death she would suggest coming along, to protect and introduce him as if he were a little kid starting school.

He considered never going near the club—just disappearing for a few hours and coming back with some story or other, and going on with the pretense until she forgot or gave up. But if he didn't show up there, word would get back through Murphy. So about midmorning, watchful and unwilling, he went through the gate and stood a minute, looking around.

Two girls were playing on the first court. They banged the ball ferociously, they ran like sprinters, they slid and changed directions and charged up and fell back, they chopped and lobbed and drove and smashed and volleyed in grim, breathless competitiveness, they chased each other from corner to corner and from net to base line. One of them, Bruce saw from her gestures, was deaf and dumb.

His heart was down. In this place where his interfering mother had got him, even deaf-and-dumb girls played with a power and skill that demoralized him. In his fraudulent white ducks, carrying his secondhand Dreadnaught Driver and his two new balls—and why had she got only two? Even he knew there should be three—he sneaked past the clubhouse and hid himself in a wicker chair under the arbor, where he became a spectator.

He had been there for perhaps ten minutes, and was thinking of sneaking out again, when Joe Mulder came out of the clubhouse. Bruce knew him from high school. He had played end on the same football team on which Chet had been a halfback, and he was captain of the school tennis team. One of the big guys, but not one of the stupid ones. He had spoken to Bruce once or twice in the halls.

"Well, hey there, Mason," he said, and gave Bruce a surprised blue glinting look from under his pink eyebrows. He flopped into

a chair and pitched his racket into another. His ducks had obviously been wadded, sweaty and soiled, into a locker. His
sneakers were so worn that only the laces kept them on his feet.
He smelled of stale sweat and stiff gym socks. The three balls he
laid on the strings of his racket were worn fuzzless. Bruce
wished he had had the wit to sit down on some curbstone and
get the seat of his new pants dirty. If Joe hadn't been looking at
him, he would have wiped his sweaty hands on his legs to dull
the whiteness and obscure the crease.

"Hi," he said.

The grass under the arbor was long and uncut, stained with
fallen druit. Wasps were busy there. Joe reached up for a cluster
of grapes, tasted one, made a face, and threw the bunch away.
"How's Chet?"

"He's up in Idaho or somewhere."

"Playing ball?"

"I guess. He doesn't write very often."

He wondered if Joe Mulder knew about the raid. There was
no way to tell.

"I didn't know you were a tennis player," Joe said, and now he
was looking pointedly at Bruce's unbaptized clothes.

"Well," Bruce said, "a little."

The deaf girl chased a ball down their way, and Joe wagged
his fingers at her through the screen. She gave him a broad grin
and heaved her arms in the air as if gesturing an explosion. She
was sweating like a man out there in the heat.

"You belong to the club now?"

"I just joined."

"Good."

He seemed genuinely pleased. For a minute they sat with
nothing to talk about, and then Bruce said, "I don't know many
members, I guess. Who's around this summer?"

"Oh, most of us. The whole East High team—Kreps and
Bailey and McBride and me. Some guys from the U. Al Anderson, you know him? Writes sports for the *Deseret News*, always
writes himself up as 'the little star,' and 'Anderson, with his
flashing all-court game.' I don't know—most of us. Chick Bel-
ton, he's state and intermountain champ. Quite a few Old Joe
Gettems that you think you can mop up on and never can. Cagey

old bastards that can't run and can't hit it and never make an
error. And some girls. Amy out there, the deaf one, ought to win
some tournaments this year. Lots of people." He picked up the
Dreadnaught Driver from where Bruce had leaned it against a
chair. "This yours?"

"Yes," Bruce said, and added, "My old one."

"Jesus, it's heavy, isn't it? That'd break my arm." ·

His arm looked about as breakable as a sawlog. Bruce was
conscious of how skinny his was by comparison, and he cursed
his mother for letting Murphy sell her an old clunker that even
Joe Mulder couldn't swing.

"My other one's got a busted string," he said. "That's lighter."

Joe Mulder's glinting, quick eyes touched Bruce's white perfection and withdrew. "What's your other one?"

In panic Bruce searched the vacancy of his mind for some
name, some scrap of information, some echo of an advertisement
or a conversation, and found nothing. He could feel his ears red-
dening. "It's a . . . a . . ."

Joe picked up his own racket and tested the tone of its strings,
laid it down to pick up Bruce's and get a duller tone. As he laid
his down, Bruce read its throat.

"It's an HA!" he said. "Spalding HA. Like yours."

"Yeah?" Joe was smiling. Bruce would have sworn that he had
lifted that racket to give him a clue. "I like an old HA, don't
you? Old pancake turner. It isn't so good for serving, do you
think? It's so wide in the top you don't seem to get as much
zing on a serve. But for ground strokes, it's the one."

Bruce couldn't have agreed with him more.

"You going to the U this fall?" Joe asked.

"Yes. Are you?"

"Yeah. Going out for tennis?"

"I hadn't thought about it."

"Nearly the whole university team graduated. Some of us
ought to have a chance to make it. Freshmen can earn a letter in
tennis. Better come out."

"Maybe I will."

"Let's take over the whole beeswax."

"You'll make it, for sure."

"I don't know. Maybe. Kreps might, too. Maybe Bailey, if he'd train a little and remember to stay eligible." Leaning, he squinted upward at the glitter of sun through the grapevines. "God damn Bailey, he's never been on time in his life. We had a date for ten. I've got to be at work at twelve. You waiting for somebody?"

"No, I just wandered by."

"Want to hit some till Bailey comes? *If* he ever comes?"

Bruce would have lied if he could. But if he wasn't prepared to play, why was he sitting there in tennis clothes, with a racket and two new balls? He couldn't even say he wasn't feeling well. Obviously, up till then, he was.

"I'm not in your class," he said, and having tried the truth with his toe, he immediately fell in all the way. "I'm just a beginner. All I'd do is make a horse's ass of myself."

A half smile was stuck on Joe's freckled, amiable face. "When did you get so humble?" he said. "I thought you were the guy that ate people alive. Once I heard you offer to tear the arm off old fat-ass Kirkham and beat him over the head with the bloody end of it. You were a *terror*, boy. Little, but oh my."

"Yeah, well, that was . . ."

"The funny thing was, he wasn't sure you wouldn't do it. You had him buffaloed." Joe laughed, made a surprised face, plucked a handful of his stained shirt away from his armpit, sniffed, and reeled. "Jesus, the Beau Brummel of the courts. It's all right once it gets warmed up, but cold it's worse than chloroform. Let's hit some before I asphyxiate myself."

"You don't want to hit any with me."

"Sure I do. Come on."

So Bruce went out and disgraced himself, hit three or four over the fence, lost one of his new balls in the vines, pushed and patted like a girl (*not* one of those on number 1), and was never once made to feel his clumsiness. Joe corrected his grip and showed him how to take a backswing and follow through. He showed Bruce where his feet should be, and how his weight ought to be coming through the ball, and how his eye ought to be on it till impact. In twenty minutes he taught him more than he had expected to learn all summer, and when Bailey finally arrived, he sent Bruce over to the bangboard off number 5, to practice what he had shown him.

"You've got a good eye," he said. "Your reactions are fast. You're coordinated. All you need to do is practice and play a lot."

From down at the end, in moments when he was walking after his ball, Bruce watched Joe and Bailey slug with one another from the base line, and he was envious but not discouraged. In a half hour, Joe Mulder had him belonging where he had never hoped to belong. By October he was taking an occasional set from Bailey or Kreps, and he had beaten one of the Old Joe Gettems that even Joe had trouble with.

Bruce Mason lifted his nose into the night wind. Bless that slovenly, confident, grinning, friendly horse. He had known Bruce Mason inside out from the first minute under the arbor, but still liked him and found him for some reason interesting and amusing. Bruce had spent that whole first day on the bangboard, and had come home blown, blistered, sunburned, soaked with sweat, just in time for supper. His mother had been delighted at the success of her plot. But it was not his mother that Bruce's heart thanked. It was Joe.

He would have played five sets barefoot on broken glass for him. Joe rescued his summer and perhaps his life. He taught Bruce not only tennis but confidence, and not only confidence but friendship. Simply by accepting that outcast, he made him over. If Bruce Mason knew anything at all about magnanimity, he learned it from Joe Mulder.

The night wind was moving the branches of the trees. The light of the arc lamp fluttered in the street. It seemed an endless way from Beirut and the terrace of the St. Georges, an incomprehensible distance from this tennis club and the fifteen-year-old who haunted it in the summer of 1925 to the State Department Building, the string of embassies, the array of foreign hotels and American compounds where accident and opportunity and perhaps the line of least resistance had later led him. The truth was, he felt at least as close, right at that moment, to the fifteen-year-old as to the ex-ambassador, the editor, the expert on Middle Eastern oil.

He opened the door and stepped out. The air was alive overhead, the shadows moved in a flow like the current of a river. He waded across the street and up onto the lawn, searching the dark beyond the building to see if perhaps they had kept the vine-covered fences. Those were a coolness in summer, a glory in fall. At any time of the year the ball came at you out of that even background in three dimensions, so plain you could read the label on it.

He bent over the sign planted in the lawn, but could not read it in the flaky light. Finally he struck a match, cupping it against the wind, and moved it along the plank in which letters had been cut with a router.

"Senior Citizens' Recreation Center," it said.

Angrily he shook the match out and dropped it. He went straight to the car and turned the switch and looked at his watch under the cowl light. Ten-twenty. Why not? he thought. If his house is dark I can simply drive past and turn around and go back to the hotel.

II

1

Back of the low outline of the house rose the gully trees. Light was shining through the side windows onto the shrubs along the drive. Almost furtively he went up the walk and stopped below the steps that mounted to the familiar door.

Ghosts watched from the shadows—Joe, Joe's father and mother and big frolicsome sisters and their young-businessman, golf-playing husbands. And the waif named Bruce Mason who seemed to live there. If someone inside should turn on the light, the whole Mulder family would be caught, not, like Jack Bailey, *in flagrante delicto,* but in their goodness and friendliness and warmth, their St. Bernard size and companionable numbers, their profound unanxious solidarity and confidence. He had the feeling that their footprints must be stamped into the cement floor of the porch like the prints of old-time movie stars in the entrance of Grauman's Chinese.

Here nothing had changed except himself. In the little light that seeped around the front drapes, it seemed that even the porch furniture duplicated the swing and chairs that they used to loll in on Sunday mornings, drinking grape juice and ginger ale, playing bridge or solo or Mah-Jongg, listening to Johnny Marvin or the Two Black Crows on Joe's portable Victrola, reading about themselves in the sports pages in the sweet morning shade.

Or attending tolerantly while Joe's father, with the nose of a ship's figurehead and the bearing of a Roman senator, lectured them on the need of eating a head of lettuce each day, or the benefits of debating societies in forming the minds of boys their age, or the superiority of good music, Grieg or MacDowell, to the popular songs they wasted their time on. Sometimes he sat down at the piano—the whole family played the piano, often simultaneously—and sang in a resonant bass,

> The hours I've spent with thee, dear heart,
> Are like a string of pearls to me.
> I count them over, every one apart,
> My rosary, my rosary!

How was it, Mason thought, standing in darkness and making no move toward the steps, that someone so supremely middle-middle, a small businessman whose imagination reached no further than family, community, and Kiwanis, and whose opinions were often as dubious as those of Harry Mason, though invariably opposite—how was it that this decent, limited, rather pompous man should have been a figure of such authority and respect? Even at sixteen Bruce Mason had known more about the seamier possibilities of human nature than J. J. Mulder would ever know, and he had thought he knew more than he did. Yet he listened to Joe's father with deference, and would no more have ridiculed or mocked or contradicted him than he would have spit on his floor.

"Bruce's God," Harry Mason had sneered once when Bruce was quoting J. J. Mulder on some subject or other. It was a revelation. Bruce understood him clear down to the ground. Jealousy. His father had never met J.J., but he felt him as a rival. That was startling, and would take some thinking about. Harry Mason resented the fact that his guarded, laughterless, irritable house should be abandoned in favor of one rotten with respectability.

How could he have expected anything else? His sons were bound to escape him as soon as they could. Chet had gone outward, flying off the edge. Bruce had gone inward, toward the re-

spectable sobriety of the Mulders. Everything they represented
—the family, community responsibility, good citizenship, ethics
—drew him as milking time draws a barn cat. From the time
when Joe first brought him home after a tennis match, all
through the years when he worked in J.J.'s nursery as handyman,
delivery boy, and salesman, J.J. had to be respected as what
Bruce thought a father ought to be, and his home as what a real
home was. He suspected that he had given more thanks and outward affection to Joe's mother than to his own, too. She never
had opinions. She was subdued to J.J.'s omniscience, and re-
tained only sympathy and kindness and a determination to fatten
up that thin Mason boy Joe was so fond of, and whose own family was somehow no good in ways that she carefully did not
inquire about.

Jack Mormons, the Mulders did not tithe or go to meeting, but
they kept the strenuous Mormon sense of stewardship. Having
talents, one improved them. Having money or position, one tried
to use it for the public good. Once Bruce had caught on to those
attitudes, he had only one way to go.

Now after long absence he stood before their house reminding
himself that they really had treated him as a son, and that he
owed them nearly everything—the job that J.J. gave him and in-
nocently exploited him in, the independence the job had promoted, the affection they let him freely share. He supposed he
was their faith in self-improvement made manifest, the object of
a Mormon proselytizing impulse not lost but only redirected. He
corroborated their belief that anyone could take hold of himself
and make himself into something better, happier, richer. It was
an American, especially a Western, as well as a Mormon notion.
Mason had subscribed to it then, and sneakingly still did. But
he had given them little in exchange for what they gave him.
In respect to his personal and family life, they must have found
him as taciturn as a paving block. It was their own openness and
generosity they liked him for.

He studied the dim light behind the drapes, either a low-wat-
tage night light or the diluted illumination from some room
deeper in the house. For a second or two he thought he heard
the murmur of television or radio voices from the back somewhere, then he didn't. Gone to bed? Not likely.

Everything in his memory rejected the notion of Joe Mulder pottering off to bed at ten-thirty. He remembered too many Sundays when, making the most of their one day off, they had got up before six to go out and play eighteen holes at Forest Dale or Nibley Park, and lunched on a Brigham Street Pharmacy malted milk so thick it had to be eaten with a spoon—tractor oil, SAE 50—and gone on to the tennis club and played five or six sets, singles and doubles, and then separated briefly for dinner and a change of clothes, to meet again and go out on a double date that kept them up till two or three. It offended his image of Joe Mulder to think of him going to bed. That engine.

It dawned on him that he was smelling the dark fume of lilacs. How exactly right! At this house the lilacs would have been continuously in bloom since the day he had first climbed its steps.

Following the fragrance, he stepped around the corner of the porch, and in the light from the side windows he saw the tapered cylinders of blossom lifting from among the crowded green hearts of the leaves. They were almost gone by. The top blossoms were browning, and only the shaded and protected ones were still fragrant. He leaned around and put his nose deep into the leaves and dragged his lungs full of the fragrance that preserved everything he once was.

All at once he was uncomplicatedly eager to see Joe, and impatient at his own evasive delays. But as he turned to start up the steps and put his thumb to the bell button he was stopped by the question of what he would say if the door opened. The patterns of communication between him and Joe would be fossilized. They would have no common language except the jargon of an antique adolescence. He couldn't imagine how he would greet his oldest friend.

Remember me? Coy.

Joe, you old scissorbill! Embarrassing, grotesque.

Or pull the old trick, crouch down low, turn up the coat collar and the face, become an upward-peering dwarf so that the opener of the door, expecting someone at eye level, would have to jerk his glance downward to the gibbering thing at his feet? Halloweenish, a shame to his gray hairs.

Maybe just silence? Stand there waiting for recognition?

He couldn't do it. Instead of mounting the steps he swerved

off across silent lawn to the sidewalk, and went walking up the
street as if he were not a visitor from a strange planet, or an
Enoch Arden peeking in the windows of the past, but only a citizen out for a pre-bedtime stroll.

His mind was busy with what might have been going on back
at the house if he had had the nerve to push the doorbell. He
finessed the greetings and exclamations and handshakes, and because he couldn't quite visualize how Joe would have aged—his
red hair would have gone rusty white, probably, and his Aire-
dale eyebrows would have grown bushier, but those details
didn't make a picture—he transferred them all out onto the back
lawn, where they sat in darkness in the warm wind, perhaps with
sweating beer cans in their hands, with their minds turned backward.

"You know, we grew up deprived," Mason might say. "Prohibition was a terrible thing. We've sat out on this lawn a lot of
nights, but never with the comfort of a beer. If we wanted a beer
we had to go down to Otto's."

Joe makes a sound like gagging. "Ether beer!"

"Black home brew with a stick of ether in it, that's right. It's a
wonder we lived."

Joe says, rumbling, "Remember the time Bailey drank milk
and gasoline because somebody told him it was intoxicating?"

"My goodness," says the faceless wife from her darkness.
"Didn't it kill him?"

"You couldn't kill Bailey with a drink. Anyway, I doubt he
swallowed any. He was gagging before he got the glass up to his
nose." Casually he adds, "What ever became of Bailey? He still
around?"

"He's around, raising as much hell as ever."

But that is not what he wants to hear. He backs up; he
rephrases the question. This time they do it right.

"Dead," they say. "Died four or five years ago."

That's better. End of story, end of grudge. All that Nature Boy
vitality, all that uninhibited machismo, gone quiet. Lounge lizard, wild partier, reckless driver, cunt-hunter, farewell.

"What is it about the Baileys?" he hears himself say. "How do
you account for their missionary spirit? Is there joy in hell when
some innocent is subverted? Bailey was the worst companion

you and I could have found, do you know that, Mulder? Alcohol, cigarettes, women, speeding, drunken driving, the works. He really was a missionary, too. In Tongatabu he just had the wrong gospel forced on him. The church wasn't his dish. But when it came to leading people into temptation he was a regular Dr. Livingstone. Nothing tickled him more than to baptize somebody."

In his dark chair Joe Mulder, hardly yet encountered, barely visualized, continues to rumble with laughter. "Remember that radiator cap? Bailey never got over it. You filled him with admiration."

It stands in his head like a scene from *The Rake's Progress:* the three of them in the hot alley parking lot, about to climb into Bailey's red bug. Bailey stops with one leg up, points, swears. "Some son of a bitch! They look, and his radiator cap is missing. Promptly, unhesitatingly, Bruce Mason, sixteen and in the first flush of being *in*, skips to a Model T touring car parked in the corner, unscrews its radiator cap, and skips back. From up on the blanket-covered board laid across the gas tank for a seat, Bailey cheers. Then someone says, from the doorway of a store that backs onto the alley, "What the hell goes on?" Angry young man in a rubberized apron, scowling in disbelief out into the glare. Bruce's perception is instant and crystalline: the young man would be coming out, but there are three of them, and Joe is as big as a house. Support makes him impudent. He says to the young man, "Somebody stole our radiator cap, and I was stealing yours to replace it." The owner's eyes bug in outrage, but he stays in the doorway. "Well, put it back, for Christ sake!" "Right you are," Bruce says, and puts it back. "O.K.?" The young man watches with his head sunk down. Joe climbs into the bug. Bruce goes to its front end, nudges the crank in until it catches, hooks his finger into the choke wire, and leans his shoulder against the radiator's beehive cells. Bailey retards the spark and pulls the gas lever halfway down. Bruce leans, lifts, jerks. One pull, and she starts. The young man in the doorway looks over his shoulder—someone is calling him from inside. Bruce waves and hops up beside Joe. Reluctantly, looking backward, the young man disappears. In a skip and a jump Bruce is back to his car. With the radiator cap in his hand he meets the bug as it

turns for the alley entrance. Bailey slows, Bruce leaps up, they
are gone. At the first corner Bailey stops and Bruce jumps out
and screws the plug onto the radiator. Bailey pounds the wheel,
delighted. "Nerve of a road agent," he says. "Mason, by God,
that *beats* me!"

"Bailey was catching, like smallpox," Mason says into the rattle
of cottonwood leaves. "I don't take much pleasure in his memory. One thing I do remember with pleasure, though—the night
you crammed him into the garbage can down at the club."

He hears his own steps in the quiet street, he is aware of the
cars that pass, brightening trees and house fronts and throwing
his shadow ahead of him down the sidewalk. The canyon breeze
flows steadily against him, a strong breeze for all its mildness. It
is dry, but fragrant with what it has blown past since emerging
from the canyons: soaked lawns, sprinklers forgotten in flower
beds and shrubbery, drives and gutters overflowing. Like a salty
cracker eaten with ice cream, that dry wind bearing moist odors
blends into a contradictory and tantalizing taste, and he is savor-
ing it even while he juggles and arranges that scene years back,
on the same sort of summer night as this, but earlier, barely
dusk:

They have been playing late, and are just coming out of the
heavy Virginia creeper shadows of the club. And here comes
Murphy's half-witted girl across the parking area. She is really
helpless. Any male who speaks to her undoes her; she can't do
anything but roll her eyes and moo. Somebody, Murphy or somebody else, has already got her good and pregnant. She must be
five or six months along. Almost every night she comes to the
club like this, and Murphy, that little five-by-five who is always
singing "O Sole Mio" or "Là ci darem' la mano" as he rolls the
courts in the mornings, is given every evening renewed cause to
sing. He will be very proud of that bastard when it is born:
"That's-a my baby!"

But now here comes this unwatched imbecile across the parking area, mooning along in no hurry through the dusk, and
Bailey suddenly gets the idea that he'd like to take her on. Never
had a feeb, he says. And look, she's already pregnant, no danger
or anything. He begins to kid her. It starts as kidding. Then

Bruce and Joe find out he means it. He wants them to go back and keep Murphy occupied for ten or fifteen minutes while he takes this poor moron under the hedge.

They laugh and refuse. He insists. They continue to refuse. He gets impatient. They try to drag him away, laughing. He will not budge, getting surly. That is when Joe suddenly folds him up and crams him into the garbage can. He comes out fighting, ready to kill Joe. Joe holds him off with one long arm until the girl gets tired of waiting and moons on into the club to see Murphy.

"Bailey was the kind that should suffer a conversion on his deathbed," Bruce says to Joe's shadow on the lawn. "He would have made a proper hero for Graham Greene. You and I are too square to get to heaven, but the Baileys are another matter. Only the real sinners give God any reason to exert Himself. No fun shooting tame hares."

"Speak for yourself," Joe says.

He has come to a place where Thirteenth East crosses the gully. The land falls away on the lower side into an unbuilt darkness that rattles with moving cottonwood leaves. Simultaneously aware of where he is, and how familiar it is, and hanging back to continue that imaginary conversation on Joe's back lawn, he feels how the whole disorderly unchronological past hovers just beyond the curtain of the present, attaching itself to any scent, sound, touch, or random word that will let it get back in. As a stronger gust rattles through the tops of the cottonwoods below him, he stops dead still to listen. Memory is instantly tangible, a thrill of adrenalin in the blood, a prickle of gooseflesh on the arms.

In the moving shade he and his mother wait for his father. (Where? Somewhere in the Sun River valley near Great Falls? Somewhere on the Frenchman or the Milk?) The horses, tied to the wheels, rustle for a last oat in the wagon box. On their backs the sweat marks have dried white under the harness. Dust is white in the cracks of the wagon, on the felloes and spokes of the wheels, in the furrowed bark of the trees. The hubs, where axle grease has been extruded, wear knobs of dust like luxuriant mold. The ground is pancaked with the dung of cattle that have dozed in this shade, and over ground, dust, dung, the litter of fallen twigs, is drifted a snow of cottonwood fluff from burst seedballs. When a sudden wind swarms through the grove, every leaf of every tree spins and rattles, accentuating the stillness that is not stillness at all, but a medley of dry sounds: crackle of grasshoppers, sawing of crickets, distant mourning of doves, and through it, over it, around it, encompassing it, the tap and clatter of cottonwood leaves. He doesn't know what he and his mother are doing there, he only knows that they wait, patient or imprisoned or entranced, immobilized in afternoon. When he looks up, the sun glints through at him off the varnished faces of thousands of heart-shaped reflectors, and beyond the dancing leaves the sky is a high pure blue crossed by traveling fair-weather clouds that darken and dissolve

become a velvet night sky with a late moon loose in it. The sound of cottonwoods has never ceased. He is aware that behind him, where their bedroll is laid out, the grove is deep black below and afire with cool shimmering light up where the wind stirs the high leaves. But he is not looking at the grove. He looks the other way, across the irrigation ditch, toward the peach orchard and the cliffs. Light like frost touches the high rim, and breaks up the face of the cliff into highlighted edges and promontories separated by depths of soft matte shadow. It falls in ragged patches between the orchard trees, and glitters and passed and is renewed on the water of the ditch. On the other side, Nola stands up, rising out of the dark pool of her clothes, facing him, dusted and hazed with moonlight, glimmering but plainly seen. The night is soft against his skin, but he is shivering, his jaw locked as if by paralyzing cold. She takes a step and dips a foot in the water. A low laugh wells out of her. "Oh, it's warm!" her husky voice whispers. "Come on." His shivering is so violent that at first he cannot move. He hears it communicate itself to the gelatinous air, and shake through the air into the tops of the cottonwoods and vibrate there, the very voice of his awe and worship and desire

The vision breaks and tears, dissolving. Below him the trees rattle and are still. Mason feels around in his mind like a blind man reassuring himself about the objects in a familiar room. The web of associations, the dense entangled feelings, are still, after an absence of two thirds of a lifetime, as intensely there as a rattlesnake under a bush. Not the girl herself; she is no more to him than a rueful shrug. But the associations, the sights and sounds and smells that accompanied her, the vivid sensuousness of that time of his life, the romantic readiness, the emotions as responsive as wind chimes—those he does miss.

Listen to those cottonwoods talking, he says to the two he left behind on the dark lawn. Doesn't that sound tell you, as much as any single signal in your life, who you are? Doesn't it smell of sage and rabbit brush and shad scale? Doesn't it have the feel of wet red ditch-bank sand in it, and the stir of a thunderstorm coming up over one of the little Mormon towns down in the plateaus? Just now, for a half second, it drowned me in associations and sensations. It brought back whole two people I used to love. When cottonwoods have been rattling at you all through your childhood, they mean *home*. I could have spent fifty years listening to the *shamal* thresh the palms in the date gardens of Hofuf, and never felt anything but out of place. But one puff of wind through those trees in the gully is enough to tell me, not that I have come home, but that I never left.

Having let it surge through his head like the wind through the branches, he takes it back. He could never say any such thing to Joe, much less to Joe's unknown listening wife. And yet there is something he wants to say. He tries again.

"Do you know how privileged you are?" he asks them. "Are you properly grateful to be living in Paradise?"

They protest, naturally. It is their belief that his life has been filled with exotic adventures and that theirs is restricted and provincial. That is one of the reasons he is only imagining himself in that back yard, and is not there in person: he hates the thought of being treated, by Joe, as The Ambassador, a visiting Distinction. That would only exaggerate the changes and the differences and the losses of forty-five years.

But Paradise. Their incredulity makes him insist. He feels that quiet back lawn as a green sanctuary full of a remote peace. "Paradise is an Arab idea," he says. "Semitic, anyway. It's a garden, always a garden. They put a wall around it because that's how their minds work, they're inward-turning, not outward-turn-

ing. Paradise is safe, not exciting. Like this. Change the mocking-
birds in that gully into bulbul birds, and put up a wall, and
you'd have it: water, greenness, coolness, peace, and all around
you the desert. The Mormons are all mixed up about heaven,
their right hand doesn't know what their left is doing. The Book
of Mormon makes heaven into a sort of New Jerusalem, with
gold-paved streets and windows of opal and ruby. But the real
Mormon heaven was made by hand, and it's this, it's an oasis in
the desert."

He cannot tell whether they accept what he says or whether
they are only being polite to the ex-ambassador, an old friend.
The scene fades, frays, is lost. A car coming along Thirteenth
East exposes him where he stands looking down into the moving
tops of the gully trees. His shadow rotates, floats outward,
stretches, dissolves. For a second or two the car occupies all the
silence, the whole inside of his head. Then its noise dwindles and
the night and his head are whole again.

He turns back. Most of the houses along the street are dark. It
must be eleven or after. A vague frustration grows in him—at
the hour, at the fact that the two back there on the lawn cannot
understand what he is trying to tell them, at the impossibility of
going back there in person at all. How will he get all the questions asked? How will they bridge forty-five years? Can he say to
Joe, outright, What *did* happen? Did Bailey and Nola stay together? When I was here for my father's funeral you said their
singing act had broken up, and you thought they had, too. But if
she didn't marry Bailey, whom *did* she marry? Where's she living? What happened to her?

He would not admit that much interest in her, either to Joe or
to himself. But he admits curiosity. That intense obsessed involvement, and then absence, silence. She managed to remain
mysterious; he would like to know about her, but he can't imagine asking. Neither can he imagine trying to explain to Joe why
in forty-five years he never wrote a single letter. He was the one
with the unstable address; he should have given Joe a chance to
keep in touch. Later, much later, he might have read about
Mason in the newspapers or got him with his breakfast orange
juice on the "Today" show, he might know exactly how time has
dealt with Bruce Mason, what he looks like, how he has spent his

life. But by the time that information might have been available, it would have been far too late for Joe to write. Pride would have intervened. I'll write the bugger when he writes *me*.

So now if Mason goes up on that porch and rings the doorbell and startles them out of their bedtime preparations—her hair in curlers, Joe's teeth in a glass—in what role does he appear? Is he the Diplomat or is he the bootlegger's boy?

It is impossible, not because he fears Joe but because he fears time, change, himself. After so long a silence, his slightest word, the answer to the simplest question, may strike Joe as being the word of a man who went away and forgot all his old friends and now comes back dropping names, parading himself rich and famous, as it may seem to them, around his home town.

Tomorrow it may be easier. Tonight he is too tired, he is not yet used to the strangeness of the once-familiar. After the funeral tomorrow he will call them, take them to lunch, spend the afternoon reaching back to what, however it may seem from his actions, means the most to him in this place.

He cuts across the parking strip to his car, and in the empty street, a street that stares like an Utrillo, makes a U turn and starts back toward the hotel.

2

The canyon breeze had died, the trees were still, the street lay
out before him, not simply empty, but blurred and ambiguous, a
double exposure, and he felt bewildered, in the strict sense, half
lost in a half-remembered wilderness, beguiled by familiar-seem-
ing landmarks as he had been when a boy prowling the willow
bottoms of the Whitemud, following the destinationless and
overgrown paths that cattle had pushed through the brush. He
clenched his eyes shut and opened them again to clear his vision,
and the street came single again. But it was the street of the
past, not that of the present.

It had the familiarity of hallucination. Its trees overhung it
with their known, late-at-night stillness, the arc lights blurred in
the leaves and cast puddles of inert dusty light on sidewalks and
parking strips and the angles of curbs. He had just dropped Joe
off after a date, and was turning home. The tiredness of a long
day and night had softened his bones. He yawned a jaw-cracking
yawn: he had not slept since 1931. Slouched in the seat,
scratchy-eyed, doped with drowsiness, he let the car find its own
way like an old buggy horse.

Not surprisingly, it took him home, and by ways as familiar as
the faces of the dreamed-of dead, past East High School's gray

barracks, site of all his subsequent flight-pursuit, corridor-and stairway, forgotten-examination nightmares; past the lunch shack, plastered with Camel and Coca-Cola signs, where they used to lunch on hot dogs and root beer, and where older boys, Chet among them, bought forbidden cigarettes and stood on the firing line just off the school grounds and smoked them with the intention of being observed.

Below the lawn, spread along the fossil beach terrace of the lake that thousands of years ago filled the valley, was a long hanging darkness, the playing field where in paleozoic gym-class softball games he had patrolled an invariable, contemptuous right field and batted ninth. Below that, the slope fell away to the crisscrossed lighted streets of the city, the bright bands of State Street and Redwood Road, the curving line of a new freeway, and far out, the darkness of the salt flats and the lake and the desert that reached to California. Up to the right, at the head of Main Street, the floodlighted Capitol stared whitely. Below it was the bloom of the business district with the spiky floodlighted temple at its upper edge.

Abruptly the capitol winked out. Its afterimage pulsed, a blue hole in the darkness, and before it had faded, the temple, too, went dark, cued to the same late clock. Something invisible but palpable, some recognition or reassurance, arced from the dark desert across the city and joined the dark loom of the Wasatch. In one enfolding instant, desert and mountains wrapped closer around the valley and around him their protective isolation.

Seen and unseen, lighted and dark, it was all effortlessly present. Here was a living space once accepted and used, relied on without uncertainty or even awareness, security frozen like the expression on a face at the moment of a snapshot. This territory contained and limited a history, personal and social, in which he had once made himself at home. This was his place—first his problem, then his oyster, and now the museum or diorama where early versions of him were preserved.

He felt its relationship to himself so strongly that he became defensive and resistant. It couldn't be that he actually yearned backward to the limited life he had known in this place. For more than forty years he had lived where the world was most dangerous, at the uneasy edges where nations slid down or were heaved up like the earth's plates in collision. He had had to devote himself to cultures and languages not his own, and to problems the very reverse of personal. He had given his life, or most of it, to social and political Medicare, he had attended a thousand meetings with his attaché case full of Band-Aids. He had been not a person but a representative, interchangeable with other representatives, trained and disciplined toward imperturbability even while being spat at for his color or for the flag on his fender, even while being driven through streets vicious with sniper fire. Yet here he had spent the whole afternoon and evening walking around the edges of this preserve of the memory, fascinated by images out of his immaturity and by the fragrance of lost possibility.

He drew down his mouth, and like some Scott Fitzgerald answering the charge of writing about frivolous things, muttered the only excuse that came to him. Maybe it's my subject matter. Maybe it's what I really know.

Remembered habit created remembered reality. His needle ran in a groove. At Seventh South he turned left down the hill, and in a few seconds was rolling slowly, almost stopped, opposite the last house where they had lived in Salt Lake City, the house of his postponed senior year in college, the duplex that was home when Nola was his girl, the happiest house, for a while, that the Masons ever had.

The roofs of other houses jutted up along the side street where there had been empty lots before, but otherwise he saw no change. The cinder-brick duplex was still jacked up above the corner by a flight of cement steps. The basement garage still opened on the side street, an excellent arrangement for a man who had cars to unload and suitcases to deliver. A man with such a garage need not fear nosy neighbors.

Unless memory was mistaken, during the year-plus-a-summer that they had lived here, his father had all but forgotten to be afraid of the law. He had made himself a place, he filled a need. Among the neighbors he passed for a traveling man. His trips were as routine as if he were making calls on hardware dealers or bookstores. His private arrangements were so neatly concealed in the basement behind a false wall of cupboards that Bruce had fixed up a basement apartment within fifteen feet of the cache, and sometimes had friends in, without causing any anxiety. Caution had haunted all their other houses like the smell of drains. Here they breathed freely.

They were like any other middle-class family. The 1929 crash happened while they lived here, and they never even noticed it. They had money in the bank and a Cadillac in the garage—one of those early models whose gas-tank pressure you had to pump up before you could start, the kind that for years afterward you saw around, indestructible, converted into hearses.

In the vacant lot out behind, his father had made a vegetable garden, and could often be seen working along his rows of lettuce, beans, and corn, sweating contentedly and kidding the passersby who kidded him about working too hard. The people in the other half of the duplex—what name? Albert Something, some French name—were quickly tested and found safe. Bruce's mother had a friend, his father had a companion with whom to share a bottle of home brew on a hot afternoon, or a gin fizz on a late Sunday morning. They experimented together with kits for making wine out of black mission figs. They went deer hunting together in the Uintas.

Contentment, of a kind, and for Bruce, too. This street where he paused, craning to look, was filled with memories of an easy belonging—smell of cured October leaves, sight and feel of frozen ruts, sting of cold clean air when he shoveled off sidewalks and driveway after a snow, smells of growth in the spring, brightness of forsythia against the dark cinder brick of the house. He traced the flight of a spiraling football as he or someone else threw a long pass diagonally from sidewalk to sidewalk, testing his arm.

The sound of his idling engine was the idling of LeGrande Benson's new Studebaker, and they were sitting in it on a bright winter morning, the exhaust steaming into zero cold, the windows fogged, the breath of the heater puffing against their shins, the radio going softly, while LeGrande told him about his rookie season with the Chicago Bears. Bruce was full of respectful, amused astonishment that at two hundred and twenty pounds LeGrande had been found too light to play tackle, and had been converted into an end. He valued the reminiscences about Bronco Nagurski and Ernie Nevers; up to that time, he had known no one so familiar with greatness. Neither had he ever seen, until then, a car with a heater or one with a radio.

This Benson, a pretty good friend of his who lived up the street, and with whom he had played club basketball, had made the giant stride out of their provincial rut. In a way that must have been deeply satisfying to him, Bruce provided the home-town audience he required for the reciting of his adventures. But he did more for Bruce than Bruce did for him. Without envy, for it had not occurred to him that he, too, might someday take such a step, Bruce listened attentively, proud to know Benson, prouder to be known.

Felicity. Life without strain. And it was more than being ac-cepted on the block and living without fear. Something in their family relationships had eased, too. Chet had lived down the anger and disappointment he had both caused and felt. Now at twenty-two a married man of five years' standing, trapped, his hopes put away or scaled down, he was living in Park City and playing baseball in summer, basketball in winter, for the Sil-ver King mine. Now and then he brought Laura and their infant daughter down and gave Bruce's mother the joy of being Grandma.

Nor was Harry Mason immune. Bruce remembered him prop-ping the baby on the sofa and pushing a cushion into her face, knocking her backward when she struggled to sit up. "Toughen-ing her up," he called it. He had played the same game with his own children. As with them, he never knew enough to quit when she was red and gurgling with laughter. He nearly always went on until he made her cry, when in baffled irritation he would hand her to her grandmother. At such moments, Bruce felt that he half understood him. He did not mean harm. He simply tested by teasing what was in a sense his, what he perhaps loved and felt responsibility for. The tests were such limited tests as he could conceive. They all failed to pass. In the end, so did he.

Almost as much as Chet, Bruce had grown past his father's ob-ligation to make a man of him. They hardly saw one another for days at a time, for Bruce was at school or work all day and out more than half the nights. If his father grumbled about his tom-catting around, he could challenge him, asking wherein he was failing. He was attending college, which nobody else in the family had ever come close to doing. He was making nearly straight A's—and if he felt that he didn't deserve his grades, considering the amount of studying he did, he carefully kept that opinion to himself. He worked a forty-hour week while going to school and a sixty-hour week during vacations. He bought his own clothes, and had bought his own car. He had a bank account that approached a thousand dollars. In that last year of school, he was editing the literary magazine and reading papers for Bill Bennion and another professor friend—how, and during what free time, only God knew. Thanks to J. J. Mulder's indulgence, he could arrange his work hours so as to play on the tennis team in the spring, and in tournaments during the summer. Though he did not point out this detail, either, his name was in the sports pages oftener than Chet's.

He said, and believed, that the more he asked himself to do, the more he could do. His mother, who never got over thinking of him as sickly and frail, protested that he would ruin his health, and when he discovered that he had an ulcer, she thought she had made her point. But he told her what he had been told: that ulcers were a young man's disease, and would pass, and anyway were no hindrance to anything but his eating habits. His drinking habits he did not mention, and his smoking habits he did not change.

Yet in a way she was right. Mason could not remember just when the ulcer had appeared. Perhaps he had had it for months before he finally took his dull bellyache to the doctor. But during the year or so of his greatest felicity and confidence, there it was, his personal bosom serpent. He supposed that retrospect should make more of it than he had made at the time.

But then, at the end of the twenties, exceeding peace had made Ben Adhem smug. It would be falsifying memory to pretend that he was anything but arrogant and a prig. Except for the notes from underground that his ulcer sent him, he was brashly confident. He thought good times were forever. He assumed that his happiness was the product of his own excellence. His father used to eye him askance when he sounded off. "You know me, Al," he would say.

Perhaps he shared some of his wife's pride in their younger son, though he would have had no way of showing it, and though Bruce (Mason admitted) would probably have become totally insufferable if he had thought he had his father's approval. And once the old man met Nola, Bruce heard no more about late hours. She broke him down like a dandelion stem. It was a queer, disquieting experience to watch the father whom he had feared, hated, and despaired of pleasing, show off before a girl—*Bruce's* girl—like a sixteen-year-old.

He had rolled almost past, and was already craning backward to see the corner and the dark house. But now he stepped down hard on the brake, for he didn't want to outrun what leaped into his mind, vivid and intact, cunningly lighted. He was improving on it, expanding it, preparing exposition and climax and denouement, even as it materialized. In the moment when it returned to him, he was already beginning to transform it from tableau to story.

The year is 1930, the season is spring, probably May. The time is evening, around eight-thirty. Though it is still light outside, it is beginning to be dusky in the house. In his dinner jacket, his breastplate of gleaming white, his smoky-pearl studs and cuff links, his Bond or Dart collar as prescribed by Jack Bailey, his hand-tied black butterfly bow, he comes into the bedroom where she lies reading. She lowers her magazine to take him in. Two weeks ago she had her left breast and all the lymph glands on that side removed, a radical mastectomy, and she is pale and thin. Her freckles show coppery across the bridge of her nose, her heavy sorrel hair is in a braid. Her eyes are always startling him—the brightest, clearest blue he ever saw in a human head. Her smile breaks out in pure pleasure.

"Oh, you look nice!"

"That's what they all say."

"I'll bet they probably do, at that. Except for your homely face, you've got to be quite a handsome boy."

"Sez you."

"Sez me."

Sometimes, in spite of what he knows about her life and the things she has had to put up with, and despite the stoic look that lurks in her face whether she is sick or well, he feels her spirit as gay and playful as a girl's. She brushes away her troubles, she makes scornful fun of illness and pain, she is resolutely cheerful even in the face of this operation, which scared Bruce's father helpless, sickened Bruce, and must surely have frightened her. Right now, though she looks white and tired, a sassy sparkle lights up her eyes. He has an intimation of how game and pretty she must have been as a girl, and he knows that he is the one who brings this out in her. He is the apple of her eye. Across the footboard and the rumpled bedclothes they smile at one another as if they had a big joke in common.

"O.K.," he says, accepting reality. "Who flutters pulses is me."

She reaches her left arm, stiff from the operation, the armpit tight with half-healed scars and adhesions, and turns the face of the Big Ben that ticks on her bed table.

"Are you going with Joe?"

"No, he couldn't get a date."

"You're starting early, for you."

"I'm on the committee. I ought to get down a little ahead of time to make sure everything's O.K. By the time I pick up Nola and get to the hotel it'll be nearly nine."

"Nola, Is she a new one?"

"Nola Gordon. No, not new—well, pretty new. I've taken her out a couple times. She's living with Holly."

"Is she pretty? Do you like her?"

He rolls his eyes toward the ceiling and licks his slavering lips.

"Does she like you?"

"Adores me. She's putty in my hands."

An amused snort bursts out of her. "It sounds to me as if it was the other way around." Looking him over with the little smile crinkling the corners of her eyes, she says, "Come here, let me fix your tie."

She sits up, and he bends over her. Because of her stiff arm, she can't quite reach, and he kneels on one knee so that she can tug the bow straight. Her face is within inches of his, intent on what she is doing. As she works, her robe falls open, and down the opening, in the V of her nightgown, he catches a glimpse of the flat, mutilated left side of her breast—a skin flap drawn across bare ribs and held by red scars like claw marks.

She sees that he has seen. Embarrassed, she pulls her robe around her and lies back. Grimacing, she says, "Don't let it get too serious, too soon. You've got too much ahead of you. You don't want to tie yourself down like Chet."

Or like me, she might have said. When she was Bruce's age, twenty, she had been married for two years.

"No danger," he says lightly.

They are both self-conscious and pretending not to be. "Try to get home early," she says. "You never allow yourself enough sleep."

"Look who's talking."

"I'd sleep if I could, believe me. Anyway, I'm not young any more, I don't need as much sleep as you do."

"I'll tell you what. I'll promise to sleep as many hours tonight as you do."

They laugh, but he is vaguely uneasy, for he has felt, like the draft from a door standing open somewhere else in the house, how the stillness and darkness of empty rooms will close around her as soon as he leaves. The people next door—Marcotte, that's the name—are away visiting their daughter. No one will drop by, no one will telephone. It will be a long, ticking time till ten, and then till eleven, and then till midnight, and then till whatever hour, one or two or three, when his headlights will sweep across the ceiling as he turns in. Shifting blame that he ought to accept himself, he says, "I should think Pa could have waited till you were well before he made his trip."

"Ach," she says. "Anybody dragging around the house makes him jumpy. He's better off having something to do."

"That doesn't mean *you're* better off."

"I'm just fine."

"Don't get out of that bed. Tomorrow I'm staying home all day and cleaning the place up and cooking you little custards and stuff."

"All right. You can baby me tomorrow."

"How *do* you feel? Can I get you anything before I go?"

"No, no. You run along and give your Nola a thrill."

"I hate to go off and leave you alone."

"Don't be silly. I'm fine."

"I'll try to get in early, but I may have some committee business afterwards."

This is a lie as ridiculous as hers about feeling fine. She knows it, and is indulgent. He knows it, and is not pleased with himself. The only committee meeting he is likely to attend will be a committee of two in a dark parked car.

Her eyes, bright as blue turquoise, go narrow with the crinkling of her smile. She makes a show of snuggling her back comfortably into the pillows, and opens her magazine. He leans and kisses her cheekbone. "Good night. I'll leave the light on in the living room."

"No need to waste electricity."

But he leaves it on anyway. It makes him feel better about leaving. Then he opens the door and emerges into the spring dusk. The air smells of mown lawns. His dancing pumps are as light as gloves. He jumps the six steps, his feet touch grass twice, he is in the car. By the time he has turned the corner he has forgotten her, he is looking ahead, not back.

Mason's foot eases up on the brake and the car begins to roll. The route is precisely the one he would have taken that night in 1930—down to Tenth East, right on Tenth East to South Temple, down South Temple to the tower house and the hotel. When he passes E Street on the right, he looks for the old Brigham Street Pharmacy, once hangout and landmark, universally known among the young as the BSP. It has become a shabby branch bank.

A block further down, he involuntarily slows as he approaches the house with the tower, as if he were indeed going to stop there, leap up lawn steps and porch steps and interior stairs as impetuously as he just now leaped from his porch, and arrive panting at the door where Nola in a party dress of green taffeta, her hair piled rich and dark on her head, his orchid pinned to her waist, will open. She has a figure more womanly than Holly's, not so pencil-thin, deeper-bosomed. Her shoulders, rising bare out of the stiff green silk, are smooth and golden. She is as full of promise as the spring night outside. He has never seen her dressed up like this. She takes his breath.

"Oh, hey, *beautiful!*"

"You like it?" She touches the orchid at her waist. "I never had an orchid. I had to try to live up to it."

"You make it look like some daisy out of a vacant lot."

He slides inside and reaches for her, but she shrinks away, laughing. "You'll smear my war paint." Relenting, she leans forward. He leans to meet her, and she gives him a soft, fluttering, puckered kiss as if she were kissing him through a hole in a curtain. Only their lips touch. He tastes raspberry lipstick, and when she goes into her bedroom to get her wrap he takes out his handkerchief and wipes a faint red stain from his mouth. The sight of it on the clean folded cloth excites him. He sits down at the piano and bumps out a mechanical bass to "Twelfth Street Rag," his total accomplishment on the piano besides "Chopsticks." In the middle of it, the other bedroom door opens and Holly comes out, dressed for a date.

"Well, hi."

"Hi, Holly."

"You've got a new talent."

True. Nola has taught him those chords so that they can play something four hands.

"No limit to my gifts," he says. She makes him nervous. It has been two weeks since he asked her for a date. After that little outburst of hers, he just dwindled away, without quarrel or explanation. He doesn't know how nonchalant or casual to be.

Something about Holly's upper lip makes her look as if she might lisp, though she doesn't. She moves around setting little things to rights, squats briefly to turn on the red lamp on the floor. Its light glows on the ceiling as if from a manhole down into a volcano. She lights a cigarette, and he smells menthol. Kools. "You're going to the spring formal, I hear."

"Yes. Are you?"

Her amused glance takes him in from his satin-bow pumps to his wing collar.

"I'm going to a party at the country club with my boss."

"Aha!"

"Yes," she says. "Aha!"

Nola comes out with a brocade coolie coat over her shoulders, its arms hanging loose, and a gold evening bag in her hand. Even in high heels she manages to move like a barefoot woman. He sees Holly's eyes stop on her for just a moment, a look as

measuring as if she were about to sit down and draw her. Then
she widens her look to include Bruce and makes a little wave
with slim fingers. "Well, have fun, kids. *Freut euch des Lebens.*"

That is a motto he and she once adopted for themselves, when
they were reading William Ellery Leonard's *Two Lives. Freut
euch des Lebens.* Live it up.

"She doesn't like me going out with you," Nola says on the
stairs.

Bruce has had the same impression. Though it bothers him a
little, nothing could inflate his self-esteem more.

The chivalric code as it has leaked down to him and his crowd
from Emily Post and other authorities is explicit about the opening of car doors, the help one should offer a lady in such matters
as sitting down, the obligation of the escort to walk on the gutter
side of the sidewalk, presumably to shield the lady from the
splashing of possible mud and slush. There is no mud or slush
this mild night, but he opens doors, holds elbows, makes sure all
feet and skirts are inside before shutting. He is scrupulously on
the gutter side from parking place to hotel entrance. He holds
the revolving door while Nola, lifting her whispering skirts,
slides in. Emerging behind her into the lobby, he sees that some
student couples are already there, watched with interest by hotel
guests sunk in lobby chairs and sofas. Who are all the beautiful
young people?

He is whacked hard between the shoulder blades, and here is
Jack Bailey, rank as a barrel in which Bourbon has been aged.
His arm is hooked into the elbow of a swamp angel, a Moulin
Rouge character so obvious in her inclinations and compliances
that she might as well wear a satin band over her shoulder like
an Atlantic City beauty contestant, saying Miss Willing. Jack in-
troduces her: Muriel Something. He says to Nola with his
burbling leer—he is the only person Bruce knows for whom
words like "burble" and "leer" are unavoidable—"Been out on
Redwood Road lately?"

She only looks at him. So does Muriel. Coldly.

"Stay away from there with this guy," Jack says. He raises his
finger like a preacher, and intones, "He knows no such word as
no!" Then, a magician patter-chorusing while he folds his hand-

kerchief, he says, "They're changing the name of Redwood Road, did you hear?"

"They are?" Bruce says. "Why? What to,"

"Taylor Walk." Jack raises his eyes up along his upward-pointing finger and wahoos into the coffered ceiling of the Utah Hotel lobby. His girl snickers, gently chewing gum. Already drunk, Jack says, "Listen. Intermission. Room 244. Eh?"

They leave him. They choose to walk up the broad steps to the mezzanine.

He keeps falling out of his time machine. Instead of ushering a gorgeous girl in by the front entrance, he drives up to the side. The attendant comes out of his glass office and Mason turns the car over to him. The lobby, instead of boys in dinner jackets and girls in party gowns, shows only bellhops and two belated couples who have been doing whatever it is one does now in the evening in Salt Lake, and who are waiting in their denim leisure suits and Hamro slacks for the elevator. Instead of joining them, Mason, too, walks up the stairs to the mezzanine.

Now it returns, now he is back there, for off to the right of the stairhead are the doors to the ballroom, where the orchestra will be arranging their chairs and wetting their reeds, and where other members of the committee will be talking to the assistant manager about dinner details or lighting, or making last-minute adjustments of the decorations (red roses on white trellises, like a garden scene from a high school play).

He goes to the doors and looks in. The past is not there, the present slaps him in the face. The big gaunt room is lighted only by orangey wall-bracket lamps whose bulbs are twisted to resemble candle flames. Folding chairs with mimeographed sheets scattered on or under them stand in broken rows where their occupants pushed them when they rose from whatever librarians' or petroleum geologists' or woolgrowers' meeting last went on here. The podium wears three water glasses, a pitcher, and a wilted microphone. The room is stagnant with dead speeches, rules of order, motions and seconds and amendments, treasurers' reports. He doesn't suppose it has been used for a dinner dance in years. Dinner dances went out with the Model A.

Yet if he narrows his eyes he can make it swirl with colored motion, a Calder mobile. His senses venture out toward the throb of dance music, he sniffs girls as fragrant as tuberoses, the whiskey breath of a grinning undergraduate spinning his girl close reeks in his face.

If Bruce Mason were with another girl, that breath might be his: he would have felt obligated to gargle. If the girl in his arms were another, say Olive Bramwell, he, too, might be charging around the ballroom like Crazy Horse surrounding Custer. But Nola has a calm that discourages boisterousness. Her dark piled hair among the shingle bobs and fresh marcels makes her seem more womanly than any girl in the room. She is not made for acrobatics or showing off; she is made for waltzes, slow fox-trots, circlings in uncrowded corners, long looks, murmured talk, serious questions, sober moments, upward smiles, communion. Her voice is husky, her laugh so warm and low that it makes the laughter of other girls sound like the cackling of hens.

Already it seems to be intermission. The musicians are setting aside their instruments, the crowd is pressing toward the doors and the punch bowls on the mezzanine. Waiters have appeared with tables that they set up around the periphery of the floor. They whip white cloths over them, lay them with silver and glasses. But these two stand talking, unwilling to break.

On the merest glance, he is younger than she—younger in years, younger in manner and self-command. He is blond where she is dark, his eyes are blue where hers are brown, he is thin and hyperactive by contrast with her composure, darkly tanned where she is golden. She makes a center, he orbits it. She smiles, he laughs. He talks with his mouth, eyes, hands, body; she listens. He whips around her as if she were egg and he spermatozoon. Utter opposites, they make a one: Yin and Yang. Their force field deflects intrusions. From the first note of the band until now, they have avoided trading a single dance.

It is the first time they have gone out together to anything but a movie. They have still many things to discover about one another—where they come from, what they like, how they feel, what they hope to do. In six dances he has painted six self-portraits, summarized his twenty years, told about his friends and his job, carefully avoided saying anything about his family, invited her corroboration of his opinions of professors and courses, discovered that in the autumn quarter, before he knew her, he graded her papers in a Victorian poets class and gave her a C plus, determined to his brief disappointment that she has no interest in Hemingway, Proust, Joyce, Eliot, or tennis. He has learned that her mother is dead and that she was brought up by her father and several aunts on a ranch in Emery County. There at the ranch in Castle Valley, on the edge of the San Rafael Swell, she has a horse named Baldy, whom she pronounces Bally. Her eyes are full of light as she tells him about all-day rides into the Swell or up onto Ferron Mountain. She adores her brother, a rodeo rider, who once competed in bull riding and saddle bronc with boils on his behind.

In return for this information he confides, since it is something she obviously respects, that he, too, is a sort of cowboy, having grown up in Saskatchewan and Montana.

He sees that the crowd has left them, that they are standing alone, and says, "There's booze up in 244. You want to go up?"

"Will it be a lot of noisy drunks?"

"Probably."

"Jack Bailey and those."

"I don't know who all. Jack for sure."

She scowls. To his fascinated eyes she has the most expressive face he has ever looked at. In an instant, Helen becomes Medea. "Jack Bailey thinks he's smart."

"Why? What's he done?"

"Nothing. But he sure tries."

He is bothered. The thought of Bailey after her in a car, really putting it to her, tail or walk, and meaning it, turns him cold. He can hardly bear not to know, though he dares not ask. She gives him a smoky glance out of the corners of her eyes and looks away, toward the doors, nursing some irritable recollection. He feels inept and junior. He wants to retrieve the moment and get the scowl off her face.

"The hell with Jack. We don't have to go up. I wish we could get somewhere away from the crowd, though."

"Ah, so do I!"

Her vehemence gladdens him. The small white scar like a check mark above her eyebrow is a deliberate defect to empha-

size her perfection. Her throat and shoulders rise from the strap-
less green taffeta like a lily from its sheath. His legs are weak
with how beautiful she is. Very lightly, tentatively, questioning
her with his eyes, he raises his hand and with the tips of his
fingers touches her bare shoulder. Whatever prince woke Sleeping Beauty touched her that way, reverently, holding his breath.
Her eyes fly to his, and hold.

Abashed, they stand smiling at one another. Her dark un-
plucked brows lift in a question. He feels that his face has gone
lopsided, like that of a wax doll left too near the fire. "We could
go outside and walk around," he says. "We could go sit in the
car."

"All right."

"Which?"

"I don't care."

The light in her dark eyes is not reflected, but comes from
within. Not breaking his deep look into them, he sees with the
lower edge of his vision the golden throat, the beginning cleft
between her breasts, and another image overtakes and over-
powers it: his mother's face so close that the freckles blur across
her nose, and the nightgown falling open to show the flatness,
the scar with its angry stitch marks.

Apologetically and confusedly (why? because he has not been
able to put his mother entirely out of his mind? because he will
use even her illness to involve this girl in him?) he says, "I
shouldn't go home with a breath, anyway. My mother's sick, and
if I come home smelling like a still she'll lie awake all night convinced I'm ruined."

Nola says with a smile, "I didn't know you were such a mama's
boy. Does she always wait up for you?"

For a moment he is angry. She is making unjust assumptions.
She doesn't know what she is talking about. "She's got cancer,"
he says. "She had one breast removed a couple of weeks ago."

He hears how bluntly his words rebuke the lightness of her
question, how ugly a sound they have in this place, and he adds,
"Not a very pleasant subject."

"Ugh, that's terrible," she says. "I'm sorry. I can't imagine anything like that. Has she got somebody with her?"

"No, the old man had to go to L.A. I'm her nurse. When I'm
home."

Now he is getting even, he is covertly blaming her for leading him to neglect his duty. It is perhaps a compliment of a kind, but she hears only the rebuke, and is upset. "You should *be* home. You shouldn't have brought me to this prom."

The moment she accepts blame, he absolves her of it. "I *wanted* to bring you to this prom. If we were missing this prom I'd cut my throat."

"But she shouldn't be left all by herself."

"She isn't that sick. She's been getting up a little every day. I told her I'd try to get home early."

Once more, unable to refrain, his fingers come up and touch the satiny, cool shoulder. "I don't know," he says, shaking his head. "I don't know if I'm man enough to dump you off on your front porch like some foul ball I want to get rid of."

"Bruce, why don't we go see her?"

"Now?"

"Right now, yes."

"We'd miss dinner."

"Who cares? Anyway, it wouldn't take long, would it? We could be back in half an hour. I hate to think of her alone and sick while we're having fun."

"I don't like it much myself."

"Would she mind, do you think?"

"Mind!" He can see the two of them smiling in at her from the doorway of her bedroom, she in her emerald silk, he in his dinner jacket, a vision from one of the glorified compartments of his life to which she has never had entry.

With his arm around her, he turns her exuberantly toward the doors. "Boy," he breathes, close to her ear. "You know something? You're some woman."

God help him, that is probably what he said. Mason moves himself out of the doorway to let them pass, ready to laugh at what he sees of himself in that callow youth, and bemused by how assumptions and usages change. In those days of innocence they did not call themselves men, as even boys did now. They were the boys. But girls were not girls, nor had they yet become babes or broads or birds or chicks. For a while there at the beginning of the twenties they were chickens, and briefly they were flappers because for a season or two they flopped around through snow and wet in unbuckled galoshes. Some were hot

mamas. But generally, to the boys around 1928, 1929, 1930, the
females they went out with were women, even if they were
hardly more than teenyboppers. I've got a date with a woman,
they said; or, I'm taking my woman to the picture show.

They would all be told now, Mason thinks, that they needed
their consciousness raised. The contemporary harpies who pass
for women would probably spit on this sexism of deference, this
disguised momism or whatever it was. But perhaps the boys
knew something that the present has forgotten: that the only
place one can first learn love is from a woman, that all tenderness, of any kind, derives from what is learned at the breast.
Given a learner as insecure as young Bruce Mason, safety may
well reside in some woman, mother or lover or wife or whoever.
Whether women have difficulty getting credit cards or not, it is
not they who racket around through empty universes hunting for
a place on which to come to rest. They are themselves such a
place.

So it seemed to Bruce Mason then. So it seems to Mason now.
From the mezzanine rail he watches this boy escort his woman
across the lobby toward the revolving doors. He is voluble,
deferential, proud, absurd. She moves as serenely as the moon.

The elevator that he enters smells lingeringly of hair spray. He
pushes the 6 button, and unreality rises under his soles. His mind
is with them in the car, heading up South Temple. When he puts
his key in the lock of 623 and opens the door, his mother in the
light of the bed lamp lowers her magazine and looks up. Her
eyes jump in alarm to the face of the Big Ben on her bed table,
and then back to Bruce.

"What is it? You're home early. Is something wrong?"

Keeping Nola out of sight, he says, "I broke my leg and they
were going to shoot me, but I got away."

"You *what?*"

"I got away. They're after me."

"Oh, poof!"

She is so easy to dismay; she is never prepared for jokes. He
doesn't suppose she would ever be taken entirely by surprise if
something drastic happened to him, for she has imagined every
possible catastrophe in the dark of sleepless nights. She has only
this one basket. He is her only remaining egg.

Now he pulls Nola into the doorway. "This is Nola, Mom. We came out to see how you're doing."

"Oh, my goodness!"

In consternation she sits up, tugs her robe tighter around her, pulls her braid across her breast, tries to smooth the mussed bed clothes, and within a second is back against her pillows, at bay. Everything she is feeling, Bruce is feeling, too. She is embarrassed to be caught unprepared and disheveled, and he shares her shame. He should have picked up the room before he went out. She doesn't want to look old, sick, faded, or mutilated to the girl who smiles at her from the circle of Bruce's arm, and he agrees: she deserves protection and disguise. He should have thought of that.

But even in her confusion she is taking Nola's measure and making note of the familiarity with which her shoulders wear Bruce's arm; and while that detail brings the ears of her apprehension pricking up, she is going pink with pleasure at having been remembered. More than that. The eyes that take Nola in are dazzled, too. He can see admiration growing in them, and right on the heels of the admiration a caution: *This is serious, he's gone on her;* and in another split second, *Oh, I don't blame him, she's lovely!*

His mother has never met one of his girls, and would be flustered even if she were not caught unprepared in an untidy room. They bring the fresh air in on their clothes; Nola's coloring is too rich and alive beside his mother's pallor. The contrast stares like blood on a sheet. And is there, in those first seconds, some contest going on? Is it Nola's natural warmth and sympathy, or is it her triumphant sense of being young and beautiful and immortal that makes her so gentle with a woman sick and perhaps doomed? It is no contest, really. They flip a coin for him, but the coin has two heads. While it is still in the air, his mother concedes, gives her blessing. She cannot help loving what he loves.

"Aren't you both nice!" she cries as Nola stands over her holding her hand. "But you shouldn't have left your dance."

"It's intermission," Bruce tells her. "We're not missing a thing except a five-course dinner, delightful company, solid-gold favors, champagne, and a few little things like that."

"Champagne? Do they really serve champagne? How can they . . . ?"

"You can't trust a word this one says," says Nola.

"Ah," his mother says. "You've found that out already. But he's sort of nice, too, don't you think? I'm just sorry you're going to lose your favor, the little compact, Bruce showed me. Don't they put those at the girls' places at the tables?"

"She'll get one," Bruce says. "Maybe three. Why else am I on the committee?"

They beam at one another, thinking of things to say. "Aren't you hungry?" his mother says. "Dancing is hard work."

"Especially with Nola," Bruce says. "It's like rocking a car stuck on dead center. Only one thing to do—put her in high and push her backwards."

"You ought to be ashamed to say a thing like that. I'll bet she's a beautiful dancer."

Nola's smile is slow and untroubled. "If I don't just plant my feet he walks all over them."

It is an extraordinarily happy moment. Their cheerfulness lights up the room. Again his mother says, "*Aren't* you hungry? You ought to have your milk every two hours—has he admitted he's on an ulcer diet? He probably wouldn't. Let me just . . ."

Bruce pushes her emerging feet back under the covers. "You want milk or ginger ale?" he asks Nola. "There are some compulsory cookies. I made them myself."

"Did he really?"

"Yes, he did. He can do all sorts of things."

"You'll make some woman a good wife."

She comes close to expressing a thought that is in all their minds.

From the kitchen, while he pours three glasses of milk and fills a plate with the oatmeal cookies he made the evening before to tempt his mother's finicky appetite, he can hear the getting-acquainted talk going on in the bedroom, one voice clear, one husky, one asking questions, one making answers. The ranch, the brother and sister, the horse Bally, school. He hears Nola say she doesn't suppose she'll ever get to go back and live on the ranch, she'll have to live in Salt Lake if she wants a job. No music down there, either, except playing for dances with the Robbers' Roosters, and she had enough of that in high school. But she loves it down there. Maybe she can get down in June, her sister is getting married again, her first husband was killed in an accident in a coal mine in Helper. But that will be only a visit, a day or two. She'll have to get a job this summer. She has another year before she gets her teaching certificate.

He hears it with his mother's ears, noting what she will have noted. One more year in school. Probably safe until she's finished college. By then he'll be twenty-one, at least, and will have saved more. With both of them through college and working, it might be all right.

That is something he knows she wants to believe. She does not like her own caution, learned from failures of too many kinds. She can't help loving what he loves, and wants him to have it.

He puts the glasses and the plate on a tray and hoists the tray on his palm and goes on in with it balanced above his shoulder. Satisfying screams tell him to be careful. Expertly he rotates it down and sets it on the bed table, shoving aside the clock and medicine bottles that he should have cleared away in advance. His mother grabs and rescues a bottle about to topple onto the floor. Then, as he straightens up, light cuts under the drawn shades and moves across the wall. Bruce and his mother look at one another. A car is idling right below the windows. While they listen, its door shuts solidly. In a moment the garage doors creak open.

"Why, that's your dad!" she says. "He must have driven straight through."

The pleasure goes out of the room. Quietly she says to him, "Maybe you'd better go let him in, he may not have his key."

Of course he has his key. What she means is that Bruce should warn him there is someone here, so that he won't come in carrying something or saying something that shouldn't be seen or heard outside the family.

He goes back to the kitchen, angry that his father has interrupted their happy little party. They should have checked on his mother and gone away again while the going was good. He switches on the stair lights and opens the door, and his father is already there with his key in his hand, in shirt sleeves, his eyes bloodshot, a two-day grizzle of beard on his jaws, his hands and arms greasy from working on the car. He stares at Bruce in his monkey suit.

"What's this?"

Bruce raises his finger halfway to his lips. "Somebody's here."

His father steps inside. "This time of night? Who?"

"My date. We came back from the prom to see how Mom was doing."

The bloodshot eyes are on him hard. "Why, is she worse?"

"No, she's all right."

Grunting, his father reaches a glass from the cupboard and draws himself a glass of water. He watches Bruce as he drinks, and when he has gulped the glass empty he wipes the back of his dirty hand across his lips. "What were you doing at a prom, anyway? You should have been home here looking after her."

The retort jumps to Bruce's tongue: Why weren't *you* here looking after her? But he keeps it in; he falls back on the watchful, obscurely sullen silence that has been his response for years. He thinks his father hears it, unsaid as it is.

His father's eyes travel down Bruce's black-and-white length. He is the kind of person for whom a tuxedo is automatically sissy or comic. Outlaw or not, within the limits of his experience and comprehension he is incredibly conservative. He accepts only what he knows. When he sees Bruce duded up in riding breeches and English boots he can't keep from chirping with his lips and slapping his leg and saying, "Giddap," laughing and looking for corroboration at whoever else is there. Now he just looks.

"Your girl's in there, you say?"

"Yes."

He works his cheeks as if they were cold. Briefly he leans to bare his teeth at himself in the mirror beside the kitchen door. He examines his greasy hands, and for a moment Bruce hopes he is going to go and wash, so that he and Nola can get away before he comes out of the bathroom. Instead, his father shrugs and pushes out into the dining room. Bruce comes along behind, apprehensive and ready to be ashamed.

His father's entrance is disconcertingly like Bruce's own of a few minutes before. He stands hidden outside the door, and intones, sepulchral and singsong,

Then I sees within the doorway of a shy, retirin' dugout
Six Boches, all a-grinnin', and their Cap'n stuck 'is mug out.

On the last words, wearing a rubber-lipped grin, he sticks his head around the jamb.

He has not yet made any sign that he knows Nola is there. Bruce watches him go in and bend over and kiss the woman in the bed—and that is surely showing off, that most certainly reflects his awareness of an audience. Except when he is showing off or clowning, he makes no such standard gestures of affection.

Bruce's mother's voice, fluty and high, is as false as his kiss. "I didn't expect you so soon. How was the trip?" Then, before he can answer, "This is Nola Gordon, Bo. These nice children left their dance to come out and see me."

Now finally he turns toward Nola. Bruce can't see her, but he can see the jolt she gives him. He has probably visualized Bruce's date as some flat-chested flapper with her hemline above her knees and her waistline around her hip bones, her hair cut like a boy's, her jaws going on a wad of gum—the whole John Held picture. He has not expected someone like this.

At once something humorous and alert comes into his dark face, his lips remain quirked into a half smile after he has said hello. Nola's low voice murmurs something. Bruce knows exactly how she is looking at his father, her eyes curious and interested, seeming to waver but actually steady, only the light in them changing. He can't stay out of it. He pushes in, crowding the little room with one person too many.

At once he feels compared and judged. Beside his father's size and weight and shirt-sleeve dishevelment he feels like the overdressed figure on a wedding cake. Though he is as tall as his father, he weighs fifty pounds less. He is not bearded, dirty, heavy-shouldered, smelling of physical exertion. The old helpless feeling of inferiority oppresses him. He is angry that he has brought Nola here and tried to mix the unmixable oil and water of his life.

In his mother's watching eyes there is an expression he cannot read. Understanding? Sympathy? Pity? Warning? In a too casual voice she says, "You're all greasy. Did you have a flat tire or something?"

It is a cue his father has been waiting for. A short laugh erupts from his throat, he spreads his hands and looks at them, he regards Nola with an indescribable waiting slyness in his face.

Bruce reads him—oh, he reads him! He has a tale to unfold. He is going to shine.

"Nothing so serious as a flat tire," he says. "I tipped over."

Bruce's mother sits straight up. "Tipped *over!*"

"Ass over teacup," he says cheerfully—and is there a deliberateness in the profanity, a calculated nudge? Bruce wishes Nola had kept her coolie coat on. Her shoulders are too naked for this room and this company. His father rolls his hands as if winding yarn. "Down the bank, clear over, and up on her wheels in the ditch."

"You could have been killed!"

"Damn right I could have."

"Are you all right? You didn't get hurt at all?"

"Nary a scratch."

"The car?"

"Few dints and scratches. Never broke a thing."

She knows and Bruce knows what he means. A broken bottle in a carload of liquor can be disastrous—you daren't even stop for gas, for fear someone will smell you.

"How?" Bruce's mother says. "Where?"

He is still speaking to Nola, not to her. "Down by Santaquin. Thunder shower wet the road where they'd been grading, left it slick as soap. I came to this curve in the dark and started to skid and straightened her right out." His muscled, oily arm shoots out, his hand makes the rolling motion. "She hit something solid and went over. Touched on her side and then on top and then came clean on over. Never even killed the engine. Bumped my head on the roof and that's all—the wheel held me in. Before I know where I am, there I'm sitting in the ditch with the old car going chug-a-chug-a-chug under me. I couldn't believe there wasn't anything wrong—that's where I got all dirty, checking it out. Finally I just drove down the ditch till I found a place where I could get back on the road, and came on in."

"Oh, you're lucky!"

"Skillful," he says, and winks at Nola, who is watching him with her expectant dark eyes and her slow smile. He sees the plate of cookies and the glasses of milk on the bed table and helps himself. "These for me? Thankee, I think I will."

"You must be starved," Bruce's mother says. "Let me get you something solider than . . ."

"Stay in bed!" Bruce says harshly. "I'll get him something, if he wants something."

Chewing a cookie, his lip stained with a crescent of milk, his father looks at him. Marksman's eyes, he has, red-streaked and steady. It is as if he were looking down a rifle barrel. A grunt comes out of him. "I can get myself something."

"We should be getting back, anyway," Bruce says to Nola. Obediently she picks up her coolie coat from the bed.

His father looks at the Big Ben, which says ten minutes to twelve. "You starting out on your party *now?*"

"We've been at the party. We just came up to see Mom. The party lasts till one. I have to be there to help close it up. I'm on the committee."

"Well," says his father with an incredulous laugh. "If you're on the *committee.*" To Nola, in that jocular, nudging tone—he reminds Bruce of Jack Bailey—he says, "Are you on the committee, too?"

"Nope. I'm just the committee's date. I go where it goes." Obviously she does not feel the bullying pressure that Bruce feels. She is pert, she looks on this as kidding.

Bruce holds the coolie coat for her to slip into it, and as she half turns and raises her arms, he sees his father's eyes on her smooth shoulders, her shaven armpits. Comprehending and feeling everything, a reservoir of understanding and concern, his mother says from the bed, "Don't stay out too late, now. I'm sure Nola needs her sleep as much as you do."

"Sleeping is what I do all day Sunday," Nola says with a smile.

"Well, it's not what your committee does," Bruce's father says. His eyes meet his son's, almost as if good-natured. "I've got work for you tomorrow, Mr. Chairman, and I don't want to have to get you up with a stump puller."

"Don't worry," Bruce says, like a sullen, dominated fifteen-year-old. The old man has made his point; he has diminished him.

His mother says, "You need some sleep yourself, Papa. You've just driven a thousand miles nonstop, and rolled over in a ditch."

"I'm setting the alarm for seven." A brag, Bruce perceives. I, the untiring, the indefatigable. I plow deep while sluggards sleep. He drags Nola from her goodbyes, they get away.

"Your mother's a darling," she says as they settle into the Ford.

"Yes."

"She thinks you're the cat's pajamas."

"Yes, poor deluded thing." He is still smarting from his father's infallible gift for making him look small. "At least she's right about one thing. She thinks you're gorgeous."

"Ha!" she says, neither affirming nor denying. After a second, when they have started up the street, she says, "You and your father don't get along."

"Was it that obvious?"

"You won't let him joke you."

"His jokes aren't jokes."

"I thought he was cute," she says—to provoke him? "So big and sort of tough. I like tough people."

"Well," he says, furious, "there's always somebody willing to kiss the cow."

"Oh come on! You're tough yourself. Feel how hard your arm is."

She snuggles against him, holding his skinny wing. Thank God it *is* hard, so hard you can barely tell the muscles from the bones they are strung on.

"Every time I spit I split a plank," he says. "Them I don't kill I cripple."

"No, I mean it. You don't quit. I'd hate to be on the other side from you if you really wanted something."

Mollified, he lets his feathers be smoothed. "Good. Because you know what I want?"

"Let me guess."

"Don't waste time guessing. Do you want to go back to the prom?"

"Do you?"

"No. The other guys can close it up. I want to go up on Wasatch Boulevard and look at the lights and taste your raspberry lipstick."

"Oh, you do." But she does not object. He swings up through Federal Heights toward Fort Douglas. As if she understands the sulky thoughts he still has not chased from his head, she leans against him and begins to sing in her husky contralto. In a moment he joins her. The city falls away behind as they climb toward the foot of the mountains. He opens the car window to let the night in.

III

1

Brushing his teeth, he remembered that he had done nothing about flowers for his aunt's funeral. As was his disciplined habit, he got his notebook out of his jacket pocket and wrote himself a reminder for the morning. Then he started to get into bed and found in the middle of it the box that he had carried from the funeral parlor that afternoon.

He had felt no curiosity then, but now as he took the box by its cord and started to set it on the floor, he hesitated, hefting it. What would the poor old thing have put away for him? An afghan, to keep his knees warm? Some crocheted antimacassars? A quilt? It felt a little heavier than any of those things that she would probably have called "keepsakes." And it touched him, now that he gave his attention to the box, that she would have put away anything at all. Gratitude he had not expected, never having given any affection. Perhaps she had felt it necessary to pass something on, for they were the last two survivors of a tribe, the last orphaned speakers of their family tongue. He had felt that bond himself, even while resenting her as a burden. Better that meager relationship than no relationships at all.

A label had been stuck to the outside of the cardboard. It curled and came off when he touched it. The ink of the writing

on it was faded and brown, evidently years old. So this was no
late senile whim. She must have boxed it up, whatever it was,
years ago. "Property of Mr. Bruce Mason," she had written on
the label.

Sighing, he crawled into bed, hoisted the box onto his stomach, and untied the cord.

Something soft and bulky, wrapped in brown paper, filled
most of the box. On top of it, sunk into depressions that had
been shaping for many years, were three books, limp-imitation-
leather Modern Library, ninety-five cents each, the backbone of
any undergraduate library in the twenties.

He stared at them, still uncomprehending. He opened one of
the books and saw his own name scrawled slanting up the inside
cover. Impatiently he yanked the brown parcel from the box and
uncovered a white sweater with four red stripes around one
sleeve. He made an astonished sound like laughter, and tipped
the box. Out tumbled two bundles of letters and a manila envelope. He leaned back against the headboard so abruptly that he
banged his head. He said aloud, "Well, I'll be damned!"

Nola had brought that box to Joe's house, where Bruce was
staying, on the morning of his father's funeral. This was a year
after they had broken up—not the June of their abrupt parting
but the next one, the very day when he should have been gradu-
ating from law school in Minneapolis. She chose to bring back
this symbolic package of repudiation not when his hurt and
anger were hot, not when his mind was on her, but when he had
got over her, after a fashion, and when he was gritting through
the aftermath of his father's last violence. He was anguished to
be done with it all, and gone. He never spoke to her: he saw
her coming up the steps and would not go to the door, but let
Joe talk to her. And he never looked in the box that Joe brought
inside. He scorned to take back anything he had once given her,
he wanted to give her no assurance that they were quits. So Joe,
after taking him from the funeral hill to the Union Pacific station, must have dropped the box with Aunt Margaret when he
delivered her to the Home. She had sat on it for forty-five years
like a hen on a china egg.

Tired as he was, he could not resist looking. What, of the
things he had given her during the time when she was an altar

he laid offerings on, would she have felt she should return to him? It was bizarre that she should have been the one to preserve the only relics of that time of his life. Everything else was gone. If he was a thing that lasted, the only documentation was what his estranged girl packed up to throw back at him. This was the total album and attic where that part of him could be found.

He picked up the little books again. He supposed that he had loaned them to Nola and urged her to read them. Perhaps she had tried to, for she wanted to please him. Now, finally, they returned to him like library books carried away accidentally or on purpose, and discovered years later and mailed anonymously back where they belonged. *Salome,* by Oscar Wilde; *Irish Fairy and Folk Tales,* edited by William Butler Yeats; *Studies in Pessimism,* by Arthur Schopenhauer.

He opened the Yeats.

> The Irish word for fairy is *sheehogue/sidheog,* a diminutive of "shee" in *banshee.* Fairies are *denee shee/daoine sidhe* (fairy people).
>
> Who are they? "Fallen angels who were not good enough to be saved, nor bad enough to be lost," say the peasantry.

Nothing there for a Jack Mormon girl from Emery County. What could he have been thinking of? He laid Yeats down and picked up Schopenhauer.

> Unless suffering is the direct and immediate object of life, our existence must entirely fail of its aim. It is absurd to look upon the enormous amount of pain that abounds everywhere in the world, and originates in needs and necessities inseparable from life itself, as serving no purpose at all and the result of mere chance. . . . I know of no greater absurdity than that propounded by most systems of philosophy in declaring evil to be negative in its character. Evil is just what is positive; it makes its own existence felt. . . . The pleasure in this world, it has been said, outweighs the

pain; or, at any rate, there is an even balance between
the two. If the reader wishes to see shortly whether this
statement is true, let him compare the respective
feelings of two animals, one of which is engaged in
eating the other.

Nothing there, either. What could she have felt when, out of
his arrogant inexperience, out of his sheer undergraduate enthusiasm for hard doctrine, or the self-pity that had made him believe he was suffering's biographer, he plucked things like this
from the great grab bag of Western culture and demanded that
she read and ponder them? He might as well have suggested
that she learn Turkish. Her mind operated on a direct hookup
with the senses, not by abstract ideas; and to suffering, any kind
of suffering, she had a cat-like aversion.

He put down the Schopenhauer and picked up Wilde,
skimmed over a few pages of overheated dialogue, and stopped
near the end, detained in spite of himself by the voice of Salome.

Ah! I have kissed thy mouth, Iokanaan, I have kissed
thy mouth. There was a bitter taste on thy lips. Was it
the taste of blood? . . . Nay, but perchance it was the
taste of love. They say that love hath a bitter taste. . . .
But what matter? I have kissed thy mouth, Iokanaan, I
have kissed thy mouth.

"Look at the moon!" Holly once read to him from that same
play. "*Regardez la lune!* How strange the moon seems. She is like
a woman rising from a tomb. She is like a dead woman. One
might fancy she was looking for dead things."

Their limited and provincial city had never given them the opportunity to hear Strauss's opera, but even if it had, they would
have heard Herod's daughter in their own way. Though it would
have delighted them, probably, to see a raging soprano stagger
and crawl around the stage, smeared with blood, clutching the
bloody head of her obsession by its bloody hair, she would have
delighted them primarily because she was a vessel of jeweled
language. In their literary way, they responded to words as in-
cantation.

Ah, thou wouldst not suffer me to kiss thy mouth, Iokanaan. Well, I will kiss it now. I will bite it with my teeth as one bites a ripe fruit. Yes, I will kiss thy mouth, Iokanaan. I said it: did I not say it? I said it. Ah! I will kiss it now.

They would have been charmed, titillated by the sound. But Nola, though she couldn't read, could have played it.

Across Mason's mind, floating in the empty room like the moon rising from a tomb, appeared the body of the dead woman he had seen that afternoon, and he felt like a ghoul or a necrophile, infatuated with corpses.

Alack. Nearly fifty years agone.

He dropped the three books over the edge of the bed and picked up the sweater, a white cardigan with a red U above the pocket and four red stripes around the upper left sleeve. The last letter he earned, part of the paraphernalia of innocent self-advertisement then universal among athletes on a campus. Mason had the impression that the letter-sweater thing was no longer fashionable, and would embarrass a contemporary jock. Then, it had been as natural as wearing shoes. The sweater was a sort of escutcheon. You could tell by the kind—cardigan, pullover— what sport was involved.

Seniors, he remembered, had had a choice between the usual red with white letter and stripes, and the dressier white with red. He had chosen white for that last one because Nola did not wear red, and this one was for her. He didn't suppose he had even tried it on. Forty-five years ago just about now, only a few weeks after the prom from which he had just returned, he had picked it up at the coach's office and carried it straight to her—his signature, label, mark of ownership; his substitute for a West Point class ring, juvenile forerunner of presidential citations and ribbons of the *Légion d'honneur:* decorations will be worn. Would you like to wear my sharpshooter's medals? Here, let me offer you my Purple Heart.

We're like sun myths, he said to the listening presence of Joe Mulder, who had come quietly into his head and stood there attending like someone watching the evening's television news. We're like sun myths in the late afternoon of a cloudy day, looking back at the morning, when we were ascendant, when our strength waxed instead of waning. Being in love with that girl was only part of it, for me. Just picking up this sweater puts me back to that time when everything was cresting.

It wasn't a time of choices, though it might seem so. The sun leaned on us, and warmed us on that side. We turned toward what shone on us, and if we leaned too far, we toppled, and toppling, toppled others. Call it the domino theory.

2

He is walking along Thirteenth East Street on an absolutely perfect morning, a creation morning. Perhaps there was a shower during the night, but it feels as if prehistoric Lake Bonneville has risen silently in the dark, overflowing its old beach terraces one by one, flooding the Stansbury, then the Provo, on which this street is laid, then finally the Bonneville; filling the valley to overflowing, stretching a hundred miles westward into the desert, lapping against the Wasatch, pushing long fjords into the canyons, washing away all the winter smoke, softening the alluvial gravels, rinsing and freshening every leaf of every shrub and tree, greening every blade of grass; and then before daylight has withdrawn again into its salty remnant, leaving behind this universal sparkle and brightness.

It is such a morning as all the old remember and only the young belong in. School is over, college is done with, summer and life are ready to begin. He drags the dewy coolness to the bottom of his lungs. His feet are light on the sidewalk, lighter yet on the parking-strip grass where he prefers to walk. In his left hand is an old canvas equipment bag, in his right a tennis racket, imperceptibly cracked in the throat from his bad habit of hitting his overhead with a lot of spin, like a second service. With this cracked but otherwise very satisfactory racket, which he hopes to sell that morning to Marv Eldridge, who is just taking up tennis and is not discerning, he takes the heads off dandelions, forehand and backhand. His footwork is nimble, his backswing fluent, his eye is on the ball, he follows through with a snap. He wears clean white cords, white buck shoes, and his letter sweater with three stripes, and every detail of himself gratifies him. He admires the springy condition of his legs and the strength of his right forearm, considerably bigger than the left. The characteristic tennis player's callus on the inside of his right thumb is like a badge.

The east side where he walks is shaded by tall houses, but between them and at intersections the sun slants through and stretches across the street to lean on eastward-facing porches where bottles of milk and rolled *Tribunes* wait to be retrieved. The cones of pink blossom on the horse chestnut trees light up like candles when the sun strikes them. The leaves around them are heavy and rich and dark.

At the drugstore on the Second South corner he turns right, up the slope toward where the Park Building's white marble front overlooks the Circle and the tree-dotted lawn. This is a different sort of morning from the hundreds when he has walked up this gentle hill toward an early class. Everything is over except Commencement, which, scornful of ceremonies, he will evade. Nothing remains but last errands. He sees only a few straggling students. The scene has been clarified and hardened into finality like a negative in the fixing bath, yet it is morning, with morning's excitement in it, and he walks toward unlimited possibility. Ahead, the sun dazzles over the roof of the Park Building and overexposes his sight. The mountains beyond are backlighted and featureless.

Now at the edge of the Circle, Maurice comes wobbling and scurrying across the grass, waving his arms, uncoordinated and ablaze with greeting. His hair is wild, the words he speaks are chewed and unintelligible. He wears his brown leather jacket and basketball shoes, and he obviously wants something. It takes Bruce half a minute to comprehend: Maurice wants to carry his racket. Given it, he is transformed. He handles it with both hands like a battle-ax, making fierce faces and sweeping the air.

Old Maurice, the campus moron, enthusiastic leader of cheers at football games, self-appointed master of ceremonies at pep rallies, front prancer in snake dances after high school basketball games, adorer of all athletes. Everybody knows Maurice, everybody laughs and groans when he goes scrambling and falling in a frenzy of school spirit out of the stands and onto the cinder track. Some people, especially girls of the snottier kind, find him disturbing and think he should be kept at home, but that would be the worst sort of unkindness. Distorted image of Bruce's own innocence, Maurice touches and amuses him. He feels protective, and kids him along. Who could resist his adoration? He reveres this hero in his letter sweater with three stripes, he is ennobled to be seen with him. Out of the corners of his odd little mismatched eyes he invites the attention of a couple of gardeners returfing a worn patch of lawn, and when they look up grinning he decapitates them with two swings in the air.

At the steps of the L Building, Bruce offers to take the racket back, but Maurice doesn't want to give it up. He will look after it. He understands its preciousness, he will take the greatest care of it. So Bruce leaves him sitting on the sandstone steps, cradling the racket in his lap and shielding it from a student who passes too close.

Bill Bennion's office, always a mess, is on this morning a total mess. The desk overflows with bluebooks and themes, the chairs are piled with books recently returned by undergraduate borrowers and not yet restored to the shelves, which anyway are too jammed with other books, cardboard boxes of notes, stacked mgazines, and wadded lunch bags smelling of banana skins to hold them. The wastebasket has overflowed onto the floor. On the window ledges and on the tops of the radiators the dust is thick over piles of mimeographed sheets that have been there in that condition ever since Bruce first came into this office as a sophomore.

He has been in it many times since that first one. A lot of literary bull sessions have gone on here. He has been introduced to a lot of books here, and has carried them out and brought them back and been profanely quizzed about them. Across these piles of themes and across the littered desk he has broadcast his share of barbaric yawp, and been set straight without impatience by the smiling man who sits across there with the morning sun pouring in on him from behind, turning his bald skull into a fuzzy golden dandelion-head and sending shafts and whorls through the smoke of his pipe.

From the equipment bag he takes Carl Van Vechten's *The Tattooed Countess* and Eliot's *For Lancelot Andrews,* and pushes clear a corner of the desk and lays them on it.

"Well," says his professor and friend Bill Bennion, watching him benignantly through his smoke. "The end of something."

"The very end."

"Now what?"

"Now what?"

"What are you going to do with yourself?"

"Oh, what a dusty answer gets the soul," Bruce says, "when hot for certainties in this our life!"

"You horse's ass," Bennion says, and takes his pipe out of his mouth to laugh. When he laughs, the slight cast in one eye is accentuated and his benignant expression is touched with completely friendly scorn. In the equipment bag Bruce finds some pages of an old theme, crumples them into a ball, looks for a place to put them, feints left, feints right, and scores with a spectacular hook shot into one tight corner of the wastebasket.

"Hey, look." He blows his whistle and holds up two fingers.

"Don't evade the issue, you cretin," Bennion says. "What *are* you doing to do?"

"What is there to do? Birth, copulation, death. Choice is an illusion."

"The hell it is. If you turn out to be a gardener, after all the effort I've put in on you, I'll staple you to a stump by the balls. Have you decided? Or haven't you put your so-called mind to it at all?"

With his hands behind his head, his arms fuzzy with pale hair all the way around, even on the inside, even on the biceps, he scowls through the smile that never leaves his face—*can't* leave his face, that's the way his face is. He has no other expression except that benevolent, interested, slightly strabismic, pleasantly scornful smile.

"God, I don't know," Bruce says. "I suppose maybe I ought to take the fellowship and get an M.A."

"In English?"

"Isn't that what you offered me one in? You didn't think I should take the one Parker offered me in philosophy."

"That's right, you shouldn't. You've got better things to do with your life than losing yourself in a subject nobody believes exists. What'll you do with an M.A. if you get it?"

Bruce shrugs, without an idea, and if the truth were told, untroubled.

"Teach?"

"I don't know. Maybe."

"Are you prepared to go on for a Ph.D.? If you're going to teach in any place worth teaching in, you'll have to have it."

"Utah doesn't give Ph.D.s."

"I know that, for God's sake. You'd have to go away somewhere."

"I haven't thought much about it."

Bennion looks upward, inviting the roof to fall on him. "Obviously," he says. "You know, you're the damnedest, most unmotivated, drifting son of a . . . Have you talked to Notestein?"

"No."

"Well, I have. I've been talking to him for three weeks, and he's been talking to everybody he knows. He's got you a fellowship at the University of Minnesota Law School if you want it."

There, just there, begins the redirection of Bruce Mason's life, but he does not realize it. He is simply astonished. "He *what?*"

"You heard me. He thought he could, and it turns out he can. He must have lied like a thief about your miserable little capacities, to get you in this late. So what are you going to do, tell him no thanks?"

"Well, but Jeez, that complicates . . ."

"You bet it complicates. It complicates you right into where you have to make up your mind, for a change."

"Hell, Bill, I never had any ambition to be a lawyer. Why law?"

"Because that's what's available. Because Notestein's a lawyer and that's where his connections are. Because he has this half-baked confidence that you might *make* a lawyer. That's the trouble with all of us. We think you're fit for something or other, and break our asses trying to set something up for you, and you don't know, you can't make up your mind, you haven't thought about it. *Well, think about it!*"

"Yes, sir."

"Look, you moron," Bennion says. "I know I offered you a fellowship, but that was just to keep you from wasting your time in philosophy. I never did think taking an M.A. in English, here, would do you any good. You've taken all our courses, you've learned anything we can teach you. You need to get out and knock your head against bigger people and bigger ideas. If you had the initiative of a banana slug, or I had, we'd both have thought of this a lot sooner, and we might have got you something at Berkeley, or even Harvard or Yale or some place East that would *really* jar you loose. But you didn't, and I didn't, so Minnesota is the only decent shot you've got."

"Yeah, but law."

"Law's one kind of education, maybe a damn good kind. You don't have to practice it, or even teach it. Just let it educate you—and don't think you're past being educated. My point is, if you don't make your break now, at the natural time to make it, you never will. You'll sit out in that nursery growing roots in your behind, and marry one of those half-mast-eyed girls you squire around, and wind up with six kids in primary school, twins in the baby buggy, triplets in the oven, your ass in a sling, and your double hernia in a nice supportive truss."

They both have to laugh. "Minnesota," Bruce says, trying out the idea. "My mother came from Minnesota. I just missed being born there, right out there in the cornfield. I haven't been that far east since I was four."

"What I'm telling you. Time you went. *Somewhere*, to study *some*thing."

"Subpoena duces tecum," Bruce says, by Joe Mulder out of his lawyer brother. "With or without the ad testificandum clause. How long is law school?"

"Two years?" Bennion says. "Three? I'm not sure."

"Good God, what would I tell my goil?"

"That's just what I thought was on your mind," Bill says, as grimly as his overweening benevolence will permit. The cast in his eye gives him a mad, squinting, leprechaunish look. "I expect you could tell her a lot of things she'd rather hear, but I know what *I'd* tell her."

"What would you tell her?"

"I'd tell her to wait."

Out on the steps old Maurice, Fidus Achates, is still guarding Bruce's racket. Bruce thanks him profusely and shakes his hand. Maurice loves to shake hands, standing to it with his chest out and his eyes front like somebody having the Congressional Medal of Honor pinned on him. Then Bruce gives him a nickel for a root beer and turns him around and starts him down the hill with a pat on the back. All the way across the Circle he keeps turning around to wave.

Leon Notestein, the president's assistant, is not in his office, but he has left an envelope for Bruce. It contains a letter from the dean of the Minnesota Law School, saying that Leon knows perfectly well it is too late to admit anyone, and much too late for fellowships, but on the strength of Leon's uncritical admiration for this boy, he is holding a tuition scholarship and will hold it for two weeks at the most. Clipped to this letter is a scribbled note: "If you want this, get the application in, with all papers and fee, *right now*. Call me Tues. A.M. if questions."

Questions Bruce has plenty of. Doubts—and this strikes him as curious—he has none. Only a sort of wonder: this is the way things will happen. From the time he left Bennion's office he has been as little complicated by indecision as Maurice on his way to the soda fountain. They put this nickel in his hand and turn him around and pat him on the back and start him on the way he is supposed to go, and off he goes, waving back bravely. Regardless of his worth or his wishes, his destiny is directed by fairy godmothers. If glass slippers are in the script, they will be his size. If pumpkin coaches roll up, he will be the one for whom their doors open.

God's fool, he floats through the errands he came to do. Marv Eldridge is not in the bookstore, where he said he would be, and after waiting ten minutes Bruce gives him up and goes to clean out his locker in the Park Building basement. Then back to the bookstore to turn in his key and get his refund. Still no Eldridge.

He goes on up to Ham Barrentine's office and picks up his last sweater. Ham gets a little sentimental over the last four years, and shakes his hand and grips his shoulder. He asks what Bruce is going to do now that he has graduated, and Bruce tells him that he is probably going to law school in Minneapolis.

Emerging from the Park Building on his way to the gym to clean out his locker there, he finds Joe Mulder sitting under a tree with his sweater box beside him, intently watching dozens of little red-and-black box-elder bugs crawl among the hairs on his arms. He offers an arm to Bruce. "Have some?"

"I wouldn't want to deprive you."

"Nice bugs. No bitee. Just friendly and gregarious. I see you got your sweater."

"Yeah."

"Giving it to Nola?"

"I guess."

"Make that girl a four-letter word," Joe says. "How about a couple of sets to wrap up the season?"

"I ought to be out to work by eleven. There's about twenty tons of bullshit to bag."

"Let Welby bag it. Break him in right. We can play a couple of sets and still get there before noon."

"O.K., but I have to allow time to get there on the streetcar. My car's in the shop."

"I've got mine. Come on, I smell the blood of an English major."

"I'll beat your brains out," Bruce promises him. "On the last day of the season Mulder learns how it feels to be number two."

It really is a solar myth morning. For five years, ever since that day at the tennis club when he was fifteen, Bruce has been giving his body his devout attention, playing basketball in Ward amusement halls and in the commercial league, seizing every spare hour at school to work out on the weights and run laps, hitting tennis balls against the bangboard, playing anybody handy, running practice sessions a set or two sets long. There is a lot of physical work at the nursery, too, and he likes it. Nobody is going to admire him for his physique, but he has labored to make them admire his old college try, and in spite of his ulcer he is in the shape of his life. That morning, a Sir Gareth out of the kitchens, he takes on Lancelot, who taught him everything he knows, and he unhorses him.

The varsity courts are cement, and very fast, made for big servers. Joe's service is not only big, it is *heavy*—it can twist your racket out of your hand. Overhead he is brutal. If you feed him a lob anywhere short of the base line you might just as well turn your back and hope he misses you. He is too high to lob over, too long-armed to pass, too severe to be outsteadied. The only way to play him, at least on these courts, is power against power, and that is the day Bruce can do it. He has modeled his game on Joe's, after all.

They are taking the net at every chance. Nobody loses any points—the other wins them. They ace each other many times, they are both bouncing smashes over the fence and punching volleys off at sharp angles. Or else getting cleanly passed. It must be spectacular, the way they are hitting them, for by the middle of the first set they have begun to draw a crowd. By the end of it the crowd is cheering every point.

When they change courts after Bruce has won the first set, Joe works his pink eyebrows at him ferociously: from here on, he will get his. Bruce shrinks his shoulders together and cringes. "Now the roof falls in," he says. He could not be more dishonest. He knows he is invincible. Joe goes on playing his best, which is good enough to beat nearly anybody in the state, and still Bruce beats him. Just to make it convincing, he aces him on match point.

Red, grinning, and amazed, as wet as if he has stood under a sprinkler, and with his hair dark red and kinky with sweat, Joe comes up to the net pretending he is going to throw his racket at Bruce's head. "God damn, Joe," Bruce says, as happy as he has ever been in his life. "Why can't I play like that every time out?"

"Because you can't be unconscious all the time," Joe says. "You silly son of a bitch, Mason, if you played that way every time out you'd be beating Doeg and Vines."

The crowd is dispersing. The sky has developed very white puffballs of cloud down over the Oquirrhs. The sun pours down, still well short of noon. Bruce falls like a tower, catching himself on his hands, and kisses the cement of the court.

The locker and shower rooms are entirely empty, hollow and

reverberant and thick with the smells of old fellowship—Ivory
soap, steam, Lysol, fresh sweat and stale sweat, the rubbery fragrance of tennis balls kept in a locker, even the lingering smell of
the shellac with which they doctor frayed strings to make them
last. They take a long, ceremonial shower, perhaps their last in
that place, and sit on the worn benches and dress without hurry.

"You know something, Mason?" Joe says. "This could be the
summer we do it. We play the way we were both playing this
morning and there's nobody around here can take us. We could
win the Adams, the State, the Intermountain, the whole shebang."

"Maybe a lot of California ringers will be coming through
looking for tournament experience."

"They won't bother with anything but the Intermountain.
They don't like the high-altitude bounce."

"All right," Bruce says. "We'll take the Adams and the State.
What the hell, why not the Intermountain, too, ringers or not.
When does it come?"

"September, I think. About the middle."

"Oh, hell," Bruce says, shot down by a thought, "I might not
be here."

"Why? You taking a Hawaiian vacation or something?"

"I might be going to law school."

Joe stares. "Don't shit me, Mason."

"I'm not. Notestein and Bennion have wangled me a scholarship at Minnesota. I guess I'm in if I want to fill out the papers."

Joe pulls on a sock, watching Bruce as if he expects him to
break out laughing. Bruce can see him begin to believe. As he
pulls on the other sock he says, "Have you told my old man?"

"No. I just heard about it two hours ago."

"*Because,*" Joe says, "he's been talking about retiring in a few
years and turning the business over to you and me."

"You mean to you."

"Both of us. He's got this plan for letting you buy in—you
know, a little at a time, out of your wages, or maybe giving you
some stock as a bonus. He thinks people work better when they
own part of what they're working at."

Bruce is troubled, for this is what in his most ambitious hour
he would have dreamed of until a few hours ago. His eyes catch

Joe's, he reaches for his shoes. "That sounds like something you dreamed up. Keeping the old team together."

"No. He likes you. He likes the way you work. Always has."

Feeling like a heel, selfish and ungrateful, Bruce says, "Well, I haven't really made up my mind. I've still got a day or two."

They are a little ill at ease, not talkative as they were only minutes ago, as they clear out their lockers and throw away stiff old gym socks and worn tennis balls. Bruce jams his stuff into the equipment bag, Joe rolls his into a wad, and they go down to the parking lot loaded with rackets, gear, and the big boxes containing their sweaters. It is getting hot. The rumble seat of Joe's Ford is an open oven. They throw their stuff into it and climb in.

"Have we got time to run down past Nola's?" Bruce asks.

"I guess so. The Temple Square?"

"No, she's moved out of there. That place was full of snoops. She's got an apartment with two other girls down on Fifth East. They're all working at Auerbach's this summer."

"What's the matter with you?" Joe says. "Letting yourself get crowded out by a couple of Auerbach clerks."

"They're protection," Bruce says. "We don't trust ourselves. It's stronger than we are."

Joe grunts. "I wouldn't be surprised, at that."

Neither would Bruce. Since the night when he played hide-and-seek with the elevator man, he and Nola have been headed toward something serious that neither of them speaks about and that both understand.

"She know you're going to law school?"

"How would she? I told you, I just heard a couple hours ago. Anyway, it isn't a cinch I'm going."

"You gonna tell her now?"

They tip down the Second South hill. Bruce punches Joe in the arm. "Listen, Giuseppe, I haven't had time to think about it. My family don't even know. No use to bring it up till I'm sure. So when we get down to Nola's, how about just unostentatiously keeping your face shut?"

One cough of laughter comes out of Joe. "My face is a lot more unostentatious shut than open. Mason, you silly bastard, you slay me."

He stops before the apartment house that Bruce points out, and Bruce hops down and reaches the sweater box from the rumble seat. It is well baked. The high sun pours down on him. The old run-down street smells of summer. The cottonwoods are shedding fluff.

"You coming in?"

Joe doesn't move. "I'll just sit out here and keep my face unostentatiously shut. But don't poop around, Mason. The old man will be out there before one, and it'd be a good idea to be busily bagging bullshit when he arrives. Or it would be, that is . . ." He leans to inspect something on the left running board. "It would be if the chance to become a partner in the Mulder Nursery meant anything to you."

He makes Bruce mad; he seems to blame, or threaten.

"Joe, you know goddamn well it means a lot."

"Fine. Glad to hear it."

"You think I don't know how much you and your dad have done for me?"

"Shit," Joe says. "Go on in and give her her sweater and kiss her tenderly a few times and get the hell back out. I'll sit here and think up a firm name to replace Mulder and Mason, Nursery Stock Bedding Plants, and Garden Supplies."

"I'll come back and be the company lawyer."

"What do we need of a lawyer?" Joe says. "The job we've got open is for an experienced bullshit bagger with a stake in the business."

3

From the apartment entrance he looks back upon the hot street, the sharp shade of trees, the old Ford with Joe's red head sticking high above the windshield, the bright morning climbing toward the peak of noon. And from far off, he looks upon himself standing there on the brink of something. A voice goes on in his head, patiently explaining, like the voice of someone explaining baseball to an Arab.

Accident, they say, favors the prepared mind. Opportunity knocks only for those who are ready at the door. If we believe the novels we read, upward mobility is always ambitious, hungry, and aggressive, or at the very least, discontented. The George Willards are forever yearning away from the spiritual starvation of Winesburg toward some vague larger life.

But that is not always the way it is. Some of us didn't know enough to be discontented and ambitious. Some of us had such limited experience and limited aspirations that only accident, or the actions of others, or perhaps some inescapable psychosocial fate, could explode us out of our ruts. In a way, I suppose I had to hitchhike out of my childhood; but if I did, I did it without raising my thumb.

The provinces export manpower, yes, as surely as atmospheric highs blow toward atmospheric lows. But the brains that are drawn outward to the good schools, the good jobs, the opportunities, don't necessarily initiate their move. It can be as unavoidable as being born. They feel themselves being rotated into position. Even if they could know what they're going to find outside, all that pain, blood, glaring light, sudden cold, forceps, scissors, hands tying Boy Scout knots in their umbilicus, they could neither prevent nor delay it. Head first, leg first, butt first, out they go.

Bruce is feeling the strains of that inevitability as he walks away from Joe, whom he has just rejected, and puts his thumb on the doorbell of Nola, whom he will leave behind. No Fates have woven him into any fabric of obligation. He was not born to found Rome, he has no specific compulsion to be rich and famous, he is incapable of calculation and strategy. On the contrary, his wishes and his visible future coincide. What Joe and J. J. Mulder have planned for him will guarantee every dream he ever had, and secure him in the middle-class security he has always coveted. He can make a decent home for his mother (in these daydreams the old man is always gone—divorced or dead, vanished somewhere). He can marry (eventually, not right this week) the girl whom he contains as a house contains a furnace. Her pilot light is never out. A slight change of temperature, a turn of the thermostat, and his heated blood clanks in his radiators.

Can he give her up, or postpone her, perhaps for years? Can he go away and leave his mother to the old man's selfishness and dependence? Can he cut himself away from everything familiar and secure—friends, job, tennis, Sundays when the whole hard week uncoils and stretches?

The answer is that he probably can, for he is tacitly planning to. But September is a long way off. Decision, though he has to sign his name to it within a few days, will not produce its consequences for three months.

Nola is a long time coming. He rings again, wondering if she may already have started working at her summer job. Then the knob turns, and he is looking at a young man whose face, strange to him, is clouded with irritability fading toward a schooled politeness.

He is so unexpected that Bruce stumbles over his tongue. Almost contemptuously the young man opens the door, and as Bruce steps in he sees Nola standing in the living room with her fingertips on the back of an overstuffed chair. Her fingers are bent backward with the weight she is putting on them. Her face is scowling, the Indian look heavy in it.

Tableau. Bruce and the young man inspect one another without making their interest too obvious, and Nola stands sullenly by the chair with the light behind her and her face in shadow. It is several hard seconds before she says, "You two don't know each other. Eddie, this is Bruce Mason. Bruce, Eddie Forsberg from down home. He just graduated from West Point."

They shake hands. Forsberg has a polite, stiff manner, and his handshake is firm and brief. Bruce has no way of knowing what Forsberg knows about him, but he knows at least one thing about Forsberg. High school sweetheart. The air is full of competitive tension, the way it is before the first serve of an important match.

"Aren't you working today?" Nola says.

"I'm on my way. I just dropped by to . . ." He carefully does not look at Forsberg, but feels his attention. It occurs to him that he ought to save the sweater for a more private occasion. It is a dirty trick to rub the guy's nose in the fact that someone else has intimate understandings with his former girl. But he has the box in his hands, and here is this rival waiting across the net. He serves, and he goes for an ace. ". . . give you the sweater I promised you."

She takes the box and sets it on the thick back of the chair to open it. Then Bruce becomes aware that Forsberg is looking at him with pale, furious knowledge. Pointedly he drops his eyes to Bruce's hand, on the fourth finger of which Bruce is wearing his West Point class ring.

In civilian clothes he is under a handicap; he would compete better in his regimentals. For all he knows, the sweater with its four stripes certifies that Bruce is some notable athlete, able to broad-jump twenty-five feet or give Nurmi a run for it in the mile. Or perhaps he isn't thinking any such thing. Perhaps he is just sick at his stomach with the certainty that he is out and Bruce is in.

He interrupts Nola's badly acted pleasure in the sweater with some unconvincing acting of his own. His face has gone pinched and pale, his voice is too loud. "Well," he says, "I see it's time for me to take my unwanted presence out of here."

Bruce would hate to have Nola look at him the way she looks at Forsberg—forbidding and uncharitable. Contributory, embarrassed, and triumphant, he stands outside the closed circuit of their tension. With his sweater forgotten in her hands, Nola says, "Will I see you again?"

"What would be the point?"

A slight, considering, agreeing, dismissing hesitation. "I'm sorry, Eddie."

"Are you?" He transfers his attention to Bruce, and he is more ham actor than ever. Bruce understands that it is his real and angry feeling that makes him sound so false. "I owe you my thanks," he says, and all but bows. "It's been very instructive."

Bruce does not answer; he is both appalled and ready to laugh. Anyway, what is there to say? Forsberg has read the situation correctly. He takes hold of the doorknob with his left hand, and salutes derisively with his right. "There are some advantages to being in the Army," he says. "Then you don't have to join the Foreign Legion." His laugh sprays around the room. "Have a *very* pleasant time down in Castle Valley," he says, and is gone, slam.

The moment the door closes, Nola spins around and with spread fingers lifts her hair off her head as if she were dying of the heat. "Hooo!"

"What's the scoop?"

"Oh, he makes me so mad! I hate people who act as if they own you."

"What's he done?"

Now her eyes lock with his, a look that is at once searching and almost furtive. "He's been after me all morning to marry him and go off to the Philippines."

This information takes Bruce's wind. It is far more threatening than Forsberg's actual presence was. The thought of his intense attempt, the intimacy and seriousness of his intention, the previous understandings it suggests, is demoralizing.

"Just out of a clear sky?"

"Oh, he's been writing. I never gave him any encouragement."

So they have been corresponding, and Bruce has known nothing about it. Bruce has understood that the ring, which he stole off her finger and which she never made him give back, was something from the past. Apparently he has been misinformed. While he and Nola have been going out, hotly kissing, touching, driving each other wild, working closer to what they both want and anticipate and don't quite know how to approach, she has been writing this other fellow. She has kept him informed of her changes of address, else how did he find her? The thought of how much he doesn't know, how much she has not told him, leaves a cold, hollow spot in his solar plexus.

"You never talked about him."

"There was no reason to. I've only seen him a few times in three or four years."

"Were you ever engaged or anything?"

"No, of course not."

"He must have thought so. Otherwise why would he think there was a chance you'd marry him and go off to the Philippines?"

"I have no idea. Why would any girl go off to the Philippines with anybody?"

"Is that why you turned him down?"

"Oh, what do you think?" she says angrily. "I sent him away, didn't I? What more do you want?"

Caution. Move softly. Lightly he says, "You ought to introduce him to Holly. She's red hot to go to the Philippines or any place else."

There is an annoyed, fuming silence. He hears himself like some bothersome insect. "Were you ever in love with him?"

"Will you let it drop!"

"All right, all right." He folds her in his arms, but she is a stiff armful. In a moment she pulls back to look into his face. "He wouldn't *believe* me when I said it was over!"

"It?"

"Oh, whatever it was! I used to go out with him in high school. He thought he could come back and I'd look at him once and that would be that."

"It was seeing me wearing his ring that convinced him."

"Yes."

"That makes me feel sort of crummy."

"Why? It's all right. He doesn't mean anything."

If he doesn't mean anything, why is she upset? Yet she did send him away. She stonily sent him away, and Bruce is in possession.

"What did he mean, have a good time down in Castle Valley?"

"I told him you were driving me down to Audrey's wedding. It was the only thing I could think of that would put him off."

"Why wouldn't he just have come to the wedding himself?"

"He's sailing from San Francisco in three days. Anyway"—she gives him a smoldering look, her face a foot from his, so that he sees the little check mark scar above her eye—"anyway, if he showed up there my father would shoot him, or my brother Buck would."

He laughs. "You're kidding. What for?"

"Because they don't like him."

"They must not like him an awful lot."

She makes a sound of irritation and turns out of his arms and goes to the window, to stand pulling the curtain aside and looking out. She is in such a state that he can almost see the sparks fly off her.

"Would they shoot me if I appeared with you?"

Flash out of the corners of her eyes. "Why, are you scared?"

"They can't object so long as my intentions are honorable."

"Are they?"

He laughs. "No."

It is not the right tone to assume. She is not in a mood for joking. Some grudge rankles in her. "That's so, isn't it?" she says. "You're like all the others. You're just after what you can get."

"For God's sake!" Were Forsberg's intentions not honorable, is that what she means? Is that why her father or brother would shoot him if he showed up? Did somebody catch them at something? How far did she let him go? Knowing his own temptations, he is clear on Forsberg's. He glares at her in doubt and suspicion.

She has tears in her eyes. She is really angry. "I should have told Eddie yes. At least he wanted to marry me, he wasn't just fooling around."

"Nola," he says, distracted, "what are you talking about?

Who's fooling round? What makes you think I don't want to
marry you?"

"You've never said one word."

"That doesn't mean . . ."

Accusingly she interrupts. "You know how it's getting with us.
I keep waiting for you to say something, but you never . . ."

He has a moment of complicated clarity. He understands that
without really telling him anything about her past relations with
Forsberg, she is using Forsberg as a lever under him. This is not
something he resents or resists—it excites him. It is clear that, ac-
cusing him of only fooling around, she would be upset if he
didn't pursue her, which he certainly intends to do. But there are
cautions in him, just as clear. He remembers that conversation
with Holly: *In the good old-fashioned way? In the good old-
fashioned way. Meaning you want to marry her? Well, sometime,
sure. Not right next week.* Bill Bennion, too: *Six kids in primary
school, twins in the baby buggy, triplets in the oven, your ass in
a sling, and your double hernia in a nice supportive truss.*

A quicksand, Bennion would call her, a swamp to drown in.
But how intolerable is the thought of not drowning! He thinks of
the folded papers in his hip pocket, and what those say about his
intentions, and is shaken. He has intended to tell her. But not
now, not now. He takes her in his arms and kisses her long and
hard, looking all the while into her wide-open eyes.

"Will you marry me?"

From the way she tries to read him, he might be in Hebrew.
Her hair is mussed from her having grabbed it in both hands
after Forsberg left.

"Yes," she says, and puts her forehead against his chest and
pounds it on him. "I'm sorry, I'm sorry, I'm sorry!"

"Sorry why? Don't you want to?"

"I made you say it."

"You never made me say anything I didn't want to say."

She rubs her nose against him. Her breath is warm through his
shirt. In a little voice she says, "I just got my grades. They aren't
very good."

"That's my fault. I've been taking up all your time."

"I took up yours, too. And you've been working, besides. What
did *you* get, straight A's?"

As a matter of fact, he did, but he lies. "Not that good."

"Whatever you got, you can do it. You're bright, and you're a man. I'll be lucky if I get my certificate, and luckier if I get a decent job. I'm twenty-two, Bruce! I don't want to spend my life clerking at Auerbach's."

"Don't worry, I'll see you don't have to."

Now she is reading him again, braced back against his arm. "You mean you'll take care of me? I wonder. You'll take advantage of me and then something will come up, some chance or other, and you'll drop me like a hot rock."

The papers burn in his hip pocket. He does not know what he is going to do about them. But what he says is: "I told you I want to marry you. What more can I say? As a matter of fact, Joe was just telling me his dad wants the two of us to take over the nursery. He'd let me buy in. I'd be a partner."

Hearing himself, he is both dismayed and thrilled—dismayed because he so falsely conceals the business about law school, thrilled because, spelled out this way, job and girl and all, the second option takes his breath.

"As for taking advantage of you," he whispers into her pine-soap-scented hair, "yes! I can't wait."

Her eyes come up a moment and are hidden against his chest again. He sees the part in her hair. Even in his heated state, as with Forsberg a few minutes earlier, he notes how false real emotion can make us appear. She *looks* coy and false.

"You, too," he tells her. "You love me. You want to. Don't you?"

She says into his shirt, "Would I be acting like this if I didn't? Damn you, you . . . You know what I was thinking when I told Eddie you were driving me down home? I was hoping you would. I kept thinking of being alone with you. I kept wanting to show you off to Buck and my father and sister and everybody. My father's always after me to marry some nice boy and settle down and quit living in apartments. He thinks it's dangerous, or immoral, or something. And I was thinking, if we did go, there might be some place . . . I know I couldn't say no to you, and I didn't know how you felt about—marriage, and everything. If I didn't say no, and then you didn't want to marry me, where would I be? You wouldn't respect me. You'd lose interest."

What he hears is unreal, like the murmured talk of a talking picture heard without seeing the picture. Laocoön in the toils of his serpent had no more pressure on his chest or thunder in his ears. He tips her chin up and stares into her eyes, to see if they are saying what her mouth is saying. But she will not look directly at him. He encloses her in a shivering, exultant hug.

"When is this wedding?"

"Day after tomorrow."

"Can you postpone starting your job? Say you're not quite through school?"

"I think so."

"I'll get tomorrow and the next day off. How far is it down there?"

"A hundred and seventy-five miles."

"My car'll be fixed by tonight. We can leave early tomorrow and camp out somewhere and come in just before the wedding, as if we'd driven straight down."

She studies him with her lower lip bitten thoughtfully under her even teeth. "I . . . can't leave early tomorrow."

"Why not?"

Her eyes hunt in his like someone hunting for a lost earring in the grass. "I have to see somebody."

"Who?"

"Why are you so inquisitive! The doctor, if you have to know."

"About what? What's wrong?"

"Never *mind*."

"Can't it wait?"

Her eyes still hunting in his, her lips bending into a smile, she shakes her head. "No."

Heated conjectures have started up in him. He is almost totally ignorant, and timid to boot, and afraid to think what his mind suggests to him. Yet the suggestion is unavoidable. Something female. Something in preparation for their trip? He knows the limerick about the girl from St. Paul who went to the birth-control ball, and about her pessaries and other accessories, but he has only a dim idea what the accessories might be, or how they work. In the world of Jack Bailey it is the gentleman who provides protection. Is she really, as coolly as this, contemplating getting herself something, knowing she intends to go all the way? The thought instantly quells desire. Then he realizes that she has no such thing in mind. She could not even conceive of taking love so coolly. She is only telling him that she has something wrong, some variety of the female troubles that the Lydia Pinkham ads speak of but nice girls do not.

"When do we go, then? Day after?"

"Can you arrange it?"

"I sure as hell *will*. And the day after, too, so we can stop somewhere on the way back." The further this conversation goes, the more unbelievable it is. He looks into the bottomless brown pool of her eyes, and what he sees there lifts him eight inches off the floor. "Do you know somewhere?"

"I was thinking. Have you ever been in Fruita?"

"In the Capitol Reef?"

"Yes. It's just a pocket in the cliffs, on the Dirty Devil. An uncle of mine has a peach orchard there. We've camped in it sometimes. There's a grove of cottonwoods, and a ditch that comes right out of the river, and an old log house that he stores hay in. Nobody lives within two or three miles. Anyway, they'll all be staying on at home after the wedding."

"Perfect!" He puts his lips to the fragrant part in her hair and whispers against her skull. "And you will. Tell me you will."

"You'll think I'm fast."

"I think you're wonderful. Gorgeous! Incredible! Beyond compare! Say you will."

"Oh, do I have to *tell* you?" She lays her forehead against his chest and immediately pulls it back. "Bruce?"

"What?"

"I don't want you to think . . ."

"I don't think anything except that you love me."

"No, there's something. . . . Why I have to go to the doctor. I've got . . . You know, something's a little wrong. To fix it they might have to . . . I might not be technically a virgin."

Full of magnanimity, he forgives her. "Who cares?"

"I don't want you to think anything."

"You're a darling."

She takes his wandering hands and holds them. "You!" she says. "You're exactly what my father is afraid I'll get mixed up with!"

"Are *you* afraid?"

Her eyes swim and change, they have suction in them, they pull him down. She is smiling. With her eyes wide open she kisses him.

Eventually, somehow, he breaks away, still leaning to kiss her one more time through the door as it closes. He is shaky, his face is stiff. What he feels as he leaps down the sidewalk is not love, not desire, not anything that simple. It is nothing that needs further gratification. It is already gratified. It is wonder.

The sun is intense and dizzying, straight overhead. The shade where Joe sits seems like darkness. When he levitates into the seat, Joe rouses himself.

"You already? You haven't been gone more than two hours. If you'd only stayed a while, Welby'd have had it all bagged."

"Bullshit."

"Pree-cisely," Joe says. Pulling away from the curb and setting a course toward Sugar House, he looks at Bruce curiously out of the corners of his eyes, but he asks no questions.

As for Bruce, he seethes behind his pretense of everyday-ness. His mind is full of reruns of the scene he has just left. He is formulating the lies he will have to tell J. J. Mulder in asking for two days off. And one other thing, one unworthy thought: If a girl were getting ready to go to bed with a fellow, and wasn't sure how experienced or inexperienced he was, but was afraid he might know she was not a virgin, she might, if she were scheming but not too clever, tell such a story as Nola had just told him.

An expert in untruths, he feels the unlikelihood of her being deflowered, at just this moment, by a doctor. It is too pat. It anticipates potential questions. And there is Eddie Forsberg, high school sweetheart, who had some reason to think she might marry him and go off with him to the Philippines. He must have had reason. But he can't pursue her down to the ranch because her father or brother might shoot him.

He dismisses these sneaky thoughts. He believes her because he wants to believe her, because he can't equate such a lie with the look in her eyes and the passion with which she kisses him. He shoves the treacherous little notion back and away, he smothers it in anticipations, he obscures it with fantasies of pure young love in a paradise oasis among the red cliffs.

4

Except for the wrinkles in it, the sweater might have been brand-new. He held it up and looked for holes, sniffed the wool for the smells of preservation: neither moths nor mothballs had been there. The thing might have come straight from its original Utah Woolen Mills box. Mason couldn't remember whether or not he had ever seen Nola wear it. At least she hadn't given it to Bailey.

Laying it aside, he picked up the two bundles of letters, one tied with string, one with a piece of brown velvet ribbon that he seemed to remember around Nola's hair, times when she let it down and bound it behind her head. When she sat at the piano it hung down her back in a thick, dark-chestnut sheaf like a horse's tail, clear to the bench.

As between those tied with string and those tied with ribbon, he chose those tied with ribbon. They were not, he saw, chronologically arranged, only bundled together. Put in order and read consecutively, they might make a sort of sickly *Sturm und Drang* novel, a decaffeinated *Sorrows of Young Werther* or *Wilhelm Meisters Lehrjahre*. He was certainly not going to read them through. He might look at the top one.

It was postmarked March 4, 1931. That would have been only

a little while after he got back to Minneapolis from Chet's funeral. At Christmas he hadn't been able to go home because the
banks had all failed, and the savings of more than four years at
the Mulder Nursery had gone in one blow, crossed out. Lesson
number one in the curriculum of growing up. The holidays he
had hoped to spend with Nola in Salt Lake he spent in Minneapolis in the company of other threadbare students, eating crackers
and cottage cheese, and milk kept cold on the window ledge,
and reading, reading, reading, boning up in hornbooks, review-
ing torts and contracts and crimes in preparation for February's
exams, and putting in a systematic three hours a day on general
books calculated to improve his mind. Aristotle just then, as he
recalled: *Poetics, Ethics,* and *Politics,* one after the other—books
he had managed never to hear of during his undergraduate
years, and as unrelated to his immediate life as the Harvard
Classics philosophers he had read when he was fifteen.

Then, at the end of January, on the eve of examinations, came
the telegram announcing the last of Chet's misfortunes and mis-
takes. Lesson number two followed so fast upon number one
that he hardly had time to set his feet. Like his catch-up reading,
his instruction in real life had much ground to cover in only a little time.

If Chet had not been generous and good-natured, he would
not have worked up a sweat on a cold and windy day, helping
dig somebody's car out of the snow at the Ecker ski-jumping hill
outside of Park City. If he had been born luckier, he would have
waited to catch pneumonia until after antibiotics had tamed it.
Being generous, unlucky, and ill-timed, he dug and pushed, he
got overheated, he fell sick, and he died within six days. "I'm
leaving you the dirty work, Ma," he told his mother a few hours
before he drowned in his own secretions. Then he escaped from
his future, which was drab, and his marriage, which was in trouble, and abandoned to the responsibility of others the daughter
he had conceived before he was legally a man.

Bruce came home to a week of clenched misery. Chet's wife
had gone to pieces, his father ate his own vitals in guilt and self-
blame, his mother tried to hold them both up, Bruce tried to
support her. It was his father who took that death hardest. He
had always liked Chet better than Bruce. Chet was an extension

of himself, wholly masculine, big-chested, unbookish, an athlete. Even after the runaway marriage and the subsidence into odd jobs and semipro baseball, the dream of the big chance, big leagues, big success, had never quite died for either of them.

It was like the game of swatting the baby with a pillow: the old man never realized it wasn't going well until it had gone all to pieces. He never knew how he felt about Chet until Chet was dead. Every night Bruce heard him moaning in nightmares, and his mother's voice as she tried to wake him to a reality as bad as his dreams.

Death closed their closed family in upon itself more than ever; they were as impervious as a spore. There was no room for Nola among them. Bruce had to find time for her separately, which was not easy. She was tied down by classes and practice teaching. He saw her only in the evening, late, when her own work was done and when his parents had gone to bed so that he could borrow the car. Their hours together were somber. Though she was sympathetic, and cried for his trouble, it was the renewed separation that she feared. She couldn't make anything out of their brief bleak reunion for thinking how soon it would end.

He could give her only scraps of himself. His mind was always back at the house where his mother would be lying sleepless, waiting for the next installment of his father's nightmare and hoping for the sound of Bruce's key in the door. Through the months in Minneapolis, Nola had been an anguish in his blood, he had been swollen with visions; but while he was at home they never even tried to make love. There was no place, and anyway Chet would have lain like an accusation between them. All they did was sit in the cold car and torment one another with abortive touching, and kisses that had in them something like a groan.

On the last night he picked her up after dinner and they sat up on Wasatch Boulevard in the white cold, under the cold mountains, huddling and kissing and promising. He talked about the next summer and all they would do, but in the middle of his Pollyanna spiel she put her hands to his face, cupping it and staring into his eyes, and cried in her husky voice, "Oh, do you *have* to go back there? I can't stand it if you go away again!"

And here, something odd. He had been utterly miserable in Minneapolis. With no gift for the law's precisions, and un-

dereducated to begin with, he had compensated by a monoma·
niac diligence. He went nowhere except to classes and the library, he took no exercise, he ate in twenty minutes in order to
get back to the books. In spite of the monotonous bland things he
ate, his ulcer was a constant reminder under his wishbone. He
was away from everything that had once given him a delusive
confidence, his heart was wrenched with more love than it could
hold, he was blackly lonesome. And yet when she begged him
not to go back, he had not a moment's hesitation. Of course he
was going back. He would stick it out, and she should, too, and
eventually they would get their postponed reward. Four more
months, and then all summer together. Another nine months, and
together for good. He would find a place in some local law firm,
or hang out his own shingle.

Mason could hardly believe his own naïveté. What had he
thought he was going to do? Arrange little divorces? Settle little
real estate squabbles? Draft little wills? Litigate little disputes
about water rights, or breaches of contract or promise? That last
was probably it. Breach of promise was very big about that time.
Many a female heart, inspired by Peaches Browning, was exposing its injuries to sympathetic juries.

It was fantastic that he should ever have thought his future
might lie in the practice of law. That was only the direction in
which he had been pushed by people eager to do him a favor.
He had no more initiative in his career than water has on a
slope. Nevertheless, once started, he would have felt it immoral
—unthinkable—to stop before the end. He would get his degree
and come back. They would be married and build a house, or
maybe only a basement at first, in the Salt Lake Depression style
—a roofed-over foundation in which they would live until they
could afford to build the first floor. Just Molly and me and baby
makes three.

Question: Why that mule headed inertia? Answer: In the first
place, he *was* mule-headed. He hated to back up, start over,
change direction. To this day he drove that way, *gerade aus* like
a German, despising the people who dart from lane to lane.
Moreover, he was used to delayed rewards. He knew something
about having to work for what he wanted, and even more about
frustrations and disappointments. He was a digger, but there

was a fatalist in him, too. He mistrusted the rewards that he would break his neck to win. He half expected to fail even though experience should have taught him that most of the time he did not. In his bones he knew that the world owed him nothing. Some part of him was always preconditioned to lose. And though he felt himself superior to his background, and capable of some vague unspecified distinction, he knew himself unworthy. He was a sticker because it was easier to dig in and be overrun than to attack and be repulsed.

To Nola he had said nothing about any of that. He didn't know himself that well. Also, he had hope. When you live by daily postponements, you had better have hope.

It didn't help that on that last night he felt he had to take her home at ten so as to spend the last hour or so with his parents. The next morning, when he kissed her goodbye at the Union Pacific station, her lips were cold from the wind, and her eyes were bottomless. Sad? Resentful? He couldn't tell. He never could read her eyes.

Now here was this letter written from Minneapolis a few weeks after he left her for the second time. He wished Aunt Margaret had managed to preserve something else, his letters to his mother or Joe, a diary, old papers, photographs, anything. To reconstruct that time from these letters alone was like trying to make a composite drawing of a suspect from the evidence of a single witness.

He is still running books past his eyes, a random sampling of the wildest variety: Longinus' *On the Sublime, Heroes and Hero Worship, The Origin of Species* and *The Voyage of the Beagle,* Freud's *Totem and Taboo,* Andreyev's *The Seven That Were Hanged.* These are his after-study-hours reading. He confides that before turning off his light about two every morning, he gives himself a German lesson, reading a page, with the help of a dictionary, from *Also Sprach Zarathustra,* Tieck's essays on Shakespeare, or Giovanni Papini's *Gog.*

Strange, strange, and far off. Even the handwriting strikes him as strange. Most people's handwriting, he believes, grows more angular and irregular as they age, like the shapes of old pine trees. His, on the contrary, has grown more precise. It is demoralizing to see this impetuous scrawl and know it for his own. It is even more demoralizing to read what this boy sees fit to say to his girl, frantically signaling from his isolation to his desire.

He is excruciating. His letter is a desperate patter chorus of puns, doggerel, snatches of languages he does not know. Embarrassed to speak seriously of what he respects and covets, he describes professors as vacuum cleaners full of air, dust, and dead flies. Poverty, exile, and the death of a brother have taught him nothing. He sounds seventeen, not twenty-one. And if Mason were the girl this boy is writing to, he would notice one thing: though he is bitter against his exile and passionate for its end, the bulk of the letter, like that score card of books he has read in the past week, is about what his exile is teaching him. He speaks less of his losses than of his gains.

Dull fare for an unintellectual girl left behind in Salt Lake City, as dull as Yeats on fairies or Schopenhauer on suffering. Would she have felt that this compulsive self-improvement of Bruce Mason's, which she cannot know is half-baked and only semi-directed, threatens what she wants and what he says *he* wants? Would she feel the torque of foreign books, foreign ideas, working on his provincial innocence?

He reminds Mason of one of those little toy apes made of cloth and fur, with painted grins and rubber-band insides. Twist the rubber bands tight and set this anthropoid on a table and he will begin to writhe and contort himself toward uprightness. A hand or foot will catch and brace, the body will lift, the head will come up. Then something will slip and down he will go again, flat on his low brow. But he does not stay there. The body goes on writhing, begins to come up, struggles to stand, is almost standing. Then flop, he is flat again, but his fixed indomitable grin is already stirring with mindless persistence upward, a paradigm of evolution.

The quintessentially deculturated American, born artless and without history into a world of opportunity, Bruce Mason must acquire in a single lifetime the intellectual sophistication and the cultural confidence that luckier ones absorb through their pores from earliest childhood, and unluckier ones never even miss. He is a high jumper asked to jump from below ground level and without a run, and because he is innocent and has the temperament of an achiever he will half kill himself trying.

And Nola Gordon is what? She has no real interest in high jumping. She likes to sit and let the sun shine on her, and sing.

What could she have made of his idiotic way of signing off? Where his feeling might be laid miserably bare, he has to ham it up. "Nola, mein Schatz, Ich liebe Dich. In fact I might say, without fear of successful contradiction, je t'aime. Or even Oás ἀλαπῶ." How preposterous. Irritated, Mason denies his acquaintance. Whatever happened to him, he deserved it.

Then he turns the last sheet over, and there is a postscript.

Ah, darling, only 87 days till the first of June! My calendar looks like the Prisoner of Chillon's. I make friends with mice and spiders to keep from thinking about you. We've *got* to go down to the Capitol Reef again this summer, or to Fish Lake, or the Aquarius, or some other place empty and beautiful. You deserve that kind of setting. I want to see you bare in the moonlight. I want to touch you—but look out. My touch would raise blisters, and the kisses I've been saving for you could cause third degree burns.

My God, it drives me crazy to think. I know a place in the Ontario Basin, just over the divide from Brighton, where hardly anybody ever goes. (Not like the last time we were in Brighton. That makes me miserable every time I remember it). Or there's a little lake halfway along the old tramway between Brighton and Park City. Even if we both have to work this summer (and did I tell you Joe spoke to his dad, and even though times are terrible he says I can have my old job back?) those places are close enough for weekends. We could drive up to Brighton or Park City on Saturday night after work, and hike in.

Oh, keep your heart warm! I dreamed the other night that I came home on a cold morning and you wouldn't start.

One letter is enough to depress him. It brings back that whole frantic, lonely, expanding winter, those ulcer-diet meals of cottage cheese and milk and mashed potatoes and bread and ice cream, those late half hours of communion each night before he climbed into bed with Nietzsche or Tieck, those bleak visits to the post office when the box showed nothing—he wrote her daily, she did well to manage two letters a week. He ties up the bundles and tips the box to put them back in.

There remains the manila envelope. When he undoes its metal clasp, snapshots slide onto the spread.

His first impulse was not to look at them. There were advantages to being orphaned away from the past. Evidence might be hard on the self-protective memory. Just now, in a single letter, Bruce Mason had so embarrassed his mature descendant that the descendant shrank from the relationship. He felt a derisive unwillingness that verged on distaste, like a Victorian cleric trying to reconcile himself to descent from an ape.

What if Nola Gordon, too, should turn out to have been an absurd adolescent, callow, provincial, not beautiful, not mysterious, not in any way worth the disturbance she caused? The memory, Mason had discovered, is deceptive and self-serving, and could blur faces as it could blur other things. What if he turned these snapshots over and found that Nola was not the dark mysterious desirable girl he thought he remembered? What if he had invented her? What if the fashions of the early Depression years turned her into a frump?

But he was engaged in laying ghosts, not only the ghosts of his luckless parents and the ghosts of old girl friends, but the ghosts of old innocence, inexperience, possibility. His innocence had always been flawed by self-doubt, and only those years of delusive security, when he had been sixteen-going-on-twenty-one, had lured him into the open. When the boot came down, he had crawled back under his rock dragging his squashed guts.

Not that he needed healing, or ever had. He took the blows that fell on his family and himself because he expected them. The world owed none of them anything, and no few years of relative grace had convinced him otherwise. He had read Epictetus; he was a Stoic by destiny and choice. And he was not, afterward, driven to wipe all that out of his mind. It was only the girl he wiped out, and her he systematically forgot not so much because love or grievance gnawed at him as because he was ashamed to have been a fool, and by no means a guiltless one.

Now he flinched away from looking at these photographs refreshing the face of his temptation. He was reconciled to having been a fool, but at least he wanted the temptation to have been irresistible.

The photographs lay face down. He turned over the top one and there she was, smiling from the doorway of a little log cabin. She wore riding breeches and boots, a white shirt open at the throat, a black Stetson pushed back on her head. Beside her, a wagon wheel leaned against the log wall; above her head, a nail wore a bouquet of binder twine. The interior of the cabin shadowed backward in dim crisscrosses of hay. The face looking at him was heavier and more Indian-looking than he remembered it, but he could see why it used to interrupt the beating of his heart. The eyes were candid under severe dark brows. The mouth was curved in a Gioconda smile.

Quickly he shuffled through the others. Only eight—one roll from his old bellows Kodak. One print was so over-exposed that all detail was washed out. Two were of a crowd—the wedding crowd—spread across the grass under the cottonwoods, self-conscious countrified strangers not even forgotten because never known, but once studied gingerly as potential relatives by marriage. When you marry into a Mormon family you marry tribes and nations.

Here are the bride and groom, she in a best dress, her hair direct from the beauty parlor, he wearing a Tom Mix shirt and a dazed smile. Flanking them, the bride's daughter, father, and brother Buck. Buck's hard face is a younger version of his father's, curly dark hair an earlier stage of curly gray. Both have the beaks of hawks and eyes that bore into the camera like the eyes of zealot grandfathers in old tintypes.

In the next one, Buck is smiling broadly, a movie cowboy. He and Nola sit their horses in front of a cross-bedded sandstone cliff on which someone has marked with chalk, for greater visibility, the pecked outlines of petroglyphs—deer with exaggerated antlers, mountain sheep with curled horns. The teeth of brother and sister are white in their dark faces. They sit their horses with the easy weight of sacked grain. Their thighs, pressed against the saddles on the side toward the camera, swell against the cloth, his against tight Levi's, hers against the tailored twill of her breeches. Riding breeches are the only kind of pants he ever saw her in. In those years women did not wear pants, even Levi's, and even on ranches.

Now here are Nola Gordon and Bruce Mason on the top bar of a corral, a picture taken by Buck just before they started back, presumably to Salt Lake. Her eyes are slanted sideward, and she is laughing. Bruce leans back, pretending to be toppling off. His face is the face of one who trusts his life. Both look clean, open, happy, and incredibly young.

Did Nola return these snapshots to remind him of something? Did she regret what she had done to him, or what they had done to each other? If so, her gesture was as futile as a telephone ringing in an empty house. Probably she was simply clearing her life of whatever trash he had left behind. He remembered her carrying that box up Joe Mulder's steps, wearing the implacable expression that had been on her face when she looked Eddie Forsberg out her door and on his way.

But then why this last picture, Nola barefooted and bare-legged, lifting her skirts high to clear the water of the ditch in which she is wading? To remind him of her body? Or of an occasion and a ceremony and a promise? The light is early, the shadows are flat and long. Above the waist she is wearing only a brassiere, and on her face is a look of laughing dismay that is not dismay at all, but excitement. In this snapshot her face is as vivid as Holly's.

If it was meant as a reminder, it was the right one. It would have reminded Bruce Mason on that bleak sunstruck day of his father's funeral, and it reminds him now: morning in Eden. Just after he ambushed her with the camera, he splashed after her and caught her in person, and in the middle of the knee-deep water, in his new exultance of possession, laid his hand on her bare midriff and his mouth on her mouth.

Mason squeezed his eyes shut, easing the strained muscles. It must be one-thirty. Enough of all this. He put the photographs back into their envelope and the envelope and letters back into the box, and set the box down on the floor. The sweater weighed on his feet, and he kicked it off. He turned off the past with the light.

With his eyes open, he watched how the blackness of the room turned imperceptibly to modulations of gray, itself like a faded photograph—vague bureau, shadowy desk and chair, ghostly doorways leading to bathroom and closet. He could not feel himself in any specific time or place. This was not the Utah Hotel in Salt Lake City at the end of May 1977, but some place that was typical without being defined. He had slept in this bed all over the world. A late car passing in the street might have been passing under the windows of a room in London or Washington or Cairo, Tehran or Beirut or Amman, anywhere along the confused unedited newsreel of his life.

The wheels rolled backward, images flowed and dissolved. He was asleep, but he might as well have been awake, for the pictures were the same, sleeping or waking—little movies in which he was both actor and camera. He took a trip he had taken before, he attended two weddings, one sanctified in shirt-sleeve piety, the other consummated in awe. Dreaming, he continued the pilgrimage that he had begun when he rounded the corner of the Oquirrhs and saw shining against its mountains the city of his youth. Sleeping, he was troubled by the same feelings of nostalgia and loss and rueful wonder that had attended him all day.

That this boy should be himself. That what he had done and felt in his naïveté and egotism and innocence should persist so long and so unchanged. That he should understand it and be cured of it but still contain it. That calf love, like childhood unhappiness and boyhood self-mistrust, like mother love and father hate, like everything else that had got fed into his computer in those impressionable years, should be so helplessly a thing that lasts.

He is flying, not at all surprised at being able to fly, with the Atman guide Khamis ibn Rimthan. His name means Thursday, and he cannot get lost. In his head is a gyroscopic compass. Set him in the middle of an unknown waste and ask the direction and distance of any landmark—anything as far as Mecca or as near as the flint desert called the Abu Bahr, the Father of the Sea—and he will point and tell you, "Till tomorrow evening in your truck," or "Six hard days by *dhalul*." He has crossed the Rub' al Khali north-south and east-west, he has guided the King

through the red Dhana sands, he has led Aramco's geologists
clear to the plain of Muttia, where the al-Murrah tribesmen
drink camel's milk because all the wells are salt. They say of him
that he could bury a rupee in a traveling dune and come back
five years later and find it.

It seems that Khamis is taking him to his native region, and
that in some confusing way he must have gone this route before, for he recognizes things. The water that spreads to the horizon, rounding its brilliant turquoise into a glittering salt plain, is
surely Great Salt Lake. And yet as they swoop over the saltworks
toward Saltair, the buildings and the long dikes of salt blur into
a cluster of *barastis* on the flats, the domed pavilion dead ahead
might be some just-not-quite-recognized mosque, the Saltair
causeway becomes an arrowy fish trap projecting into the Per-
sian Gulf, and Arabs are washing ticks off their camels on the flat
shore.

Now all that falls behind. They are flying against a stiff wind
in a country of cliffs. Their robes flatten against them—like
Khamis, he is wearing the *agal*—and he can distinctly hear the
edges of the cloth pop and flutter as they speed along. But it
cannot be cloth he hears. It is the noise of his old Model A,
laboring along a desert track, in immense highlands, up a slope
that steepens and steepens toward the vertical. In alarm he looks
at Khamis, but Khamis nods and smiles and motions him on. His
hands are frozen to the wheel. What was terrifyingly steep is
near vertical, past vertical. The earth curls backward like an
enormous river wave, the Ford goes on pulling this impossible
grade, they curve smoothly up and over in a loop that is never
completed. Gravity is in abeyance, panic locks his guts. Are they
flying again? No, far under him, or above him, are the trestles of
the Saltair roller coaster, and the thunder that he hears is from
wheels, and the whistle of air past his ears is remembered from
his first ride on this coaster, soon after they arrived in Salt Lake
from Montana. Weightless, drunk with space, terrified, he soars
up and over, endlessly over, looping the loop, wheeling with the
universe.

They they are still. Somehow they have surmounted or escaped it. They stand on a terrific rim in a wind that blows
silently out of time, silently but so strongly that they stoop and

cling to avoid being blown off the earth. All around the edges of the world, concentric lines of cliffs rise rim beyond rim. Their colors are red-gold, rust, chocolate, sulphur yellow, coppery blue-green; their profiles are familiar and evasive. The rock they stand on, he sees, is a cameo butte, all that is left at the center of an eroded dome as long and wide and high as a mountain range. He is uneasy, as in a game where he doesn't know the rules, and he asks Khamis, "Where are we? Circle Cliffs? Tuwaiq Escarpment?"

Instead of answering, Khamis points down. Down there a half mile, a mile, sunk in the sunny stone, glows a tiny green spot, a Memling miniature landscape. He sees it with the eye of an eagle or buzzard, uncannily sharp and precise, clearly lighted: green meadows, buildings and roofs, a double loop of creek, the angular sculpture of corrals, even tiny animals of a remarkable verisimilitude. Recognition and gladness come together. It is the remembered place of his boyhood, the sunken river bottoms of the Whitemud, in Saskatchewan.

He says something to Khamis, and finds that Khamis is slyly smiling. With the changefulness of water flawed by wind, his face alters and softens, his hawk's beak gentles. He puts up a hand and removes the *ghutra* and reveals under it long red hair in a braid. His smile is complex; he looks at Mason with his mother's blue eyes. The wind, blowing against him, outlines under his robe the breasts and hips of a woman.

"Ah!" Mason cries in love and relief. "They told me you were dead!"

Displeased, she frowns. The wind presses her robes against her and shows the flatness where her left breast should be. Her brows are dark, level, and severe; her hair is not red, but brown and shining. Her eyes come closer, growing larger until they fill his whole vision. As if he were an insoluble puzzle, they search, probe, question, wonder. They are waveringly steady; the light in them darkens and changes but the insistent gaze is not withdrawn. Softly, in a voice of husky sweetness, she begins to sing. The tune he knows but cannot name. The words he recognizes: "I have kissed thy mouth, Iokanaan, I have kissed thy mouth!"

As smoothly as an elevator they are sinking down. From below, deep in its protected pocket, the Memling landscape rises toward them, growing swiftly larger, and as it rises it changes through a series of recognitions. The enclosing walls are the bench hills above the valley of the Whitemud, then they are the cliffs behind the ranch house in Castle Valley, and almost at once they rise grandly in the red, white-capped wave of the Capitol Reef. The green core rushing upward burns an ever more intense green. It rushes toward him, or he toward it—safety, illusion, lost Paradise, whatever it is. He is filled with anticipation and dread.

The screen breaks up in shapes of flame. Everything is a red flickering. He is in a movie theater, and in the projection booth the film has caught fire. Aware of the cold, he looks around him and sees that he is alone in the theater.

Groggily he gropes and finds the edge of the blanket and pulls it up. The pillow is wet from his mouth, and he rolls over. Almost admitted, not wanted, the hollow hotel room hums and recedes. The dream, if it is really a dream and not unsleeping memory, comes back as documentary.

5

Like a curious dog, the camera comes hunting along the welted bank of a ditch. It is in no hurry. Moving close to the ground, it inspects close-to-the-ground details. It dwells on the slow, spinning surface of tea-colored water, it notes the dimpling tracks of skaters in the eddies, and the wakes that V down from rocks and clumps of half-drowned grass. It is not above spending a few seconds on a darning needle that sits on air for a moment and darts away a few feet to sit on other air. It wonders that a jimson weed is able to extract such rich dark foliage and such creamy trumpets of flowers from arid sand. It ruminates without comment on an old boot, curled and mummified, beside the path.

Now it arrives at a pole bridge, and above it a weir and the headworks of a branch ditch. The upper plank of the weir is raised, and water falls in a smooth curve over the lower one. The pool above is solid with watercress. Into the visual dream, stirred by some foot that the camera never discloses, and perceived by a nose for which there is no assignable body, rises the smell of mint.

The camera lifts its glance, and sees that all along the left is a cliff of cross-bedded sandstone, frozen dunes in whose base the wind has eroded caves. Men have improved them by building corrals around them, trapping for the use of stock shallow areas of shelter. Two corral-caves are open and empty. In a third, a mare stands hipshot above her sprawled sleeping colt. In a fourth, three calves lie chewing the cud. With the same unlocated nose that detected the mint, we know the smell of those caves: horse and cow dung both dry and fresh, the sun-dried reek of urine, dust, some residual odor of sage and juniper. The sun falls straight down; the band of shade in the caves is only eight or ten feet wide. Half buried in the pinkish sand is an Orange Crush bottle.

Poking along the cliff beyond the caves, the camera comes to a place where the face is vertical and stained with desert varnish. In this dark glazed surface primitive men have pecked the outlines of deer and bighorn sheep, which modern hands have reinforced with chalk. Below the chalked petroglyphs is a band of handprints in red ocher. A sun-steeped richness of life pervades these noon corrals, this quiet ditch, this billboard cliff. The fingers (though there are no fingers) feel how tepid-cool the water would be if one stooped to dip a hand in it.

The camera pans along the cliff, up it to its rounding rim, and with a gust as sudden as a wind that blows an umbrella inside out, we are looking high upward, away upward, to the rim of a level, lava-capped, spruce-spiked plateau. From a mile up, it looks down over this fertile desert. The interdependence is obvious without a caption. Up there is snow shed, summer range, a subalpine climate, recreation, coolness, relief. Up there is the source of this ditch that makes the desert live.

Withdrawing, the camera inspects the sod-roofed stable, two long haystacks, and the pole corrals that lie below the main ditch, with the branch ditch flowing past them. Beyond is an alfalfa field, intensely green. Out in the open valley, whitefaces are gleaning a stubble field, perhaps winter wheat, that ends at a barbed-wire fence. On the other side of the fence, a car tows a horizontal funnel of dust along a road, and beyond the road, another line of cliffs holds the valley in on the south. This is not rounded and domed and monolithic like the cliff on the north. It has been eroded into a line of gargoyles and hoodoos, all leaning southward.

The camera reasons that these are remnants of the outer shell of an enormous dome which wind and water have dissected to its salmon-pink heart, leaving the shell like a broken wall around the wilderness of stone inside. In there, the distance is hazed with transparent blue. It trembles with familiarity. Its cliffs and cameo buttes have been seen only moments ago. The mind gropes for identification, and finds it: The San Rafael Reef, leaning inward toward the waste of the San Rafael Swell. Robbers' Roost, Butch Cassidy's country. The camera surveys it with respect, withdraws to the safe ditch bank marked with the tracks of men and horses, and moves on until it is stopped by a fence made of slabs of ripple-marked sandstone set on end.

Path and ditch go through the fence; the pole gate is down. In the slabs to which gateposts have been bound by windings of baling wire (Mormon silk, says some amused folklorist at the dream's core) there are brown ribby shapes of fossil fish, some of them a foot long. Inside the gate is deep shade. We are looking into a half acre of big Fremont poplars that lean over a log ranch house and all but obscure the cliff behind. Through the grove, quicksilver bright, the ditch flows through grass that must be periodically flooded to keep it so green. Scattered and clustered through the grove are fifty or sixty people. They make a picture like a Renoir picnic or a Seurat promenade *sur l'herbe*, but different, special, simpler and homelier, quintessentially redledge Mormon.

The camera recognizes ranchers, farmers, dealers in alfalfa seed, coal miners from Helper or Sunnyside, beauticians from Price, schoolteachers from Castle Dale or Emery, rangers from the Manti-La Sal National Forest. Whoever they are, the women have been weathered by the same dry wind, and have bought their dresses from the same J. C. Penney store in Price, or from the ZCMI in Salt Lake at Conference time. Whatever trade the men practice, they all dress as cowboys, in boots, washed and ironed and faded Levi's, and shirts with yokes and snap buttons.

There are children of all ages, the boys small replicas of their fathers, the younger girls in white dresses with white stockings grass-stained at the knees. The yard has been raked and mown, but it is uneven, worn bare in spots, and already gathering a new drift of cottonwood fluff. Three old women sit in a swing lounge in the deepest shade. From a tree over by the cliff, an automobile tire has been hung on a lariat, and girl children are pushing each other in it. They swoop across the ditch, set feet against the cliff, and push out again, shrieking. Up the ditch, some boys throw a shepherd pup into the water. He crawls out dripping, yapping, and agog, and shakes himself on them. Yelling, they grab him and throw him in again. He loves it. He would happily drown, object of so much attention.

In this crowd the camera finds the city boy, Nola's young man, marked by his white corduroys and white buck shoes. The old women discuss him, girls eye him as they help set the long trestle tables near the house. He stands talking to Nola's father about cattle, and alfalfa, and grazing permits, and water rights. The camera understands that these subjects are not those on which he is prepared to be voluble, but he listens well, and he remembers enough from Saskatchewan and Montana to make an occasional sensible remark. When someone calls Nola's father away, the city boy falls into talk with her brother Buck. Their subject is bulldogging and roping and bronc riding, and here he does better, since he has an honest admiration for any athletic skill and is, moreover, much less wary than with the old man, who makes him nervous.

Soon the city boy and Buck go through the stone fence and on down to the stable. The old women watch them out of sight; the camera watches the old women. Then we pick up the two around the stable corner. Three others are there, sneaking cigarettes. The city boy offers Buck a Lucky and takes one himself. Buck winks and leans and pulls out of the manger a partly emptied fifth of unlabeled red-eye. It goes around until it comes to Bruce Mason, who declines, using his ulcer as an excuse. The others clearly do not understand about ulcers and look at him as if afraid he might be pious.

"I tell you, boy," Buck says, "you ain't gonna survive this struggle just on brute strength."

"Don't encourage him," another man says. "More he don't drink, more they is for us to. I dearly love a man that don't drink, myself."

The bottle goes around again. The next-to-last man, sensing shortage, takes it from his mouth, looks at it against the light, takes one more small sip—a tablespoonful—and regretfully passes it to Buck, who drains it and throws it over his shoulder without looking. It smashes against the log wall. "Who flang that?" a man asks. They laugh.

One of them leans around the corner to look. "About ready to start, up there, I guess."

"Maybe we better git back," Buck says, and steps on his cigarette. "Come on, boy, you're family."

He whacks Bruce on the shoulder and leaves his arm there as they walk together back to the sandstone fence and into the shade. The old women watch, noting the fraternal acceptance.

A sort of order is shaping out of the colored chaos under the poplars. Like particles in a kaleidoscope, people arrange themselves around a large genial man in white shirt and arm garters —the bishop—who pushes and pulls at the air, beckoning them in or moving them back. Women leave their work in the kitchen and at the tables and come over, untying apron strings and looking around for their children. The three men whom Bruce and Buck have left behind at the stable come up the slope and drape themselves warily on the sandstone fence at the very edge of things. Chatterers bore on into the growing quiet until they become aware and fall still. Women stoop and fiercely yank up their daughters' stockings and yank down their dresses. A loose aisle has formed, leading toward the kitchen door. The white-shirted bishop folds his arms and waits, smiling.

Heads turn like sunflowers, and the bride is at the kitchen door, in soft focus behind the screen. Her dress, greener than the grass, is unkind to her coloring, which is doubtful in any case because her brows are dark like Nola's and her hair, marcelled as rigid as tin, is newly blonded. Though she is weathered and not young, is really quite a homely woman with bony, too large features (that Southern Paiute inheritance?), the camera notes her resemblance to Nola. A stranger might think her Nola's mother. Her smile is tense.

She opens the screen and steps down onto the sandstone slab that serves as a doorstep. Coming after her, the groom lets the screen door slam, and winces at the noise, raising his narrow shoulders and grinning guiltily and drawing sympathetic laughter.

He is the only person there who wears a coat. He wears, in

fact, a suit, black and ironed stiff. His boots, new, are outlined under the narrow legs of his pants. Through the collar of his checked cowboy shirt he has run a necktie from behind, so that in the opening where there would normally be a knot there is only a band of patterned silk. The ends of the tie must hang down his back, under his coat, like pigtails. The sun has reddened without tanning him. His hair is sandy and plastered down. His upper lip is cracked, and he keeps touching it with the tip of his tongue.

The screen opens again and Nola and Buck, maid of honor and best man, step down behind the bride and groom. Buck's maroon silk shirt glows against the gray logs like an exotic flower. Nola in a dress of soft yellow looks cool, serene, removed from all the stress of this marrying. The camera suffers a pang of pride and love, just looking at her.

Without intending to, she makes the bride and groom look like yokels. Her eyes go out over the crowd until they find Bruce. Then she smiles a small private smile, throws it like a rosebud, and as he catches it he is enveloped in blue static. She should be the bride here. Is. Will be. There is only one marriage scheduled, but there will be two honeymoons.

Buck has observed that smile, and who caught it. He says something to his sister out of the corner of his mouth, and she gives him an admonitory nudge with her shoulder, not looking at him, still smiling her inward smile.

The bishop nods, and the four on the doorstep, not unanimously, start forward. The bride turns her ankle in the rough grass and makes an exasperated, self-conscious grimace. In the front row of watchers a girl of twelve or so stands up with a gasp and a sob. The bride's daughter, even more tense than the bride. Promptly the woman above her wraps the girl in against her skirts. Pale, trapped, brimming, the girl watches as if at a hanging.

Her mother stops before the bishop, adjusts her feet in the grass, squares her shoulders, looks around helplessly for some place to lay her bouquet, and with abrupt decision hands it back to Nola. The bridegroom, tonguing his cracked lip, leans forward slightly and peeks down the front of his trousers.

"Darrell's nervous," the bishop says. Laughter, quickly hushed.

Barely moving her lips, the bride says something, and the bishop nods. Aloud, he guesses comfortably that folks all seem to be here, they might as well get started.

A random puff of wind moves and dies in the high tops of the poplars. A watching woman bats cotton out of her face without taking her eyes off the drama before her. The camera strays past the principals, looks out from the shade across the glaring valley and sees the leaning reef of hoodoos and goblins, and away beyond, the Swell crawling with heat, the color of cliffs and canyons almost discharged in the steep light. The clouds in the visible arc of sky are rounded white above, flat below.

"Now, before we get down to the proceedings, let me remind you of what we were saying before," the bishop says. He speaks conversationally to the bride and groom, ignoring the spectators. "When you're married and settled down over there on the Minnie Maud, or for that matter if you should move anywhere else, whatever place you live in, become a real part of that place. Mmmmmm? Dig in and work and belong in it and do your share."

They stand before him like culprits, wearing the look of good Mormons hearkening to counsel. The camera, meantime, interprets Bruce Mason's feelings. He looks upon his girl's sister and her husband-to-be as hicks. He feels superior to them and to everyone there unless perhaps Nola's father and brother. The father strikes him as a tough old bird with a gimlet eye, the brother as a good egg, skilled, worldly, and reckless. The rest are yokels. Yet he may not smile at these country Mormons, because they are her people, and she is loyal to them.

All her life she has been the darling of this tribe. Her sister mothered her, half a dozen aunties anxiously spoiled her. She was the one who could sit down at the piano, even as a little girl, and play by ear any tune you wanted to name. She was the one who would pick up a guitar, or an accordion, or whatever was lying around, and by suppertime be playing the thing. She was the one who went off to the university in Salt Lake. He has seen the fond and yearning looks they give her. Because of her, they deserve his politeness if not his respect.

He has also caught the women watching him, and seen their

speculative eyes. How serious are those two? Is he good enough for her? Somebody said he isn't LDS. That's bad. But perhaps he could be brought to receive the Word? He seems in other ways like a well-spoken, pleasant young man.

An impostor, he knows that every single aspect of his background, if it were known, would be a black mark against him, and their solidarity makes him half envious. He feels how satisfying it would be to belong to some tribe or family, and though he feels superior to this one, he does not dismiss the notion of a not unfriendly alliance. Can he imagine being married here himself —in this grove, before this shirt-sleeved bishop? Would he bring his own family? His mother, yes, she could make contact with anybody. Chet would be at home with the boys back of the stable. But his father is unthinkable here. He belongs out in the Robbers' Roost, not in this green and pious oasis.

"This marriage isn't just yours, you see," the Bishop is saying. "I'm sure you both understand that. Other people have an interest in it, too. Mmmm? The community has an interest in it because you'll be part of it, and it has a right to expect you to live up to your obligations. The state has an interest in it because it'll have you registered, all your records will be there. And the Church has an interest in it because through it your marriage is sanctified."

Around the edge of the bridegroom's hair, like a scalping scar, runs a line of unsunburned white. This is probably the first time he has had his hat off, except to sleep and get his hair cut, in weeks. The barber has shaved his neck round. Down by the corrals a calf is bawling. The woman with her arms around the bride's daughter frowns in annoyance, willing the creature still.

"All right, then," the bishop says. "You understand all that. Now, Darrell, you take Audrey by the right hand. Audrey, you take Darrell. That's it. Now. By the authority in me vested as an Elder of the Church of Jesus Christ of Latter-day Saints, I declare you man and wife."

It comes too quickly. Everyone is confused, including the principals. They look uncertainly at the bishop, who has to motion Buck to step forward with the ring. The bishop takes it from him and hands it to Darrell, who fumbles and nearly drops it from his tonglike fingers, and then has trouble shoving it over Audrey's knuckle.

"Darrell *is* nervous," the bishop says with a wide smile.

A black cat with its tail in the air walks around the corner of the house and across the grass. Scare flares in the eyes of one of the watching women, and with her skirts she tries to shoo it back. But her move is too hesitant, inhibited by the occasion, and the cat comes on down the line, rubbing against legs, watched by all, until a little girl stoops quickly and lifts it. Its hind legs and tail hang down, an inert weight, against the white confirmation dress.

The bride's daughter weeps steadily, copiously, not quite silently. The woman holding her makes an exasperated face and hands down a wadded handkerchief. The girl takes it, weeps, wipes.

"You may now kiss each other," the bishop says.

Violently the bride flings herself against the bridegroom's chest. The contrast between her worn vulnerability and Nola's composure confirms for Bruce Mason how far she has outgrown her origins. All around, those origins are wet-eyed.

Sheepishly the husband wraps his new wife around. Suspended, with drowning eyes, the daughter stares. It is a very swampy occasion. For relief, Bruce looks toward Nola, holding the bridal bouquet on her arm, but her eyes are for her sister, not for him.

The crowd stands, embarrassed and fulfilled. Nobody dares to break the tableau. Then Audrey pulls her homely wet face away from Darrell's Tom Mix shirt and cries accusingly, "Well, why don't somebody *say* something, instead of standin' there watchin' me cry!"

Laughter is sympathetic and relieved, inertia is broken. The daughter comes running and desperately clings to her mother's leg. Nola, then Buck, then their father, kiss the bride. The women kiss embarrassed Darrell, the men pump his hand. Two women quietly retrieve their aprons from behind the swing and, tying strings as they go, head for the kitchen.

"Look this way, Audrey," a woman says, and raises a camera. People fall back out of the line of fire. A man says, "It's too dark in the shade here, Ede. You won't get nothing," and the camerawoman says, "No, it ain't, I've got this *thing*."

Near her a half-grown boy, serious as a dynamiter's assistant, holds aloft a tray of flash powder. People back off further, respectful of advanced technology, while the bride assembles herself, dabs, blinks, laughs, grabs Darrell on one side and her daughter on the other, and freezes as stiff as the girl from whose head the crack shot shoots glass balls in a Wild West show.

"Wait!" Darrell says. He tears off his coat and rips the necktie out of his collar and tosses them to someone in the crowd. Cheers.

"Smile, now," the camerawoman says. "Say 'prunes.'"

She peers, squints, is on the brink. Prunes. Click, but no flash. Uncertainly she looks up. "Didn't it go?"

Voices assure her that it didn't. She winds the film. The boy stares aggrievedly into his tray of flash powder. "Try it again."

Fixed smiles. Prunes. Click. Again no flash. "Why, what's the matter with the blame thing?" the camerawoman says.

Buck disconnects the flash boy, to the boy's disgust. "Try it over in the sun, where you don't need that contraption. Come on, Aud, get that lucerne-wrangler over here."

Bruce follows along, opening his camera. At the grove's edge the bride, with restrained violence, wipes her daughter's nose and hisses at her to stop her bawling. The three freeze again, then unfreeze while Buck waves his father into the picture.

"Where's Junior?" somebody asks.

"Hell," Buck says, "you won't get *him* in this." He looks down into the finder. "Hey, Aud, can't you laugh?"

"I'm *smiling*," Audrey says grimly.

Bruce, after a couple of frugal snapshots, saving his film for better things, comes up behind Nola and stabs her between the shoulder blades with his finger. She turns with a smile which his instinct tells him is too open. Those old women don't miss a thing. Yet he couldn't be happier. It thrills him to have her turn to him that way.

"I've got to go help with the food," she says a little breathlessly. "Save us places. Right at the end of the second table, there, by the ice-cream freezers."

"O.K. When do we start back?"

"They'd think it was funny if we didn't stay a while. They'll cut the cake right after we eat. Then I thought you and Buck and I might take a ride."

"All right. But don't forget we've both got to be back so we can get to work in the morning. Your aunties wouldn't want you driving late, without a chaperone."

They have drawn back against a tree, out of the crowd. Her eyes as she studies him are full of light, and promises, and secret understandings. "You devil. You've been down with Buck, sneaking drinks behind the stable. He came up smelling like a saloon."

"Not me. I copped a smoke, is all. I observe the Word of Wisdom."

"Yes, just the way the rest of·them do." As if the answers to important questions were written on him, she studies him. "How's it going? I saw you talking to Dad."

"We had a good talk about alfalfa and peaches and whiteface cattle and I told him about my childhood in Saskatchewan. He thinks I'm a reformed cowboy."

"Reformed! How do you think the wedding went?"

"Fine. It got a little juicy there for a minute."

"Poor Audrey. She's scared."

"Scared why?"

"She was really in love with Elmo. She'll never get over him. But she needs. somebody to help bring up the kids. It was no good when she was working in Price. That's a tough town."

"Darrell looks O.K."

"O.K. Not very exciting." Like a child with a secret she smiles at him. "Not like what I've got."

"You know something?"

"What?"

"You're a darling."

"Just you keep thinking so. Do *you* know something?"

"Probably."

"They like you. Buck thinks you're O.K. And Dad was leery about what I'd bring down, but he told me you're a very pleasant young fella."

"Isn't that kind of minimal? Didn't he find me exciting?"

They commune privately under their tree while the crowd mills and jabbers. Seriously she says, "How does it seem down here to you? Do you like it?"

"Like it? Sure, it's great."

"It's better than great. Would you like it if we could run the ranch sometime?"

"A reformed cowboy like me? Sure. Is there a chance?"

"I think Dad's about given up on Buck."

"What's the matter with Audrey and Darrell?"

"They've got all they can handle over on the Minnie Maud."

"I'm a heathen. Wouldn't that bother them?"

"Not for long. Anybody that's good enough for me is good enough for them."

"Ah," he says. "*Am* I good enough for you?"

Her light frown warns him: somebody heading their way. He looks, and it is one of the men who helped kill Buck's bottle. His Levi's have been shrunk to his skinny legs. He has ten inches of wrong-side lighter cloth turned up for a cuff around his boots.

"Well," Bruce says, "we'll have to see about that on the way back."

Her hand squeezes his arm, she turns and leaves him, moving with her incomparably physical, barefoot-woman's walk. The lean man arrives and props himself against the tree and breathes upon Bruce his most un-Mormon breath. His eye is on Darrell, growing more uninhibited now that the formalities are over and his coat and tie off. Audrey stands at his elbow, hooked to him like a gate to its post.

The lean man shakes his head. "Another good man gone wrong."

The camera wanders off among the million leaves of the grove, with only glitters of sun coming through them. Eventually it comes to rest on a length of railroad rail that hangs on a wire by the kitchen door. A hand bearing a tire iron comes into the picture and beats with vigor on the rail. Men stand up with alacrity, the old women rise from their swing, children come pouring from all directions. Bruce Mason reaches the end of the second table just in time to save the end place, and then the one to the right of it, from a twelve-year-old boy who, twice balked but hardly noticing what has balked him, promptly dives under the cloth and comes up on the other side next to the bride's daughter and two of her girl friends.

Women, Nola among them, make a procession from house to tables, bearing platters of fried chicken and corned elk, washbasins of potato salad, dishpans of hot biscuits, bowls of watermelon pickle, chokecherry jelly, pickled peaches and apricots. One stands by a milk can of lemonade, filling pitchers with a dipper. Close behind Bruce four ice-cream freezers, though covered with a yellow horse blanket, radiate cold.

Plates and platters go down the table, are emptied, are retrieved and carried back to the house for refilling. Eventually the procession slows. A woman sits down to eat, then another, only two or three anxious aunties standing ready for whatever need arises. Nola comes hurriedly to her seat, and Bruce stands up to tug her chair into place on the uneven ground. The bride's daughter watches, fascinated, this demonstration of big-city *politesse.*

On both sides of her, her girl friends are gnawing drumsticks and talking through them. One place down, the twelve-year-old is gobbling as if this might be his last chance for a square meal until the Fourth of July. For a minute the bride's daughter watches her friends with distaste and him with loathing. Unable to bear more, she leans around the girl next to her and says to him, "Eat with your fork!" Her eyes, seeking corroboration and approval, come around to Nola, who smiles, and Bruce, who winks. Conspiracy of good manners.

Now the feast is finished, the littered tables are abandoned. The freezers once filled with homemade peach ice-cream stand tilted and empty in their melting salt water, drawing flies. The drying shepherd pup is seeking out morsels under the tables. Audrey, with Darrell's hand guiding hers, has cut the cake, and girls have carefully wrapped their pieces with the intention of taking them home and sleeping on them.

There has been a lot of competitive pie-sampling: Elverna's apple, LaVon's peach, Aunt Vilate Chesnutt's coconut cream. Before the men and boys have quite finished with that, Audrey in a crowd of women and girls has thrown the bridal bouquet. But she has not given everybody a fair chance. She has grooved it like a three-and-nothing fast ball into Nola's hands.

Tearfully now she makes her way around family and friends, her bony face blurred with crying, and kisses each in turn, some several times, crying, "Oh, God love you, God love you!" She stands for a moment before Bruce, leans and kisses him quickly, says to him tensely, "I think it's great! You be good to her!" and goes on by. The crowd lines up before the rarely used front door, making an aisle from it to the sandstone fence, on the other side of which waits Darrell's pickup, the honeymoon vehicle. Buck, as best man, was supposed to guard it from pranksters, but instead has helped hang it with banners saying "Just married," and through the holes in its perforated solid-rubber rear tires he has helped string tin cans on baling wire. With his own hands he has tied a chunk of Limburger, imported from Salt Lake for the occasion and kept carefully hidden in the springhouse, to the exhaust manifold.

Now the run through showers of rice, the yelled good wishes, the pandemonium as the pickup jerks away with its wheels trailing tin cans. Men whoop, women scream, dogs bark, dust rises in clouds. Safely down past the stable, Darrell hops out and yanks the wires loose from the wheels and hops in again. Audrey is wadding the "Just married" banners in her hands. They start up, a wadded banner flies out, Darrell raises his clenched fist and pokes it at the sky. Their dust goes down the valley road toward some destination which Darrell has been too cagey to reveal even to his treacherous best man.

Dissolve. A moment of quiet. The dust settles.

It is not the newlyweds who drive down the valley and whose dust drifts southward across the reef. It is not early afternoon, but later, five or six o'clock. The light is growing flatter, the shadows are beginning to reach out from buttes and promontories. It is not a black pickup that the camera follows, but a gray Model A coupe with fender wells and a rear-bumper trunk, quite a snappy little heap. The two who ride in it, sitting close together in spite of the heat, are not sheepish or tearful, but young and glorified. The girl holds a bridal bouquet in her lap.

The dreaming eye follows their dust down to a junction, turns right with them up a long hill, passes the summit and swoops with them down the switchbacks on the other side. When the driver has to double-clutch and shift down on a steep turn, taking them smoothly around without so much as a minimum skid in the gravel, the girl hugging his arm hugs it tighter. "Good skinner," she says.

The camera loses them in a canyon and picks them up again as they top out at a great distance, buzzing along an elevated sagebrush plain above which rise the rounded shoulders of a higher plateau. Aspens are just leafing out on the high slopes, and in all the north-facing hollows there is snow. They drag their balloon of dust through little towns—Fremont, Loa, Bicknell—which seem to be inhabited exclusively by children on horseback who want to race. They round a corner under the colored cliffs of Thousand Lake Mountain, they pass through Torrey, they bore like a corkscrew into the rock along the Dirty Devil. On their left, the Capitol Reef rises. Its lower cliff is already in the shadow of the western wall; its domed white rim is still in light so brilliant that the eye squints against it.

The canyon widens and flattens. They are in a pocket of green among red cliffs. A dusty track turns off left. "Here," the girl says, and the driver swings the wheel. They bump down the ruts toward a grove of trees and stop against a ditch.

The leaves hang heavy, individual, heart-shaped, dark green, utterly still. The ditch runs clear knee-deep water. Across it, filling the bottomland to the foot of the cliff, are spaced peach trees, braced and propped against the weight of ripening fruit. Just between cottonwoods and orchard is an old house of squared logs, doorless, its inside crammed with hay, a broken wagonwheel leaning against the jamb, a clutch of binder twine on a nail above the wheel. There is a dense, unnamed familiarity: we have known this place before.

Into the stillness that sifts down on them like feathers, a canyon wren drops its notes, musical as water. The ditch chuckles and guggles to itself under its banks. Down the canyon from the high plateaus, feeling its way toward the desert, comes the first stir of evening breeze.

The dreamer yearns and strains against an overwhelming sensibility. He is as susceptible as poor homely Audrey. He leans to kiss the girl beside him, but there is an encumbrance, and looking down, he sees with a shock that he is holding something alive and crippled, a big fierce scared bird that struggles against his hold and pecks his hands. In the enclosed car he can't let it go, and yet it struggles so powerfully that he has great trouble hanging on to it. Indecision rises toward panic. What will he do with the thing? Open the window and throw it out? Wring its neck? Cram it down between brake and gearshift and put his foot on it?

The girl's eyes are on him, full of growing aversion, and he is ashamed.

His shame awakens him, but he resists being awakened. With his knees under his chin he burrows back and down, wanting to pick up the dream where it was broken, deal with this buzzard or whatever it is, take that look off Nola's face and get on with the consummation he knows is coming.

But though his half-conscious mind can remember it, his unconscious refuses to dream it. Some censor forbids this movie. Dream and girl repudiate him, or he them. He finds that he can't evoke her face, much less her body, shivering and damp and goose-pimpled from their dip in the ditch, crowding against him, growing warmer, stopping her shivering, on the bedroll under the broken shadow of the cottonwoods. She blurs and evades him until in the end he lies quiet and lets her go.

The room hangs in its small-hours stillness above the stillness of the street. He feels bleak and old, done with, excluded and a failure, and is angry with himself for feeling so. For the dream, now that he has come fully awake, he neither wants nor believes. It lies to him about himself and it lies about the episode it pretends to recall. Some inferiority or self-doubt has been warping the facts in order to prove something. There was no repudiation then, and no failure. However fumbling and green he was, he was not unsuccessful, nor was Nola unwilling. The end of that initiation was not disappointment but a great grateful tenderness. Still the censor bans the rerun.

The trouble with the censor is that it knows too much. It has another, and much longer, and presumably far more important life to remember and keep under control. It is wary about accepting the illusion of wholeheartedness that would have to accompany this uncensored dream. It knows that the girl and first love are both victims, and so is the boy who took them joyriding. They cluster at the edge of consciousness like crosses erected by the roadside at the place of a fatal accident.

6

"So what are you saying?" asked some interlocutor in some an-
teroom of sleep. "That it wasn't just a Dear John situation? That
you got really hurt?"

"No," Mason said. "That's not what I'm saying."

"She left a mark on you."

"A heart with an arrow through it."

"If she didn't mean anything, why couldn't you finish that
dream?"

"Embarrassment. I'm too old to be having erotic dreams. And
of course she did mean something. She meant a great deal, then."

"You keep saying you're a thing that lasts. You know what the
Red Queen said to Alice."

"What?"

" 'It's a poor sort of memory that only works backwards.' "

"What's that supposed to mean?"

It must mean something, or he would not have worked it into
this conversation. But he couldn't make sense of it, and let it go.
Finally his interlocutor—he perceived that it was both Holly and
the woman of the St. Georges terrace, and that she was smiling
at him with a certain fondness and with an air of sympathetic
and ironic knowledge—said, "You're like a nailhead that's been

painted over. You think you're all covered up, but I can still see you under there. She was the biggest thing in your life, and she threw you down."

"And I recovered. I'd have recovered faster if she hadn't chosen to unload me just when my family was being wiped out, too."

"But you worshiped her, didn't you? When she let you go to bed with her it was like a religious experience."

"Yes. All right. But let's not talk about a bloody nose as if it were a broken head. She wounded me where I was most vulnerable, in my vanity and my self-confidence. She preferred another lover. She was a grown woman with a body and I was a boy with brains. The body always says hurry, the brains may say wait. When I went away she found out that she hated being on the shelf like a purchase with a deposit on it. She had desires that wouldn't let her wait. I could have waited indefinitely, no matter what I said or thought."

"Could you? You just admitted she was like a religious experience. You think sex is holy, don't you?"

"Not the way I see it in the movies and in the lives of my junior colleagues."

"*Ought* to be holy, then."

"Sure, it ought to be. I'm that old-fashioned. Mystery, the profoundest agitation and self-sacrifice. Nothing to be cheapened or played with. Not just a jazzy incident on the pleasure circuit. Not the great god Orgasm."

"That's what you didn't like about Jack Bailey."

"Didn't like but couldn't help being fascinated by."

"Why didn't you ever marry?"

"Mainly because as soon as I got out of law school I took a job off in a country where the native women went veiled and stayed behind walls, and where there weren't any others. Even if I had been anywhere where I might have met a woman I wanted to marry, Saudi Arabia was no place to take a wife. By the time it all opened up after the war, I was petrified in my bachelor habits. Get it out of your head that Nola spoiled me for all future women. We had a brief affair."

"Was it so brief? All summer. You went to that wedding at the beginning of June and you didn't go away to school until September."

"But it was 1930," he reminded her or himself. "In Salt Lake City. You girls had this thing called a reputation to be careful of. Nola's apartment was always full of roommates and their dates. In those days there weren't any motels. In a hotel, in a town the size of Salt Lake, you were bound to run into someone you knew. You didn't take her home, the way they seem to now, and expect your parents to bring the two of you breakfast in bed. That left the automobile. You remember how it was."

"I wasn't prying after details. I only said it mattered to you."

"There's no reason you shouldn't know the details. Such as how many times I slept with her altogether. Six or seven? I wasn't much of a tempest in her teapot."

"If this is bothering you I'll stop."

But of course he couldn't let her stop, because he was inventing this conversation, he needed her questions so that he could answer them. Also, as his invention, she was properly sympathetic and friendly. She thought of him as a man who had modestly distinguished himself, and she knew this episode in his past that she thought intimate and touching. She wanted the Nola episode to demonstrate something about his sensitivity, or constancy, or character. She wanted to believe that a deep distress had humanized his soul, and also she wanted him to have been Nola's innocent victim. Even while he estimated her misconceptions with a good deal of irony, he wanted to keep her there, talking.

The sound of a car—police car? someone running from the police?—came fast up South Temple from the direction of the Union Pacific station. He heard the foot come off the throttle as the car swerved around the Brigham Young monument, and then come down hard again. The sound hummed away eastward, diminishing, gone.

He said, "If I tell you this sad story will you quit trying to invent it? Physically it never amounted to much. There just wasn't opportunity. We didn't want to be the kind of people who left used condoms in lovers' lanes."

She was not bothered by his bluntness. She said, "I thought she went to the doctor."

"I don't think she had herself fitted, if that's what you mean."

"Why did she go, then?"

"I doubt that she did."

"Why did she say she had to?"

"I don't know."

"What do you think?"

"What do I think? I think Forsberg had had her virtue, and she didn't dare tell me. I think she cooked up that doctor story so there'd be an explanation in case I noticed."

"She was lying to you from the beginning."

"That isn't fair. She was in love with me. She had this indiscretion in her past and couldn't tell me because she knew I couldn't take it."

There was a further question hanging in the dark between them, wherever they sat talking. *Did* he notice? *Was* it a virgin he lost his virginity to, down on that bedroll in the moon-flecked shadows of the cottonwoods beside the guggle of an irrigation ditch under the Capitol Reef?

Evidently she didn't feel that she should ask. The answer, in case she did, would be yes, he did notice, and no, she was not a virgin. *Some* doctor had done his job.

He turned on his side to woo sleep. His body ached with tiredness, he pressed into the mattress with a ton's weight. But in a moment this companion—interlocutor, old girl friend, lost possibility—came snuggling up, fitting herself to him, warm and comforting and female. It was unfortunate that she took that way of declaring herself, because her presence and her gesture told him something about himself, and moreover brought back that bedroll, that warm night, when after their second lovemaking Nola had crowded against him in exactly the same way, her breasts against his back, her breath warm and drowsy, her lips kissing the back of his neck, and on the verge of sleep murmured, "This is a nice formation."

He noted the terminology. He had noted it then, but chosen not to acknowledge what it suggested. Formation. A military term.

"You were going to tell me about it," Holly said.

"There's nothing really to tell. A piece of banal juvenilia. Summer love affair. Dates every night. Movies. Once in a while we'd go dancing at the Old Mill, that open-air place at the mouth of Mill Creek Canyon. Shirt-sleeve summer nights, big moons floating up over the Wasatch, lots of close-harmony singing. Lots of necking, seldom consummated. Standard erotic obsession."

"But you were working. You played tennis."

"Not much tennis. Joe and I entered two tournaments and didn't last three rounds in either one. Joe was disgusted. So was his father. I was so groggy for sleep I was worthless. If I hadn't been going to quit soon, I think he'd have fired me. I definitely wasn't the industrious young man he'd thought of taking into the business."

"But you *were* ambitious. You were going off to law school. When did you tell Nola about that?"

"Late. Very late. August. I made it sound as if the chance had just come up and it was such a great chance I couldn't refuse it."

"You weren't very honest with her, either."

"Each of us had something to tell the other that we were afraid the other couldn't accept. We were both right."

"But you both had to accept it."

"I don't know. I never admitted what was actually very clear. She never reconciled herself to my going away. It made a difference. She'd get black moods. It changed there, toward the end. A sort of desperation came into it. We did some unlikely things."

She waited, it seemed to him, in some hope that he would be explicit. He found that, though he had inked out that episode almost immediately, he hadn't obliterated it, and that he regretted it as much now as he had then. He felt like taking out his pen and scratching over and over it until it was nothing but a rectangle of solid black.

"You can't want to hear every shabby detail," he said.

"Only if you want to tell me."

"I don't."

"All right."

But he couldn't let her back off so meekly. Apparently he still needed her for antiphonal purposes. "We double-dated one weekend with Jack Bailey and his swamp angel. Bailey had the use of somebody's cabin at Brighton. We went along and shacked up with them."

"With that . . . !"

"Cunt-hunter, yes."

"Oh, Bruce."

"I know. I was supposed to spread my cloak over mud puddles, not drag her through them."

"Why would you take her? Why would she go? She despised Bailey."

He rolled onto his back and opened his eyes. The room was as dusty with shadows as his mind. "Desperation?" he said. "The feeling that every day brought calamity closer? We were obsessed with one another, we couldn't ever seem to be alone or free. So when Bailey came coiling down out of his cinnamon tree and whispered in my ear, I heard him as an opportunity. I had these visions of pines and stars and darkness, another round of Capitol Reef. So did Nola, I suppose. We thought we could ignore Bailey, or put up with him, and his girl as well, even though we both thought she was a disgusting chippie."

"Why would Bailey ask you? How did he know you were . . . you know, intimate."

"On matters like that Bailey was infallible. He thought when we disappeared from the prom we gave ourselves away. He was wrong about the circumstances but right in general."

"You put yourselves right in his hands."

"Yes."

"What happened, an orgy?"

"It would certainly have been called an orgy in 1930."

"All together?"

"Good God, you have got a lurid imagination. No. But not quite the Capitol Reef, either. There were two double beds in this one-room shack, with a blanket hung over a wire between them."

"It sounds so vulgar and grubby."

"It was all of that."

And when he came back from school the following June, starved for that girl, strung up like a fiddle string, denying the intimations of petulance and rejection he had been getting from her letters all through the spring, planning the surprise he had to propose—that she go with him to Reno, where his family had moved, and spend the summer at their cottage on Lake Tahoe; when he pulled up at her door after dark, dinnerless and bleary-eyed and hallucinating after eighteen hours on the road, expecting that the evening would be his and that the blackboard could be cleaned of everything and now at last the ordeal of absence was over; when she opened her door to him and he found that instead of spending the evening with him she had to sing with Jack Bailey out at the Old Mill, was already in evening dress with her smooth shoulders bare—for Bailey—and really couldn't, now how could she? Their act wasn't over until one—see him afterward, she'd have arranged it otherwise but he hadn't said he'd drive straight through, she hadn't expected him until tomorrow —why, right then his mind had gone back to that shack in Brighton and arrived at a conclusion like a calculator flashing its instant sum. It went back now, and the sum was the same that had sent him off to Reno, alone, before noon the next day. Zero.

7

He can hear them through the door and through the years—the laughter, exclamations, screams, rebel yells. Reluctantly he puts his thumb on the latch and steps in on their party.

The air is thick with cigarette smoke, but even smoke that thick can't obscure the musty odor of the place itself. It is a smell that rises from corners, lies like a gas along the Congoleum floor, sifts down from rafter angles where pack rats have left accumulations. Put your nose to the rough studs and you smell it. It is the smell, among other things, of mice in various forms and stages: living nests of shavings and chewed rags, with a core of pink newborn things as naked as worms; abandoned nests stained with tiny urinations and peppered with tiny turds; old carcasses, paper-dry, found where the poison left them, or flattened in traps. Each is a special staleness, together they compose the total odor of a species: birth, copulation, death. Into their pervasive blend, like pigments into a mixing base, are wrapped other shack odors; dust, oilcloth, kerosene, candle wax, the linseed-oil fabric of the window shades, even a wholesome memory of spruce gum from studs and rafters.

In this unbreathable atmosphere, made worse since they shut the door and windows against the night cold, and growing more

unbreathable with every butt they add to the overflowing sau-
cers on the floor, they are sitting cross-legged around a blanket
playing strip poker. They have been playing for some time, for
all are partly undressed. All are shoeless. Bailey has both socks,
Bruce only one; the girls are barefoot. Both boys are bare to the
waist. Nola still wears her skirt, but has lost her blouse. She manages to look modest in what he thinks he remembers was called a
teddy.

But Muriel. Well, Muriel has not been holding good cards. She
is a large, well-padded girl even in her clothes. Now she sits, a
creature out of a Turkish dream, in the puddle of her own flesh,
held in from deliquescence only by her arms, crossed over her
breasts, and by her straining panties.

Leaning against the proscenium arch, the stage manager who
has revived and is directing this period piece, he can read her
mind. Why not? She is playing the part as he directs her to. She
is conscious both of her charms and of the interest they arouse,
but she would like it a lot better if Nola wasn't sitting over there
with her back straight and her face expressionless and everything covered up.

Muriel doesn't like Nola, or think she is so good-looking. She is
willing to bet that when the time comes to peel, Nola will
chicken out. And she is annoyed at the way Bailey, dealing a
new hand and singing as he deals, raises his eyes to Nola at
every card and puts a burbling emphasis into the words of his
song.

> Though down in her heart I *knowwww*
> She's not slow *slowww*
> And *ohhh*.
> Those eyes!

What does he have to keep looking at *her* for? There's plenty
to look at here, for God's sake.

> Like the waters still
> She's *very deep,*
> She knows a heap
> I've found.

She's got that *meet-me-later look*
And oh, she knows her book
That little Quaker down
In Quakertown.

Deep my eye. She came up here to sleep with Bruce Mason. Where does she get off, trying to be demure? And where does Jack get off, watching her with that smirk on his face and his mustache twitching like a rat's whiskers?

Muriel has trouble picking up her cards without exposing herself. She has to lean over and scrape them up with her fingertips, not uncrossing her arms for a second. She sees Bruce's eye wandering her way, and shoots him a look like a butcher knife. Let him watch his own girl, if he's so hot to see something.

Something is tickling the side of her breast where it bulges out under her arm. She jerks away with an exclamation from Jack's stockinged foot. "Keep your old feet to yourself!" she says, and hugs herself tighter, the cards in her fingertips right in front of her nose. Her skin twitches as if the eyes on her were flies. She reminds Bruce of the kind of postcard for sale in places like Medicine Bow, Wyoming—an old cow stepping on her dragging udder, over the caption "You think *you* got troubles!"

Next to her Bruce is studying his cards, but his mind is readable, too. He is a chemical machine, and every gland in his body is pumping into his blood the stimulants that the species has evolved to ensure its perpetuation. But if a machine, how complicated a machine! Assuming that the others are as complicated as he, this powwow across a gray army blanket is as intricate as anything in the universe.

Muriel is hard to ignore. If he doesn't keep his eyes open, he might miss something spectacular. Also she has a large, loose mouth, and some folklore rumor floating in his head speaks of the sexual apparatus and appetite of women with large mouths. Though he knows this is probably as reliable as the folklore about Chinese women, still he is intensely curious. He wishes he were sitting across from her, rather than next door, so that he could see without appearing to look.

Standing by the door, qualmish with distaste, Mason tries to remind himself that this is Utah, 1930, long before *Playboy*, skin flicks, and the porno revolution made the female body as exciting as a meat market and sex as momentous as blowing your nose. This boy has never seen a naked woman, even Nola; their lovemaking has taken place in darkness or illusory moonlight, and in a blind fog of adoration. He never had a sister to surprise or spy on. Except for a few French postcards he has probably never seen a completely revealing photograph. And he is only a few years removed from the hilarious hormone-tormented shrimp who was tempted into copping feels in a Saltair crowd. But he has read books. The literary word that bulges in his mind is "pneumatic." To his eyes, casually slanted in quick glances, Muriel looks as pneumatic as a pile of graduated inner tubes. Like the Michelin ad. When she moves, she afflicts him with all the symptoms of detached retina.

That is one element of his complexity, that sexual excitement over a girl he is contemptuous of, that alertness to catch the most fleeting moment of revelation if Muriel should drop her arm. He is ashamed of his excitement even while it is as wild in his blood as an eel in a washbas'n, for on his left, within two feet of him, her knee touching his, sits Nola, also partly undressed and in full jeopardy. If they were alone, he would be worshipping her calm brow and her golden arms and the hair that falls in dark waves down her back. But as it is, his interest in her is postponed or suppressed, almost denied, and is certainly secondary to his interest in the gross provocations of Muriel. In fact, he is glad that Nola is neither as undressed nor as sensual as Muriel. He feels toward her a protective, fatherly-brotherly-husbandly concern.

At first, he was as enthusiastic as Bailey about this game, and he has cooperated with Bailey's outrageous cheating. The girls are pathetically easy to cheat. Neither knows the least thing about poker; they don't even know the value of their hands. Right under their noses he and Bailey have dealt off the bottom, drawn extra cards, and picked up cards they wanted from the discard pile. In the interest of mere plausibility it has been necessary to cheat themselves now and then, and lose a shoe or a shirt with roars of dismay.

But the closer Muriel comes to the naked truth, the more complex Bruce's response has become—all the more eager to get on with it, troubled at what is happening. Much as it arouses him to

think of them sitting under the one hanging bulb as naked as
newborn mice, and avid as he is to examine all of Muriel, it
makes him stern and gloomy to think of Nola undressing in front
of Bailey. Intimations of his own bad judgment and treachery
bother his mind.

Bailey has been working on Nola, not by being pleasant and.
trying to charm her, but by a steady, bright-eyed, knowing attention, ironic compliments, baitings, innuendos, dares. He makes
her pay attention by exaggerating precisely what she least likes
in him. Every word is suggestive, every smirk a dirty joke. But
he has been very John Gilbert about it: his mustache twitches
like an eyebrow. What his effect has been it is hard to say. When
he calls her Brown-Eyes, she gives him a smoky glance of contempt. When he sings to her one of his double-meaning snatches
of song ("Mine in May, his in June"), she ignores him. But this
afternoon, when they rode up to Solitude, and Bailey started rac-
ing her on the trail, she would not let herself be passed, and half
killed her rented horse beating him to the lake.

As she gathers her cards she ignores his Quakertown crooning,
and there is a smolder like resentment in the olive skin of the
cheek turned toward Bruce, and her eyes are veiled. She looks resentful, yet Bruce is uneasy. Outrageous as Bailey is, he gives off
sparks. Things happen around him. He is wild in something like
the way of Nola's brother Buck, whom she adores.

The truth is, it is Bailey, not Bruce, who has called the tune
throughout this excursion. Bailey brought that color into Nola's
cheekbones and that set to her jaw. She came to be private with
Bruce, but she has spent her whole time fending off Bailey's kidding or ignoring Bailey's off-color remarks. Now here she is in
danger of undressing in front of him—and it is she for whom the
strip poker was proposed, Bruce is sure. Bailey doesn't have to
go to all this trouble to get the clothes off Muriel.

Muriel twitches like a horse, and Bruce's eyes shift. Nothing
but the extruded side of her water-balloon breast and her instant
hostile glance. His own glance is opaque and indifferent as he
turns it to Nola.

By their rules, any item of clothing equals any other. Right
now, she would have to risk her skirt to win one of Bailey's
socks. What else has she got on? The teddy, a brassiere, perhaps

underpants. Or does the teddy take care of those? Three items, at most four. One loss will have her in trouble. Two, and she will be right where Bailey wants her.

Will she strip, if it comes to that? As it will?

The tip of her tongue is against her upper lip as she arranges her cards. Her eyes meet Bruce's, and she smiles lightly. She has the exhilarated, heightened look that she sometimes has while singing.

"Cards," Bailey says. He holds the deck in his left hand and with the thumb and forefinger of his right he riffles the edges. They are new cards, and the sound is peremptory. Like a self-conscious shark, he smiles. "How many, Muriel m'love m'love?"

Without moving her arms from their cross on her breast, Muriel sticks out three fingers, letting three unwanted cards dribble onto her thighs.

"Three," Bailey says. "For your sake, Sister Snow, let us pray they're good ones." Deadpan, he inserts the three cards into her extended fingers, and then with a sudden thrust is inside her fingers, under her hands. She shrieks and bends away. "Get *out* of there, you . . . !"

Bailey withdraws. "Oh boy," he says with utter unenthusiasm. "Hot dog."

Furiously Muriel stabs him with her eyes. She holds her cards against her collarbone and is dignified.

"Brother Mason," Bailey says.

"Give me three, Bishop Bailey, and give them your blessing."

"*Three?* Too bad, pal. It pains me to see you brought so low. Here's some extra-heavy ones."

He whacks the cards down on the blanket so hard that two of them jump face up. Before the others have settled back from their startlement at his violence, Bailey is as inert as the Buddha.

Confirming that the cards which fell face up will not help his hand, Bruce refuses them and demands two more. After an argument, Bailey passes him two, which turn out to be four. They don't help his pair of nines either.

"And now we come to Sister Gordon," Bailey says. "Sister Gordon is sitting there hiding something. What can Sister Gordon need to make her even happier?"

She gives him a level glance and slides one card onto the blanket.

Bailey clasps his brow in consternation. "One? Brown-Eyes, what are you doing to us? What have you got there? Two pair? Possible straight? Possible flush? Four of a kind? Oh, Brother Mason, hang on to your pants!"

Nola picks up the card he conspiratorially deals her, looks at it, and folds it into her hand.

"It suits her!" Bailey cries. "God, Mason, we're ruined. She's sitting there with a Farmer Brown and she's got designs on our most per-sonal and pri-vate garments." His black widow's peak moves down and then back, his eyes are bright and full of glee. He looks over at Muriel's quivering flesh with compassion. "Kiddo, what are you gonna do when she comes on with a straight flush? We'll be looking up your old address."

Muriel crosses her eyes and sticks out her tongue. Bailey reels, and then stiffens with resolve. "Unless the Great Bailey can catch."

"What difference does it make who I lose to?" Muriel says. "Anyway, who says I'm gonna lose?"

"Ah," Bailey says sadly. "She caught, too, Mason. We're surrounded. All right, boy, the old spirit. Better death than dishonor." He consults his hand. "The Great Bailey will take two."

With his eyes closed, he lays his cards down on the blanket without discarding any, and gropes until his hand finds the deck. How many cards he takes is not clear—three or four. Keeping these palmed, he picks up the original hand and fuses it with the new one. Immediately he begins to laugh silently, bending his forehead clear to the blanket. His fist holding the cards pounds the floor. In a single motion he comes out of his cross-legged squat. A certain number of cards hit the discard pile, but only Bruce sees them. The girls are watching Bailey leap for the two-by-four above him. His shadow heaves on the wall as he chins himself furiously—three, four, five, six, ten times. Dust shifts down, so that Nola leans away, protecting her hair. Bailey goes on chinning. His biceps bulge, his chest is luxuriant with black hair, spittle comes out of the corner of his mouth, he chortles as he chins.

Bruce watches, hating what he sees. Three times during the poker game Bailey has exploded into one of his spasms of energy and challenged him to an arm wrestle. Three times Bruce has waved him off. He tells himself that he can beat Bailey at practi-

cally anything, from tennis to pitching pennies, but that truth
abides in him sullenly and without satisfaction. As Bailey's legs
go up and down, as his swollen neck is hauled up to the brace
for the fourteenth, fifteenth, sixteenth time, the old clammy inferiority comes on. He could not match Bailey in chinning any
more than in arm wrestling. His chest is ribby and hairless, he
has little of Bailey's wadded muscle. The old cold self-knowledge
of the runt suggests to him that as a lover he may not match up
either. Muriel, he is sure, thinks so, and somewhere in the middle
of her self-contained quiet Nola may suspect it, too. Perhaps she
feels protective about him, as he feels about her. The thought
makes him die a little.

And this is another element of his complexity. He no more
wants to strip in front of Bailey and Muriel than he wants Nola
to. He wants no comparisons. Mason, his survivor, watching
from the doorway, shares his inadequacy and self-contempt.
They understand, as the strong and beautiful do not, that though
clothes may serve important functions of warmth, ornament, and
modesty, their principal function is that of disguise.

Bailey crashes down, blowing, and without comment sweeps
up his hand. He has a face like a Hawthorne Mephistopheles—
not a face, a *visage*, gleaming with wicked delight. In his whole
life it has never occurred to him to doubt himself for a second,
which means that both memory and thought are short-circuited.
Yet Bruce feels sullenly that confidence like Bailey's, however inferior morally and philosophically to his own self-doubt, is probably attractive, perhaps irresistible.

He wishes passionately that they were somewhere else—
anywhere else, even in her apartment with her featherbrained
roommates around, even parked on Wasatch Boulevard with the
cloud of his departure growing darker between them. Anywhere.

"And now, Brothers and Sisters," Bailey says, "everybody
should be getting ready to lay down." He raises a finger. Everything about his face is pointed—eyebrows, cheekbones, chin, the
sporty little mustache, ears, the light reflected in his eyes. Glee
grows in his face like flame in kindling.

"It isn't fair," Muriel says with her cards held against her chin.
"If you guys lose, you just lose a sock. I'd lose *everything*."

"You've already lost everything, baby." He pats her thigh, but
his eyes are on Nola, and he is saying to her silently: You too,

kid. Don't pretend around me. You lost it and liked losing it. "Everybody set?"

A knot has gathered under Bruce's breastbone. He has to break this up, but how? Bailey will never let them forget it if they back down. But if they don't back down, there goes Nola's skirt or brassiere. Bailey sits there with a straight, a flush, a full house. With all those cards, he has to have something good. For a second he wishes he had cheated as wildly as Bailey, and yet, as Muriel says, what difference would it make? He can't beat Baily without beating Nola, too. The only way she can get out of this is to beat Bailey herself, and she isn't going to do that with the two pair she probably holds.

Expose Bailey's cheating? He hasn't been the only one. Still, that may be the only way. Let it break up in accusations and denials. He lights a cigarette, takes a drag or two, and passes it to Nola. The fog around them is thick and blue.

Muriel is still grumbling. "I don't care! You get all the good hands. You'll beat me and say I should take everything off, and I'm not going to be the first."

Bailey can discern an injustice when one is called to his attention. "Two to one, I'll bet you. How's that?"

"Two socks against my pants!"

"Two socks *and* my pants?"

The look of a sly bargainer comes into her eye. "You'd still have your shorts, and I wouldn't have anything."

Bailey, after a moment of thought, smacks his knee. "All right! I'm ahead, like you say. I've got the biggest stack." Mirth convulses his face and is at once wiped away. "Here's what we'll do. This is the last hand. Everybody bets whatever he's got left. Brother Mason shoots his wad, Brown-Eyes risks her all, Muriel hangs her last rag on the line, the Great Bailey puts everything at hazard."

He says it to all of them but he is talking to Nola. Bruce can see her face settling into stubbornness, resentment, and determination. She thinks she has a chance. But why is *he* staying? What does he expect to do with his pair of nines?

Abruptly he throws down his cards. "Not me. I'm out."

Bailey is scandalized. The honor of the company. The code of the sportsman.

"No," Bruce says, shaking his head. "I fold."

He will not look at Nola. He looks at Muriel instead, and Muriel is as scandalized as Bailey. "Well, *all right!* If that's the way you . . ."

She makes a gesture of throwing in her hand, too, and Bruce's hope leaps up. But Bailey has grabbed her wrist. For a moment a pink nipple-eye goggles free and is clapped under again.

"Wait, wait," Bailey says. "You can't, Mason."

"Why can't I? Why should I stay with a pair of nines?"

"Because this is the last hand. If you back out now you're a welsher."

"You're darn right," Muriel says. "You get me practically naked and then you quit. I'm not undressing unless the rest of you do."

"Somebody won't," Bruce reminds her. "Somebody's going to win this pot. Guess who. He called it the last after he saw he had it cinched."

"Who says he has it cinched?" Muriel says. "I'm still playing, if the rest of you are."

"I'll tell you what," Bailey says. "I'll strip anyway, even if I win. Whoever wins has to strip, too."

"Then what's the use of playing the hand?" Bruce says.

To his dismay, Nola says in her husky whisper, "Come on. Are we playing?"

Bailey is galvanized. "Now you're talking! You're damn right we're playing. I'll bet you, by God. Everything against everything. Showdown. Brown-Eyes, I think you'd like to see me put up or shut up."

"Just once in your life." Nola says.

She gives Bruce an unreadable sidelong look. Anger glows in her temple. She twists to free the ends of her hair from under her, and pulls a sheaf of it forward over each shoulder. Perhaps that is what she is counting on, like Lady Godiva. She has more nerve than Bruce has. He feels desperate and put in the wrong, and it gives him a pang to see her there, proud, erect, stubborn, sure to lose.

"Let's see," he says, and leans against her to look at the cards she spreads slightly to show him. What he expected. Two pairs, kings and sevens.

"Mmm?"

He shrugs, carefully noncommittal, hoping that his lack of

enthusiasm will warn her. But his mind has seized on a fact: in the hand he just threw away there is a king.

"I don't know," he says, and picks up his cards again. "Maybe I ought to stay in."

Muriel squawls in outrage. "After you've looked at her hand? Oh, no sir, I'm not going to . . . !"

"Keep your shirt on," Bruce says, and looks at her and snickers. He throws down the cards, but now the king is in his palm. Again he leans against Nola to look. He takes the cards from her, dropping a kiss onto the point of her shoulder, and studies them and passes them back with a shrug. Bailey might still have her beaten, but at least now she has a chance. Leaning back and stretching, he manages to scuff under the blanket the five of clubs he has removed from her hand.

"Are you ready, finally?" Bailey says. "Christ sakes, Mason, she's already said she's in. She doesn't need your chicken advice. Are you betting us, Brown-Eyes?"

"I'm betting you."

"Yahoo!" Bailey says, and lifts his pious eyes. "This may be the greatest unveiling since they took the sheet off Brigham's statue and found the coconuts. What've you got you're so proud of?"

"What have *you* got?"

"I dealt. Here, we'll do it in order. Muriel, lay it down."

She lays it down, leaning far forward and endangering herself at several points. "Three eights?"

Bailey shakes his head sadly. "Too bad, kid. Nice try."

"You haven't won yet. What've you got?"

"Wait. First Miss Coverall."

"Two pairs," Nola says.

"Two *pairs*? Is that all?"

"I guess it's enough."

"Mason, Mason," Bailey says. "Why didn't you instruct this innocent Sister better? Your two pairs don't even beat Muriel's three eights."

Nola's eyes fly to Bruce's. The color in her temples spreads slowly into her cheeks. "Don't they?"

For some reason Bruce leaves her exposed. She has put down her cards, face up, but not spread, so that not everything shows clearly. He compresses his lips and shakes his head, trying to read in her wide eyes what she will do if she loses, as she thinks she has, and may yet. Or what she would do if she won, and Bailey started stripping off there, six feet away. But he can't read her. Her eyes tell him no more than an animal's would. They glisten, that is all.

Bailey is weaving back and forth like a cobra. "What a pity, *what* a pity! Oh, Sister Gordon, if you had only sought the right counsel. Because . . . I've . . . got . . . here . . . in . . . my hand . . ." He lays down the nine of hearts, then the ten, then the jack, then the queen. Their eyes are on the withheld last card. Bailey's eyes bug out, his mouth opens, he slams the card down with a yell. Deuce of hearts. "A flush," Bailey says.

Sweet, wonderful triumph has replaced the tension in Bruce's insides. He is in no hurry. He stays leaning back on his hands while Bailey stops his weaving and says, "Now, ladies and gentlemen! See it here! See it all! Spectacular, revealing, first time in the Western Hemisphere!" Beatifically he smiles. "Losers first."

Nola looks at Bruce, then at Muriel. Muriel looks at Nola. Muriel sets her mouth and stares with dislike at Bruce and hugs herself tighter. "Not me. Not in front of him. He backed out. He has to leave."

Disgust makes Bruce move more violently than he planned to. He jerks forward onto his knees and with his fingers spreads Muriel's hand, three honest eights. He spreads Bailey's dishonest but undeniable heart flush. Then he spreads Nola's full house, and his eyes find Bailey's and hold them. He says nothing.

Bailey leans and stares. "You stacked them!"

"The hell I did. She just misread her hand. Ha, ha, you old bugger, you walked right into it. Off with the duds, Bailey old boy. Off with the last rag, Muriel. We'll run it up on a pole as a signal of distress."

But Muriel, sitting angry among her inner tubes, spits out, "I'm not undressing in front of you!"

"You stacked them when you looked at her hand," Bailey says.

"Horsefeathers, Bailey. You lost. You called me chicken, what are you?"

Promptly Bailey tears off a sock, then the other. "Don't call *me* chicken!"

"Oh hell, who cares whether you peel or not?" Bruce says. "Come on, Nola, let's get some air."

He pulls her to her feet, suddenly shocked at seeing her in her underwear. She grabs up her blouse, then his shirt and sweater, and comes along. Barefooted, they go out into the mountain night, so clean and cold after the shack that he feels his first lungful as a sword swallower must feel the steel. The stars are blue-white and brilliant, the sky is narrowed by the dark spiked tops of firs. On the doorstep they struggle into their shirts. He hands her his sweater and she pulls it over her head. He kisses her as her head emerges.

"Wait."

Reaching back inside, he picks the flashlight off the bench by the door and slams the door shut. Following the path that leads out to the road, they walk behind the yellow puddle of light.

"Why did you put that king in my hand?" she says.

"Because he'd have beaten you if I hadn't."

"I thought two pairs was a good hand. I wanted to beat him so bad he'd crawl."

"You couldn't have beaten him. He was cheating."

"How do you know?"

"Because I saw him."

"Why didn't you call him?"

"Because I'd been helping him. The whole game was crooked."

She says nothing. Hunting smooth ground for their bare feet, he squirts the flashlight ahead. As they come out on the road the big old abandoned Silver Lake Hotel looms in the starlight, and beyond it, like a watermark on the sky, the dim granite of Mount Majestic. A meteor streaks down the sky and leaves a living blackness where it was consumed. He feels sad, old, guilty, and misunderstood.

"Why?" Nola says tightly. "Were you that anxious to see Muriel?"

"Why would I want to see her?" he says violently. "That cow. I don't know why. I ought to have my head examined. Bailey can get you doing things you'd never do. I wish we hadn't come up here."

"So do I."

"Would you have undressed, if he'd won?"

"I suppose I'd have thought I had to."

"Even though he was cheating."

"I didn't know that."

"No," he admits, and then, overwhelmed by guilt, "I was the one who knew that! Oh, I'm sorry, Nola! Why did I get us into this? I hate to take you back in there."

"I know."

They stop at the edge of the clearing to cling and kiss. Her hair is clean and slippery under his hands. All around the cirque the mountains stand high and dim. There are only a few lights, and no sounds. It is late. Mason, who has followed them here, feels how love, which was first a wonder and an awakening, has brought them already to a kind of desperation, a kind of pollution, a kind of woe. Innocence would have been their happiest choice. In the dark path he rocks her body against his and feels the hot stir of desire and knows that they have brought death into the world.

At last she says, "We'd better go back. I'm cold."

"Why don't we just get in the car and go home?"

"What would they do if we stranded them?"

"Probably just what they're doing now."

"How would they get back?"

"That's their problem."

"If we did that to them, they'd talk to get even."

"They'll probably talk anyway."

"Maybe only to me. Jack thinks it's smart to pretend he knows everything you do. He likes to get the goods on people. He wants everybody to be as dirty as he is. But he might not talk except to me."

"Damn Bailey."

"We should have known better."

"I should have, you mean. I know the bugger. I've known him from away back."

He is shivering, running his hand up and down her back, his nose in the fragrant part in her hair. "Can you imagine us making love in there while those two listen? With nothing but that curtain in between?"

She makes no response for a long time. The response she finally does make has a grudging, argumentative quality: "They'll be too busy to pay attention to us."

"Maybe." Overwhelmed again, he cries, "Ah, why isn't it like the Capitol Reef?"

"It will be again."

"But we've only got two weeks more!"

In his arms she goes quiet. It is the wrong thing to have said. For at least a minute he stands there crowding her against him, kissing her, moving his hands on her back and sides, trying to revive the passion that was there only seconds ago. But he seems to have put it out. Finally her husky whisper says, "Let's go. I'm cold."

In silence, following the slash of the light, they go back into the woods along the narrow path. Short of the cabin Nola stops. "Give me the flashlight."

He watches the disembodied blob of light float and waver down toward the privy. When it disappears, he relieves himself in the bushes. Under the firs it is very black, with only two or three brittle stars showing through the roof of trees. It is as still as it is dark. All Brighton has gone to bed except the two of them, who most want to. In his thin shirt he is shivering. His feet are icy, and sore from the rocks and twigs of the trail. He is glad when the light blooms again down in the blackness, and comes toward him darting left and right until it finds him and holds. When she arrives, he folds her once again into a shivering, miserable embrace. But she doesn't respond. In a moment she is leaning back with both palms against his chest.

"Bruce."

"What?"

"I hate to tell you. I've got the curse."

"Oh."

Stupidly he stands there. For just an instant he wonders if she is lying, if this is punishment. Then with a bitter, strange, husky little cry she lays her face against his chest. "Oh, damn, damn, damn!"

The father-brother-husband in him has already stepped forward, perhaps too promptly, to replace the lover. He is concerned and practical. "Well, did you . . . ? Are you prepared?" (And if you are, says some subliminal prompter, why did you let me bring you up here?)

"No, I'm not due. The altitude must have brought it on. Sometimes it does."

The little things one learns about women.

"Maybe we *should* go in."

"No. I can cobble something."

"But . . . in there? With them around? It's all name and no game!"

"If you don't want to," she says.

"I could take you home and come back tomorrow and get them."

"Oh" she cries huskily. "Can't you get it through your *head?* I don't want to leave you! I don't want you to leave *me!*"

Her violence awes him. He stands and has nothing to say. Then her whisper asks, "Could you go in and get my little overnight bag?"

"Sure."

"It's on the bed."

Concerned with what he may interrupting, he knocks several times. Then he pushes open the door. "Here I come, ready or not." He shoots the flashlight beam across the shack to the right-hand bed. The air in the shack is so bad that he turns his mouth inside out. "Gahhh! How do you stand it in here?"

"We were doing fine till you came along," Bailey's voice says. "You finally coming to bed?"

"I just came in to get something."

He gets it and turns back. The diffusion of the light, just before he turns it off, shows their noses, side by side. On second thought he revives the light, returns to the bed that he and Nola will share, kneels on its sagging mattress, and heaves the window above the bed wide open till it sticks.

"What the hell you doing?" Bailey says.

"Opening up. It smells like a fox farm in here."

"Then when you get through opening up what are you gonna do? I don't want to seem inquisitve, Mason, but are you gonna be in and out all night?"

"Don't mind me. Go right ahead with whatever you were doing."

"Sure. What are *you* doing, out in the cold and dark?"

"Looking at stars."

"Oh yeah?"

"Yeah."

"Well, for Chrissakes settle down. You could interrupt something important."

"I doubt that. We'll give you ten minutes and then we'll be in."

He finds the door, and closes it on their grumbles and murmurs.

Nola stands where he left her. She takes the bag and flashlight and says,

"Go a little way away. I'll whistle."

So he gropes along what he thinks is the path, stumbles into bushes, stubs his feet on rocks and roots, and at length stands staring into blackness that writhes with dim shapes as much in the eye of the beholder as beauty is supposed to be. At length her low whistle summons him.

"Bailey's going to give us a bad time when we go in," he says.

"Let Bailey look after himself and we'll look after ourselves."

"All right. I'd better give him a warning, though."

Again he knocks, and again he waits before he pushes the door open. He and Nola do not speak. With a slash of the light he shows her where the bed is, and after a second or two gives her another wink to make sure she has found it. The bed complains when she sits down on it, and his heart flinches. They won't be able to so much as roll over without those two assuming things.

Softly, feeling with distaste the grittiness of the floor under his bare feet, he finds his way across the cabin without the light and sits down beside Nola. She is already undressed, and she comes against him bare and loose when he touches her. From the other bed, a few feet away behind the blanket, Bailey says, "Pardon my curiosity, but it just occurred to me to wonder where you two were gonna sleep. Don't tell me you're gonna climb into the same bed."

"Shut up, Jack."

Snickers, murmurs. "I never would have believed it," Bailey says.

"Pipe down."

"So much a lady. So resentful of vulgar slurs."

"Shut up, you son of a bitch, or I'm coming over there with the ax. I'm not kidding."

A moment's silence. "Why, he's offended," Bailey says. "Chivalry is not dead." Murmurs. Snickers.

Nola lifts her knees and slips into the bed. "Once more," Bruce says furiously. "I'm warning you, Bailey. Once more." He waits. Nothing but rustlings and smothered laughter. He slides his pants down and off and gets in beside his true love. She turns to him and they meet, silently grappling. He feels the barrier she has built against him, and it only makes more excruciating his desire. Their springs do not talk, as those of Muriel and Bailey do. There are no murmurs and snickers from this side. He goes into her arms the way gophers used to go into his little Oneida jump traps back in Saskatchewan—head first, and were gone.

Kissing her, he finds that her face is wet. Her nails dig into his back. The other bed is silent. Some uncounted time later it awakens again to creakings and rustlings that soon steady into rhythmic squeaking. Bruce and Nola lie locked in their hard unrewarding grapple. His arms are dead and his side aches from the unrelenting rigidity of his position. He feels that this balking of desire is somehow his fault. He hopes that Nola is asleep, and so will not stir and risk wakening her. Listening to Bailey and Muriel make their carnal love, he is fascinated, and filled with disgust, and bitterly ashamed. And he is not at all sure that Nola is not listening, too, and somehow blaming him.

BAM!

Someone has shot through the shack with a shotgun. Bruce is sitting up with his feet over the edge, every hair on end and his heart, after one enormous bound, thudding in his chest. He is aware that Nola is up on her elbow behind him. A paralyzed silence has overtaken the rhythmic squeaking next door.

"Holy Christ!" says Bailey's voice out of the dark. "What was that?"

Bruce, glaring around in blackness, groping for the misplaced flashlight, feels how comprehension struggles by slow osmosis from capillary to capillary.

Mason, too, up on his elbow in the dim hotel room, struggles toward the same realization, or an equivalent one.

Someone down in the street has shot off a gun.

The window above them, jammed open without a prop, has let loose and dropped with a bang.

He eases back down. Bruce says to Bailey, "The window fell shut."

It is all fading, dimming, slowing down. His heart slows from its painful pounding. Off in the dark behind the curtain he hears the rustling begin again. Bailey snorts through his nose, laughing, making a sound as if he is talking with his face between breasts. His whisper is confidential, amorous, nuzzling. "Jesus, that's a new one. How'd you *like* that, kid? Coitus alarmus . . ."

Mason feels for the girl who was lying beside him, but she is gone.

IV

1

He awoke at seven with a headache and the feeling that there
was something he was supposed to do. It took a moment to
think: flowers for the funeral. Not an errand important enough
to wake a man up after only four or five hours of disturbed sleep.
But he was used to waking with jobs on his mind. Mornings had
always been his best time, his day-organizing time. His friends
used to be amused at his little black book, in which he jotted
down appointments, reminders, obligations, shopping lists,
which, as soon as each item was taken care of, he inked out so
blackly that they could not be read. He was a man, they said,
indifferent to where he had been, interested only in where he
was going. Thinking with some irony that they would have had
to change their description if they could have been in his head
for the last eighteen hours, he got out his book and set up the
morning.

Flowers
Settle with Philips at the Home
Funeral: be there 11:30
Call Joe

Not much. He wished there were more. Sight of the sweater and box beside his bed suggested to him that if he didn't have things to do, he could again be seduced into messing around in the past like a scavenger in a dump. For a man uninterested in where he had been, the broken newsreel his mind had played through the night was as disconcerting as a failed lie detector test. He got into the shower and washed all that away.

He was already in the hall, and closing the door on his way to breakfast, when the telephone rang. Surprised, suspicious, his responses leveled out to flat caution, he went back and answered it.

"Mr. Mason?"

"Yes."

"Can you hold for Mr. Richards?"

He held, wondering what Mr. Richards, and then he came on: Herbert Richards, one of the Assistant Secretaries of State. "Hello, Bruce?"

"Yes. Good morning. What's up?"

"I'm sorry to hunt you down on the road, especially since your secretary said you're on an unhappy errand."

"It's all right. A mercy, as they say. She was very old."

"Still. No fun."

"No. Were you calling to commiserate with me?"

"All right, Your Excellency. No, as a matter of fact. I'm calling to see if you'll help us out for a month or so."

"Help you out how?"

"Covering the OPEC meeting in Caracas."

"Don't tell me you haven't already got that covered. It comes up in two weeks."

"I know. Sure we've got it covered. How's your Spanish?"

"Terrible."

"Doesn't matter. There are plenty of people to look after the Venezuelans and Ecuadoreans. It's the Arabs we're worrying about, and we haven't got an Arabist who comes close to you. How about it?"

"June 14 is pretty close."

"I know," the earnest electronic voice said. "We were going to go with Henry Knoll. He isn't Bruce Mason, but he knows his way around. But Henry just came up with bleeding ulcers. He doesn't need an OPEC meeting. So we had a huddle last night and asked ourselves why not the best? You worked for Aramco for years, you've served in both Saudi Arabia and Iran, you know all the Middle Eastern countries, you're fluent in Arabic, you know Yamani and most of the others, you're not now officially in the Department, your magazine is influential. You won't be exactly invisible, but at least you'll have a front. And they'll talk to you. They trust you. You represent a friendly and informed constituency. Don't say no. You're the only one who can do this."

"I'd have to be briefed."

"And debriefed. We figure a month altogether."

Mason ran a calendar through his head, estimating. "I drove over here, wanting to see the desert again. That means I have to drive back. I couldn't get to California before tomorrow night, even if I left right after the funeral. Today's what? Wednesday? Say this afternoon and tomorrow to drive back, and Friday and Saturday to get the office squared away. The earliest I could fly to Washington would be Sunday, the earliest I could be in the office would be Monday morning."

"Monday morning is great."

"Well, all right, then. Do I come as a consultant, or do I get briefly hired as a Department employee, or what?"

"Can we leave that till you get here? We want to do it the best way for you."

"All right."

"You're already cleared as a consultant, anyway. Have you got TR vouchers?"

"I think so, yes."

"Good. Just come on, then. I'll look for you Monday morning. If you get in early on Sunday, call me at home. Come out and stay with us in Bethesda, if you'd rather."

"A hotel's easier on both you and me," Mason said. "I'll have my secretary try the Hay Adams. Otherwise the Shoreham. I'll see you Monday morning."

"Great. I'm absolutely delighted you'll do this."

"Did you really have any doubts?"

"No," Richards said, and laughed. "Bring your black book."

"I'm making an entry in it right now."

"Marvelous, marvelous. Till Monday, then."

"*Hasta luego.*"

"*Hasta la vista.* Goodbye. Thanks, Bruce."

"Goodbye. Thanks for thinking of me. This could be fun."

The Middle East pursued him. While he was breakfasting in the coffee shop he read in the *Tribune* that Adnan Khashoggi, who had been investing Saudi petrodollars in the United States for years, had yesterday opened an International Trade Center out on the flats beyond the Jordan. Mr. Khashoggi was not personally present for the ribbon cutting because he had been subpoenaed in the Lockheed bribery affair, and was staying out of the country. Nobody quoted in the *Tribune* seemed disturbed by this cloud on the Trade Center. In Utah, apparently, a petrodollar was a dollar.

It amused Mason to find Khashoggi active in Utah. He had known Khashoggi's father years ago, when he was court physician to Ibn Sa'ud, back in the time when Socal, the forerunner of Aramco, was hauling Saudi Arabia hand over hand into the twentieth century, and when Riyadh was a mud fort with neon quotations from the Koran around its walls. Now here was the son planting a piece of the Saudi-owned twenty-first century on the banks of the creek where Mason had caught suckers when he was thirteen or fourteen—a creek called the Jordan by zealots who compared themselves to the Children of Israel, and took it as a sign and a wonder that their promised land, like that to which Moses led his people, lay at the far edge of a biblical wilderness on the margin of a dead sea.

Wilderness no longer. The air outside was city air, the heat was city heat. The night's coolness was already shriveling upward along the faces of buildings, and the crowds hurrying to work sought, as Mason did, the shady side of the street.

The flower shop to which the doorman had directed him turned out to be run by a Nisei woman with mainly gold teeth. She was so prompt with suggestions, and so sympathetic to his needs, that within twenty minutes he was writing her out a check, and her son in a denim apron had begun to lay out the order on the table at the rear of the shop. The flowers, they promised, would be delivered within an hour.

Mason opened his black book and drew a rectangle around "Flowers" and inked in the rectangle until it was solid black.

Now item two. It had been on his mind as a mildly distasteful duty that he would have to go up and sort out his aunt's few shabby possessions, give to her friends, if any, what they could use, if anything, and dispose of the rest to the Goodwill or the Relief Society or the trash can. Philips, the director, had forestalled him by sending down to the funeral parlor his aunt's watch and wedding ring, along with Nola's conscientious box of returnables. But there were still his aunt's last bills, the closing out of the account. He borrowed the Nisei woman's telephone and made a call.

Philips, it turned out, had already taken steps. Mr. Mason had got the personal belongings, the watch and ring and such? Yes. And the box of his own belongings? Yes. The rest was so minimal that he had taken the liberty of giving it either to her friends or to the Goodwill.

Mason hung up feeling vaguely rebuffed, as if Philips had failed in cordiality. But he drew a rectangle around Aunt Margaret's problems and inked them out. Now there was only the funeral, nearly three hours away, and the calling of Joe, which he began evading as soon as he thought of it. He felt half irritable, nursing his shadowy headache. He wished he could dispose of these trivial details and get started back to San Francisco. He was already thinking ahead to Washington and Caracas, leaning into the routine preoccupations and challenges of his life. At the same time, he was thinking almost aggrievedly that Aunt Margaret was a true Mason. She left nothing, not even duties. No will to read, papers to sort, house to clear out and sell, lawyers to see. Where she went down there was not even an oil slick.

Unexpectedly given three free hours in any other city, he would have visited a museum or toured the monuments. Here the museums contained mainly pioneer relics, and he knew the monuments. Without much wanting to, he found himself driving around town in that state of mixed recognition and bewilderment that had possessed him in every unoccupied moment since he arrived.

The city was bigger than he liked, and its expanding edges were indifferent to his insistent recollection. The university had grown so much that the old Circle, once the heart of the place, looked lost and apologetic, a survival. His impulse to go in and see if Bill Bennion's office was still there withered. His suggestion to himself, that he find a telephone book and see if he could locate Bill himself, lasted only as long as it took him to recollect that if Bill were alive he would be past eighty, perhaps senile, surely forgetful, with no such memories as Mason had of the times when Bill had taken a can opener to his mind and let in the air of books and ideas. Many bright students had gone through Bennion's life, each occupying three or four years. He could hear Bill's ironic voice: "Jesus? Jesus of Nazareth? I do not call him to mind."

He drove on up toward the mountains and found that much of old Fort Douglas had become a golf course. The apricot orchard through which he had unreeled his tardy telephone wire was a fairway bordered by bungalows. The firing range where he had shot the nick out of Colonel Waterman's hat had vanished under lawn and sand traps. And up on Wasatch Boulevard where he and Nola had used to park, he got totally lost, and was swept into a freeway that took him clear to the mouth of Parley's Canyon before he could turn off.

Making his way back through Sugar House, he drove past the J. J. Mulder Nursery and found that someone (Joe?) had face-lifted its sagging vine-covered front and transformed it into a glass-and-redwood palace call the Tree Farm. Was this the place to try to renew contact with Joe? He hesitated, almost turned in, turned back out again. There would be all the interruptions of customers and phone calls. Joe might not even be there, might have retired. And anyway, Mason wanted to see no Tree Farm; he wanted to keep the Mulder Nursery as he remembered it.

Coming in on Seventh South along Liberty Park, he drove slowly, looking for the first house they had lived in in Salt Lake, the one with the bullet hole beside the door. He recognized nothing.

Down Ninth South to State. Now Automobile Row. Once he had haunted the State Street corner of the old ball park, waiting to chase down one of the balls that got hit over the fence in batting practice. Turned in at the wicket in the left-field wall, such a ball got you a free bleacher seat. Long gone—gone, he realized, well before he had left Salt Lake. Gone, too, naturally, the Night Owl, where at one or two of a Sunday morning after a date he and Joe used to stop for a pork tenderloin and a milk shake.

But when he turned up West Temple he could tell from the feel of his insides that this was where he had been headed all along. After two blocks he slowed to a crawl. Mid-block, on the west side, there should be a brick apartment house. There on the southeast corner, ground floor, after two months of hard trying, his mother had died in October 1931.

It wasn't there. What was there was a two-story, balconied motel, a square U with its opening to the street, cars angled in against the walks, its office showing a lighted neon sign: VACANCY.

Like his father's fleabag hotel, the place of her dying had been swept away and replaced, and in the process her very existence had been made dubious and unverifiable. Nothing here confirmed what he had carefully inked out but not forgotten.

Vanished or not, this was what he had been inexorably returning to—this misery, this wreck of everything. He had lost his brother, his savings, his safe place in the world, his girl. He had never had a father. He was losing his mother day by day as the codeine and then the morphine dehumanized her. Happiness, confidence, security, hope, were delusions. Pain was real, and shame was real. He withdrew into endurance, he avoided old friends, even Joe. He embraced dull sorrow.

Now none of that existed. In their Chamber of Commerce zeal for progress they had modernized him out of his profoundest life.

"Unless suffering is the direct and immediate object of life," Schopenhauer had once tried to teach him, "our existence must entirely fail of its aim." Did he believe that? He didn't know. Or rather, he did know, of course he knew. He didn't believe it for a moment. Nevertheless, he resented being cheated out of what he had finally made his way back to.

His father could not bear to go on living in the apartment where she died. Neither could he bear the doldrums and bad times that the Depression by then had brought on. An entrepreneurial frenzy moved him, he was uptown all day working on schemes. Within a couple of weeks of his wife's death, he and Schmeckebier had leased the old pool hall and were working all hours cleaning it up and painting. Expenditures brought on economies, and soon they had given up the apartment and moved into that cheap hotel uptown, sharing a single room. The fall tipped toward winter, the smoky blanket thickened over the city. Bruce walked around in a spiritual coma, unconscious.

Behind him a car blasted its angry horn. He took his foot off the brake and turned in against the curb. Turning, he looked into a face contorted with improbable fury. An arm in a loud sport shirt was shaken at him, a voice yelled something: *thellryuhdoin!* The car peeled past, roaring.

Salaam. Peace. The face, the disproportionate fury, might have been his father's.

Why hadn't he left at once? The Mulders would have taken him in. J.J. might even have found work for him, Depression or no Depression. Or he could have found pickup work at the university, reading for Bill Bennion or others. Or he might have gone back to Minneapolis and starved it out there until the new term opened.

But he stayed, sleeping in that shabby room where the other bed groaned with his father's cigar-soaked dreaming weight, and by day hanging around the pool hall.

The sun was like a burning glass on his arm, lying along the car door. The pavement writhed with heat waves, and his mind with ambiguous recollections. He tried to remember how he had finally broken away, and could not be sure. Did he make a brutal scene? Did he throw up to the old man, before they parted, everything he had ever held against him? Did he say, *You made her live half her life without friends, and never even realized, because she was loyal and wouldn't tell you, what you did to her. Me, too, you shamed me in front of my friends so that I can't face them, and can't live in this town. Chet, too, if you'd been any kind of father he wouldn't have got that start he could never recover from.* Did he say any of that? And did he go on and say, *Yes, and when she was dying, did you try to help her and make it easier? Or did you groan around about expenses till she felt she couldn't afford to be sick? You know what you did. You stayed away all day, day after day, hanging around the New Grand Hotel trying to make a quick buck and investing in gold mines that eventually broke you. And two days before she died you all of a sudden had to go to Los Angeles for a load of whiskey—nothing could wait. What you were doing was running out. You were leaving her to die alone, or with only me. And you*

*already had that henna-haired floosie. Mother told me. She said
she could smell her. Hard times! While your wife died by inches,
with only me to help, you were already being consoled by
that . . .*

Had he said any of those harsh things, or only rehearsed them
sullenly, wanting to say them? He had an image of his father's
face convulsed with rage like that driver who had just peeled by,
furious at six seconds' delay. But there was another image, too,
the hard face crumpling, going to pieces. Which was more intolerable?

The feelings of that miserable time came out of the gray past
and overwhelmed him.

2

Still in waders, with the string of ducks across his shoulder, he stood hesitating on the sidewalk in the cold November wind. His knees were stiff from being cramped up all day in the blind, and his feet were cold. Today, all day, he had been alive; now he was back ready to be dead again.

Lights were on up and down the street, and there was a rush of traffic and a hurrying of people past and around him, yet the town was not his town any more, the people passing were strangers, the sounds of evening carried no warmth or familiarity. He admitted acquaintance with none of it. He had shut himself off.

Then what was he doing here, in front of this pool hall, loaded down with nine dead ducks? What had possessed him in the first place to borrow gun and waders from his father, and go hunting? If he had wanted to breathe freely for a change, why hadn't he kept right on going? What was there here to draw him back? A hunter had to have a lodge to bring his meat to and people who would be glad of his skill. He had this pool hall and his father, Harry Mason, Prop.

He stepped out of a woman's path and leaned against the door. Downstairs, in addition to his father, he would find old

Max Schmeckebier, who ran a cheap blackjack game in the room under the sidewalk. He would find Giuseppe Sciutti, the Sicilian barber, closing his shop or tidying the rack of *Artists and Models* and *The Nudist* with which he lured trade. He would probably find Billy Hammond, the night clerk from the Windsor Hotel, having his sandwich and beer and pie, or moving alone around a pool table, abstractedly whistling, practicing shots. If the afternoon blackjack game had broken up, there would be Navy Edwards, dealer and bouncer for Schmeckebier. At this time of evening there would be a few counter customers and a cop collecting his tribute of a beer and the other tribute that Schmeckebier paid to keep the cardroom open.

And he would find, sour contrast with the bright sky and the wind of the tule marshes, the cavelike room with its back corners in darkness, would smell that smell compounded of steam heat and cue-chalk dust, of sodden butts in cuspidors, of coffee and meat and beer from the counter, of cigarette smoke so unaired that it darkened the walls. From anywhere back of the middle tables there would be the pervasive reek of toilet disinfectant. Behind the counter his father would be presiding, throwing the pool-hall light switch to save a few cents when the place was empty, flipping it on to give an air of brilliant and successful use when feet came down the stairs past Sciutti's shop.

The hunter moved his shoulder under the weight of the ducks, his mind full for the moment with the image of his father's face, darkly pale, fallen in on its bones, and the pouched, restless, suspicious eyes that seemed always looking for someone. Over that image came the face of his mother, dead and six weeks buried.

His teeth clicked together. In anger he turned, but the thought of going to the hotel room curdled as it was forming. And he had to eat. Broke as he was, a student kept from his studies, he had no choice but to eat on the old man. Besides, there were the ducks. He felt somehow that the hunt would have been incomplete unless he brought his game back for his father to see.

His knees unwilling in the stiff waders, he went down the steps, descending into the light shining through Joe Sciutti's door, and into the momentary layer of clean bay-rum smell, talcum smell, hair tonic smell, that rose past the still-revolving barber pole in the angle of the stairs.

Joe Sciutti was sweeping wads of hair from his tiled floor, and hunched over the counter beyond, their backs to the door, were Schmeckebier, Navy Edwards, Billy Hammond, and an unknown customer. His father was behind the counter, mopping alertly with a rag. The poolroom lights were up bright, but when he saw who was coming he flipped the switch and dropped the big room back into dusk.

As the hunter came to the end of the counter their heads turned. "Well I'm a son of a bee," Navy Edwards said, and scrambled off his stool. Next to him Billy Hammond half stood up, so that his pale yellow hair took a halo from the backbar lights. "Say!" Max Schmeckebier said. "Say, dot's goot, dot's pooty goot, Bwuce!"

But Bruce was watching his father so intently that he hardly heard them. He slid the string of ducks off his shoulder and swung them up onto the wide walnut bar. They landed solidly—offering or tribute or ransom or whatever they were. For a moment it was as if this little act were private between the two of them. He felt queerly moved, his stomach tightened in suspense or triumph. Then the old man's pouchy eyes slipped from his and the old man came quickly forward along the counter and laid hands on the ducks.

He handled them as if he were petting kittens, his big white hands stringing the heads one by one from the wire. "Two spoonbill," he said, more to himself than to the others crowding around. "Shovelducks. Don't seem to see many of those any more. And two, no three, hen mallards and one drake. Those make good eating."

Schmeckebier jutted his enormous lower lip. Knowing him for a stingy, crooked, suspicious little man, Bruce almost laughed at the air he could put on, the air of a man of probity about to make an honest judgment in a dispute between neighbors. "I take a budderball," he said thickly. "A liddle budderball, dot is vot eats goot."

An arm fell across Bruce's shoulders, and he turned his head to see the hand with red hairs rising from its pores, the wristband of a gray silk shirt with four pearl buttons. Navy Edwards' red face was close to his. "Come clean, now," Navy said. "You shot 'em all sittin', didn't you?"

"I just waited till they stuck their heads out of their holes and let them have it," Bruce said.

Navy walloped him on the back and convulsed himself laughing. Then his face grew serious and he bore down on Bruce's shoulder. "By God, you could've fooled me. If I'd been makin' book on what you'd bring in I'd've lost my shirt."

"Such a pretty shirt, too," Billy Hammond said.

Across the counter Harry Mason cradled a little drab duck in his hand. Its neck, stretched from the carrier, hung far down, but its body was neat and plump and its feet were waxy. Watching the sallow face of his father, Bruce thought it looked oddly soft.

"Ain't that a beauty, though?" the old man said. "There ain't a prettier duck made than a blue-wing teal. You can have all your wood ducks and redheads, all the flashy ones." He spread a wing until the hidden band of bright blue showed. "Pretty?" he said, and shook his head and laughed suddenly as if he had not expected to. When he laid the duck with the others his eyes were bright with sentimental moisture.

So now, Bruce thought, you're right in your element. You always did want to be back with the boys in the poolroom, pouring out to see the elk on somebody's running board, or leaning on the bar with a schooner of beer talking baseball or announcing the weight of the big German brown somebody brought in in a cake of ice. We haven't any elk or German browns right now, but we've got some nice ducks, a fine display along five feet of counter. And who brought them in? The student, the alien son. It must gravel you.

He drew himself a near beer. Several other men had come in and he saw three more stooping to look in the door beyond Sciutti's. Two tables had started up; his father was hustling, filling orders. After a few minutes Schmeckebier and Navy went into the cardroom with three men. The poolroom lights were up bright, there was an ivory click of balls, a rumble of talk. The smoke-filled air was full of movement.

Still more people arrived, kids in high school athletic sweaters and bums from the fringes of skid road. They all stopped to look at the ducks, and Bruce saw glances at his waders, heard questions and answers. Harry's boy. Some men spoke to him, deriving importance from the contact. A fellowship was promoted by the ducks strung out along the counter. Bruce felt it himself. He was so mellowed by the way they spoke to him that when the players at the first table thumped with their cues, he got off his stool to rack them up and collect their nickels. It occurred to him that he ought to go to the room and get into a bath, but he didn't want to leave yet. Instead he came back to the counter and slid the nickels toward his father and drew himself another near beer.

"Pretty good night tonight," he said. The old man nodded and slapped his rag on the counter, his eyes already past Bruce and fixed on two youths coming in.

Billy Hammond wandered by and stopped by Bruce for a moment. "Well, time for my nightly wrestle with temptation."

"I was just going to challenge you to a game of call shot."

"Maybe tomorrow," Billy said, and let himself carefully out as if afraid a noise might disturb someone—a mild, gentle, golden-haired boy who looked as if he ought to be in some prep school learning to say "sir" to grown-ups instead of clerking in a girlie hotel. He was the only one of the poolroom crowd that Bruce half liked. He thought he understood Billy Hammond, a little.

He turned back to the counter to hear his father saying to Schmeckebier, "I don't see how we could, on this rig. That's the hell of it, we need a regular oven."

"In my room in back," Schmeckebier said. "Dot old electric range."

"Does it work?"

"Sure. Vy not. I t'ink so."

"By God," Harry Mason said. "Nine ducks, that ought to give us a real old-fashioned feed." He mopped the counter, refilled a coffee cup, came back to the end and pinched the breast of a duck, pulled out a wing and looked at the band of blue hidden among the drab feathers. "Just like old times, for a change," he said, and his eyes touched Bruce's in a look that might be anything from a challenge to an apology.

Bruce had no inclination to ease the strain between them. He did not forgive his father the cowardly flight to Los Angeles only hours before his mother died. He did not discount the possibility that his father's profession might have had the effect of making Nola reconsider whom she wanted to marry. He neither forgot nor forgave the henna-haired woman who several times had

come to the pool hall late at night and waited on a bar stool
while the old man closed up. Yet when his father remarked that
the ducks ought to be drawn and plucked, he got to his feet.

"I could do ten while you were doing one," his father said.

Heat spread into Bruce's face. Carefully not looking at his father, he sat down again. "All right. You do them and I'll take
over the counter."

So here he was, in the pool hall he had passionately sworn he
would never do a minute's work in, dispensing Mrs. Morrison's
meat pies and tamales smothered in chili, clumping behind the
counter in the waders which all day had been the sign of his
temporary freedom. Leaning back between orders, watching the
Saturday-night activity of the place, he half understood why he
had gone hunting, and why it had seemed essential that he bring
his trophies back here.

That somewhat disconcerted understanding was still troubling
him when his father came back. The old man had put on a clean
apron and brushed his hair. His pouched eyes, brighter and less
houndlike than usual, darted along the bar, counting, and across
the bright tables, counting again. His eyes met Bruce's, and both
smiled. Both, Bruce thought, were a little astonished.

Later, propped in bed in the room, he put down the magazine
he had been reading and stared at the drawn blinds, the sleazy
drapes, and asked himself again why he was here. The excuse he
used to himself, that he was only waiting for the beginning of
the new term before returning to school, was only an excuse. He
knew that he stayed because he either couldn't get away or
wouldn't. He despised the pool hall, hated his father, was contemptuous of the people he lived among. He made no move to
be friendly with them, or hadn't until tonight, and yet he darted
around corners to avoid meeting people he really did care about,
people who had been his friends for years. Why?

He could not hold his mind to it. Within a minute he found
himself reading again, diving deep, and when he made himself
quit that, forced himself to look steadily at his father's bed, his
father's shoes on the floor, his father's soiled shirts hanging in the
open closet, he told himself that all the home he had any more
was this shabby room. He couldn't pretend that by staying he
was holding together the fragments of home and family. He

couldn't fool himself that he had any function in his father's life, or his father in his. He ought to look for a job so that he could at least keep his self-respect until February.

But the very thought of the effort it would take made him sleepy, and he knew what that was, too. Sleep was another evasion, like the torpor and monotony of his life. But he let drowsiness drift over him. Drowsily he pictured his father behind the counter tonight, vigorous and jovial, Mine Host, and he saw that the usual fretful petulance was not in his face.

He pulled off the light and dropped the magazine on the floor. Then he heard the rain, the swish and hiss of traffic in the wet street. He felt sad and alone, and he despised the coldness of his isolation. Nola crept into his mind and he drove her out as he would drive marauding chickens from a vegetable garden. Even brooding about his father was better than that. He thought of the failing body that only months ago had seemed tireless and bull-strong, of the face before it had sagged and grown dewlaps of flesh on the square jaws. He thought of the many failures, the self-deceptions, the schemes that never paid off, the jobs that never worked out, the hopeful starts that had always ended in excuses or flight. He thought of the eyes that had once filled him with fear, but that now could never quite meet, never quite hold, the eyes of his cold son.

Thinking of all this, and remembering when they were a family and when his mother was alive to hold them together, he felt pity, and he cried.

His father's entrance awakened him. He heard the fumbling at the door, the creak, the quiet click, the footsteps that slid and groped in darkness, the body that bumped into something and halted, getting its bearings. He heard the deep sighing of the other bed as his father sat down on it, his father's sighing breath as he bent to untie his shoes. Feigning sleep, he lay unmoving, breathing deeply and steadily, but an anguish of fury had leaped up in him, for he smelled the smells his father brought with him: wet wool, stale cigar smoke, liquor, and above all, more penetrating than any, spreading through the room and polluting everything there, the echo of cheap musky perfume.

The control Bruce imposed on his body was an ecstasy. He raged at himself for the weak sympathy to which he had yielded earlier. One good night, he said to himself now, glaring upward. One lively Saturday night at the joint and he can't contain himself, he has to go top off the evening with his lady friend. How? A drink in some illegal after-hours bar in Plum Alley? A drink in her room? Maybe just a trip to bed, blunt and immediate?

His jaws ached from the tight clamping of his teeth, but his orderly breathing went in and out, in and out, while the old man sighed into bed and creaked a little and lay still. The taint of perfume was even stronger. That was what his mother meant, that she could smell her. The sow must slop it on by the cupful. And so cuddly. Such a sugar baby. How's my old sweetie tonight? It's been too long since you came to see your baby. I should be real mad at you. The cheek against the lapel, the unreal hair against the collar, one foot coyly lifted, the perfume like poison gas tainting the clothes it touched.

The picture of his mother's bureau drawers stood in his mind, the careless simple collection of handkerchiefs and gloves and lace collars and cuffs neat among dusty blue sachet packets that gave off a faint fragrance. They were all the scent she had ever used.

My God, he said, how can he stand himself?

After a while his father began to breathe heavily, then to snore. In the little prison of the room his breathing was obscene —loose and bubbling, undisciplined, animal. After quite a time he woke himself with a snort, murmured, and rolled over. With an effort Bruce relaxed his hands, arms, shoulders, head, feet. He let himself sink. He tried to concentrate on his breathing, but his father rolled over on his back again and once more the snoring burst out and died and whiffled and sawed and snorted.

By now, he had resolution in him, or around him, rigid as iron. Tomorrow, for sure, for good, he would break out of this catalepsy. He would go and see Joe. Joe would lend him enough to get him to Minneapolis. Not another day in this hateful city. Not another night in this room.

He yawned, surprising himself. It must be late, two o'clock at least. He ought to get to sleep. But he lay uneasily, his mind tainted with hatred as the air was tainted with perfume. He tried cunningly to elude his mind and go to sleep before it could notice, but no matter how he composed himself for blackness and shut his eyes and breathed regularly, that awareness inside was

out again in a half minute, lively as a weasel, and he was helplessly hunted again from hiding place to hiding place.

Eventually he fell back upon an old device.

He went into a big dark room in his mind, a room shadowy
with half-seen tables. He groped and found a string above him
and pulled, and light fell suddenly in a bright cone from the
darker cone of the shade. Below the light lay an expanse of dark
green cloth, and this was the only lighted thing in all that darkness. Carefully he gathered bright balls into a wooden triangle,
pushing them forward until the apex lay over a round spot on
the cloth. Quietly and thoroughly he chalked a cue; the inlaid
handle and smooth taper of the shaft were very real to his eyes
and hands. He lined up the cue ball, aimed, drew the cue back
and forth over the bridge of his left hand. He saw the balls run
from the spinning shock of the break, and carom, and come to
rest, and he hunted up the yellow One ball and got a shot at it
between two others. He had to cut it very fine, but he saw the
shot go true, the One angle off cleanly into the side pocket. He
saw the cue ball rebound and kiss and stop, and he shot the Two
in a straight shot for the left corner pocket, putting drawers on
the cue ball to get shape for the Three.

Yellow and blue and red, spotted and striped, he shot pool
balls into pockets as deep and black and silent as the cellars of
his consciousness. He was not now quarry that his mind chased,
but an actor, a doer, a willer, a man in command. By an act of
will or of flight he focused his whole awareness on the game he
played. His mind undertook it with intense concentration. He
took pride in little two-cushion banks, little triumphs of accu-
racy, small successes of foresight. When he had finished one
game and the green cloth was bare, he dug the balls from the
bin under the end of the table and racked them up and began
another.

Eventually, he knew, nothing would remain in his mind but
the clean green cloth traced with running color and bounded by
simple problems, and sometime in the middle of an intricately
planned combination shot he would pale off into sleep.

At noon, after the rain, the sun seemed very bright. It poured
down from a clearing sky, glittered on wet roofs, gleamed in

reflection from pavements and sidewalks. On the peaks east of the city there was a purity of snow.

Coming down the hill Bruce noticed the excessive brightness and could not tell whether it was really as it seemed, or whether his plunge out of the dark isolated hole of his life had restored a lost capacity to see. A slavery or a paralysis was ended. He had been for three hours in the company of the best friend whom for weeks he had been avoiding. He had been eyed with concern, he had been warmed by solicitude and generosity. In his pocket he had fifty dollars, enough to get him to Minneapolis, where he could renew the one unterminated possibility of his life. It seemed to him incredible that he had buried himself in dismal hotel and dreary poolroom for so long. He could not understand why he had not, long before this, moved his legs in the direction of Thirteenth East. He perceived that he had been sullen and morbid, and it occurred to him that even Schmeckebier and Edwards and the rest might have found him a difficult companion.

His father, too. The fury of the night before had gone, though he knew that he would not again bend toward sympathy. He would never think of his father without smelling that perfume. Let him have it. If that was what he wanted—after what he had had!—let him have it. They could part without an open quarrel, but without affection. They would part right now, within an hour.

From the alley where he parked, two grimy stairways led down into the cellars. One went to the furnace room, the other to the pool hall. The iron railings were blockaded with ash cans. Descent into Avernus. He went down the left-hand stair.

The door was locked. He knocked, and after some time knocked again. Finally someone pulled on the door from inside. It stuck, and was yanked irritably inward. His father stood there in shirt sleeves, a cigar in his mouth.

"Oh," he said. "I was wondering what had become of you."

The basement air was foul and heavy, dense with the reek from the toilet. Bruce saw as he stepped inside that at the front end only the night light behind the bar was on, but that light was coming from Schmeckebier's door at this end, too, the two weak illuminations diffusing in the shadowy room, leaving the middle in almost absolute darkness. It was the appropriate time, the proper place. The stink of the prison was persuasively concentrated. He drew his lungs full with a kind of passion, and said, "I just came down to . . ."

"Who is dot?" Schmeckebier called out. He came to his door, wrapped to the armpits in a bar apron, with a spoon in his hand, and he bent, peering out into the gloom like a disturbed dwarf from an underhill cave. "Harry? Who? Oh, Bwuce. Shust in time, shust in time. It is not long now." His lower lip waggled, and he sucked it up.

"What's not long?" Bruce said.

"Vot?" Schmeckebier said, and thrust out his big head. "You forgot about it?"

"I must have. What?"

"The duck feed," his father said impatiently.

They stood staring at one another in the dusk. The right moment was gone. With a twitch of the shoulder Bruce let it go. He would wait a while, pick his time. Schmeckebier went back inside, and as he walked past the door Bruce saw through the doorway the lumpy bed, the big chair with a blanket spread over it, the rolltop desk littered with pots and pans, the green and white enamel of the range. The rich smell of roasting came out and mingled oddly with the chemical stink of toilet disinfectant.

"Are we going to eat in there?"

His father snorted. "How could we eat in there? Old Maxie lived in the ghetto too damn long. My God, I never saw such a boar's nest."

"Vot's duh matter? Vot's duh matter?" Schmeckebier said. With his lip jutting, he stooped to look into the oven, and Harry Mason went shaking his head up between the tables to the counter. Bruce, following him, saw the three places set up on the bar, the three glasses of tomato juice, the platter of olives and celery. His father reached with a shaker and shook a little salt into each glass of tomato juice.

"All the fixings. Soon as Max gets those birds out of the oven we can take her on."

Now it would be easy to say, "As soon as we eat I'll be shoving off." He opened his mouth to say it, but was interrupted again, this time by a light tapping on the glass door beyond Sciutti's shop. He swung around and saw duskily beyond the glass the smooth blond hair, the even smile.

"It's Billy," he said. "Shall I let him in?"

"Sure," his father said. "Tell him to come in and have a duck with us."

But Billy Hammond shook his head, was shaking his head as he came through the door. "No, thanks, I just ate. I'm full of chow mein. This is a family dinner, anyway. You go on ahead."

"Got plenty," Harry Mason said, and made a motion to set up another plate.

"Who is dot?" Schmeckebier bawled from the back. "Who come in? Is dot Billy Hammond? Set him up a blate."

"By God, his nose sticks as far into things as his lip," Harry Mason said. Still holding the plate, he roared back, "Catch up with the parade, for Christ sake, or else tend to your cooking." Chuckling, he worked his eyebrows at Bruce and Billy.

Schmeckebier had disappeared, but now his squat figure blotted the doorway again. "Vot? Vot you say?"

"Vot?" Mason said. "Vot? Vot? Vot? Vot does it matter vot I said? Get the hell back to your kitchen."

He was in a high humor. The effect of last night must still be with him. He was still playing Mine Jovial Host. He looked at the two of them and laughed so naturally that Bruce almost joined him. "I think old Maxie's head is full of duck dressing," he said, leaning on the counter. "I ever tell you about the time we came back from Reno together? We stopped off in the desert to look at a mine, and got lost on a little dirt road, so we had to camp. I was trying to figure out where we were, and started looking for stars, but it was clouded over, hard to locate anything. So I ask old Maxie if he can see the Big Dipper anywhere. He thinks about that for maybe ten minutes with his lip stuck out and then he says, 'I t'ink it's in duh vater bucket.'"

He did the grating gutturals of Schmeckebier's speech so accurately that Bruce smiled in spite of himself. The old man made another motion with the plate toward Billy Hammond. "Better sit down and have one with us."

"Thanks," Billy said. His eyes had the ingenuous liquid softness of a young girl's. "Thanks, I really did just eat. You go on, I'll shoot a little pool if it's all right."

Now came Schmeckebier with a big platter held in both hands. He bore it smoking through the gloom of the pool hall and up the steps to the counter, and Harry Mason took it from

him there and with a flourish speared one after another three
tight-skinned brown ducks and slid them onto the plates set side
by side for the feast. The one frugal light from the backbar
shone on them as they sat down. Bruce looked over his shoulder
to see Billy Hammond pull the cord and flood a table with a
sharp-edged cone of brilliance. Deliberately, already absorbed,
he chalked a cue. His lips pursed, and he whistled, and whistling, bent to take aim.

Lined up in a row, they were not placed for conversation, but
Harry Mason kept attempting it, leaning forward over his plate
to speak to Schmeckebier or Bruce. He filled his mouth with
duck and dressing and chewed, shaking his head with pleasure,
and snapped off a bite of celery with a crack like a breaking
stick. When his mouth was clear he said to Schmeckebier, "Ah,
das schmeckt gut, hey, Maxie?"

"Ja," Schmeckebier said, and sucked grease off his lip, and
only then turned in surprise. "Say, you speak German?"

"Sure I speak German," Mason said. "I worked three weeks
once with an old squarehead brickmason that taught me the
whole language. He taught me about *sehr gut* and *nicht wahr*
and *besser I bleiben right hier,* and he always had his *Frau* make
me up a lunch full of *kalter Aufschnitt* and *gemixte Pickeln.* I
know all about German."

Schmeckebier stared, grunted, and went back to his eating. He
had already stripped the meat from the bones and was gnawing
on the carcass.

"Anyway," Mason said, "es schmecht goddamn good." He got
up and went around the counter and drew a mug of coffee from
the urn. "Bruce?"

"Please."

His father drew another. "Max?"

Schmeckebier shook his head, his mouth too full for talk. For a
second or two, after he had set out two little jugs of cream,
Mason stood watching Billy Hammond as he moved quietly
around the one lighted table, whistling. "Look at that sucker. I
bet he doesn't even know where he is."

By the time he got back around to his stool, he had returned
to German. "*Schmeckebier,*" he said. "What's that mean?"

"Uh?"

"What's your name mean? Tastes beer? Likes beer?"

Schmeckebier rolled his shoulders and shook his head. The sounds he made eating were like sounds from a sty. Bruce was half sickened, sitting next to him. He wished the old man would let the conversation drop, but apparently a feast called for chatter.

"That's a hell of a name, you know it?" he said, and already he was up and around the end of the counter again. "You couldn't get into any church with a handle like that." His eyes fastened on the big drooping greasy lip, and he grinned. "Schmeckeduck, that ought to be your name. 'What's German for duck? Vogel? Old Maxie Schmeckevogel. How about number two?"

Schmeckebier shoved his plate forward, and Mason forked out a duck from the steam table. He waited with his eyebrows lifted, and then forked out another. Bruce did not take a second.

"You better have another," his father said, "You don't get grub like this every day."

"One's my limit."

Mason came back around. For a while they worked on their plates. Back of him Bruce heard the clack of balls hitting, and a moment later the rumble as one rolled down the chute from a pocket. The thin abstracted whistling of Billy Hammond broke off, became words.

Annie doesn't live here any more.
You must be the one she waited for.
She said I would know you by the blue in your eye . . .

"Talk about one being your limit," his father said. "When we lived in Dakota we used to put on some feeds that were feeds. You remember anything about Dakota at all?"

"No."

He was irritated at being dragged into his father's reminiscences. He did not want to hear how many ducks the town hog could eat at a sitting.

"We'd go out, a whole bunch of us," his father said. "The sloughs and the river were black with ducks in those days. We'd come back with a buggyful, and the women folks'd really put us on a feed. Fifteen, twenty, thirty people. Take a hundred ducks to fill 'em up."

He was silent for a moment, staring across the counter, thoughtfully chewing. Bruce noticed that he had tacked two wings of a teal up on the frame of the backbar mirror—small, strong bows with a band of bright blue half hidden in them. The old man's eyes slanted sideward and caught Bruce looking at the wings.

"Doesn't seem as if we'd had a duck feed since we left there," he said. His forehead wrinkled, he rubbed the back of his neck. Meeting Bruce's eyes in the backbar mirror, he spoke to the mirror, ignoring the gobbling image of Schmeckebier between his own reflection and Bruce's.

"You remember that set of china your mother used to have? The one she painted herself? Just the plain white china with one design on each plate?"

Bruce sat stiffly, outraged that his mother should even be mentioned in this murky hole—and after last night. Gabble, gabble, gabble, he said to himself. If you can't think of anything else to gabble about, gabble about her. Drag her through the poolroom, too. Aloud he said, "No, I guess I don't."

"Blue-wing teal," his father said, and nodded at the wings tacked to the mirror frame. "Just the wings, like that. Awful pretty. She thought a teal was about the prettiest little duck there was."

His vaguely rubbing hand came around from the back of his neck and rubbed along the cheek, pulling the slack flesh tight and distorting the mouth. Bruce said nothing, watching the pouched hound eyes in the mirror.

It was a cold, skin-tightening shock to realize that the hound eyes were cloudy with tears. The rubbing hand went over them, shading them like a hatbrim, but the mouth below remained distorted.

With a plunging movement his father was off the stool. "Oh, God damn!" he said in a strangling voice, and went past Bruce on hard heavy feet, down the three steps and past Billy Hammond, who neither looked up nor broke his sad thin whistling. Schmeckebier had swung around. "Vot's duh matter? Now vot's duh matter?"

Bruce turned away from him, staring after his father down the dark pool hall. Orderly things were breaking and flying apart in his mind. He had a moment of blind white terror that this whole scene whose reality stared and glittered was no more than a dream, a reflection from some dark mirror. Centered in that mirror was the look his father had thrown at him, or at the glass, just before he ran.

The hell with you, that look had said. The hell with you, Schmeckebier, and you, my son Bruce. The hell with your ignorance, whether you're stupid or whether you just don't know all you think you know. You don't know enough to kick dirt down a hole. You know nothing at all, you know less than nothing because you know things wrong.

He heard Billy's soft whistling, watched him move around his one lighted table—a well-brought-up boy from some suburban town, a polite soft gentle boy lost and wandering among pimps and prostitutes, burying himself for some reason among people who never even touched his surface. Did he shoot pool in his bed at night—or in the morning, whenever he *got* to bed—tempting sleep? Did his mind run carefully to angles and englishes, making a reflecting surface of them to keep from seeing through them to other things?

Almost in terror he looked out across the sullen cave, past where the light came down in an intense isolated cone above Billy's table, and heard the lugubrious whistling that went on without intention of audience, a recurrent and deadening and unconscious sound. He searched the gloom at the back where his father had disappeared, and wondered if in *his* bed before sleeping the old man worked through a routine of little jobs: cleaning the steam table, ordering twenty pounds of coffee, jacking up the janitor about the mess in the toilet. He wondered if it was possible to wash yourself to sleep with restaurant crockery, work yourself to sleep with little chores, add yourself to sleep with columns of figures, as he knew you could play yourself to sleep with a pool cue and a green table and fifteen colored balls. For a moment, in the sad light, with the wreckage of the duck feast at his elbow, he wondered if there was anything more to his life, or to his father's life, or to Billy Hammond's life, or anyone's life, than playing the careful games that deadened you into sleep.

Schmeckebier, beside him, was still groping in the fog of his mind for an explanation of what had happened. "Vere'd he go?" he said, and nudged Bruce fiercely. "Vot's duh matter?"

Bruce shook him off, still watching Billy Hammond's oblivious bent head under the light. He heard Schmeckebier's lip flop, he heard him sucking his teeth.

"I tell you," the guttural voice said, "I got somet'ing dot fixes him if he feels bum."

He, too, went down the steps past the lighted table and into the gloom at the back. The light went on in his room, and after a minute his voice was shouting, "Harry? Say, come here, uh? Say, Harry."

Eventually Harry Mason came out of the toilet and they walked together between the tables. In his fist Schmeckebier was clutching a square bottle. He waved it at Bruce as they passed, but Bruce was watching his father. The old man's face was crumpled, but rigid in its collapse, like the face of a man in a barely controlled rage. He would not look back at Bruce.

"Kümmel," Schmeckebier said. He set four ice-cream dishes on the counter and poured three about a third full of clear liquor. His squinted eyes lifted and peered down toward Billy Hammond. "Let him alone," Bruce said. "He's walking in his sleep."

So there were only the three of them. They stood together a moment and raised their glasses. "Happy days," Harry Mason said. They drank.

Schmeckebier smacked his lips, shook his head in satisfaction, and waddled back toward his room with the bottle. Harry Mason went around the end of the bar and began to draw hot water. With the tap rushing and steaming, he scraped plates into the garbage pail.

In the quiet which no clatter of crockery or hiss of water or whistling from Billy Hammond could penetrate, Bruce said what he had to say. "I'll be starting back to Minneapolis this afternoon."

But he did not say it in anger, or with the cold command of himself that he had imagined in advance. He said it like a cry, and with the feeling he might have had on letting go the hand of a companion too weak and exhausted to cling any longer to their inadequate shared driftwood in a wide cold sea.

Was that the way it was? Mason hoped so. It lived so circumstantially in his memory that it seemed plausible. On the other hand, that whole script might be a creation of revisionism and guilt. In view of what happened the following June, he did not want his last words with his father to have been furious or full of recrimination and contempt. His break with Nola Gordon had been that way, and even after he had recovered from her, he had never been able to feel good about the way he had gone out—wronged lover, angered ego, even falser and more histrionic than Eddie Forsberg.

The duck feast with its troubled and nearly compassionate ending was at least as convincing as its alternatives, those confrontations and cold accusings, that list of grudges and outrages, that he had run so many times through his sullen projector that he couldn't tell, finally, whether he remembered them or had invented them. Which parting *did* he invent? And why, sitting outside the obliterated place of his mother's death, did he remember or invent a parting from his *father*, and not the desolate hour when his mother sighed and stopped?

He thought he knew. He had known all along. She lay quiet, the old man did not. She was loss, he was failure. Whatever he remembered about her was clear and unambiguous. Anything he remembered about his father might be pure fiction.

Without some external evidence, he had no way of sorting out truth from wishfulness and self-deception and grievance; and of his whole early life, up to the time when he started back eastward, presumably forever, he had now no external evidence except the memorabilia of a love affair that, compared with the death of his mother and his total failure to be reconciled with his father, had come to seem minor, even trivial. He told himself that it is easy enough to recover from a girl, who represents to some extent a choice. It is not so easy to recover from parents, who are fate.

The door, when he moved his arm, was hot enough to raise blisters. Through the windshield, still dusty from the desert, he looked across the street overexposed in hot light. An undocumented life had its limitations, but also its advantages. He was not bound by verifiable facts. What he liked about the past he could coat with clear plastic, and preserve it from scratching, fading, and dust. What he did not like, he could either black out or revise. Memory, sometimes a preservative, sometimes a censor's stamp, could also be an art form.

He seemed to have shut off the engine. Now he started it again and pulled away from the curb. He went up to South Temple and turned right past the temple and the monument, the hotel and the historic Mormon buildings, the slick new ZCMI Center, the funeral parlor where at the moment they were probably readying Aunt Margaret for her last excursion. At O Street he turned left up the hill, and when he reached the edge of the City Cemetery he turned left again until he found the corner and the gate.

This documentation, at least, would be intact. Graves lasted longer than either buildings or unpleasant memories, and death could not be revised. Up there in the family burial plot, the only piece of ground they had owned since they left Saskatchewan for Great Falls and the whiskey business, the three of them would be waiting for him.

But he needed directions, after all those years. There was a building inside the entrance, and a yard full of tombstones, and a greenhouse with a manure pile. As he parked and stepped out into the glare he saw that it was just past eleven. In a half hour he was supposed to be at the funeral parlor, lining up in a three-car procession.

There was no point in driving down there only to drive right back. When he had found the sexton in his office, he borrowed the telephone to call McBride and say he would meet the funeral at the grave. Then the sexton took him to a map on the wall and showed him where the Masons were to be found. He went out and climbed into the oven-like car and drove up steep, curving roads until he found the place.

3

Three times before he had stood on that hillside with an open grave before him. This time the scene was tidier than on any of those other occasions. Those who mattered were underground, and their graves were long healed. Except for what lived in his mind, they might have been under the grass forever. The new grave, an afterthought, almost an irrelevancy, was made temporary by its frame and sling, and its raw dirt was covered with a rug of Astroturf.

Each time the weather was different. His brother had been buried on a bleak, damp day of spitting snow, and clouds that snagged on the bare trees. His mother had been lowered into the mud in a steady rain that streamed off the expensive copper coffin with which his father had tried to buy forgiveness for more things than any coffin, no matter how expensive, would cancel out. The old man himself had gone down on a morning of such transcendent early-June brightness as might have been ordered for the funeral of a hero.

Aunt Margaret seemed likely to make her exit accompanied by a totally inappropriate thunderstorm. Thunderheads were piling up beyond the Oquirrhs, another quite separate set had gathered along the crest of the Wasatch. Twin Peaks and Olympus had lost their tops, a lurid storm-light lay over the end of the valley

at the Jordan Narrows. The sultry morning tasted of brass, the
air was stagnant, the sky rumbled. From straight overhead a con-
suming sun burned down.

Mason didn't begrudge his aunt the orchestral accompaniment
and the stage lighting, nor did he begrudge her a place in the
family burial plot, which would hold six. In her persistent,
cracked way she had attached herself to them, for lack of anyone
closer. She was welcome to the room she needed. He was not
going to use it.

Nevertheless, he could not look upon her burial as anything
more than a continuation of the long obligation her life had
been. If there had been any family left besides himself, he would
not have thought he owed her anything. If he had not had the
impulse to revisit Salt Lake anyway, her death would not have
brought him: he would probably have left her to one of those
quick-disposal organizations that would collect and cremate and
scatter you, all within a few hours and at minimal cost.

Sitting coatless above the graves, under a box elder tree whose
leaves broke and scattered the fierce sun, he brooded about burial customs. The Mormons, who expected to inherit heaven in
the flesh, probably felt when they laid the dead away that they
should be kept intact, so that they could leap to reassemble
themselves when Gabriel, or Moroni, or whoever had the assign-
ment, blew the trumpet. The Parsees who exposed their dead to
the buzzards on the towers of silence were harder to understand.
How had that appalling custom ever got started? Was it like
cauterization, was it to obliterate identity and discourage memory? It didn't appeal to Mason, for his dead or for himself.

But neither did the modern way of being parceled out to the
organ banks and the transplant operating rooms. Who wanted
immortality as spare parts? Who could feel anything but
haunted if he met his brother's eyes in another head, or heard in
the pulse of a stranger the heart that had once made rosy the
face of a child now lost? The towers of silence were better than
that. Scattering was better. The grave, where the dead stayed
put, where the living could sit on the ground and say, "I wish, I
wish, I wish!" or "I'm sorry, I'm sorry, I'm sorry!" or "There, I've
done everything, I've observed all the forms, and we're quits, lie
still"—the grave might be best of all. Even if the trumpet never
blew, the grave at least granted memory its illusions.

When he had run from that place on the day of his father's funeral, wanting never to return, Mason had abandoned his unitary family to the empty universe, and become himself a sort of asteroid, wandering outside all gravitational pulls. Yet he felt those durable identities underground, he was troubled by a sense of continued presence, of immanence and possibility.

If he turned his head he could see up to Eleventh Avenue and the bare mountain behind it, where new raw houses were being erected on new raw streets for the living of new raw lives. Some grudging graveyard-school poet in him all but said, "Wait. Wait a while." But he reminded himself that they were as entitled to their innings as he had been, or any of his people here under the grass. It was an amateur, pickup, playground game, and few got many solid hits, but anyone was entitled to his time at bat.

Down the other way, spreading toward the edges of the great valley, the city simmered in yellow-brown smog. The storm-light at the Narrows had become a heavy smudge. The thunderheads continued to pile up, fronting one another, mountain to mountain. There were flashes in the murk beyond Bingham, and answering flashes above Long Peak. Between the cracks and rumblings of distant thunder he heard the city's traffic like a big steady engine. The air did not move, but he had the impression that the blue overhead was closing in from the south.

When he lay back on the grass, the zenith even through the leaves was too bright to look at, and so he rolled over onto his stomach and propped himself on his elbows, prone, memory-prone, inhibited like a nickel-cadmium battery by past failure and incomplete use. Below him were the graves.

The first one said:

SON
CHESTER LAWRENCE MASON
APRIL 19, 1907–JAN. 24, 1931

The second said:

MOTHER
ELSA NORGAARD MASON
SEPT. 1, 1881–OCT. 24, 1931

The third said nothing. It was only an area of turf whose out-line he would not see at all if its shape were not suggested by the two named graves beside it, and by the small aluminum marker, stained with weather and stamped with a meaningless number (he had looked), where a headstone might be.

What should that third grave say? HUSBAND? His mother, con-ventional, forgiving, and loyal, would have put up such a stone over him if he had died before her, but it would have been gross mislabeling. FATHER? Surely piety did not require that conces-sion. If Mason had felt obligated to order a stone for the old man's grave before he took off into world-space, he would proba-bly have specified a blank slab. He would have treated his father like an entry in his reminder book—drawn a rectangle around his name and blacked it out. Did.

Yet Harry Mason's only definition, now, was given him by the relationships he lay beside. Without them he would merge with the universal grass. In his life it was the same. The family that he created and bungled and abused and betrayed was his only ac-complishment.

Was that why Mason had felt he must come back? *Him?* Did he think he owed his father something? Acknowledgment, was that what had always been missing? Or had the old man marked him so that even forty-five years after his death the son still craved his approval? Was he here to show off the accom-plishments of a diligent life, the souvenirs of upward mobility, from sharpshooter's medals to the rosette of the Legion of Honor, not to the girl on whom he had once heaped these trin-kets, not to the friend whose tennis cups and football trophies had stirred him to emulation, but to the father who had been as omnipotent and as full of faults as Jove? Was he in this town, on this hillside, for the same reason that he once took nine dead ducks into a pool hall he despised?

A funeral procession, a hearse and three cars, so meager a cor-tege that it had to be Aunt Margaret's, turned in at the gate and started the circling climb up the hillside. The headlights were pale and blind in the brightness of sun that still fell on the hill. Mason stood up, tightened his tie, and put on his jacket.

The southern end of the Oquirrhs was gone, and a wall of black rain was advancing through Murray. The towers of cloud

above the Wasatch were miles high, brilliant at the edges, black
in the folds. Holladay and East Mill Creek, along the foot of the
range, were overrun as Mason watched; the sunlight shrank toward him along the freeway leading to Parley's Canyon. Then
the darkness marching up the valley was split like the House of
Usher. The hot fork vibrated yellow on the air and then blue on
his inward eye, and he counted: one, two, three, four, five. The
five was drowned out in an appalling crash.

The hearse and limousine pulled up on the drive, followed by
two cars. Out of the limousine, hurrying and with his eye on the
sky, got McBride, followed by another man. Out of the hearse
got the driver and a dark-suited assistant. Out of the two cars
crept, stiff and slow, four old ladies, helped by two men, one of
whom had to be the Home director, Philips. They clustered on
the grass like leaves that the next wind would blow away.

McBride came half trotting across the lawn. "I hate to put it
this way, but if we don't get through here in about five minutes . . ."

"Let's get on with it."

"I was thinking of the ladies from the Home."

"Quite right. They mustn't get wet."

"I brought umbrellas. But still."

"Absolutely."

"Thank you," McBride said. "You have every right to expect a
simple, dignified service. But we can't always . . ."

Distracted, he smiled at Mason and waved his helpers on,
beckoned impatiently at the people from the Home. While the
old ladies were assisted tottering to the graveside, the funeral-
parlor people opened the back door of the hearse and got Aunt
Margaret rolled into the open. They couldn't have moved with
more driven speed if they had been sailors lowering a lifeboat.
Across the grave Philips lined up the four ladies, clucking and
shifting their uncertain feet. Running, he went to the car and
brought back umbrellas, opening them and putting one in the
hand of each lady. The ladies, who had probably anticipated the
funeral as an outing, eyed Mason with interest and the sky with
uneasiness, the coffin with the wincing sympathy of premonition.

A gust of wind came up the hill and blew the ladies crooked
and passed. The air was still again. The blue had all but closed

overhead. Out of its edge, apparently aimed like an artillery
shell, a lightning bolt jagged down. It struck somewhere east,
near Fort Douglas. The funeral-parlor people, McBride included,
were struggling to get Aunt Margaret's coffin straight in the
sling. The moment it was steady, and McBride stepped back,
two helpers darted to the hearse and came back bearing flowers
which they piled on the rug of Astroturf beside the open hole.
The man who had ridden in the limousine with McBride, and
who it seemed was some sort of house preacher, stepped forward, smiling thinly on the handful of spectators and waiting for
the thunder to roll away.

It was a service almost as lame as Mason remembered his father's, when a lurid murder-suicide had presented the preacher
with an impossible task. This time the preacher offered up a
short prayer asking rest for this humble woman who, having long
ago lost husband and children, had been blessed with one affectionate and loyal friend, her nephew, Ambassador Bruce Mason,
here today. He threw name and nod across the grave at Mason,
who stood impassively and despised him for a toady. Through
the kindness of that one surviving relative, this poor woman was
enabled to live out her life in comfort and security, and to make
new friends in a strange city. (Thunder, two claps of it, one on
top of the other, and such a rolling barrage that Mason heard
nothing else for a full minute. When words were distinguishable
again, that meek and humble woman Margaret Webb had borne
her infirmities as patiently and as long as God in His infinite
mercy required. She had felt her loved ones waiting on the other
side, and was going home.

Mason did not recognize in any of this the stubborn and demanding old woman who had been his aunt, but he acknowl-
edged the convention. *De mortuis,* and good luck to her. The un-
felt and not very appropriate words of the funeral parlor's
all-purpose preacher produced in him a shabby sort of pity, and
a wish that he had shown the poor old thing a little more personal attention. At the same time, the preacher's complimentary
allusions to the affectionate nephew (read Visiting Dignitary)
annoyed him, and he wanted the charade over.

The preacher opened his Bible and spread it across his left
palm. Mason would have sworn he saw air made visible as a new

flurry of wind rushed up the hill and snatched the pages upright
and fluttering. The dresses of the old women were plastered
against their bones. Philips grabbed his hair and held it on with
one hand, standing with his eyes slitted and his lips drawn back
from his teeth. While they fought the gust, lightning struck
somewhere on the mountainside with a demoralizing crash. They
waited till its noise rocketed away and was absorbed into the
general rush and grumble of the coming storm. Then the
preacher found his place again and began to read, or pretend to
read what he knew by heart.

The 23rd Psalm, predictably. He raised his voice nearly to a
shout in order to make himself heard. As he was leading them
through the valley of the shadow of death, the clouds overhead
rushed together and wiped out the last streak of sun, and darkness poured up the hill, right on cue. The ladies, with little cries,
huddled and clung and braced their frailty against the weather.
From two of them Philips took the umbrellas, apparently afraid
that if he didn't, the wind would blow ladies and all away. The
air was prickly with imminent rain.

The preacher beat it to the finish line, but barely. His "forever" was hasty, blown away on a gust. It was hardly out of his
mouth before Philips and McBride, folding down umbrellas as
they went, were herding the ladies toward their cars. Just as
frantically, the preacher, the hearse driver, and the black-suited
assistant cranked Aunt Margaret into the ground, as if to get her
to shelter before the deluge. The moment they had her down,
they ran for hearse and limousine.

Hurried, windblown, still deferential, McBride came back to
shake Mason's hand with his strong birdlike claws. His forehead
was wrinkled; he seemed genuinely distressed, and Mason
thought in a moment of friendlier feeling, *Why, he's a person.
God help us, maybe we all are.*

"I'm so sorry," McBride was saying. "I so wanted things to go
well. But sometimes the weather . . ."

"Don't worry. Everything's fine. Do we have any more details
to settle?"

"No. I have your check. You have the things Mr. Philips
brought down. I hope everything was satisfactory in spite of this
storm."

"Perfectly," Mason said. "Many thanks. Goodbye."

"Goodbye, sir."

Sir. He did not feel like "sir." He felt like the last survivor of a star-crossed family. He felt like the puzzled son of a feckless father—boomer, dreamer, schemer, self-deceiver, bootlegger, eventually murderer and suicide, always burden, always enigma, always the harsh judge who must be appeased. He felt like the last remaining spectator at the last act of a play he had not understood.

McBride hung a moment as if he wanted to say something more, and then ran. Now came Philips, his charges safely put away in their cars, still holding his hair on with his left hand. "What a shame about the weather! I hoped we would have some time—I expected to see you at the funeral parlor."

Attentive, flatly smiling, Mason heard the rebuke: Where *were* you?

"The ladies have been anxious to meet you," Philips said. "Margaret often spoke of her nephew the ambassador. She was very proud of you. Could you perhaps come by this afternoon and have tea with us?"

"I'm sorry. I have to start back to San Francisco this afternoon."

Frowning, wagging his head, Philips acted out his resigned disappointment and the disappointment of the ladies. A drop of rain splashed the left lens of his glasses.

"Well, then it's all finished," Philips said. "I'm glad to have met you, finally."

"Thank you for taking care of her. I'm sure she found a real security with you."

"She was one of our family," Philips said. "We shall miss her." He looked at the sky and fled.

Mason ran, too, and made his car with the rain already spattering him, his shoulders and glasses wet, his skull stinging with cold drops. Before he could slam the door, the sky bellowed and opened. Rain burst on the roof and drowned the windshield. There was such a roar that he could not hear the engine when he started it. One look out past the overwhelmed wigwag of the windshield wipers told him that he did not want to drive in that

downpour. He shut off the engine again and let the wipers die
and sat as immersed as if he were in a bathysphere on a sea bottom. The ruby taillights of the funeral procession winked on in a
blurred row, but did not move.

For a good fifteen minutes everything outside was wiped out
in water. The windows steamed up and when he tried to open
them the merest crack he was sprayed with fine drops. Water
rushed and thundered on the roof, artillery duels went on in the
sky. Rubbing the steam from a peek-hole space, he could see
nothing but the smeared red of the taillights ahead of him, and
the vague swirling rush of gathering water in the road. He felt it
push at his wheels as if it were going to sweep him away down
the hill. The old ladies marooned in their cars must be in a twittering panic. Poor old Aunt Margaret must be afloat in her
flooded grave.

Eventually the downpour slackened. Opening the window a
few inches, he saw the hearse and the three cars still waiting.
The drive was a river six inches deep that went around the cars
as if they were rocks in a rapid.

Then smoke puffed from the hearse's exhaust, and the hearse
rolled away cautiously downstream, throwing up rooster tails of
water from its rear wheels. The limousine followed. The moving
lights went around a rain-swept corner of trees and shrubs and
were gone. The cars from the Home sat on. Thunder, still heavy
but receding, marched around Ensign Peak and started up toward Ogden. Far down over the Oquirrhs, a gap of blue had
opened. The sound of the rain on the roof was less than the
sound of the flooded road.

Five more minutes, and the Home cars started and pulled
away, turned around the corner of shrubs and trees, and disappeared. Mason sat on in the diminishing rain, looking out the
cautiously half-open window at Aunt Margaret's flowers beaten
down on their bed of Astroturf beside the frame and sling. In a
little while, probably, the sexton's truck would come up the hill
and remove the machinery, and a couple of men would shovel
the mud into the hole until Aunt Margaret was safe with the
others.

The light was growing overhead, the rain had all but stopped.

Blue was reclaiming the sky down the valley. In the wet, polished granite of the headstones above his mother and brother, Mason saw reflected blue, and the limbs of the box elder tree moving as if in water.

Should he put a headstone over Aunt Margaret? God would not need it to find her, in case He ever wanted to summon her to immortality. And no one was going to come to her grave on Memorial Day and put a little glassful of fresh flowers there. The Genealogical Library of the Mormon Church, busily compiling its lists of everybody who ever lived on earth, even families as migrant and meaningless as Margaret's, would get her name from the cemetery records or from whoever kept the records of births and deaths. There was no need of a stone.

Nevertheless, he sat with narrowed eyes and visualized how three identical stones would look there in a row. Let her in, why not? Establish a quasi-eternal territory for the family, give it the appearance of having been united and complete. According to the best traditions of American mobility, and in conformity to his own status as orphan, he himself would end up somewhere else, probably scattered out beyond the Golden Gate somewhere, and no one would have to make these empty decisions about him. He was the last. No one would have to propitiate him, or make a place for him. But Aunt Margaret, who had wanted in, might as well be given what she had wanted.

The wet granite of the two stones reflected the moving branches, the expanding blue. Beside them, hardly bigger than the tags they had used to wire onto shrubs in gallon cans at the Mulder Nursery, he could see the aluminum disk that marked his father's two square yards of grass.

He was conscious of no decision. He simply started the engine, drove down to the building by the gate, found the sexton eating his lunch, and interrupted him long enough to order two headstones identical with the two already set up over the family. He wrote out a check for the sum the sexton added up on his order blank. He wrote out on two 4×6 cards what the stones should say.

One was to say only Margaret Mason Webb, and her dates, which Mason did not have but which the sexton said he would get from the Home. The other was to say:

FATHER

HARRY GEORGE MASON

MARCH 12, 1870–JUNE 3, 1932

"Any sentiment?" the sexton said. "'Rest in peace,' anything like that?"

"No," Mason said. "That will say it."

"It will take six months or so. The new grave has to settle."

"That's all right. Can you let me know when it's done?"

"Yes, sir," the sexton said. "I can do that, if you want."

"I'd appreciate it. Well, thank you very much."

"You bet," the sexton said, and turned back to his lunch.

Mason had his reminder book out, and was scratching back and forth and up and down over the entry that had read "Funeral: be there 11:30." When nothing could be read, when it was only a black rectangle, there remained on the page the last thing he had contemplated doing: "Call Joe."

"I wonder . . ."

"Mmm?"

"No. Nothing. I can do it from the hotel."

He lifted his hand to the chewing sexton, a man with a good appetite and a good conscience, and went out into the washed, dripping glitter of noon. His mind was running ahead as he drove out the gate and down the hill to South Temple. If he had a quick lunch he could be on his way by two, and with any luck, and the hour gained on the time change, he could be in Elko to sleep, and have a relatively easy drive home tomorrow.

And Joe? What about him? Was he going to call from the hotel? He knew he was not, almost before he asked himself the question. He had known all the time that he would not. However much Joe had meant, however warm and loyal it had been of Joe to try to reach through to him, it wouldn't do, it would only be a frustration and a disappointment. Whoever had lasted in Bruce Mason, it was not the young man who had once been best friend to Joe Mulder, any more than it was the one who had cracked his heart over Nola Gordon. They would have nothing in common but that adolescence with its games and its love affairs and its sun-myth conviction of power and growth. What they had once shared was indelible as if carved on a headstone, and was not, after so long a gap, to be changed or renewed.

As he drove down to the hotel and turned his car over to the youth in the glass office, he was busy in his head with one final check-off. Around Bruce Mason as he once was, around the thin brown hyperactive youth who had so long usurped space in his mind and been a pretender to his feelings, he drew a careful rectangle, and all the way up on the elevator to pack his bag he was inking it out.

FOR THE BEST IN PAPERBACKS, LOOK FOR THE

In every corner of the world, on every subject under the sun, Penguin represents quality and variety—the very best in publishing today.

For complete information about books available from Penguin—including Puffins, Penguin Classics, and Arkana—and how to order them, write to us at the appropriate address below. Please note that for copyright reasons the selection of books varies from country to country.

In the United Kingdom: Please write to *Dept. JC, Penguin Books Ltd, FREEPOST, West Drayton, Middlesex UB7 0BR.*

If you have any difficulty in obtaining a title, please send your order with the correct money, plus ten percent for postage and packaging, to *P.O. Box No. 11, West Drayton, Middlesex UB7 0BR*

In the United States: Please write to *Consumer Sales, Penguin USA, P.O. Box 999, Dept. 17109, Bergenfield, New Jersey 07621-0120.* VISA and MasterCard holders call 1-800-253-6476 to order all Penguin titles

In Canada: Please write to *Penguin Books Canada Ltd, 10 Alcorn Avenue, Suite 300, Toronto, Ontario M4V 3B2*

In Australia: Please write to *Penguin Books Australia Ltd, P.O. Box 257, Ringwood, Victoria 3134*

In New Zealand: Please write to *Penguin Books (NZ) Ltd, Private Bag 102902, North Shore Mail Centre, Auckland 10*

In India: Please write to *Penguin Books India Pvt Ltd, 706 Eros Apartments, 56 Nehru Place, New Delhi 110 019*

In the Netherlands: Please write to *Penguin Books Netherlands bv, Postbus 3507, NL-1001 AH Amsterdam*

In Germany: Please write to *Penguin Books Deutschland GmbH, Metzlerstrasse 26, 60594 Frankfurt am Main*

In Spain: Please write to *Penguin Books S. A., Bravo Murillo 19, 1° B, 28015 Madrid*

In Italy: Please write to *Penguin Italia s.r.l., Via Felice Casati 20, I-20124 Milano*

In France: Please write to *Penguin France S. A., 17 rue Lejeune, F-31000 Toulouse*

In Japan: Please write to *Penguin Books Japan, Ishikiribashi Building, 2-5-4, Suido, Bunkyo-ku, Tokyo 112*

In Greece: Please write to *Penguin Hellas Ltd, Dimocritou 3, GR-106 71 Athens*

In South Africa: Please write to *Longman Penguin Southern Africa (Pty) Ltd, Private Bag X08, Bertsham 2013*